"Anne de Graaf is a consummate storyteller, taking us far beyond our comfort zones to places in the world—and places in our hearts—where we've not traveled before. Her fast-paced style keeps the pages flipping, while her careful historical research makes us want to slow down and take in all the fascinating details of a time and place few Americans have experienced. Thanks to Anne's fine work, we can immerse ourselves in postwar Poland and strengthen our own faith in the same way her endearing characters do."

LIZ CURTIS HIGGS
Author of *Mixed Signals*

"Anne de Graaf has an extraordinary gift. She SEES. Where others see only historical data, Anne sees a tapestry. She sees glimmers of hope in broken hearts. She sees eternal truth within a story begging to be told. And what the heart sees, it never forgets."

ROBIN JONES GUNN
Author of forty-five books, including THE CHRISTY MILLER SERIES

"Anne masterful[ly] transport the reader into a time and place whe[re] [mi]ght fear to tread. Her desire to understand the t[...] [...]ons of Eastern Europe is increasingly evident i[n] [...]l; and her historical research is impressive! Coun[...] [...]ide a truly engaging and informative read."

MELODY CARLSON
Award-winning author of over thirty books

"Anne de Graaf is a master storyteller who weaves history, inspiration, and memorable characters into a generational-spanning saga of epic proportions."

Reviewer's Bookwatch
August 1997

"Anne de Graaf keeps readers turning pages."

Librarian's World

The Hidden Harvest

Bread Upon the Waters

Where the Fire Burns

Out of the Red Shadow

OUT *of* *the* RED SHADOW

A Novel
by
Anne de Graaf

BETHANY HOUSE
PUBLISHERS
MINNEAPOLIS, MN 55438

Out of the Red Shadow
Copyright © 1999
Anne de Graaf

Cover design by Koechel Peterson & Associates

Scripture quotations identified NASB are taken from the NEW AMERICAN STANDARD BIBLE®, Copyright © 1960, 1962, 1963, 1968, 1971, 1972, 1973, 1975, 1977, 1995 by the Lockman Foundation. Used by permission.

Published by Bethany House Publishers
A Ministry of Bethany Fellowship International
11400 Hampshire Avenue South
Minneapolis, Minnesota 55438
www.bethanyhouse.com

Printed in the United States of America by
Bethany Press International, Minneapolis, Minnesota 55438

Library of Congress Cataloging-in-Publication Data

De Graaf, Anne.
    Out of the red shadow / by Anne de Graaf.
        p. cm. — The hidden harvest ; bk. 3)
    ISBN 1–55661–620–1
    1. Poland—History—1945– Fiction. I. Title. II. Series: De Graaf, Anne.
Hidden harvest ; bk. 3.
    PS3554.E11155 O97   1999
    813'.54—dc21

                                        99–6418
                                          CIP

To
Erik

ANNE DE GRAAF is the author of more than sixty children's books and three novels. More than four million of her books have been sold in over sixty languages. Her first novel, *Bread Upon the Waters*, is published in seven countries, including Poland and Germany, and its sequel, *Where the Fire Burns*, enjoys similar success. *Out of the Red Shadow* is the concluding novel of THE HIDDEN HARVEST series. Anne de Graaf has also worked as a journalist and economics translator for the Dutch government. Born in San Francisco and a graduate of Stanford University, she has lived the past seventeen years in Ireland and The Netherlands with her husband and their two children.

Acknowledgments

Special thanks to my father, John Davoren Bowden. As the record of our trans-Atlantic phone calls will testify, you showed unflagging interest as I struggled with this last story in the series. Your love and confidence in me encouraged more than you will ever know. You have always been there for me. Thanks, Dad.

As with the other two books of the series, I owe a special debt of gratitude to Elżbieta Gajowska. She read various versions of the manuscript, checking the Polish and all historical references. Most importantly, she put me in contact with people who could tell me their true stories. Part of the rich circle of friends she has welcomed me into are two people who helped me verify actual prison conditions and other circumstances during Poland's martial law era. Małgorzata Pawińska and Wojciech Charkin, thank you for so generously looking things up and asking questions of others in order to answer my own. You are both treasure troves of information.

Anne Christian Buchanan is my gifted editor and talented friend. Without you, this story would not sing.

I am grateful to Terry McDowell for his editing skills, for showering me with kind words, and for understanding the power of this story.

Many thanks to my dear friend Laurel Anne Dukehart, whose encouragement and wisdom upheld me on a day-in, day-out basis.

Julia and Daniël have grown into young adults as I wrote this series. My pride and joy in you both knows no end. Thank you for your laughter and your love.

This book—and this series—is dedicated to my husband, Erik. You showed me the bright side of the moon.

A Word From the Author

This series is based on true stories. The first book, *Bread Upon the Waters*, was largely a fictionalized documentary of the difficult conditions in Poland during and after World War II. As the series has progressed, however, I've embellished more and more in order to protect the anonymity of people still living in Poland. In *Where the Fire Burns*, the relationship of Amy with Piotr and Jan, the persecution sequence in the final chapters, and the events of December 1977 were entirely fictional. In *Out of the Red Shadow*, only the circumstances and historical background of the *Solidarność* movement, as well as the physical conditions of martial law, are factual.

Although I invested a great deal of time and energy interviewing the men and women of these times and places and traveling back and forth to investigate archives and look at old photos so that I could more accurately describe Poland, any similarity between the characters of this book and true-life stories is purely coincidental.

Having said that, I want to add that the words in italics following the headings for each new Part are direct quotes from interviews I had with the character I've called Hanna. This is also the case for much of the dialogue in chapters 34 and 38. The last time I saw her, she said, *"I pray fervently that even these experiences of mine might help someone to trust the Lord in life's difficult situations."* Her indomitable spirit inspired these books, and I pray I did her courage and faith justice in my rendition of all she endured in this life. Her words haunt me still, even as her presence permeates every page.

I promised her I would tell her story. If only one heart has been touched as deeply as mine was, then she smiles today in heaven.

Anne de Graaf,
Hoek van Holland, The Netherlands

"Every good thing bestowed and every perfect gift is from above,
coming down from the Father of lights,
with whom there is no variation, or shifting shadow."
—James 1:17

EUROPE 1976-1988

Moscow ✹

(R U S S I A)

R.

Katyń
● ●Smolensk

I A)

S.

S.

UKRAINE)

Artemovsk ●

Stalingrad ●

(GEORGIA)

Black Sea

TURKEY

✹ Ankara

Prologue

September 1976

They freeze in the memory, those moments when everything changes forever.

Even as the scene moves forward, it seems to hang suspended, each word and each expression existing for an eternity, endlessly repeated.

He stands there before them, their suspicious gazes falling on him like snow. Soft, unfelt, but he can still smell the doubt, the well-placed distrust.

Jacek stares back at the old man. *Old, ha! Old like me.* At the old, feeble woman—*once so beautiful. The years have not been kind to her.* At their son—*what was his name? Jan?* And then to the other woman, their American daughter-in-law.

Amy. My Amy.

Daughter.

But she doesn't know. None of them know. He has only known it himself for a matter of minutes.

"I've heard enough." He sounds far more certain than he feels. How long can he keep the mask up? "I've noted the names you gave me...."

"Name," Amy corrects him. "I'm only looking for one man."

"Yes, of course. *Name.* Skrzypek, wasn't it? Jacek Skrzypek?" How long has it been since he heard that name?

He is still trying to grasp the truth—that this woman talking to him in heavily accented Polish really is his Amy, brought back from the dead. *They told me she was dead.* And she is pleading with Jacek Duch, a stranger, a minister in the Polish government, to find this

15

Jacek Skrzypek, her father, who left her behind in America before she was even born.

He struggles out of habit to maintain his mask of indifference and looks for reassurance to the mirror on the opposite wall. Staring back at him is a well-dressed man in his sixties. Salt-and-pepper hair cut very short. Eyes of obsidian. Wrinkled face set in stone. No sign of the realization that is crumbling his carefully constructed defenses.

"Is everything all right?" Piekarz is asking. "Has Amy told you everything?"

I could ask you the same question. For Piekarz and his wife and his son have just returned to the room. They did not see the silent exchange of moments before that is still part of the frozen scene in Jacek's mind.

They did not see the dark young man who appeared for just an instant in the doorway—striding in, then freezing still at the sight of him and Amy. Intense, wary. *An outlaw.*

They did not see, as Jacek did, the look the young man threw his daughter before he vanished.

The look she returned.

A part of Jacek still lingers on what the look told him: *She loves him. But who is. . . ?*

The family is waiting for his reply. Amy fixes him with dark, familiar eyes. Those eyes could be his undoing.

He coughs abruptly. "Yes, well, I think my business here is ended. I must go."

Piekarz nods and holds Jacek's coat for him. On the way to the door, the old man asks, "Do we have an understanding?"

He feels his vulnerability now. The upheaval inside separates him from his usual calm. *Must get out of here, at any cost.* "Yes, of course. But you must *never* contact me like this again. You will not see me again."

Door closes. The frozen moment thaws with a rush, and Jacek allows its full impact to wash over him in a great, tumultuous wave. He steadies himself and sees a gloved hand against the wall. His own. In the darkness descending, he knows. He knows too well. He has known it since the moment he recognized her.

My daughter. Not my daughter. She must never know . . . .

Even now, the web of lies he has spun so carefully for so many years prevents him from telling Amy who he is. The truth would be too dangerous for both of them.

"My daughter, not my daughter," he mumbles, hearing his breathing turn into a pant. Blindly, he gropes his way down the dark stairway. And then, before him like a ghost in the dark corridor, he sees a shaded figure.

Who?

Frantic now, he struggles to discern the shape of the shadows, and for shifting seconds he thinks he sees them all.

Monika? No. Ina? Izzy? Gabi? No! Barbara. . . ?

Ghosts all, *where?* Dead. Impossible. And yet . . .

Betrayer, betrayed, Jacek knows with devastating certainty that now he must pay the highest price of all for the choices he has made.

PART I

---◦∞◦---

BREAD OF TEARS
Psalm 80:4–5

September 1976 – June 1979

*Now the danger is greater because we cannot see
the enemy. He is not as well defined as before,
more subtle, and so, more dangerous.*

1

Images from past and present merged. *No one can know the fear.* Jacek Duch drove like a madman up the tortuous switchbacks. The roads were bad in this southeasternmost corner of Poland among the *Bieszczady* Mountains that ringed him now like old friends looking down on a fallen comrade.

Jacek had come here often on his hunting trips with the other Party officials. Those had always been times of great caution. Like hawks circling wolves they had eyed one another, measuring each other's strengths and weaknesses. Often enough, the Party hierarchy for the next five years had been agreed on over a bottle of vodka during such weekends.

But now Jacek Duch was alone. He had only been driving for a few hours, but it felt like longer. The ridge before him marked the Soviet border, where the Ukraine met Poland. He looked at that ridge longingly, like a doomed man running out of time. He focused on those rocks and told himself that if he could reach them, if he could just hang on long enough to navigate the car up the rest of these treacherous roads, he might be able to save himself from disaster.

Perched on top of the ridge before him stood the stone lodge. Jacek could not see it from where he drove, but he knew exactly where it nestled between the twin groves of yellow oaks, waiting for him.

"I don't know anymore," he had told Roman.

"What don't you know anymore?" The other man bent over Jacek. "You're trembling, man."

Jacek looked down at his hands, which shook like small animals in his lap. His heart would not stop pounding.

Already he had broken the only unbreakable rule in this business. He had panicked. And yet in his panic, he had turned to the one man who might be able to save him. Ironically, he was also the man who had the power to destroy him. Roman was an officer in the *Służba Bezpieczeństwa*, or SB, the Polish secret police, the Security Service. He had long employed Jacek to spy on his colleagues in the Polish government. And at least once before, suspecting that Jacek was also a spy for the West, Roman had almost killed him.

Jacek looked at the face so close to his own. He could smell Roman's stale breath. "Look at us," he said. "Two old men."

Roman would not be misled. "What don't you know anymore?"

Jacek shook his head and said nothing, thinking, *I don't know how I got away from the apartment building in Gdynia.*

"What else haven't you told me?"

I haven't told you that they could bring me down, that old man and his wife.

"Who has approached you about this?"

Jacek caught himself flinching from Roman's voice as the words pummeled him harder. He tried to focus on damage control. *That outlaw—he is the first one I must eliminate.* Jacek did not want to slip into the subservient stance that had saved him the two previous times the KGB and their Polish counterparts had captured and interrogated him. Jacek knew Roman would like nothing better than to be proven right in his previous suspicion.

"Tell me, Duch. Tell me why you're doing this?"

To save the life of my daughter. The thought startled Jacek, it came so suddenly. Involuntarily he bit his tongue.

"I have to admit, you lied better the first time we did this. Now tell me." Roman pulled up a chair and sat across from Jacek, staring at his face as if examining it for hidden clues. Jacek would not meet his gaze. "Duch, we've known each other a long time. This request of yours—to halt a surveillance campaign you yourself put into motion—is highly irregular. You know that, don't you?"

"Of course." Jacek reached for a cigarette and started bringing it toward his mouth. His hand stopped in midair as he watched it shake so badly that the cigarette dropped to the floor.

"Here, let me." Roman reached down and picked up the cigarette, then blew it off. He put it into his own mouth, lit it, inhaled, and passed the cigarette back, all in the same space of time it took Jacek to return the matches to his pocket. Jacek envied Roman's steadiness at that moment.

Jacek remembered the stairs cloaked in shadows. That was where the outlaw, the dark young man who had stood in the doorway, had threatened to expose him for what he was—a spy for the West. Where he had looked Jacek in the face and called him what he was—Amy's father. Where he had hissed in Jacek's ear the news that the entire conversation in that cursed apartment had been taped by Roman's own men.

The outlaw had blackmailed him, demanding he call off the hunt for instigators of the recent strikes. It was impossible. Jacek knew that, and he knew the young man, a leader in the new underground, must know it, too.

And yet the other demand Jacek could meet. Perhaps. He had to admit that his attempt to get attention off himself by setting up a minority segment of the population for persecution had backfired. Jacek was quickly losing control. The edifices of falsehoods he had so painstakingly erected during his thirty-five years as an undercover agent in Poland were fast contracting into shadow-thin walls. *My life has been nothing but a simulation.*

"Did you hear me?"

"What? No, sorry." He would have to get himself under control or Roman would soon wear him down. Worse, he might slip up himself. With a monumental shift of will, Jacek closed his mind to the events that tortured the edges of his consciousness and focused on the present, on the next moves he must take if he were to survive.

"You are badly shaken, my friend." Roman's tone sent an involuntary shiver down Jacek's spine. He straightened his shoulders as Roman continued in the same deadly, hushed tone. "I was wanting a little more information about why I should halt the surveillance of the Protestant groups in this country."

"It's served its purpose." Even as he spoke, Jacek surprised himself with the idea of using the truth as a shield. "I knew your men would be watching me after the arrest in *Brześć*." He rubbed his stiff knees. Both of them had been broken in that city after Roman had baited Jacek and caught him, then been unable to prove his status as a double spy.

"Go on." Roman's voice was barely a whisper.

Sense the kill, do we? "I needed a way to throw them off the scent, so to speak, to distract them away from me."

"So you threw us a bone."

"Well, yes. There's no better way to ingratiate yourself with someone than to expose their enemies."

"Even if they're fictional enemies."

"Well, we didn't know that for sure, now did we?" Somewhere inside, Jacek knew he was winning, if also taking a huge chance. Yet he had dealt with Roman before. He knew the man liked taking risks. Admired the big game. Rose to a challenge. If anyone could, Roman would believe the bigger lie. Now Jacek issued just such a challenge, summoning what little self-control he still could command and returning Roman's steady stare.

A moment passed. Jacek smelled the sour sweat all over him, running down his back, his chest, inside his leg. His chest contracted with the same desperate feeling that had gripped him in the cramped stairway of that cursed apartment building.

Finally, Roman broke the silence. "I take it back. Duch, I see you haven't lost your touch. All right, I'll buy it. And I don't know why, except that I'm curious what your next move will be, so I'm calling off the witch-hunt. I tell you, I almost bought your rattled nerves. Anything else I can do for you?"

What price will I pay? Jacek thought fleetingly. But a more pressing need urged him on. He knew he only had a few moments before the façade of control he had managed to erect would crumble. He saw the pending disaster spelled out in his shaking hands. He was almost finished. Just one thing more, a place to go. "The hunting lodge."

"What?"

"The hunting lodge. That's the big favor. The small favor is I want to resign my post, take a leave of absence, a furlough, whatever you professional bureaucrats call it. My health's not so good, and the doctor says I need some time away. Anyway, I thought I might write a book."

Roman stared at him incredulously, then broke out laughing and slapped Jacek so hard on the back, Jacek nearly fell off his chair. "Of course, comrade," he boomed. "Of course. Here." He rummaged in the desk drawer and threw a set of long keys at Jacek. "The lodge is yours for as long as you need it to . . . er . . . write

24

your book! You'll be as alone as you choose to be. Duch, you never cease to amaze me! Nice touch that, the book."

Roman started to leave the room, then turned in the doorway. Jacek did not trust his expression, so he made a show of bending over to pick up the keys he had missed.

"Oh, and, Jacek?"

"Yes?"

"Happy hunting."

When Jacek stood, Roman had disappeared. He let himself out of the house and nodded at the bodyguard at the entrance. Once in his car, Jacek carefully started the engine, backed out of the lot, and drove two streets, then turned into a deserted alley. Only when he had pulled the hand brake did he allow his head to rock forward and hit the steering wheel.

Sixty-six years old, and I have lost everything. Jacek surrendered to the shakes as the rest of his body trembled uncontrollably. Then he heard a truck stall at the entrance of the alley. He looked up at the rearview mirror just in time to see the truck move past. His focus shifted, and he saw his own wild eyes staring back at him. A small smile played on his lips as tears began to gush over his cheeks. The scarred cheeks, eyes wreathed in lines, folds in old skin—all reminded him of no one. Jacek took a deep breath. He could not afford to break down.

Not yet, he promised himself. Then he began to smile, despite his shaky condition. He had forgotten that magic touch of Roman. The first time he met the man had been on a hunting trip in the same mountains he planned to return to now. Roman had set a series of traps for him during that week as well. Jacek must have passed with flying colors, since, by the end of the visit, Roman had offered Jacek a position with the secret police. It was a dream-come-true for any espionage agent already working for the other side, and a mere stepping-stone to the position he had now thrown away, assistant minister in a communist government of Poland.

Why hadn't Roman even questioned Jacek about his resignation? It was as if he already knew—or maybe he wanted Jacek out of the way for a little while. Jacek didn't care. He knew there were many things he should worry about, but he also sensed he had the energy to do only one thing.

To drive all night.

Get away. He pulled out of the alley and headed for the route leading out of the city, the pounding behind his temples forcing him on like a cattle prod.

He drove as if chased by demons that night. He drove erratically, dangerously, swerving up mountain roads, overtaking trucks, swinging way over into the left lane to avoid the slower cars. *Go, go, get away.* Jacek drove to reach a destination. With each curve, he focused on the lodge as a place to arrive when there was nowhere else. It brought bitter comfort to be able to say over and over again to the rhythm of the windshield wipers, "I know where I'm going. I know where I'm going."

Jacek stopped only once that night, at the curve in the road just before the ridge. As he stepped out of the car, the cold wind bit into his lungs. He walked shakily toward the cliff, tempted by the darkness beyond. Then he closed his eyes and loosened his neck muscles so his head rocked backward. Standing there, whipped from all sides by the oncoming storm, Jacek opened his eyes and was surprised to see stars. The weather had grown colder and more fierce as Jacek climbed higher. Storm clouds raced in and out of the twinkling lights. But the stars, spread out in a patch directly above him, still promised more than he had hoped for. He stared up at the riot of light and repeated the mantra that had gotten him so far that night. *Go, go.*

With a huge effort he rejected the cliff and its cold comfort and sank back behind the wheel of his car. He drove the last leg of his journey with his focus on the center line of the road, a part of him knowing that on either side the road dropped off sharply.

And then he was climbing stiffly out of the car again and opening the great wooden door of the lodge. As Jacek felt the coolness of the huge brick building on that storm-choked night, he found the strength to do one thing more, and that was to take out the blankets from the locker beneath the long couch. He wrapped these around his body like old friends, hugging them close. Only then did Jacek collapse.

2

Lord, be my vision, supreme in my heart

When Jacek finally woke again, he had to remind himself that he had arrived safely at the mountain lodge. The loud pounding in his head all but drowned out the birds outside. Jacek sat up and groaned, cradling his throbbing head. His neck ached, his back knotted into spasms as he stretched, trying to straighten his spine. "My God. I hurt." The croak in his own voice was Jacek's first clue that he had slept too long.

Jacek looked around the room as he tried to massage some feeling back into his right shoulder. Strips of low sunshine split the large main room into cubicles. He held his wrist up into one of the sunbeams and held it far away so he could focus on the date his watch showed—three numbers higher than when he had left *Warszawa*. "Three days. No wonder nothing works." He lowered his arm and held it down with the other hand, trying to control the spasm that shook it still.

The throbbing stopped. Jacek sighed out loud, the sound whistling through the empty space. The thought of having to stand and open the door to let some air into the dust-coated place filled Jacek with a surprising fear.

Would Roman be standing outside the door? Or his CIA controller?

A part of Jacek recognized his emotional state and the symptoms as those of a classic nervous breakdown. The shakiness, the clammy feel of his skin, the sweat running in still, cold rivulets over his body—he knew it all meant he had gone too far, had reached the limit of what his mind and body could endure. He could diagnose the illness and recommend a treatment: Go into hiding, regroup, heal alone. See if time could mend the fabric of his being. He prescribed the rest he just woke up from. *One step at a time*, that part of him advised.

But the rest of Jacek still stood in fear as he realized he viewed the door in terror, imagining all his allies and his enemies—for in his business they were often the same—lined up outside. Jacek exhaled and crossed the musty room, then let his hand fall on the latch.

Unlocked for three days.

In one motion he threw the door open, unable to keep his other arm from coming up to protect his head as he cowered instinctively. Like a shot, the wind caught the door and banged it open against the wall. He could hear dry leaves rustling in the fresh wind. Was this the tail end of the same storm he rode up here in? Jacek stood and stared, his eyes raw and red, as the pounding in his head resumed.

This, then, is beauty. The thought came unbidden. Soft as morning mist, it made its way past the pinnacles of pain, unseen, unfelt until it laid the scene before him as a peace offering for the torment he could no longer outrun.

When Jacek finally dared to lift his eyes, only the trees stood waiting with a welcome of multicolored banners. They stood still as sentinels, their leaves dancing in the crisp mountain air, waving at him in encouragement. Jacek swung his eyes right and left. *No one. There's no one here, you fool.*

An eagle called out, its cry high-pitched and haunting, piercing the stillness. Jacek raised his eyes to the light. The mountains rolled before him, unfolding one into the other, a thousand shades of color marking their distance.

Jacek felt his muscles loosen. Finally, he could relax. The part of him that cared for the broken parts took note that this was how his reinvention would happen. Or where it would happen. If any place could heal him, these mountains would. Jacek had known that instinctively when he had begged Roman for the keys.

Roman. Roman was the only person who knew he was there. But Roman would leave him alone. Jacek knew this, hoped it, was able somehow to count on it. He took another deep sigh and began to nudge his fuzzy brain toward constructing some sort of framework for the next weeks. He stepped down from the porch and walked over to the car. He needed that—structure to feel safe in.

Jacek was thinking that he should be amused at the fact that he still wore his shoes. He looked down at the pine needles muffling the first tentative steps away from the lodge and wondered if he would have slept any better on a bed of needles. When he reached the car, he sucked in his breath. Had he also left it unlocked? Well, no one would take anything in these mountains. The closest village was forty kilometers away. And he had been in a desperate state when he arrived.

Three days ago. He allowed himself an incredulous shake of the head. *How is it possible?*

Then he noticed something besides the unlocked door and his bag on the front seat where he had left it. On the backseat stood a wooden crate with packets of sausage and cheese wrapped in newspaper. And a loaf of bread. Jacek straightened and surveyed the lodge, the spaces between the trees. No one. And the door to the lodge had been unlocked. Had someone come in? Seen him?

A still voice broke through his confusion. *Roman must have called the post office in the village and left a message that there was someone in the lodge needing regular supplies.* The realization brought Jacek untold relief. Roman's thoughtfulness would spare him trips to get food, trips that would have brought him in contact with people, trips away from the lodge's safe haven. And that was what he needed, too—to stay put, not to force himself to push beyond the boundaries his shaky psyche had erected for itself.

With some effort, his stiff muscles protesting, he hefted the crate from the backseat and lugged it over the carpet of needles to the lodge. It seemed far heavier than a carton its size had a right to be.

Jacek's days soon blended one into another. He cared for himself. He cleaned the two rooms of the multistoried lodge that he intended on using, then closed off the rest. He raked the pine needles into piles, then left the piles like prehistoric mounds protecting the space he could feel safe in. Every day he awoke and stared at his hands, willing them to stop shaking.

When a first snowfall further magnified the surrounding beauty, Jacek summoned his courage and took a walk. It was something he had been working toward for weeks—a milestone in the program of healing he had laid out before himself as a country to be conquered. As he cut and stacked wood for the shed behind the lodge,

Jacek found a walking stick. At nights, by the fire, he sat and carved a handle at the right height.

Walking out into the new snow, he almost felt like a child again. The years dropped away. To the feel of the wood warming his palm, he stepped out toward the woods with a confidence he had forgotten could be his own. Snowflakes brushed his cheeks like tears.

Hushed, the forest seemed to open its arms and welcome Jacek on that day. He walked through dense wood and along meadows where sheep sheds stood empty. And as he hiked, he slowly, carefully allowed his mind's door to swing open to the day that had reduced him to such a state.

Since arriving at the lodge, he had purposely shut out the events leading up to his self-imposed exile.

Only now would he remember. But he would remember in his own time, and he would remember to move on.

Most important, he would remember Amy.

As Jacek moved silently past the trees, he finally opened up to the discovery that had cost him his nerve.

Amy.

That afternoon in that cramped apartment in Gdynia was the first time he had actually seen her. Before that she was a tattered baby picture sent him long years ago by his now-dead wife. The picture, too, was long gone. But now, somehow, his Amy was back in his life.

He had gone to the apartment because her father-in-law had summoned him with the threat of blackmail—stop the persecution of Protestants, or Piekarz would tell what he knew about Jacek. The secret the old man had kept all these years was that Jacek, wounded and delirious during the war, had spoken English, betraying his connection to the West. He also knew that Jacek had advance knowledge of the bombing of Dresden. This combined knowledge in the hands of Hanna and Tadeusz Piekarz had seemed too dangerous for Jacek to ignore. His first thought upon hearing it was to wonder how he could have the old couple eliminated.

It all seems so long ago, Jacek thought now. *How can the past betray me like this?*

Then Hanna and Tadeusz had asked Jacek for help with another matter. Amy, their American daughter-in-law, was searching for her father, a man who had disappeared somewhere in Poland during the war. They called her in to meet Jacek. And even before she spoke the name he had grown up with—Jacek Skrzypek—he had known, known beyond any shadow of a doubt, that the woman standing before him must be his Amy.

He remembered staring at her dark beauty, mesmerized by her hair, the same blue-black tone as his own, long and straight. Her olive skin, the expression unsure and searching. Her deep black eyes, the tall posture, a soft voice like that of her mother, Barbara.

Thirty years earlier he had given her up for dead, because the men who were Jacek's lifeline to America had lied. They told him that his daughter and ex-wife had been killed in an automobile accident. And he had believed them, although he also knew they wanted him to cut off all ties with the West. They thought his position as an undercover agent was too valuable to jeopardize with family feeling. Apparently they had thought the end was sufficient to justify the means. Now, even as his resentment rose toward his handlers, he wondered if he had let his own success sway him into believing too easily.

He shook his head, unwilling to let such thoughts topple his still-shaky composure. Carefully, deliberately, he pushed the focus of his concentration back to Amy, to the fact that somehow, against all odds, he had her back—even if she would never know him for her father. He added up the years mentally. *She must be thirty-seven.*

Jacek smiled despite the lonely scene around him. He had just managed to scale a rocky cliff he had often stared at from the lodge's porch. Now he stood high, surveying the surrounding hills.

He was taking care of himself now; like a dedicated nurse, he made each act one of nurturing. That morning he had packed a bag with food and water, extra socks, his binoculars. He took the time to settle on a boulder and let the winter sunshine warm his back.

He had already walked a good distance. Yet even more strenuous had been the mental effort of reconstructing the confrontation he had been running from ever since he left Gdynia.

Jacek had been lucky to escape the apartment, only to encounter that outlaw in the stairwell. *Who is he?* Jacek's training told him that this was the player who did not belong. Eliminate the man who threatened him there, and the rules of the game would become clear. That man and his mad guesses posed a danger both to Jacek and Amy. He must be silenced, kept out of Amy's life so he wouldn't endanger her further. Let his daughter learn to create for herself a life of domestic security he had never known. Such a thing would not happen with a lover waiting in the wings.

On that mountaintop then, Jacek made a vow. To tell Amy who he was would put her life at risk. His identity was a lethal weapon for both sides. But he had power. His years in the government had allowed him to build up a network of favors owed. He had it in his power to protect his daughter. Jacek took hold of this newest cause with the fervor of a drowning man trying to keep afloat.

The part of him he had turned to for rescue resurfaced. He purposely turned away from the premonition that, as a betrayer, he was doomed. No matter, as long as Amy did not pay. Protecting his daughter, then, had become the primary directive.

That decided, Jacek knew he had one more thing to do. He made his way back to the lodge and arrived just before dark. Despite the fatigue that had crept into his joints, Jacek headed straight for his car, now parked behind the shed. He opened up the trunk for the first time since arriving two months earlier.

He stared at the cardboard box for a few moments, almost afraid it would jump out at him. The box was open, its contents spilling over the edges, just as it had been when he had hurriedly tossed it into the car the afternoon he made his escape from Gdynia.

For he *had* gone back. The outlaw had made sure of that. When the young man told Jacek he knew who he was, knew what he was, *knew the apartment was bugged*, Jacek had managed to keep the panic at bay long enough to realize what must be done.

He had stood there long after the young man disappeared into the shadows, long after the door downstairs clanged shut. Jacek had stood with his back against the same wall the dark man had thrown him against, and he had plotted out, step by step, what must be done if he was to survive.

First, he would have to get hold of the surveillance tapes. So Jacek had reclimbed the stairs and shown his SB identification to the neighbor who lived to the right of the Piekarz apartment. To the left lived a friend—he knew that much from the conversation he had had with Tadeusz Piekarz. When he had sent his son Jan to fetch Amy, Tadeusz had nodded toward the left.

So Jacek had let his training take over. If the place was under surveillance, one of the neighbors on either side was the likeliest stooge working for his own SB. "I've come for the tapes," he said simply. When the old man stared at his credentials, then nodded, Jacek knew his hunch had paid off.

"You're not the usual man," the neighbor had said.

"No, I'm not," Jacek answered. He followed the man into a cubicle built behind a bookcase on the common wall with the Piekarz apartment. *Standard issue*, Jacek thought.

As the old man looked on amazed, Jacek had removed the reel-to-reel recorder and the stack of tapes and thrown them all into a box under the table that was already almost full of tapes. He kept telling himself, trying to convince himself, there was no way anyone could catch him doing this. "You'll get new equipment next time around. We have a more pressing job somewhere else," he said more confidently than he felt. When the usual person came for the tapes later, Jacek would be long gone. With the tapes missing, no one could place him at the apartment. Jacek told himself these things over and over as he walked out the door.

Jacek had carried the heavy burden down the seemingly endless flights of stairs, cursing every step, then back to his car. And then he had headed for Roman's to finagle the leave of absence and the keys to the lodge.

Now Jacek stood shivering in the snow, surveying the spaghetti-like tapes spilling out of the carton. He still panted from the hike back to the lodge as he leaned over and heaved the box out of the car, then shut the trunk.

Once inside, Jacek saw that his hands shook as he built a fire in the fireplace. That hadn't gone away. *Not yet*, he promised himself. The thought of hooking up the recorder and inviting strange voices into his space filled Jacek with the same gut-twisting fear as the idea of driving down to the village and confronting people. He counted himself lucky enough that he had managed to walk so far away from the lodge that morning. The breakdown was taking more out of him than he had ever imagined possible.

So Jacek waited. One thing his sojourn to this remote place had taught him was that he could not rush himself. His mind and body needed time and space to recover. He would deny them no longer. So he plugged in the recorder and organized the tapes according to the dates scribbled on their square boxes—four months' worth, starting with June of 1976. Then he ate some cheese and bread and went to bed.

In the days that followed, Jacek eyed the tape recorder suspiciously, like some sleeping warden sent to watch over him. If he should wake it by pushing the start button, it could shoot him down in the ensuing confusion.

I can wait, he told himself again and again. Jacek had time on his side in this place all his other worlds had forgotten.

3

Jacek marked each passing week with the discovery that yet another crate of supplies had been left on the porch. The delivery occurred every Monday morning. The first time, he surmised, the food had been put into his car so it wouldn't be raided by animals.

Now that Jacek rose early each morning, he always waited to go outside on Mondays until after he had heard the groan of the man who carried his food up the hill, presumably, a man on Roman's payroll. Then Jacek heard a thump as the crate hit the porch, and the man went away.

It didn't matter to Jacek that he had to hide like this. He knew he must keep himself sheltered from the outside world. And this was also his reason why, despite the weeks slipping by like pebbles through his fingers, he still could not summon the courage to listen to the tapes. Instead, he concentrated on his immediate surroundings. It seemed enough to dare to venture from the lodge on fine days.

He tried to notice something new in the woods each day. On one of his walks during what had become the dead of winter, Jacek heard a wolf for the first time.

At the moment he heard the sound, he had been thinking about a decision he had reached just that morning—to destroy the tapes. He would throw them into the fire and smell their melted plastic that very evening. And having spent weeks wrestling with that decision, he had made up his mind to take a different route on his afternoon walk.

The new direction took him along a high ridge. In the winter it looked different, but he could have sworn it was the same place where he and Roman had shot down an elk so many years before, during his first encounter with the SB.

Jacek stood still in the winter landscape, watching the whites around him shift from one shade of shadow to the next. With the wind at his back, chilling his legs, Jacek moved a quarter turn, and that was how he heard the wolf's howl. The wind brought it to him like a small gift.

The snow crunched beneath his boots as he headed toward the sound. He had heard that these mountains held lynx and wolves as well as the elk he had hunted here before. Jacek forced his legs to pump as he climbed another hill. Once on top, he pulled out his binoculars and fixed them in the direction of the sound, stronger now that he faced the wind.

A single animal, its head tipped back howling in the daytime, and no sign of a pack—these facts alone made the event unusual. Then the animal lowered its head and turned in the direction of Jacek's ridge, staring straight into his binoculars. *I'm too far away, and I'm upwind*, he told himself. Still, the white eyes bored into Jacek, seeming to penetrate what few layers of protection he still could wrap around his perception of himself.

"That wolf can't see me," he said out loud and turned away.

Late that afternoon he finally arrived back at the lodge. A storm had followed him in, and the wind was already blowing sharp gusts of ice and sleet into his face. He stamped the snow from his feet and entered the lodge, heading first for the fireplace. The box of tapes stood near the kindling, where he had placed it that morning. Jacek added wood and stirred up the embers, then leaned back on his heels, eyeing the square, wafer-thin boxes. As the heat from the flames started melting away the stiffness in his joints, Jacek picked up the loose tape that had no box, the last reel, which he himself had removed from the machine.

With a sigh, he carried it back across the room where the tape recorder sat on the table. Then he placed it into the machine, rewound it, and watched the tail flap around the reel, around and around. Seeing the wolf had somehow shifted his focus. Now, for some reason, he thought he could do this. "Just this one, though," he said out loud as he fed the ribbon into the empty reel.

Voices filled the lodge for the first time since Jacek's arrival. As

Jacek listened in on his own conversation with the old man and his wife, he slowly started to relax. The content of the tape told him nothing he didn't already know, and during the period preceding his visit, all he heard was loud music from the radio. *So they know they're under surveillance*, he thought. The part of the tape following his visit was blank. He removed the tape and brought back the entire box from near the fireplace. It landed with a thud on the table.

Jacek rummaged around the bottom of the neatly stacked rows. Then he pulled out the first box of the series and opened it. A full reel faced him, the ribbons of tape tempting him like the unraveling of a mystery. And yet he hesitated still, fingering the reel, wondering to himself why he was so reluctant to run the tapes.

Jacek had few compunctions about whether to listen in on private words spoken behind closed doors. The first tape Jacek had listened to was, in fact, of a conversation he had participated in, so in some ways he had a right to hear what was recorded. Besides, Jacek had been an operative in the field too long to be bothered by invasions of privacy. So what *was* bothering him? He was shakier than ever because of the breakdown. Was this continued hesitation just another associated fear? Yet another paranoia for something unknown?

Yes, the fear was there. *Always there*. He was genuinely afraid of becoming involved, of what he might discover, and of what further revelations might do to him. He realized this even as he began threading the thin brown tape into the machine. The discovery that he had a daughter, that she was here in his Poland, had sent him literally over the edge. Any further discoveries hinging on her existence might repeat the same damage to the frail recovery he had managed to pitch for himself in the last months.

Even as his actions denied his thoughts, somehow he realized that to listen to these tapes would be a conscious step in acknowledging someone he had rarely known. Not *hardly known*—not Amy. But rarely known—the real Jacek Duch. Who he was, not for one government or the other, one movement or another, but for himself. He was doing this for himself.

A part of him whispered the message to his brain as the shaking hands, specked with age spots, continued their task. And then, when he pushed the play button, and heard his daughter's voice, Jacek knew it was already too late. There would be no turning back now from her words.

"Jan, I had no idea he had kept these. He wrote them before we were married. Jan, listen. . . ."

"You told me he no longer cared."

"I thought he didn't. *He* was the one who would not see *me*. Piotr broke it off, Jan."

"Then why didn't you tell me he came back that Christmas to mend it? What else haven't you told me?"

"You don't trust me. Oh, Jan, you *must* believe me. *I didn't know.*"

"You did know. And you said nothing. You let me marry you. My brother still loved you, and you said nothing. Did you still love him?"

"I'm sorry, Jan. I swear to you there's nothing else. You know everything about Piotr now. There aren't any secrets between us, and there won't ever be, Jan. You can't keep bringing this up; it's destroying us. You have to put this behind us, Jan. *I love you.*"

"Do you still love him?"

"How can you ask that? Jan, we've been married more than two years. We have a child. Doesn't that count for something?"

"I don't know, Amy. You say you want to put this behind us. All right. We won't ever, ever bring it up again. Throw these letters in the fire if you must, but you can't lie anymore to yourself or me."

Jacek sat mesmerized by the words, the picture they inspired unfolding like a film in his mind's eye. He rewound the tape and listened again to the conversation, thunderstruck by its implications. And as the tape played on, Jacek could hear the babbling of a toddler somewhere in the background. Jacek shut down the machine and sat in the dark, shivering still.

This, this must be Tomek. This was his grandson. *I didn't know.* His grandson. Jacek shook his head. The knowledge that he was not the last—not nearly so, thanks to Amy and the little boy he had heard on the tapes—that knowledge threatened Jacek like no weapon ever had. This is precisely why he had feared the effect these tapes could have on him.

Somewhere far away he was conscious of a decision to choose this particular battle as one he would fight to the death. And he was ready to take the first step. But as with so much he had chosen to do lately, he would have to do it slowly and not overburden the part of him that had shattered from the encounter with Amy.

He made a conscious effort to calm his emotions. *Something else. Think of something else.* It was a discipline like so many others he practiced as a daily routine. But Jacek's mind would not let go of the argument between Amy and her husband.

Piotr. Piotr Piekarz! So the outlaw Jacek had met on the stairs was none other than his Amy's brother-in-law. That's who the mysterious player was. That's why he hadn't belonged. That's why he had walked into the apartment as if he lived there, then slipped out again with Amy his only knowing witness. So the game was a different one than Jacek had first sensed. The stakes were much, much higher.

Ah, a dangerous game, my Amy, loving two brothers. He smiled, though, enjoying their similarities. Dangerous games were his business. They were part of what he had always enjoyed about his job—working both sides, watching for his advantage and choosing the precise moment to take it.

And yet at the same time he ached for his daughter, knowing she must be tormented by the loves in her heart. He had seen that much on her face when she caught sight of Piotr. Jacek got up and began to pace back and forth in the great hall.

Then he heard a sound above that of the howling wind. He rose, his joints stiff all over again, since the fire had gone out and he had not moved for so long. Slowly he opened the door, resisting the wind as it tried to jerk the handle out of his hands. There it was, above the wind—another howling. A wolf's.

Had the same animal followed him? *Has it sensed I'm an old man, alone, separated from the protective pack, not unlike itself, a lone beast?* Jacek pushed aside the thought. He shoved the door shut and bolted it. He waited a few moments in the dark. His shaking was worse.

Then he went to bed and dreamed disjointed, troubled dreams.

Somewhere in the early morning, Jacek woke up to the sound of his own voice. He sat straight up in bed and listened to the storm groan among the trees. He heard a beating sound. A knocking sound. He pulled on his socks and crossed to the window, putting both hands up to peer outside.

Shapes and shadows. How could there be moonlight during a storm like this? When his muscles began to ache, Jacek returned to bed. The beating sound persisted. Like something he knew. Like carpets being beaten by old women in a city courtyard. This was Jacek's last thought before sleep overtook him once more.

In the days that followed, as the storm raged around the building, bringing layer upon layer of snow and leaving him cabin-bound, Jacek gave in entirely to the lure of the tapes. He saw the little ribbons of truth as able to unravel the players' identities in this particular game. He would insist on calling it a game. On impulse in a flight of panic that lifetime ago, he had snatched up the one thing—these tapes, the thread—that bound all the secrets together.

Day followed day followed day as Jacek inflicted a mental torture upon himself surpassing anything the Soviets had attempted during his years in labor camp. The denial broke over him like a crystal glass, shards of regret cutting into his memories of years— all the bitterly wasted years.

And all the betrayal. But it had been necessary, hadn't it? Necessary for Poland, for America, for his work. He had kept himself sane for so long by hanging on to that. And yet now, with his defenses shattered, he didn't know anymore. All the failures and betrayals kept coming back to haunt him in his dreams. At night the shades and specters tormented him—a strange parade of faces he had loved through the years. They had reentered his consciousness as if the tapes had unleashed them on his soul. When the snow should have muffled all sound, Jacek heard every creak, every moan, during the night.

The nightmares gripped him tightly, and the memory of them haunted his mornings.

Again, he saw his Barbara waiting for him, holding down the home front, waiting tables, as he plunged deeper and deeper into the embrace of war and espionage. In his dreams he saw her waiting and waiting and waiting until finally her image faded into nothingness.

Again, he watched from a tiled rooftop in *Kraków* as the Nazis dragged his Ina, the brave partisan, off to a concentration camp and certain death. He watched and did nothing, her prison photo resurfacing on his desk after the war.

Again and again, he returned to Monika, too late, and saw her lying where the Soviet soldiers had left her in that basement room in *Gdańsk*. Body ravaged, eyes open and accusing. Alive, yet not alive.

And then he was touching his fellow agent Izzy's blood, her beautiful body still warm, just moments after she was shot. And Gabi's strange disappearance that same night, the night he had escaped in the Warszawa sewers.

The knocking sound continued, and each time he opened the

door, he expected to see these faces. Where was the branch that must be causing that sound?

Soon he did not dare to sleep. He could not bear the eyes, their eyes as they stalked him in and out of the dreams. So he stayed awake and listened to the tapes.

As the sounds of his daughter and her baby son filled the hollow lodge, Jacek grew more and more tormented. Drugged by lack of sleep, he sat for hours staring at the fire, listening to his daughter's voice, willing its sound to banish the ghosts. Again and again he reminded himself, *Dead.* But the wind whispered back, *Returned.*

Finally there came a night when the howling wind died down and Jacek rose to pull open the heavy drapes. He knew the snow covered the pane outside, weighed down the rogue branch. As he held the flashlight up high, Jacek hoped the white darkness could reassure him of his true place in time. Instead, faces stared back at him. Jacek froze at the sight of dark eyes, blue eyes, unmoving lips. Eyes that bored into him, gripping his heart, tearing apart the modicum of sanity he had thrown together.

After that, Jacek only remembered waking up with the feeling of his muscles cramped in a sitting position. He came to and moved his head. It hit something hard and cold. He opened his eyes and found he was sitting crouched in the corner beneath the sink. "This cannot continue." His own voice sounded foreign.

He rose and flicked the tape recorder back on.

"Try again, Tomek," Amy laughed. *"Jeden, dwa. . . ."*

"Trzy, cztery, pięć!"

"Oh, you're such a clever boy to count to five." Amy's voice again.

"And he's just a two-year-old," Hanna said.

Then Jacek heard the boy chortling and both women laughing as Amy added, "Who likes to be tickled!"

As the little boy's giggles rolled off the tape, Jacek brought a hand up to his face and felt the smile on his lips, the stubble on his chin. *How many days old?*

He felt calm, the panic gone. He tried to picture the apartment in Gdynia as he remembered it. *I was there.* The sofas against the walls. The kitchen in the corner, with a curtain that could be drawn around it. A rack of dishes drying above the small sink. Shelves across one wall with books and glassware. A worn carpet. The door to another room. Plants by the window.

"You'd better go now, Amy, or there won't be any fish left at the market. I'll watch this little man." Hanna again.

"Are you sure it won't be too much trouble? Oh, that's a silly question. Just look at the two of you. *Cześć, Mamusiu.*"

Jacek saw the boy on Hanna's hip and Amy closing the door behind her, a cloth bag in her hands. Then a thought occurred to Jacek.

This is what counts. Yes. This can even help me.

There he was, dreading the emotions their words could recall in him. Still, his shaking was less. So why had he insisted on listening to them over and over again? The truth was, he was soaking up the trivial dialogues of this household, a home of love he had never known.

It does not have to torment me.

In all his long life, he had never heard such conversations. Words tumbled over each other as he listened in on family prayers, mealtimes, arguments, groans of pain, all mixed with the laughter that seemed to carry his Amy's new family from day to day.

Maybe now I'm finally past the torment and these words can help me.

Always that laughter, and more often than not, he heard it as a consequence of something little Tomek had done.

"Tomku, no. That's not for you. Tomku, I said *no.*" Jan's voice, affectionate but firm.

"Tomek's. Mine. More!"

To Jacek's ears, the toddler sounded so breathless, bursting with a strong will. Crying every time he did not get what he wanted.

"More? I'll give you more. Come here, you, and I'll make you fly in the airplane!" The boy's giggles.

Tadeusz's tired voice. "Ah, Jan. I used to do that with you and your brother. Oh, how Piotr loved to fly through this room."

At the mention of Piotr Piekarz, Jacek listened and learned. First he listened as a professional and learned there was nothing here the SB would find interesting. If he had not met Piotr in person, he would never have been able to link the family with the man's underground activities. It was obvious from the tapes that Jan's brother no longer had contact with his family. No, the true identity of an underground leader was a convenient piece of information for Jacek alone. Except for the tape recording of Jacek's own conversation with the Piekarz family, there really was nothing harmful here.

Once he had established that, Jacek allowed a part of himself to learn that never had. Now that his confusion had cleared, he could *embrace* the existence of Amy and Tomek. The fear set aside, Jacek became caught up in the drama unfolding with each tape he placed in the machine. After all his torment, now Jacek finally began to listen with all his heart.

"Which hymns for Sunday, Hanna?" Tadeusz out of breath, coughing.

"What does the rota say? Poor Danusia will be struggling. It was a year ago that her Karol left. Let's choose at least one of her favorites."

In this way Jacek learned who Tadeusz Piekarz was, a Protestant pastor, strong of spirit but physically weakened.

"Come, Amy. We only have one morning when the pool is opened. I'm sure Tomek's cold won't get any worse at Irena's. The exercise will do you good."

Jacek grasped Hanna's pivotal role in the family. Tadeusz's wife was a strong woman, but sick. Seriously sick with something that brought her a great deal of pain and made walking difficult.

He heard who Jan Piekarz was, his daughter's husband, dutiful and loving, even though tormented with his own doubts and insecurities. For his strength and faithfulness, Jacek was thankful. But the often dull exchanges he listened to were merely a backdrop for a devastating realization that began to dawn on him as he learned who his daughter was.

Jacek could not deny the bitter truth that Amy was nothing like him. She was, in fact, everything that Jacek was not.

"I told you not to bring Piotr up anymore." Jan's voice.

"He's your *brother*." Silence. "Just a little longer, Jan. I've almost got this ironing done."

"Leave the ironing, Amy. Look at this sunshine. Come on, let's take Tomek for a walk."

"Ah, Jan."

Tape by tape, he learned about Amy's patience, and he learned about her devotion to Jan and Tomek, but also about her silent suffering in a relationship where trust could not be taken for granted.

Jacek listened and slowly dared to wonder, *How could I have been such a fool? My life has been for what? For what?*

The question pounded its way into Jacek's vulnerable consciousness. Having been thrown into a chasm of uncertainty when he first met Amy and then plunged back into the dark depths by his reaction to the tapes, Jacek now felt himself again losing the hard-won ground he had gained in scrambling out of the pit. His breakdown was not yet over, the confusion not yet conquered. As he continued listening to the tapes, inflicting the tableau of family life on his fragile psyche, parts of Jacek broke in new places.

Outwardly he crumbled. Often he would look up after a tape had finished and find his head resting in hands, his hands wet with tears. How much time had passed? As the tape end flapped around and around, Jacek faced only his hands and his tears.

Jacek had never cried before, not that he could remember. Not when his father pushed his mother over the balcony, not when the blue-uniformed men took him to the first of many foster homes, not when he received the news that Barbara was divorcing him, or read of her and Amy's death in a tragic car accident. Jacek could not get past the calamitous loss of his own life as he now saw it, reflected in the light of someone he was slowly learning to cherish.

That reflection of himself showed only waste. The tapes revealed this to Jacek. He desperately sought the meaning to his life that this family and their simple daily life had eclipsed. Jacek rethought his life, cautiously venturing into corners he had shut away from himself decades ago.

Who have I been? What have I done?

Murder, lies, deceit, betrayal. Tentatively, he stepped toward the faces. One by one, he touched their loss in his heart, explored the reasons why. And gradually, in revisiting his crimes, he found a place to rebuild his own perception of himself. Guilt and denial reared, but he tamed them with acceptance.

Carefully, step by step, he moved backward in time. *When Gabi disappeared, was it because she killed Izzy? Did I kill Izzy with my carelessness? Did I say too much when I was drunk and blow her cover?*

Barbara. Ina. Monika. He had loved each one. "I *wanted* to love each one," he said out loud.

No, I loved Barbara, but I left her for too long. And Monika . . . I loved Monika. . . . In the final days of the war, hiding from the bombardment of Gdańsk in the basement of her father's shop, Jacek had known love. He could have built a life with Monika, loved her in a daily way like these people loved one another. *Could have.*

The more he faced up to his losses, the loss of time measured in decades and of life measured in love, the more Jacek gained a vision, learned to see, really see, who he could be, what his purpose could become.

Jacek emerged from his passage holding on tightly to two resolutions. He accepted the facts that he was a father, was, in fact, a grandfather. Not healed, but purged, he sensed the price this realization would cost him. He'd see to it that no harm ever came to Amy or to Tomek. No matter what lay ahead, he would now channel all his training, all he had learned, all his contacts, direct all his energies on this one mandate: His family's safety.

His resolution emerged from having a name for the source of tension between Jan and Amy: *Piotr Piekarz*. Jacek realized all too well the threat this Piotr posed to his daughter and grandson. In vowing to protect them at any cost, Jacek realized he would have to neutralize this threat. For not only did Piotr Piekarz represent a threat to his daughter's marital happiness, he was also the only one who knew Jacek's relationship with Amy. And if Jacek was to succeed in protecting her fully, Jacek had to prevent her from ever finding out his true identity.

For this, Piotr would have to be removed from the playing field—a regrettable but necessary precaution. If that meant having him killed, well, it would not be the first time Jacek had been involved with such measures.

Jacek Duch had built a successful career in espionage by knowing when and how to change sides. In making these two resolves, though he hardly realized it, he was changing his allegiance yet again. Only this time, for once, he would be working for his own cause. As before, he would do whatever it took to fulfill the new mission he had given himself. He would work on whatever side, tell the lies, betray others or himself if needed.

But Amy and her child would survive. That mission he would not betray.

Jacek pulled his car over onto the cliff and climbed out to stretch his legs. He lit a cigarette and held it between his thumb and index finger. In another hour he'd be out of the mountains and back in the real world.

Real is relative, he reminded himself.

Jacek took a long drag on the cigarette, then tipped his head backward and exhaled slowly. A little over a year ago he had stopped in this same spot as he had headed into the mountains.

Now he shook his head in wonder. The autumn colors had never looked so riotously beautiful. And the blood reds, russet golds, and pale yellows that painted the leafy landscape below had been saluting him all morning, a farewell-to-arms.

How often had he stood on the front porch there and stared outward, concentrating on this very place on the road?

Even now, in his mind's eye, he could still see the deck floor. The wooden slats of that porch were ingrained in his memory, he had stared down at them so often, day in and day out, as he slowly hammered his sanity back into shape.

Jacek leaned back against the car and let the air out between his lips with a long, low whistle. He had paused one last time to see the place for what it was, to put it behind him along with the unsteadiness of the past year.

It had taken Jacek many months to reach the place of psychological safety where he could finally admit these things to himself. Once he did so, he had worked hard to see, really see, the wasteland his life had been, to accept it and then move on into a cognizant pattern of putting himself back together again.

Jacek had known when he arrived here all those months ago that he would leave it either back in balance, or not at all.

Yes, he had been desperate, desperate to the core. As Jacek threw the cigarette onto the ground and crushed it with his heel, he wondered if desperate was also relative.

More desperate than when I lost Ina to the Nazis after the assassination attempt? More desperate than when the Russians chased me with tanks during the war, when I was with the Polish underground? Was I more desperate than—no, he corrected himself, just as desperate as—*when the Soviets threw me into a pit and left me there to rot?*

After all the years of running, of turning his back on the women who loved him, of betraying the causes he had fought for and been betrayed by, Jacek had finally found a reason to take a stand. Jacek, who had always had a love of women and had always known how to be left alone. In the final season of his life, he had found this reason. Another woman, this time his daughter.

How dare he play the part of guardian angel? The thought sliced through him, cold and icy as a steel knife blade. Jacek hesitated, his hand on the car door. At the same moment, the hair on his neck stood on end.

Someone is watching. He turned slowly and surveyed the hillside. Nothing. Then he opened the car door and reached in for his binoculars. He raised them to his eyes, and right away a movement on the canyon wall caught his eye.

Jacek held his breath. There, right where the lodge should be, between the grove of oaks, he saw a wolf. And the wolf was staring in Jacek's direction.

It couldn't be, Jacek thought. He couldn't tell if it was the same old dog he had sighted the previous winter. He hadn't spotted him since. There had been plenty of packs, sighted on his many walks all year, but never again a loner.

Now, from where Jacek stood, it looked as if the animal really was watching his every move. And yet all logic told him it was impossible, that he was too far away. Then the wolf was gone.

Jacek turned back to his car, intent on the purpose of this moment. He would drive back to Warszawa for the first time since his breakdown. Before he turned the ignition, though, he did a mental check.

Yes, his hands were steady. He breathed deeply, feeling the new strength in his muscles, the balanced beating of his heart. He was calm. He was back in control.

He was ready for the last assignment, the only one that counted.

Jacek sighed as the car tires crunched the gravel and he headed downward. He would miss these mountains—the air, the peace, the animals, even the howling of wolves at night.

This place, where he had arrived blind, had helped him see, to refocus.

Here he had learned to love.

4

The first thing Jacek did after returning to Warszawa was check in with Roman. "I don't need to tell you, your old ministry post has long been refilled. I do need you, though, for a few behind-the-scenes projects."

"That's fine," Jacek said. The more low-profile his activities, the better position he'd be in to pursue his own agenda. Neither man mentioned the year that had passed since they last saw each other. *It's as if the lodge does not exist in this dimension*, Jacek thought as he placed the keys back on Roman's desk.

Roman's hand covered his own as he took the keys from Jacek. Without a word, he held Jacek's hand up to the light. Jacek wondered if he was checking to see if the shaking had stopped. As he left the office, he could hear Roman throw the keys back into the drawer.

In his own mind, Jacek cynically referred to his return to the *normal* world. Once Roman had taken him back, Jacek spent the following weeks and months plotting ways to keep Piotr Piekarz quiet.

His network of contacts within the Polish secret police proved more than helpful. Jacek had recognized Piotr as one of the organizers of the workers' protests in June 1976 at *Radom* and *Ursus*, a year and a half earlier. Within a month of his return, Jacek discovered the man and his friends had not been idle during Jacek's year in the mountains. From SB agents planted as moles within the underground movement, Jacek learned that the violent suppression of those strikes had fostered a new alliance between Polish workers and the intelligentsia.

Traditionally, these two groups had never trusted each other, never found a way to work as one. And this had been fine with the government, since the communist leaders had long ago realized the wisdom of a divide-and-conquer policy.

Jacek knew the workers of Poland traditionally held a measure of power in their potential to strike. By closing down mines or calling a general strike, the workers could cripple the country's economy. They had done it before, and the government had responded as ruthlessly and violently as possible. Jacek's Party bosses realized that if they ever hoped to retain their stranglehold on the country, such strikes had to be stopped. If the people ever fully realized the power they possessed in the form of nationwide industrial action, they would be that much more difficult to control.

But now, it seemed, a crossroads in history had been reached, for that realization was being taught to them by the intellectual faction of the underground leadership. Until now, the territory of these men and women had traditionally been the universities, where they had conducted their secret lectures, encouraging students to march and protest against the communist state.

Jacek had done his homework well. It seemed that the ferocious suppression of the strikes in June 1976 had caused a backlash. The intellectuals and workers had reached out to each other, the one offering the power of its strikes, the other offering organization and vision and strategy. Jacek wondered if he was the only one to suspect that such an alliance would prove a deadly combination for the government.

He returned to Roman. "I've been doing a little nosing around on my own," he said.

Roman leaned back in his desk chair and put the fingers of both his hands together at the tips. "So I've heard," he said.

Jacek lifted an eyebrow. It was the old game of wondering who was watching whom. He ignored the remark. If he could get Roman to take the bait, Piotr Piekarz was as good as dead. He said, "I thought you'd be interested in some of my findings."

"Cigarette?" Roman leaned toward him, offering an open pack.

Jacek knew Roman was playing with him. Both men remembered too well Jacek's shameless loss of control the last time he had smoked in this office. He allowed himself to reach forward. "Thanks."

In the next moment, Roman shook his head and chuckled as if

laughing at a private joke. Then he motioned with his hand that Jacek should continue.

"You liked that one, huh? Listen, Roman, you probably already know about a new group launched by Polish intellectuals."

"Yes," Roman said. "It's called the *KOR, Komitet Obrony Robotnikow*, or the Worker's Defense Committee."

"Right. They support the workers and their strikes by helping the ones who are not arrested and keeping the movement alive while its leaders are in prison. They're pooling their resources, Roman."

"We're aware of all this. What are you really trying to tell me?"

"That this new cooperative effort between the workers and intellectuals could very well spell the eventual downfall of the communist regime."

"Heresy, my friend. You speak of heresy. Well, I can see you are back to your old tricks and maybe even have learned a few along the way. Why the sudden interest in the movers and shakers of the underground? Anyone I know?"

Jacek paused for a split second. The truth had always proven to be his most deflective form of armor. "Piotr Piekarz."

Now it was Roman's eyebrows that shot up. And in answer to the unspoken question Jacek knew his superior was thinking, he answered, "Private reasons." *He's taken the bait*, he thought.

"Often the best, my friend. Very well, what is it that you see forming here?"

By investigating his private vendetta against Piotr, Jacek had stumbled on facts the SB was already aware of, but did they realize the potential danger? "I know these findings won't be popular among my former colleagues, the ministers in government. But you've always had an inside track to the men with real policy power among the leadership. What do they think of this KOR?" Jacek asked.

"Well, as you suspected, most just laugh at it as another weak attempt to 'overthrow the masters.' But I take it you see something more—a framework?"

Jacek nodded. "Well, more of a potential pattern." How could he put it without riveting Roman's suspicion on himself? All he wanted was to stop Piotr. But any assassination order had to come out of this office or one higher. Otherwise, inquiries would be made about Jacek's personal involvement. He could not afford to have anyone asking too many questions, since those might lead the investigators to Amy's doorstep. No, what he wanted to do here was simply move Piotr higher up on the SB's *Most Wanted* list.

"I think *they* don't even realize the potential of what they've put together here. Can you imagine what could happen if someone thought of organizing the strikes on more than merely a wild-cat basis? If a strategy starts to emerge that the people can rally around, it will be that much harder to suppress. You saw what happened in '76. No, I think this is a particularly lethal combination, mine workers and former university professors. Others are laughing at them, but I would recommend the KOR be shut down now, *before* it becomes a threat."

"Our moles within the organization say it's under control. We can't go around stifling every movement that springs up. Total control is too expensive. Unlike our neighbors to the east and west, we don't have security as a number one financial priority. But I don't have to lecture you about politics, do I, Jacek?"

Jacek smiled at the irony of what he was about to say. "I'd be the last one to advocate total repression. It's just this particular branch of the underground, this peculiar alliance could prove lethal. I say nip the KOR in the bud now before they realize what they can do. Have you considered what the addition of just one more player could do to this country?"

Roman looked him straight in the eyes. "The church. Yes, now wouldn't that be the most unholy of alliances. But it will never happen, Jacek. Never in a thousand years."

With those words ringing in his ears, Jacek left his boss's office. But he left satisfied. His ploy had worked. The name *Piotr Piekarz* would now receive a higher urgency rating on the list of people sought throughout the country by SB agents. If anyone saw him now, instead of bringing him in for questioning and general harassment, then releasing him, as was often the policy, Piotr would be imprisoned. At the very least. And the rest Jacek could arrange himself.

The next item on Jacek's personal agenda was to reestablish contact with his CIA connection. Jacek had deliberately waited until he knew where he stood with Roman before he checked in with his U.S. controller. Now he had something definite to offer them. He knew from his many years of service that he would have a lot of explaining to do. An agent in the field didn't just "disappear" for a year, as he had. And they didn't need to know about his nervous breakdown in the mountains.

Even during the war, his first priority had always been communication. Against all odds, he had survived a death march and an internment in a Soviet labor camp. Even then and throughout the six long years of war, his prime directive had always been to maintain contact with someone connected with military intelligence.

Only now he didn't have the war as an excuse. And he couldn't even claim to have been taken prisoner. The more he thought about it, Jacek had to admit his case looked extremely suspicious. He would have a hard time convincing the Company he was still reliable. Despite his nearly four decades of valuable service, he might even come under suspicion as a double agent. It had happened before. And he had sworn never to let his guard down against it happening again.

Jacek thought back to the events of years earlier, when his own contact had been murdered by a double agent. At least that was what he had always suspected. Izzy had posed as a prostitute in Warszawa. Together, she and Jacek had worked the communist leadership for espionage information for the West. She had been a professional.

More than that, Izzy had provided Jacek with an anchor during a personal storm. She had helped him survive the aftermath of being posted back in Gdańsk during the fifties. That had been a bad place for Jacek. During the final days of the war, he had spied there for the Soviets, then abandoned his lover during the so-called liberation. *Monika.*

Jacek's nightmares about what the Russians had done to her only grew worse during his time back in Gdańsk. He'd almost gone crazy from the guilt. For a while, he had seen her everywhere he went. When he finally returned to Warszawa after that assignment, mentally unstable, Izzy had helped him to steady his course when he hadn't known anymore which direction was real, which was worthy.

Not unlike what Amy and the tapes have done for me in the mountains, he reminded himself.

At the time, Jacek had been arrested and questioned by Roman. After his release, his housekeeper, Gabi, had nursed him back to health. Thanks to the torture Roman's men had inflicted on him,

Jacek had been unable to walk for months. Following his lengthy recovery, he had sought out Izzy, only to find her body. Someone had murdered her only a few moments earlier. After that he never saw Gabi again. Jacek had always assumed she had been working both sides, then turned and hit him at his most vulnerable point by eliminating Izzy.

Jacek had never forgotten the coldhearted response of his superior in the field when he finally was contacted after Izzy's death. "She had been expendable." And now that was what Jacek feared would be decided about him.

He was staying in his old home in the suburbs, by the airport, and knew if the house was being watched, someone would already know he was back.

He left a message at the usual drop point, then began the tedious job of waiting to be contacted. "Back from the dead," he wrote on the note. He left the red-colored paper in the trash bin in the park by the fountain. And he returned to the spot every Tuesday at noon and six in the evening. Since Izzy's death and Gabi's defection, he had yet to see the man who had taken Izzy's place as area chief. Most of his communication was done in writing and left in this same spot on Thursdays. Since Jacek's ascendence into the government as assistant minister, the Company had felt he was in too high-profile a position to warrant face-to-face contact.

He still did not know who it was when he heard a familiar voice at his back as he stood feeding the ducks. It was an old man's voice, like his own. But it *was* the same one who had warned Jacek not to get too attached to Izzy.

"So, were you in hell or heaven?"

Jacek smiled. *At least they're still interested*, he thought.

"You said you were back from the dead. So which was it? You know, Duch, we were searching everywhere for you. The least you could have done was let us know you were planning to disappear. What happened?"

That's odd, Jacek thought. *He shouldn't be asking for details, not here.* "I didn't plan it this way. I . . . had a situation. I'm afraid the pressure of a twenty-year-long surveillance and the . . . er . . . related incident several years ago proved too much."

"You're referring to Izzy here. But you still don't know all the facts. All the players involved." The man's voice dropped an octave.

"I don't? I know that Izzy was a trusted colleague. And Gabi..."

"What about her?"

Jacek almost didn't dare to verbalize the questions. "How does she figure in the picture? A double agent? Did she eliminate Izzy?" *If she did, someone should hunt her down.* "Shouldn't she be targeted?"

The man laughed. "What? You want revenge? I don't think so. I speak from *personal* experience. Believe me, you're talking about things you know nothing of."

"Am I?"

"Operation Guardian Angel," the voice said.

"Excuse me?" Jacek asked.

"Nothing. I just wanted to let you know you're not alone in all this. And what happened to Izzy was for the best, I assure you."

Jacek would not let it go. "And Gabi? What happened to her? Was she Izzy's assassin? Does she work for us as well as for them?"

As soon as the words were out, Jacek knew he had gone too far. But a burning need to hear the truth drove him on. One of the many revelations he had experienced during the last year was that too many questions about the pivotal events of his life had gone unanswered far too long.

Jacek heard his reply as a searing hiss, "See, this is what I mean, Duch. You're a loaded gun about to go off. It's not like you. Listen, you reported years ago after the situation with Izzy that you were feeling more secure. I don't buy it. What happened to send you off running to God knows where? *Where* were you?"

He's changed the subject again. More details. Nonetheless, a part of Jacek was relieved that he was getting off so lightly. After all, he had just made the monumental mistake of questioning the allegiance of a colleague. "I needed some time out. I went to a place where I knew I'd be safe and tried to get my bearings."

Silence.

He doesn't buy it, Jacek thought. *I know I wouldn't.*

"You could have told us. We would have taken you out of the field."

Discontinued the program, in other words, Jacek thought. *And maybe me, too, in the process.*

The voice continued in a monotone. "Well, what now? At least you had enough presence of mind to resign your post with the SB.

We knew that much. And now you've come back, so we know you didn't defect, right?"

He's pausing just a little too long.

"Duch, I'll level with you. You worked hard to maneuver yourself into that position. But you've been gone too long now. How can you possibly still supply the merchandise?"

Information. "Exactly because I have a lower profile, I'll be in a better position to assess behind-the-scenes activities. I'm still in solid with the SB leadership. I do what I do for you, for them, and whatever I learn I'll pass on, just like always." It was crucial to his own plan that he retain his credibility with these people.

For Amy's sake. It was all for Amy's sake now.

A silence followed. "You want to continue in the field." It was more of a statement than a question.

"Yes." Jacek held his breath and then heard the empty laughter, a dry cackle of cynicism.

"Duch, you're too old. There are plenty who think you need time out *now*. A permanent time out. Don't you understand? It's time for you to retire. We want to take you out and bring you stateside. You've earned a rest. You have a service record that few can match. Thanks to your SB resignation and yearlong absence, it will be easier to get you out without anyone discovering what you've been doing all these years."

"But my orders . . . " Jacek's voice sounded weak. He coughed and tried to put the authority back into his voice. "I have always worked to position myself so I could spy on the leadership of this country. During the war that was the Home Army. After the war, that was the communists. Now it is the secret police. You cannot remove me, not now."

Not now, he thought.

For most of his adult life, Jacek had wondered what it would be like to leave Poland and go back to the U.S. But after he reached the age when he had spent more years out of the U.S., he had somehow known he would never go back. *And I'm not leaving Poland now! Not when I have finally found the reason why I'm still here.*

"You're right. But there are orders. And the order now is to get you out of the field in one piece."

Ironic that I would have jumped at this ten years ago, but not now. "You're not listening to me. I've *already* contacted the SB leadership and reported for duty. Don't jeopardize all I've worked for on a question of age."

"No, Jacek."

He's using my first name for the first time. Standard procedure for closing in to kill. Jacek's body tensed instinctively as the voice continued.

"There is no room for negotiating here. We thought you were dead. And now it would be best if that indeed appeared to be the case. Long-term operatives all have difficulty withdrawing. But we'd rather get you out now, alive. We might not have another chance like this."

"Don't threaten me," Jacek said. And at that moment he turned. It was against procedure, but Jacek had to be sure, had to look this man in the eyes to know what he really intended. He could no longer afford to take the usual risks now that the lives of a family— *his* family—were involved.

He stood very still, taking in the face across from his own, a face that had seen as many years as Jacek's, a face he had seen before.

"Jurek?" He whispered the name, a name from thirty years before, from during the six years of war, from Home Army days, a name of a writer friend in the days when it had been so clear who the enemy actually was. Jacek let the name pass between his lips and then regretted his slip, his second in almost so many minutes. But the man nodded.

"Yes, all these years, my friend, you have not been as alone as you thought. How else did you think you received those communiqués during the war? Surely you didn't think you were the only one in-country?"

"No, I . . ." Jacek was truly dumbfounded. He made no pretense of covering his surprise. Time seemed to stand still as he remembered so many events in the past years. Had Jurek seen it all with him, walking parallel paths, covering him in the shadows? Most importantly, *Can he be trusted?* Jacek no sooner thought the question when he knew his answer.

Jurek said, "Come, let's walk. It won't do to have you standing here gaping at me like that."

As Jacek matched the stride of the man beside him, he wondered what would happen if he switched into English. His conversations with contacts had always been in Polish. The one time he unconsciously slipped into English, Tadeusz Piekarz had heard him.

Though that had been very long ago, he was still living the rami-
fications of that incident.

No, he didn't know what Jurek knew about him. Maybe he
thought Jacek was Polish, just as Jacek thought that of him. Somehow though, at some time during the war, this partisan friend had
been brought over to the side of Allied Military Intelligence. Had
he, too, been recruited off some university campus in the U.S.? Left
a wife behind? Jacek doubted it.

Jurek said softly, "You know, they're taking us both out. Come
with me. Who else do you have now?"

He addressed Jacek as an old friend. *Who else indeed?* He still remembered the detached coldness with which this same man had
just referred to Izzy's death.

"You still don't understand. I *can't* go now."

"Give me one reason why."

"I'll give you two. The workers' protest in Radom and Ursus
was the catalyst for a cooperative effort instigated by a group of
Polish intellectuals."

"Tell me something I don't know. The KOR. It shows great
promise."

"Well, the SB is targeting the leaders of the group. They want to
quash it."

"They'll be protected. They're not your responsibility."

"Is there anyone else on the inside of the SB as high up as I am?
Anyone who can know who will be arrested before the agents
doing the arresting?" Jurek's face told him his answer. "I thought
not. Listen, you still need me there. Here," he corrected himself.

"What's the second reason?"

It went against everything in Jacek's cautious nature to trust a
stranger, even a stranger who used to be a friend. But he needed
time. He needed to buy time desperately. And for this, he needed
a desperate reason. So he did something almost equally dangerous.
He swallowed, stopped, squared his shoulders, and lied.

"I've been given an assignment by the Polish secret police."

"To hunt down the KOR leaders?"

"No. To assassinate Carter when he visits Poland next month."

5

Bid every rival give way and depart

Jacek had determined one thing for certain. It was imperative that no one find out about Amy, least of all Jurek and his other CIA bosses. That the Piekarz family was under surveillance by the Polish secret police was bad enough. But if the CIA ever got whiff that an American married to a Pole was related to an operative in the field, there was no telling what would happen. His resolve to protect his daughter at all costs strengthened. If the CIA could still use him, then Jacek could still use them. He was no longer working for the Company. It didn't matter if a friend from the past had appeared in the form of Jurek. After all his years of loyal service, Jacek now had every intention of making the Company work for him.

The bombshell he dropped detonated and cleared his field of further obstructions. Jacek told Jurek that if the KGB was using President Jimmy Carter's scheduled visit to Poland in December 1977 as an opportunity for assassination, then who better to control the situation than the one hired to do the job? Even Jurek had agreed.

"And by the way," Jacek had added. "This all ties in with what I wanted to tell you in the first place. I admit I *did* disappear for a year. The SB sent me as some assassin-in-training to a special KGB camp near the Caspian Sea." Jacek was fairly certain his controller bought the story, especially after he provided some details gleaned from a report he had once read in Roman's office.

When the time for the presidential visit arrived, and Jacek saw the amount of security surrounding the American commander in chief, it certainly appeared that Jurek had believed him. The agreement was that he would abort his assassination attempt because of all the tightened security. This way the CIA would believe in his usefulness and that he was saving face with the KGB because of the excuse of too many security men. And the SB didn't even know there was a would-be assassin in the room.

It was a superb plan, Jacek thought to himself at the time of the state dinner. He sat at the back of the room, across from the stage. Gold-gilded chandeliers hung above them, and heavy lead-glass mirrors reflected the backs of the men sitting opposite. Jacek sat at a table with men he did not know. Minor players in the government, a little in awe of Jacek's past status. He had a reputation for knowing when to change sides ever since he had switched his allegiance in the fifties from the military to the Party. In a clique as small as Poland's government one, a move like that, though twenty years old, still won him friends among certain Communist Party factions.

Jacek sat through the dinner and listened to the preliminary speeches, and listened to the translators, enjoying the English. Especially enjoying the soft accent of the president himself. Strangely, with the arrival of Amy in his life, Jacek felt more vulnerable, but more inner strength, as well. His year of solitude in the lodge had been spent cultivating that very strength, but also accepting the new weakness his daughter had wrought in him.

Listening to Carter that night, Jacek allowed his guard to drop slightly. He leaned back and swirled the cognac in the Russian crystal glass. Although he never drank the stuff anymore, he was considering making an exception this one time, for this one evening he seemed in perfect control. Jurek had believed the necessity of keeping Jacek in the field. He would continue to believe it, too. Jacek would see to that. Jurek must have tripled the security around the president, per his request.

Roman had singled Jacek out for the KOR job, which would enable him to get his hands on Piotr without arousing suspicion. And since no one could make a connection between Piotr and Amy's adopted family, she would remain safe.

Perhaps it was the English. Perhaps it was the president's southern accent as he droned on about international loans and a false economic prosperity. Where did he come from again, Jacek asked himself. *A peanut farmer from Georgia. Only in America.* He shook his head and smiled. The charming childishness of his homeland. Then the image returned, the image of his wife, Barbara, who had spoken with a soft accent from the south, his own Cajun beauty from Louisiana.

Jacek let his mind wander and had the strangest sensation that the decades no longer separated his last glimpse of Barbara. He allowed himself to ask the forbidden two words, *What if?* Words whose power he had learned to disarm. What if he had stayed with her? What if he had told the truth to his controllers and returned home the year before war broke out? What if he had raised Amy himself?

These were hard and painful questions he had refused to ask himself ever since the war. And yet he had dared to ask them recently during his year in the mountains. Somehow he had summoned the strength to face the fear they exposed. Now he asked himself again, when *had* he seen Barbara last? Why did it seem so recent? It must have been after training in Virginia . . . before the war. . . . The last time had surely been when Amy was conceived. And then it dawned on him. *That* was why he felt he had seen Barbara so recently, when in fact it had been forty years. He had seen Amy only fifteen months ago. And in Amy he had seen Barbara.

Jacek sighed. Roman caught his eye from the other side of the room and brought his finger up to his ear. He was making fun of Carter's secret service men standing at all the exits. Small wires threaded their way down the left sides of their necks, connecting a hearing device in their ears with a microphone pinned somewhere to their blazers. It was the latest in communication technology, but it meant most of them were walking around with one finger pressed to the backs of their ears the whole time.

Jacek allowed himself a wry smile. *If they only knew.* The president was finishing his speech and smiling with more teeth than Jacek had seen in a long time, when suddenly a single shot rang out.

A mirror shattered and one of the wives at a table to Jacek's left screamed. A waiter dropped his tray. Jacek scraped back his chair and watched his hand freeze in midair as the cognac glass dropped from his fingers. It shattered into a hundred shards as the golden fluid spotted his shoes.

Instinctively, Jacek reached for his gun and drew it out of his shoulder strap. "Get down, get down, everyone on the floor!" he yelled in Polish at the other men at his table.

As a volley of shots rang out, Jacek whirled toward the sound.

It was coming from around the corner to the left, from the kitchen entrance. In one motion he swung low and moved to the wall nearest that corner of the room. As he did, Jacek glanced at the stage and saw two men lying on top of the president, while what looked like another five knelt in a circle around him, guns pointed outward.

Impressive, the professional in Jacek thought. A bullet shattered the mirror opposite him just as Jacek went down on all fours. The sound of breaking glass mixed with the screams and shouts filling the room. Jacek crawled around the corner as more shots whistled over his head. Whoever it was, he was aiming at the stage. Jacek saw the kitchen door standing open. The sniper must be just inside, leaning up against the wall by the doorpost. Jacek focused his energy, then ran through the entrance, gun drawn, swirling to the left, then to the right. No one. Not any gunman at all. He looked at the surprised faces of the kitchen staff, spread out on the floor at the other end of the stoves.

"Where did he go?" Before any of the men could answer, Jacek felt an enormous weight batter into his back. He went down with a thud, his right arm twisted behind his back by rough hands, the gun removed by prying back his thumb. Jacek could hardly breathe with the body sitting on top of him.

"It's just an old man," a voice said in a flat American accent. He heaved Jacek to his feet and shoved the right side of his face up against the tiled wall. Jacek could smell the tomato soup and the stale breath of the behemoth who had tackled him. He could say nothing with his mouth shoved up into his cheek like that.

To Jacek's relief, Roman appeared a second later, rounding the corner with a skid. Then Roman stared at Jacek, taking in the situation at a glance.

"Get those people out of here," Roman ordered. As the chefs and waiters were taken past the entrance, one by one, they did not stare at Jacek as they should have. *Why won't they look at me?* A slow panic started to crawl into Jacek's gut as it dawned on him why he continued to be held this way. What had Roman's man whispered to them? A threat? Wild ideas hurled themselves through Jacek's mind. *Why don't they tell the truth, that I arrived too late!* But he knew the answer. He could tell by the roughness of the gorilla holding him that the Americans thought *he* was the assassin!

Jacek grunted and Roman looked his way. Their eyes locked,

and Jacek could see Roman was unsure of what to do. Would Roman just sacrifice him like this?

"Send a translator in here!" Roman shouted above the crowd filling the narrow passageway. Then to Jacek in a tone barely above a whisper, "Don't worry, I saw."

Relief flooded Jacek, making his knees go weak. Roman would stand by him. When the translator finally arrived, Jacek recognized him. He had been onstage at the side of one of the men Jacek had last seen lying on top of the president.

"The perpetrator?" the secret service man asked.

Roman answered him through the translator. "There's been a terrible mistake. I'm afraid this is one of my men. Release him, please."

The man nodded at the one holding Jacek. Jacek brought his hand up to his face and rubbed his jaw. He quickly told Roman what had happened. "You saw it. *They* saw it," Jacek said, indicating the kitchen crew who had just left the hallway. "I thought I had the sniper, but he disappeared. Question the staff. I'm sure you can still get a description. . . ." Jacek's voice trailed off as it occurred to him from the expressions of the men around him that there wouldn't be a description. No one wanted a description of the man who had attempted to assassinate the president of the United States during his landmark visit behind the Iron Curtain.

Roman's slow shake of his head confirmed Jacek's suspicion. The news of this incident would remain in this building. That's what the kitchen staff and the rest of the hotel would be hearing at this moment. In a few hours the shards of glass would be swept up, and no one would be able to see that the attack had ever taken place.

Jacek understood. He said for emphasis, "*I* wasn't the sniper."

"Of course you weren't," Roman said. Then he turned to the American man in charge and explained through the translator, "He was going *after* the sniper, don't you understand?"

"Well, where is the man who did it, then?" the agent demanded.

"We don't know. He escaped the building as your men were closing in on this man. One of the chefs says he left by the delivery exit."

This was news to Jacek.

"You're *certain* this man is innocent."

"Of course." Roman narrowed his eyes in a way Jacek knew meant the American was in danger of going too far.

"All right." The man brought a finger up to his ear. "One of our men we had posted on a roof across the street just confirmed your story. A man did leave from this side of the building. All right. Yes," he answered into the pin on his lapel. "Mr. President is safe, so I must leave. It's *not* been a pleasure. I have to say this, I'm afraid, diplomatic courtesy or not . . ."

That was it. Roman turned on his heel and left the big American still talking as he steered Jacek away by the elbow. Under any other circumstances, Jacek would have enjoyed the confrontation.

At the moment, however, he was replaying the events leading up to his arrest. Suddenly Jacek knew. There was no doubt whatsoever in his mind that he had been framed. The question was, by whom? Had he really been framed by his own? Who had given the secret service man the order to arrest him? How had they known he would enter the kitchen? Who had ordered the others to wait? How did Roman's men fit into this? Was this the Company's way of forcing an unwanted retirement on him? The questions turned this way and that like the walls of mirrors that now showed him crossing the banquet room at Roman's side. He had to find a way out of this maze.

Roman touched Jacek's arm briefly and whispered, "I'm getting you out of the country, *fast*. The KGB won't like what it appears you did today, my friend. And you can be sure they will tell some of my SB people to keep an eye on you or worse. Do you understand? *I have a source who says you were indeed planning an assassination attempt.* You must leave the country. Get out fast."

Jacek nodded. So he was still to blame. He blinked twice. What had Roman said? *A source.* That meant someone in the CIA had told Roman he had said he had orders from the SB to shoot the president. It was getting too complicated too fast. *Leave.* Yes, it was good advice.

So it was happening. He was finally leaving. But not for the Company, for the SB. For Roman, the man who had connections with the KGB, who had once tortured Jacek. For Poland.

For Amy, the thought came to him as surprisingly as the clean beauty of the snowfall waiting for him on the other side of the revolving glass doors. Jacek could see the snow outside from where he waited with Roman for their coats.

He was just about to respond to Roman, when he heard the man who had collared him call out, "Hey, you forgot your gun!" Jacek bit the inside of his cheek in an effort to mask his recognition of the English. He willed himself not to turn back toward the open doorway he had just passed through that connected the banquet room and foyer. Instead, he waited for the translator's voice to call him, and only then did he acknowledge the request. Jacek turned and reentered the dining room. The translator pointed to the hallway where the agent who had arrested him stood holding his gun. Jacek crossed the parquet one more time, glass crunching under his shoes, accepted his gun, then looked up to nod at the agent. As he did so, he looked past the secret service man down the passageway to the kitchen door, now closed.

In the small window at its center, Jacek saw a woman's face watching him. *Gabi!* His heart skipped a beat. But her brown eyes, the nondescript hair, the face that would disappear in any crowd, he could not forget her. *Impossible.* And just as he started breathing, another face replaced the woman's, and this time Jacek was sure who it was.

He turned away quickly, hurrying to catch up with Roman. Even when he stood outside, feeling the snow against his cheeks, Jacek could not stop feeling the eyes of Jurek watching him from that window.

Only later on the train out of the country did Jacek ask himself why he had been the only one in a roomful of security agents, KGB, SB, and American secret service, to go see who was firing the shots. Why had Jacek been the only one to try to put a halt to a presidential assassination attempt?

6

Only by accident did Jacek discover the plane ticket. He reached into his inside pocket for a pack of cigarettes and found instead the narrow envelope. Someone must have slipped it into his coat before he reclaimed it from the clerk in the hotel lobby. He fingered the carbon copies, stapled one on top of the other. Jacek recited the pink-typed stopovers softly to himself like a litany. "Vienna, Paris, New York, Chicago. Vienna, Paris, New York, Chicago."

Why Chicago? he wondered. Because half the city was Polish, maybe? It didn't matter. Someone had wanted to give Jacek the unmistakable message that time had run out. He was going back to the States, and he was going back now, or he was going nowhere. An implicit threat, especially when coupled with that evening's events. Ironic that both sides wanted him to retire.

Jacek thought back on what exactly had happened in that hotel dining room, and no matter how he lined up the facts, they all pointed in one direction. He had been framed, and by his own. The secret service man who had collared him was almost certainly told that Jacek would be the one to make an assassination attempt. He was too quick.

After all, it would be a good way for the Company to get what they wanted. That's why he had this ticket now. It all made sense. That night they had made him out to be the assassin, pinned him, and now he conveniently disappears.

Well, that isn't the way it's going to come down. Not this time. Jacek read through the ticket's itinerary one last time, then slowly began tearing it up into fine strips of paper. When he had finished, he opened the train window, cold air blasting into the empty compartment, and let the paper slip through his fingers, bit by tiny bit.

If the CIA considered him dangerous, why should he disappoint them, he smiled. No, instead of disappearing to some destination of their choice like Chicago, he'd go one better. They had liked his disappearing act so much the first time. Now let them think he really was dead.

The plan was perfect. Roman wanted him out of the country, too.

Jacek made up his mind right there. As soon as the train stopped, he got off and caught the next one headed for Warszawa. Then he went straight to Roman's apartment and told him what he wanted to do. "Let me disappear my way. If you ever want me, contact me in East Germany. I'll let you know how and where in a few weeks. And tell *anyone* who inquires that I was eliminated as too big a risk."

Roman stroked his chin for only three seconds before nodding. "Look, we go way back," Roman said. "To tell you the truth, I don't care what you do, as long as you do it far away from me. There's some serious fallout from this so-called assassination attempt, and I don't want to be the one who has to explain why one of my operatives was suspect. Understand?"

Jacek nodded. "In other words, you'll be glad to get rid of me for a while."

"Right."

So it was settled. Roman thought Jacek was disappearing in East Germany. The CIA thought he was disappearing in Chicago, but when he didn't show up, the answers to their inquiries would all point toward a SB elimination of a rogue agent. Then they would think that particular problem had been solved . . . permanently.

Only Jacek knew where he was disappearing to, and it was a destination of his choice, no one else's. He stooped slightly on the train he'd taken out of Warszawa after his conversation with Roman. Almost twenty-four hours after the assassination attempt, he caught sight of the sign at the train station he was just pulling into. *Gdynia.*

This was to be his new home, then. Born in Gdańsk, Jacek had returned to the same Baltic coast to finish his days. He would be sixty-nine next year and did not want to spend the final years of his life anywhere but in Poland. Poland was his home, where his newly discovered family was. He knew this country like no one, the hiding places in the woods, the rivers where you could catch the largest trout. And no one, least of all the U.S. government whom he had served faithfully all these years, was going to make him leave. Not now.

Jacek had not even stopped first at his home in the outskirts of Warszawa. He did not even go back for his personal things. He made a clean break. The CIA must think he was truly dead. And as a dead man, he had every intention of never returning to any of the various worlds he had ever inhabited.

There would have to be another war for that to happen. And that wasn't likely.

No one would know him, no one would notice him, he would be invisible to all those around him. Jacek wanted only one thing now, and that was to see Amy and her son as often and for as long as his old age allowed him.

He sighed as the train screeched to a stop at the station. It was good to be on his own again.

Jacek spent the next weeks getting settled into an apartment above a bakery across the street from the Piekarz building. With a little bit of luck, he thought as he looked around the one room he was renting and smelled the bakery below, this was where Amy bought her bread every morning.

Once he had a place to live, Jacek took a few days off to travel to East Germany. There he set up a drop point where Roman could leave messages for him. As soon as he had established a circuitous route for those messages to reach him in Poland, Jacek returned to Gdynia. Now no one could find him. And only Roman could contact him.

On his first morning back, Jacek was staring out the window, counting the floors to the seventh one, when he saw Amy turn the corner of the building. His heart raced at this first sighting. It was all he asked of life anymore, to see her and little Tomek now and then. He quickly got out his binoculars and focused them on Amy's face. She didn't look well. And the child she pushed in the stroller was not Tomek, but a younger girl. *Her daughter?* As he watched Amy stop and tie the hood of the pink snowsuit under the chin of the little girl, a warm glow settled over Jacek. He had a granddaughter. *Two grandchildren.*

Then, even as he smiled from the thought, the old woman, Hanna Piekarz, and Amy's husband, Jan, appeared with Tomek holding his hand and *pushing a pram*. *No, it can't be.* Jacek was beside himself. He counted backward mentally. He had seen Amy for the last time in September 1976. And now it was January 1978. Yes, it was possible. In the more than two years since his confrontation with Tadeusz and Hanna Piekarz, Amy had had two more children. *Three grandchildren.*

Jacek fixed the binoculars on the entire family, all waiting to cross the street. Only then did he notice that the adults were dressed in black. A funeral? Why was Hanna alone? Where was Tadeusz? Jacek thought he probably knew. He put on his coat and left the apartment to follow them.

Jacek had originally planned not to go outside and take the chance of being recognized when any of the Piekarz family were there. Not until he looked significantly different than he had two years ago. When they had met him, his hair was black, streaked with gray and very short. In the years that had elapsed, it had now turned snow white. Jacek intended on using that feature to disguise himself in his new life. A full head of white hair and a white beard would make it very hard for anyone to recognize the old Jacek Duch.

But today Jacek thought if his suspicion proved right, then a beardless risk would be worth taking. He followed the family, and the more he observed them, the more mixed his emotions became. What he had feared became increasingly obvious. Tadeusz Piekarz had died, and this was his funeral.

This piece of news, coupled with the astounding discovery that his daughter had three children instead of one, filled Jacek with a storm of conflicting emotions. At the graveyard, he stood apart from the crowd, amazed at the hundreds of people who had come to pay their respects. Jacek allowed his own feelings to reflect those around him. Tadeusz had been a comrade-in-arms of sorts for Jacek, as well. The man had saved Jacek's life during the war. But more importantly, he had kept his promise all these years.

Tadeusz had gone to his grave and not given away Jacek's secret. Piekarz had never told anyone but his wife, and maybe not even her, about Jacek calling out in English when delirious as a Polish partisan. Tadeusz had never betrayed Jacek as the American spy he was all during the war. That day, Jacek stopped thinking of Tadeusz and Hanna as the old man and woman who could bring him down. As he watched hundreds of people attending the funeral, Jacek doubted that Tadeusz Piekarz had ever betrayed anyone.

He stood beside a grove of trees and couldn't help but wonder what sort of funeral awaited him. He saw himself as a man who had betrayed everyone, including himself. In a flash of prescience, Jacek saw his own life in stark contrast to that of Tadeusz. The difference consisted of much more than just the homage being paid here today. There was the love of one woman, his Hanna. Jacek knew the bent old woman he saw here today, clinging to her son, had once been very attractive. Hanna had, in fact, attracted him, dark curls framing her face, a full figure, yet petite. He could still feel the rough wool of her suit when he met her for the first time, and touched her, in the Kraków train station during the last days of the war. *So many years ago.* Jacek shook himself.

Then there was Tadeusz's family life, children, and grandchildren. And his profession as a lecturer and pastor. But the disturbing realization on Jacek's mental tally sheet was Tadeusz Piekarz's cause. He and Tadeusz had both lived for a cause. And when Jacek looked at where his cause had brought him, left him, abandoned him, Jacek had no choice but to admit, *Tadeusz, yours was the better choice.*

It was a revelation Jacek wouldn't have allowed himself to acknowledge two years earlier, but in light of his treatment by both sides during the recent Carter visit, Jacek could see more clearly now where the choices in his own life had led him. And compared with the abundant harvest in Tadeusz Piekarz's life, the few grains Jacek was left with were meager and bitter reward.

He thought on all these things as he watched the people file by the grave. Jacek could not hear the words of tribute or the blessings, but he saw. He saw the expressions of old and young. He saw Hanna crumble into Jan's arms and have to be carried off. He saw Amy struggling with the three children until a friend came and took the two oldest ones from her. The one in her arms must be practically a newborn.

And then he saw him. *The outlaw.* Jacek shook himself and wished he had his binoculars as he peered at the man. There was no mistaking him, dark, young, and totally intent on Amy. He had found her in this crowd and chosen the ideal moment to approach her, as she stood helpless, with the baby in her arms.

So Piotr was still a plague in her life, Jacek thought. Maybe his end-of-life goal would have to expand and readmit the objective of eliminating this man. Jacek shook his head. He had thought getting Piotr bumped up on the SB's *Most Wanted* list would have been enough to remove him. But the man was still at large. Worse, he was still harassing his Amy, tempting her probably, and upsetting the very family life Jacek so envied.

I won't let it happen, he vowed. Now he would keep an even closer eye on Amy and, with a little bit of skill and patience, bring this man down. For although Tadeusz had proven worthy of the secret he had held over Jacek, his son was a different case altogether. This Piotr could and would use his information to ruin the hidden life Jacek had so recently won for himself.

At the very moment of his decision, Jacek saw them both turn and look right at him. He held his breath. They were too far away to recognize him, and too many people stood milling between them. All the same, Jacek had seen enough. He ducked behind a tree, then slowly made his way back down the beach.

In the weeks following Tadeusz Piekarz's funeral, Jacek concentrated on what he came to see as the most important stakeout of his life. He had decided not to risk accessing the tapes of the Piekarz apartment. That trick had worked once, and although he still had all his passports, identification, and passes for the SB, as well as the CIA, he couldn't afford anyone finding out his whereabouts. So he forfeited all his privileges, including admittance to the local censor office, where he could have read their mail. Jacek didn't want anyone to know where he was. So any information he gleaned would have to be done through good, old-fashioned spying.

He spent countless hours by the window, staring through the binoculars, fixed always on the seventh floor, and caught only glimpses of figures walking by the window. At night, he read books, sometimes three or four a week. He read endlessly, and anything he could get his hands on, in Polish or German. He even read bits of the Bible but didn't get past the first book of the New Testament. But always in those long hours of loneliness, like a parallel life, he imagined what the conversations in that apartment might be, based on the daily rhythm he had learned to recognize from the tapes he had listened to in the lodge.

And more than once during that winter, he wondered if he was only deluding himself that his existence had any purpose. How could he protect Amy by simply watching her from a distance? Tadeusz's funeral had proven a turning point. Once he allowed a single doubt in, they stung him in swarms.

When the warmer weather finally did arrive and Amy could take her children for walks, Jacek discovered a fresh torment at being so near, but so bound to anonymity. He tried to convince himself that he was lucky to get even this in retirement. To be left in peace and watch his grandchildren grow up, surely that was more happiness than many men like him could claim.

Jacek followed Amy as she made her shopping rounds. His favorite time was when she brought the children to a little playground in the nearby park. He would wait until she arrived and then go sit down on a bench with a newspaper or a book and pretend to read. He wore glasses to read because he was farsighted, and then he could peer over the glasses to watch the antics of little Tomek and Żanetka and even little Baby Gonia as she learned how to crawl. He had learned the two younger children's names by painstakingly eavesdropping the first few times he was able to tail Amy.

Jacek spent many of those moments, hiding behind his glasses and white beard, fantasizing about telling Amy who he really was. It became almost an obsession for him, an ache that only intensified as the weeks and months passed by. At the same time, he realized with relief how glad he was to finally be out of the game, deeply grateful for this second chance at peace.

Sometimes during that summer and autumn, as a means of fighting the growing urge to tell Amy who he was, Jacek would leave Gdynia. He traveled to all his favorite spots in Poland, the remote corners where time had stood still for centuries, where the old women wore scarves and sat beside each other on benches at the edge of fields, where eagles still called to each other over pristine lakes.

Jacek always returned to his one-room apartment in Gdynia, but these trips fed a part of him, a deep love for this country and its remote, natural beauty. Yet whenever he found himself back on *his* same park bench, watching his three grandchildren again after such a trip, he tormented himself with more fantasies. What would it be like to teach Tomek how to fish? How did Żanetka's hair smell after it was freshly washed and shone that ember red in the sun? More than once, as the months became a year, Jacek wondered if he was suffering from a sick obsession. Then just as often, he decided there were worse ways to end one's days. Unlike many of the unpleasant things he'd done in his life, there was no crime in watching these children play.

During his second winter in Gdynia, Jacek consoled himself with the thought that if his life seemed to consist of meaningless routine, then so were the days of most people his age. At least here in Poland, most elderly men and women had families around them, neighbors helping, family meals, and Name Day celebrations.

And Poland's economy seemed to be only improving. Despite his knowledge of why the economy seemed to prosper, Jacek felt a certain pride to see the progress.

By the time Jacek had spent a year and a half in Gdynia, he had settled several of these issues within himself. He had learned contentment, and he had discovered a deep joy at witnessing the growth of little Tomek, Żanetka, and Gonia.

For the first time in his long life, Jacek's wish had come true. He no longer felt all alone in the world and had a measure of peace. Amy and the children had become the focal point of his life, even if they didn't know it. And he had finally accepted their ignorance of him as the price he would have to pay in order to enjoy his daily glimpses of their little lives.

It was enough.

One warm day in June, Jacek sat on his bench, enjoying the sun and the children's laughter. Little Gonia had discovered butterflies and was crawling around the grass trying to catch them. Jacek sat clear on the other side of the playground and couldn't hear what they all were saying, but he attracted no attention as an old man sitting in the sun. There were enough others like him in the park that day.

And then, only moments after he had closed his eyes to take a little nap, Jacek felt a ball hit his ankle. He *had* fallen asleep. He looked up and Tomek stood before him, a vision straight from his own private daydreams. He stared at the boy, mesmerized by his proximity. All he could think was that Tomek had just turned five the month before. Jacek had even bought a present for him—a small red fire truck—a silly gesture, really, since he'd never have the chance to give it. Jacek had the toy in his apartment on the table.

Now Tomek smiled at Jacek. "Excuse me. Could I please fetch the ball out from under your bench?"

Jacek couldn't help himself. He said, "Here, let me get it." Then he bent over, retrieved the ball, and handed it to Tomek with one hand.

With the other hand, he reached out, over the distance of all his hopes and fantasies, and touched the boy's arm. Jacek felt the bone, the small muscle, stroked the skin, brushed against the tiny hairs, could even smell the little-boy sweat in his hair, memorized every detail he could in that split second.

Then Tomek said, "Thank you, sir," and was gone.

PART II

—————————— ❧ ——————————

DAILY BREAD
Matthew 6:11

January 1978 – April 1982

Yes, this is the same sort of hope as after the war, a
normal hope for one's children, the same as what
we used to hope for ourselves, but never had.

7

You my best thought in the day or the night

Tomasz's very first memory was of his youngest sister's birth. It was as if Gonia's entrance to life marked Tomasz's own entrance into consciousness; she was the first entry into his memory. What did he remember? Like any three-year-old, bits and pieces, impressions, emotions, sharp noises.

His mother with the baby in her arms. Too tiny for him to hold. Not allowed. Still, he liked her toes.

No memory of little Żanetka, who would have been almost a year old and still a baby herself. But if you asked Tomasz what Gonia had on the day she came home from the hospital, he could still describe the little colored bows on the outer blanket they had wrapped her in.

They all stood around his grandfather's bed. His father and mother leaned over to show Gonia to him, but all little Tomek's grandfather could do was make terrible snoring sounds.

"Look, *Tatusiu*. This is our little Gonia. *Małgorzata*." Amy looked up, uncertain. Tadeusz lay so still.

Tomek did not think he could ever hear her.

"Go on," Jan said, coming up behind her.

"I'm so thankful for God's gift of a new heart. Now you have two granddaughters. Żaneta, Elżbieta, in English *Elizabeth*, the message-bearer, and tiny Gonia. Tatusiu?"

And me! Tomek wanted to yell. But even though his grandfather couldn't hear them, everyone kept telling Tomek to be quiet.

So he hadn't yelled.

Tomasz's next memory after the birth of his sister was of meeting his uncle Piotr. Well, of a special day for his uncle and the rest of the family. Piotr's wedding day. Tomek was six and could remember many things about that day. It started with him standing on a chair and helping his mother and grandmother bake.

Good smells wafted all around him as his mother said, "Do you think we'll ever be able to fit everyone here for the reception after the wedding?"

Babcia gave the spoon from the cake batter to Tomek and winked at him. "Oh, Amy, it will be just like when Tadeusz was alive and our home was filled with visitors from all over Poland and the world. Today our friends and Piotr's will make this a home bursting with love." She reached out her hand and squeezed Amy's. "It's been eight long years since we last saw Piotr."

Then the door to the other room flew open. This was where his parents slept with the baby and Żanetka. Tomek was big enough now to sleep in the living room with his grandmother. The stove and sink were part of his room.

In the doorway stood his father with the funniest expression on his face. A big smile. Then *Tatuś* started singing the first line of Tomek's favorite song. All five faces turned to him in surprise. When Jan saw their expressions, he burst out laughing so hard, he forgot the next line.

Little Żanetka smiled at him and pointed a flour-covered finger as if she were conducting an orchestra. Then, in her tiny three-year-old voice, as clear as a bell, she finished the song for him.

Then Jan swept Baby Gonia up and started dancing with her. Hanna shook her head from where she sat in the wheelchair, beside the sink. "What on earth are you up to? My son has lost his mind, Amy. I'm sorry."

Amy wiped the flour off her hands and laughed. "Its all right, Mamusiu. My husband will find it for him."

"Oh, you're so clever," Jan said, sweeping her into his arms as well. "Who taught you to speak Polish so cleverly? Huh? *Her* crazy son, that's who."

Amy almost tripped in the small room. "And you did a fine job too," she smiled at him. Tomek smiled with his parents when they looked at each other that way, with his mother's eyes dancing like her feet.

Later that morning the downstairs neighbor carried Babcia

down all seven flights, since the new elevator was broken again. Then they walked over to the church, but without his father, since he had already left. The church was where the wedding was going to be, and Tomek's father got to do the wedding. Piotr had written about that as well. He wanted to see Jan first, then the rest of the family. That's what his mother had said.

When they went inside the church where his father said a sermon every Sunday, Tomek ran straight up to Jan and took his hand. A man who didn't look anything like Jan stood beside him.

Tomek's eyes grew round as he watched a tear form in one of his uncle's eyes. He looked over and saw it was because of Babcia. As the man walked slowly down the aisle toward her, he kept staring at the wheelchair. Even Tomek knew you weren't supposed to do that.

Then his uncle knelt at Hanna's side, placing his head on her lap.

"I'm so sorry, Mamusiu. So very sorry I wasn't there when Tatuś died."

"He knows. He knows." Tomek saw his grandmother crying for the first time ever. Each tear rested on the clear skin, as thin as parchment. "Oh, he knows. And so do I, Piotr. I only wish you didn't have to see me like this. But when my Tadeusz died, so did these old muscles, I'm afraid."

When Piotr straightened, Amy greeted him with outstretched arms. Before she could say anything, he put a finger to his lips and shook his head. "A new start, agreed?"

Amy shot Jan a relieved look. He could only smile back. "Yes, of course, a new start," she answered.

"Besides," Piotr continued, "how else could I respond when I see how happy you've made my brother, and with *three* children." He turned around and stooped down again, this time in front of Tomek.

"You, young man. I've been wanting to meet you for a very long time."

"Six years, sir." Tomek swelled with pride that he was the eldest.

"Yes, six years," Piotr answered as he took Tomek's outstretched hand.

"And these young ladies, they're like twins, one dark, the other light."

Tomek looked at the two heads of curls and realized for the first time just how much Gonia and Żanetka really did resemble each other. The shape of their faces, their height, their chins. They were the same in everything except hair and eye color. "No, they're not twins," Tomek said in his important voice. "This is our baby, Gonia. Well, we call her our baby. She's almost three."

"But she'll be three in a month. *I'm* already three!" Żanetka held up one thumb and two fingers, while her other hand held down the remaining two fingers.

"And what is your name, little red-haired princess?" Piotr asked.

She pretended to look shy. "Żaneta. Well, really I'm Elżbieta."

"And who knows my name?" his uncle asked.

"You are our uncle Piotr," Tomek spoke up. "And you have been doing secret, dangerous things to throw out the communists so now Poland can be free."

Everyone stared at him, then laughed. Tomek wasn't sure if he'd said the right thing until his uncle looked him straight in the eyes, as if they were both men.

"Tomku, I'm not a hero. But I can tell you a story about something I saw yesterday, made for real heroes."

"You were in Gdańsk then yesterday?" Jan asked.

"Yes," Piotr said, standing back up. "Halina and I both wanted to attend the dedication of a monument honoring the workers killed there during the riots of 1970."

"Ten years ago," Hanna said wistfully. "And all these years the poor families have been trying to mark the spot with handmade wooden crosses."

Piotr nodded. "Yes, where these men were murdered by *milicja* forces. Crosses had cropped up overnight, only to be removed by government forces. Now three iron crosses rise high above them all. Mamusiu, they seem ordained by God himself. They reach to the very heavens. As I stood in the shadow of the great crosses, structures no one would ever again remove in secrecy, I wondered if they symbolized man touching his Maker, or was God bending down to help?"

Tomek stared up at his uncle. He could preach just like his father. "Was that the story?" he asked.

"Yes, Tomku. And someday I'll take you there to see them."

"It's so strange," Amy said. "Since the Gdańsk agreements were signed at the end of August, *Solidarność* has been legal, it's as if a terrible darkness has lifted. Here it is December 1980, a half year later, and Poland is still free, well, almost free. A year ago the workers' crosses could never have been erected in public like that. Why, now there's no more reason to fear being associated with the underground. I suppose that's why we finally heard from you, Piotr?"

He nodded. "There isn't even any underground anymore. It *is* the Solidarność movement. We never dreamed we'd get such across-the-board support so quickly. But now that we have the clear support of all levels of Polish society, from peasant farmers to mine workers to university intellectuals, and even the Roman Catholic Church, there's no stopping us. The way it looks, soon, very soon, the Soviet-run communists will have no choice but to surrender the remaining control of Poland back to the Poles."

"You and Halina were very lucky to witness that dedication yesterday. A historic event," Jan said.

"But we're missing someone here," Hanna broke in. "When do we get to meet the lucky girl? You orchestrated all our meeting times for this day, but I still haven't had a chance to approve of my future daughter-in-law." Her eyes twinkled. "Then again, Piotrek, when have I ever been able to deny you anything?"

The family laughed again as Hanna reached up to stroke Piotr's hand.

"Uppy, uppy!" Gonia reached out her arms toward Piotr.

"She wants you to pick her up," Tomek translated.

"Yes, it's English," Amy laughed. "Well, sort of English."

"*Po polsku*, Gonia," Tomek said, then to Piotr he explained, "She doesn't know the difference yet."

When Gonia put her legs so she could ride on his hip, they all laughed at Piotr for not knowing how to carry a small child. But Gonia would not let him go. As Piotr stroked her soft arms and let her tiny hands play with his hair as he stood there, Tomek saw the same kind of dancing light in his uncle's eyes that his parents had shared that morning.

Later that afternoon, the church was packed for the wedding. Tomek didn't like having to wear a tie. It made his neck itch. Up front he could see his new aunt Halina in her pretty dress. She was as small as Babcia, but looked much younger than his own mother, and she had blond hair. After the service, her hand was sweaty when he shook it. She had wanted to kiss him on the cheek, but Tomek was quick to stick his hand out first.

The rest of that day passed in a blur. The reception at the apartment was even more crowded than the church. People everywhere! Tomek was lucky. He was small enough to slip between all the legs and sneak as much from the food table as he wanted. His parents were too busy to keep an eye on him. Moving around like he did, he heard plenty.

His mother said to their neighbor, "The two rooms are packed. Look at all these people. Jan's congregation, all our friends, together with Piotr and Halina's friends. I just hope there's enough food."

Tomek looked at the table. Still full of salads and cake and a wondrous assortment of good things that kept appearing out of the strangest corners and their neighbors' apartments.

Beside him, his uncle had just brought two other people over to meet his parents. "These are good friends of mine. Bogdan, my brother, Jan, and his wife, Amy. Ewa, this is Jan and Amy."

Jan took Ewa's hand and brought it to his lips. Tomek didn't like to think he'd have to do the same with any girls he met when he was older.

Tomek noticed Ewa had dark eyes like Amy's as his father said, "Friends of Piotr. I'm honored."

The man called Bogdan squinted at Jan. He wore glasses and took these off now to clean them. "I *think* your brother and I already know each other, Piotr."

Jan looked at him more closely. "Sixty-eight?" he asked uncertainly.

Bogdan nodded. "Yes, you were the graduate student who didn't want to get involved."

Jan smiled. "It all seems so long ago. You've accomplished a lot in twelve years."

"Not me, Poland," Bogdan said. "And others like my lovely wife here, Ewa. But we're not there yet."

Tomek wondered if this meant these two were heroes like his uncle.

Suddenly from the door came the sound of a man shouting in English. Tomek made his way through the crowd and saw a tall, balding man who wasn't Polish getting lots of hugs. Thanks to his mother reading and playing games with him in English, Tomek could understand what he said.

"What on earth is happening, Jan? I thought I'd drop in on your quiet, sober family, and I walk into the wildest party in Poland! Is this all in celebration of Solidarność?"

Before Jan could answer, Piotr came up behind them and said, "I'll answer that, thank you. Well, yes, we are celebrating Poland's freedom. But we're also celebrating my wedding! Welcome!"

Tomek liked the way Piotr engulfed the man in a great hug. Then the man looked from Jan to Piotr, then back again. "I don't know what to say. Wedding? You, Piotr? And it was today? And you two, ah, you two are back together. And my Hanna. Oh, she must be very happy, very happy indeed. Why didn't anyone tell me?"

Piotr said, "Well, no one really knew about this, including me, until a few weeks ago." He laughed. "Look, there's Halina. I'll introduce you to the bride. Halina, this is Aad, an old Piekarz family friend from The Netherlands."

"In Holland we always kiss the bride three times," Aad said, and everyone laughed as Halina let herself be kissed. "This is quite a day for you," Aad said. "Congratulations."

"Yes, thank you. I'm a bit, well, overwhelmed. It's hard remembering who's who."

"Well, this one you won't forget, Halina," Piotr said. "Aad is what Jan would call a missionary brother. He's been visiting our home for decades. Of course, he's a little older now, a little balder, and maybe a bit heavier." Piotr jabbed Aad in the stomach and they both laughed.

Then Jan added quietly, "But this tall Dutchman's smile can still warm a room. When Piotr and I were growing up, Aad was a dear friend to both our parents, always bringing whatever was needed, medicine, vitamins, training materials, and Bibles. He's one of the few men from the West I've met with the gift of coming alongside to discover what pastors in the East needed most. He doesn't try to impose anything. He's just there, and at the oddest moments, like now."

Aad laughed and looked embarrassed. "That's enough, Jan. Don't give away too many of my secrets."

Halina said, "No, I had no idea Piotr's family was involved in such things."

Tomek saw his uncle glance at his father and say, "It's more than that, actually. Jan is a pastor like my father was. But thanks to Aad, Jan was able to set up a link between the Warszawa church he worked in during the early seventies and a church in Albania."

"Why would you want to do that?" Halina asked Jan.

"We supply them with what Aad supplies us with, teaching materials, Bibles, medicine. But Piotr shouldn't be talking like this about it. I guess I'm not quite used to this new spirit of openness. It's strange not having to be afraid anymore of who will hear what. Well, besides, Halina, you're family now. And we have no secrets from you." Jan smiled at her.

Aad said, "Well, I like to think I brought more than books to the Piekarz family." He paused and grinned.

Piotr added, "Yes, on one of Aad's trips he brought Amy with him. And because of Aad's friendship with my father, Jan had the chance to meet Amy and get to know her during one of their Bible-smuggling trips to Moscow. Yes, we owe this man a great deal."

Everyone was quiet for a moment. It felt to Tomek like someone had said something wrong. Then Halina said, "Oh, look, there's someone putting those gifts in the wrong place. Will you excuse me?"

Jan went off to go help Amy. Tomek stayed near his uncle and heard Aad ask, "So you two have been reconciled?"

Piotr answered, "It was incredible, Aad. When I saw Jan, he just bowled right into me. I was so nervous about apologizing and then *bam!* he thudded into me and was talking about how sorry *he* is. I had completely underestimated how good it would feel to be back with the family again."

"Eight years of separation is a long time."

"You've known our family so long, Aad. You've always been there for us, even when I wasn't."

"You did what you had to."

"No, I had convinced myself I could survive without them. But when I saw Mamusia sitting in a wheelchair, I knew at what price."

Aad nodded and put a hand on Piotr's shoulder. Then he leaned forward and said softly, "And Amy?"

Piotr nodded. "I'll admit, seeing Amy was hard, but I have Halina, so I'm over Amy. Then seeing her and Jan's children was even harder. I tell you, Aad, their faces turned something over in me. I don't know..."

"What?"

"Well, Tomek is a strong boy, a good boy, I could see that much in his eyes. The red-haired daughter looked like she doesn't even belong in the family, and she was so quiet. But those green eyes take us all in."

Aad smiled. "It's true, that's little Żanetka, all right."

"But I have to admit, the baby is my favorite. Have you seen her eyes? They're hazel-colored, and she has dimples on both cheeks. When I held her, it was almost as if I'd never paid a price for leaving them at all."

"Children have a way of doing that, smoothing time over. Well, Piotr, let's hope you and Halina can share the joy of children some-day soon."

Piotr took a step backward and laughed. "One thing at a time, all right? I just got married today!"

Tomek had heard enough. Here he thought his uncle was going to be *his* friend, and it turned out he liked Gonia better. He headed for the food table, where Halina was passing out cake.

"Tomku, I know you've had more than one piece already, but you've been a good boy, haven't you? Here." She gave him another piece and smiled at him. Then Tomek walked down to the end of the table, where he saw Gonia with a piece of wedding cake in her mouth. When no one was looking, he grabbed it away from her. He thought she'd probably had too much to eat anyway and could get sick from too much cake.

"Mine! Mine!" Gonia stood holding on to the table edge and screamed as loudly as she could. Beside her Tomek stuffed his mouth full of the white cake he had helped his grandmother dec-orate. Then he took his own piece and started eating that. When he looked up, Tomek saw his father frowning at him.

Tomek said, "She's always screaming, *it's mine*. Halina said it was mine. She cut it for me and said it was *mine*."

"Give it back to your sister. And leave something for our guests, Tomku."

"No. It's *mine*." Tomek felt his eyes narrow. It wasn't fair.

His father said in the soft, stern tone that meant Tomek was really in trouble, "All right, young man. Now you've gone too far. Come with me. We're going outside to have a talk."

Tomek's face burned with shame. He put the rest of the cake into his pocket and slid away along the wall. Maybe he could lose him-self in the crowd again. He saw one of the old ladies from the church pick up Gonia and start crooning over her until little smiles replaced her tears.

When Jan started to follow Tomek, Aad placed a hand on his arm. "I notice he took the second slice of cake with him."

"Yes, I should follow. He's a very selfish boy. I'm embarrassed you had to witness that, Aad. The girls aren't like that at all. Tomku, you come here right now," he called after Tomek.

Aad said, "No, they never are."

Then, as fast as he could, Tomek took off like a shot, running out the door and down the stairs.

Jacek looked up, blinking into the sun, deeply thankful for this first contact with Tomek. It was more than he had ever hoped for. He looked in Amy's direction. She had her back to him, busy chatting with one of the other mothers. Then he stood up and left the playground, looking back in time to see five-year-old Tomek pulling on his mother's skirt and pointing in the direction of Jacek's empty bench. *But now I'm gone.*

The incident reminded Jacek of the family's vulnerability. His very reason for being there was to make sure they remained protected. But Jacek now wondered if he had been deluding himself. Amy didn't need him in her life. He wondered more often lately if his presence might only bring her more danger. The Piekarz apartment was bugged. If anyone in the family mentioned his name even once, the SB would be on to him as a Western agent. They wouldn't hesitate to use Amy and the children as a means of breaking Jacek. Years of experience told him that Roman would stop at nothing.

Yes, but so far, so good, Jacek tormented himself. *Yet I can't afford to be selfish like this afternoon even one more time. I will not take chances with their lives.* It was the only rule, his last rule, after all the rest had been discarded. This was all he was left with, a desire to remove himself as a threat in their lives. That and to remove the only other person who threatened his family's safety, Piotr Piekarz. For Jacek was still obsessed with hunting down the outlaw.

Then that same night, as if the day had been marked somehow by the movement of planets or the fullness of the moon, Jacek heard from Roman. After a year and a half of silence, Roman wanted to bring Jacek back from the dead. The reason was the new Polish pope's visit to his homeland in June.

As Jacek stood in his one-room apartment, staring at the paper with Roman's order in his hands, he resisted its message down to the very core of his being. Everything in him screamed not to return to the SB, but Roman made it clear he had no choice.

So Jacek left his apartment. He left Gdynia. He left his family behind. He left his life. And every day, he thought back on the touch of little Tomek as the farewell gift it had become.

When they met, Roman looked even older than Jacek felt. He'd gone completely bald and gained some weight around the middle. His face was covered with baggy shadows. The first thing Roman said as they met in a restaurant in the Old Town of Warszawa was, "I noticed you weren't around much. I mean at the drop point in East Germany. *Rostock*, wasn't it?"

"No, Dresden," Jacek said, thinking, *The games never end.* "Since when do you trust the *Stasi*?" Jacek asked.

Roman laughed. "You're right."

Jacek knew that among the SB there was a certain honor among thieves. The general feeling toward the East German security services was that they were robots. Even the KGB was more human, in a savage sort of way. It was the reason Jacek had chosen a contact point in the DDR. He knew nine out of ten East Germans worked for the Stasi, and each of them could be counted on if bribed.

"So what's so urgent that you couldn't do without me?" Jacek asked.

"Well, you were just too smart. One of the very scenarios you once sketched for me years ago has actually happened."

"Don't tell me," Jacek said. "Growing support of the Roman Catholic Church for overthrowing the communist hold on Poland."

"Well, wherever you've been hiding out, it hasn't been where they censor the news. Anyway, the new pope's visit this month could blow up in our faces if we don't handle this right. With the church behind the underground, there's no telling how far the resistance in Poland can go."

"Bold words from one of the security service heads," Jacek said. "Tell me what you're planning."

Roman explained the strategy, and Jacek added a few details of his own. The crowds would be massive, they knew that much already. And the potential was explosive.

Jacek had his own risk potential now that he was back "in the open" again. He kept his longer white hair but shaved off the beard and shaped the rest into a bushy mustache. He wanted to fit in with the style of the day. This was important because he still had to hide from the CIA.

The same men and women who had supported his network with the Company were now the very people Jacek must avoid and fool. The CIA thought he was dead. It would be better for everyone if that remained so. Jacek knew he must keep an extremely low profile. As he prepared himself for this latest mission, Jacek, who thought he had left this all behind, realized with some trepidation that he would now be required to play his most subtle role yet. He would have to hide from the very masters he used to serve. And this time, everything was at stake.

During the last half of 1979 and the first half of 1980, in the year after Roman recalled Jacek, everything the government security forces tried failed. The more they attempted to quench the new Solidarność movement, the farther the flames seemed to spread. A spark of hope had caught among the people as Poland began to struggle, yet again, to free itself from the mantle of oppression.

In that year after Jacek had felt Tomek's touch, he spent all his working hours with a team of political analysts. How he longed for the simple days of sitting in the sunshine in the park. He often thought back to those quiet days in Gdynia during the endless arguments over policy. His assignment was to come up with a strategy aimed at eliminating the threat of Solidarność.

"The communist government considers the new church support as intolerable." This was the latest memorandum, issued in early 1980. Jacek was in the unfortunate position of being able to say he had tried to warn them years earlier. His reward now was being forced to listen to the so-called experts say the same things over and over again.

All the while, Jacek waited for the part of him that missed the action. He needed that part to rise up and lend a sense of purpose to what he was doing now. In Gdynia he had been prepared to accept the quiet life. Secluded there, in anonymity, he had thought all he wanted was peace.

But as he watched Roman line up the big guns of the secret police, and as his team of analysts hammered out a strategy for cracking down on the population before this Solidarność got out of control, Jacek sickened at the thought of what he worked for now.

Jacek could accept that behind the scenes, spying on preparations for a harsher treatment by the milicja, or government police force, of all levels of the population seemed to be his destiny. Then why couldn't he thrill to the chase like in the old days?

The answer lay much closer to the surface than Jacek was willing to admit. Perhaps the disillusionment that had seeped into every one of his days that year was simply because his spying served no purpose now. He had no one to report to anymore.

And in the heat of this latest battle, Jacek had now become a member of the old communist guard.

He heard his voice during these meetings, saying they should have targeted KOR as he had suggested back in November 1977. Now it was out of hand. Yes, they all agreed. But *now* the government ministers faced an escalated situation.

Around and around and around they went. The question on everyone's mind until August 1980 was how to put the flames out before the communists got burned.

8

A month after his uncle's wedding, in January 1981, Tomek's father went to America. He traveled with that tall man Aad, and Tomek stayed at home with all the women.

"Tomku, don't look so glum," Babcia said. "We need you here. I'm glad we have at least one man in the house." Tomek was helping his grandmother fold laundry. He sat on the couch beside her, while his mother kept the girls in the other room, where she was ironing.

"But I wanted to go with him," Tomek said.

"You're so much like your uncle Piotr. Did you know that? I see it now that Piotr is back in our lives again."

Tomek looked up and saw his mother standing in the doorway to the other bedroom, her mouth open.

"No, Mamusiu, that's not true. He's not at all like Piotr. Why, Piotr is much . . . moodier, don't you think?" She brushed past them to put away some clothes in the dresser in the corner.

Tomek looked at his grandmother, but she didn't answer.

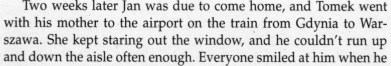

Two weeks later Jan was due to come home, and Tomek went with his mother to the airport on the train from Gdynia to Warszawa. She kept staring out the window, and he couldn't run up and down the aisle often enough. Everyone smiled at him when he did it, as long as he didn't make a lot of noise.

At the airport, his parents hugged and kissed, holding each other for way too long. Then, during the five hours on the train ride back home, Tomek couldn't get the giant jets he had seen out of his mind. "I want to fly, too. Why didn't you take me, Tatusiu?"

"Someday I will, Tomku."

"Now, tell me everything. How was the trip? Was Aad pleased?" his mother asked.

"Aad is always pleased," Jan laughed. "But I wanted to make sure I was worth the planefare that the mission put up, so I let him schedule me for as many preaching engagements possible. I think a lot of money was raised. Americans are so generous, but I knew that already." He smiled and squeezed Amy's hand.

"Strange, isn't it? Aad brought me east. Now he brought you west. With the new freedom, it only took two months to get you a passport and visa."

"Well, having an American wife helped."

"Was it hard, preaching in English?"

"Well, Aad said on the first day, 'You can do it. Those Americans will just think your accent is charming. The thing is, people need to hear from a Pole, not a Dutchman, how in this new year of 1981 Solidarność has changed some things, but not everything. There's still as much a need as ever. And just because doors are opening doesn't mean it's time to stop going through them.' "

"Well, tell me all the places you went. I want to hear it *all*."

"Me too," Tomek said as he crawled onto his father's lap.

"We started in Los Angeles, then worked our way up the length of California, then flew home. Aad said the West Coast is enough for one trip. And because there were two of us, we could appear at twice as many churches. Some of the congregations had been supporting Aad's work here for decades. Aad went with me the first week, then once we reached northern California, he let me conduct meetings on my own."

"Did you go to Yosemite? I've always wanted to go there."

Jan paused, then said softly, "Yes. Amy, I had no idea all the *things* you left behind. I've never seen such extremes. Yosemite was breathtaking in its natural beauy. And I couldn't believe how open people were everywhere we went. Total strangers came up to us spontaneously and talked about their sicknesses, their grief, their intimate losses, as well as great joy and blessings.

"The wealth I saw in San Diego and the communities around San Jose was beyond belief. I've never seen such big houses and expansive land. Like *cattle on a thousand hills*."

"What else?" Amy gently prodded.

"In the cities of Los Angeles and San Francisco, I saw incredible poverty. Women and children, as well as men who looked sick and wasted, were sleeping on the streets, under bridges, in doorways. I . . . hadn't expected that in America."

They were silent for a few minutes, then Mamusia asked, "What did you preach about?"

"Well, I had a fresh new audience, didn't I? I used some of my old favorites that our own congregation has already heard. Maybe it was too much, but Aad said I could say whatever I felt moved to. And this was the other extreme I witnessed that was disturbing to me."

"What was that?"

"Extreme judgmentalness. For all their generosity, Americans are also very critical, even of themselves. So I said we should beware of judging ourselves too harshly. And others. There was only one group of people in the Bible Jesus could not . . . how did I put it in English? *Stomach*. Good word, right? And that was the educated Pharisees. They thought they knew so much and were always quick to judge. Only against them was Jesus ever angry. Do you think that was too much?"

Tomek looked at his mother. She was crying, but with a soft smile on her lips. "No, Jan. I don't think that was too much. Tell me more."

"I did recognize a lot of what I love in you. Many Americans are like children. We've lost this innocence in Poland. The spontaneous way these Americans take strangers to their hearts, it's almost . . ."

"Naïve?" Amy said.

"Well, no. I don't know. It's no problem. I mean, look how incredibly they give, in heaped-down and overflowing measures. They're so generous. And so loving and so funny sometimes. I see how you are like this too, with your giving heart. It's just that they . . . have so much.

"I can say this to you, Amy, but these people have gone into my heart and I fear for them. '*And from everyone who has been given much shall much be required.*' "

Amy did not answer but just nodded. "I don't know," Jan sighed. "I'm empty after everything that's happened. I'm just *so thankful* to be back with you and the children." He gave Tomek a big hug.

Tomek thought this might be his chance, so he asked, "Did you bring me back a gift, Tatusiu?"

Jan started to frown and Amy said, "Now, Jan, he's excited."

His father nodded and reached into his small bag. Tomek so wanted a new battery-operated race car. He had asked his mother if they sold them in America, and she had said she thought so. Now he wondered if a race car wouldn't get crushed in the bag his father was searching through.

Then Jan pulled out something flat and white, wrapped in plastic. "Here, I bought you a T-shirt, Tomku. You'll be the only boy at your new school with 'I love San Francisco' written across your chest."

Tomek burst into tears.

"What is it? You don't like it? You should be more grateful. Tomku, sometimes I just . . ."

"I wanted a race car," Tomek said between sobs.

"It's my fault, Jan. I think I gave him the wrong impression."

"But you just said they have so many *things.*" Tomek brushed away his tears. He hated it when he cried.

"Yes, they have *things*, Tomku. But things aren't what's most important in life. And you have every *thing* you need. Your mother and I make sure you never go without. It's a pity you were too young to go with me on the trip to the Ukraine in the Soviet Union last year. Then you'd be more thankful for all that you have.

"There the people can't even move from village to village without permission from the police."

"You have to give your passport back to the police in Gdynia when we get home," Tomek said.

"You know this? Then you're a clever enough boy to know we may not have total freedom yet, but we have *more* than the people in Russia. And as far as things are concerned, the people I met in the Ukraine live off the food they grow in their own gardens, like ours along the railway tracks. Some people can listen to Polish radio, and they know we have it much better. *All* their shops were empty."

Everyone was quiet for a moment. Tomek was glad no one else sat in their compartment to hear his father preaching to him like this. Then an idea popped into his head. "Will you take me to America someday, Tatusiu?"

"No, son. I think I'd better take you on a trip to Russia first."

93

"You never take me anywhere. I wish I could travel."

"That's enough, Tomku! You're tired and that's why you're talking this way. Why don't you lie down over there and try to sleep," Amy said.

Tomek climbed off his father's lap and curled up on the seat opposite his parents. Then he pretended to go to sleep, but he could still hear it when his father sighed and said, "Amy, I had no idea all you gave up when you came here, came to me. The wealth, the space, like Tomek says, the *things.*"

"Hush." She placed a finger over his lips. "Don't. Just don't. Here I have you. You and our precious children. I prayed for you every day. Your day, my night."

"My day, your night," he answered. And Tomek was afraid they would kiss again.

Tomek stood next to the globe in their neighbor's living room. It was a huge, brown globe with all the countries outlined in black with giant sea monsters coming out of the oceans. *Pani* Irena said it was all right. Żanetka spun the globe, and Tomek told her the names of the countries his finger landed on.

"If I could go anywhere, I'd go . . . there!" Tomek said. "I'd go to America. And I'd go to Australia . . . there!"

Żanetka said, "Where's Bethlehem? I want to go see where Baby Jesus was born."

Tomek frowned at her. "You're only three."

"I'm almost four!"

He took over spinning the globe, then stopped it with his finger on top of one of the dragons. "I would go to islands where pirates have buried treasure . . . there!"

Their grandmother appeared in the door. "Żanetko, it's time to come home."

"Where would *you* go, *Babciu*?" Tomek asked.

"I would go to bed if I were you two. Come on now, enough world traveling for tonight."

From August 1980, Jacek inwardly rejoiced with the rest of the country. The passion he held for Poland ran just as deep as in the days when he fought alongside the partisans in the Home Army.

Outwardly, Jacek's colleagues, the other superior officers in the SB, saw the new freedom of Solidarność as a massive opportunity for gathering information. "Let them think they're free," Roman told them all. So while the communists regrouped to map out a new plan of attack, the secret police had never been so busy. Their agents spent the entire Solidarność period, starting at the end of August 1980, getting to know the enemy.

And all the while, the Soviet Union put pressure on the Polish government to act. Do something, anything, but get the country back under control. Those were the orders. Finally, in March 1981 the Russians threatened to invade Poland.

9

Waking or sleeping, your presence my light

"Tell us, Uncle, please!" Tomek chanted. Then Żanetka joined in, and they both made their voices bounce off the tiled walls at the ice cream parlor. "Tell us, Uncle, please!"

They sat together, all of them eating different flavors out of glass bowls. Tomek's grandmother was back home with his mother and Gonia. Tomek had promised to bring them back some of their favorite ice cream. Tomek's Name Day was coming up on September 22, so they were going to have a big picnic next week. Their uncle had taken the four of them out to celebrate, and they now sat around a little marble table, with ice cream running down their chins. They were the only customers.

"My teacher says *Lech Wałęsa* is a hero," Tomek said. He was *very* proud of having started school on the first of September.

His father shook his head. "I remember when I was seven. My teacher would *never* have called Wałęsa a hero. Ha, that would have been a joke!"

"You sound so bitter," Piotr said.

"I'm not bitter. Not really," Jan said.

"Why wouldn't your teacher be like my teacher?" Tomek asked. He was using his spoon to make stripes of chocolate sauce throughout the ice cream. When he finished, he was going to mush it all together and see how dark the ice cream became.

"Well, for one thing . . ."

"Don't go there, Jan," Piotr said.

"Why not? The boy *needs* to know. Then maybe he won't take so much for granted."

Tomek looked up, his spoon halfway to his mouth. *What have I done wrong?* They were just having fun, eating ice cream, and he wanted his uncle to tell about Wałęsa. Now his father sounded angry.

"When I was seven, things were much different in Poland. Everyone was very afraid of the secret police. There was a bad man in Russia called Stalin. He made sure people even as far away as Poland were afraid of him. His secret police would break into people's homes in the middle of the night and steal them away, and sometimes they'd never be heard of again."

"It sounds like one of Babcia's fairytales. Like . . ." Tomek hesitated.

Żanetka said, "Like Hansel and Gretel!"

His father didn't even look at Tomek. "Back then there were a lot of rules. And if you broke the rules, people were punished. But the rules were bad. One of the rules was you couldn't have a Bible in the house. We had the big Bible our father brought home from the war."

"He kept the inside of a church Bible and used the leather cover to make shoes for a man in prison camp," Tomek told Piotr proudly.

"You know this story?" Piotr asked, smiling at his brother.

"Just the shoe part. Babcia told me."

"Well, did she tell you about your grandfather being arrested in the middle of the night when I was seven?"

"No," Tomek said softly.

"Then she also didn't tell you why our Tatuś was taken away for two years. It was because of me. When I was your age, I talked too much to my teacher. I told her about our big Bible. And then she went to the secret police and told them. The secret police came in the middle of the night and took him away. And for a long, long time, I thought it was my fault."

Tomek felt sad for his father. "So she was like a spy," he said feebly. No one answered. Żanetka got off her chair and went over to Jan, then gave him a kiss on his cheek and went back to her chair and ate her ice cream.

Piotr coughed uncomfortably. "But he came home again to us. And I had been born in the meantime. And then we lived happily ever after."

"Until he died," Tomek said. He couldn't remember anything but the one time when his grandfather lay in bed, snoring so loudly, when Gonia came home from the hospital.

"Tomku! You should show more respect."

I didn't mean anything bad. "But I don't see how this has anything to do with me and my teacher."

"Jan, he doesn't mean any harm. Come on, we're celebrating his Name Day here." Piotr coughed.

Tomek wasn't sure what was safe to say anymore.

Tomek heard her loud and clear. "I've been *here* before," Halina's voice rang out over the water so even the people along the beach who didn't know them turned to stare.

The whole family looked up as his aunt and uncle arrived at the picnic. Piotr went over to Hanna's chair, parked under a tree. Tomek and his sisters sat at her feet, cross-legged, eating barbecued sausage. Tomek liked all their greasy faces. He smiled. "Uncle Piotr!"

"Cześć, Mamusiu. I'm sorry we're late."

Halina came up behind him and greeted them all. Then she went off a short distance, stripped down to her bathing suit, and stretched out on the pier.

"Halina has a headache. And I'm afraid we forgot her cake," Piotr told them.

"I heard that," Hanna said. "Well, it doesn't matter. Look at this glorious weather. The summer's not over yet."

"Go on, Babciu. Finish your story," Żanetka said.

Hanna looked at Piotr and nodded toward Halina, but Piotr just shook his head. She turned to the children. "Where was I, then?"

Tomek piped up, "You were telling us about riding underneath the train."

"Tomku, you're getting ahead of the story. You should be the one telling it. I can tell you were listening the last time you heard me talk about this, though."

Tomek smiled. "No, *you* tell the story, Babciu."

"All right. So there I was, at a lake just like this one, all alone. The war was over, but I had lost my own mother. I had lost your dear grandfather. The only person I hadn't lost was your father, who was safe in my tummy. I came to the lake and was exhausted from walking and hitching rides all the way from Czechoslovakia. When I got to that lake, I fell asleep under a bush."

"What kind of bush?"

"Żanetka dear, I don't remember."

"How different does this lake look now?" Tomek asked.

Piotr looked over at his brother. Jan stood with his arm around Amy, both of them trying to keep from laughing out loud. He coughed and said, "Yes, Mamusiu, how different?"

"Oh, you three are worse than the children. All right, I'll tell you how different. See that pier Halina's on? When my father taught me how to swim here, that pier wasn't here. And there were no rowboats either. So there!"

"Go on, Babciu!" Żanetka said.

"All right. You have to understand that because of this place, I had good memories of being at a lake. And so when I made it to that other lake, something in me just knew I would make it back home. And with God's help I did."

"What was it like riding under the train? After the lake." Tomek asked.

"The train wasn't the most important part of the story, Tomku."

"No, but it is one of the most exciting. It was my favorite part of the story when I was six too, Tomku," Piotr said.

"I'm *seven!*"

"Of course. Excuse me, young man."

"Now *you* tell us a story, Uncle Piotr. Tell us about fighting the communists. Tell us about Wałęsa."

"I think I liked the days when we did everything in secret better."

"What did you do secretly?" Tomek asked.

"Wouldn't you like to know? Now, why don't you show me how fast you can get your parents wet. Maybe then I'll show you how to swim. First, let me put on my swimming trunks."

"I already *know* how to swim." Tomek stood up and grabbed hold of Piotr's hand. He wanted to drag him down to the water.

"Oh no, you don't," Jan called out, running toward them and splashing when he got there.

Amy and Hanna laughed, but Halina was less amused. She got off the pier and took out her towel to dry herself off. "I think you did that on purpose," she said to Piotr.

Tomek was glad when his uncle stayed for a little while at the water's edge, watching him and Jan splash each other. "Come join us!" Jan called to him. Piotr waved back.

So Jan and Tomek came and sat down beside Piotr. Tomek stretched out in the sand and bombarded ants with an avalanche of sand from his hand. His father asked, "Is everything all right, Piotr? I don't want to pry, but if you need someone to talk to, I'm still your brother."

Tomek wondered if he should leave. No one said anything to him, so he thought he'd just try to be quiet.

His uncle sighed. "Oh, I don't know, Jan. It's funny. My own personal life seems to mirror the newfound one of Poland. The first few months following the Gdańsk agreements were a honeymoon period.

"At first, I woke up each day thankful for Halina's presence beside me. Just to no longer be alone was a gift in itself. But . . . well, it's embarrassing. Anyway, it seems now there's this distance between us."

"You sleep apart, then?"

Piotr nodded. "I wonder just how long we actually were happy? Was it really only a few weeks? Perhaps a month. I guess I just don't understand. I honestly believed I was in love with Halina. Every time I visited you and Amy this winter, I felt only admiration and respect for how Amy has fit in. She's worked hard as a wife and mother, but also as a daughter to Mamusia. I *wish* Halina would make an effort like that.

"Jan, I can't tell you how grateful I am to have you and Amy as friends. Ever since March, it seems both the country and my marriage have been threatening to fall apart."

"What about the Soviets? I wondered how much of what we heard rumored was true. Was it as bad as it seemed?"

"Worse." Piotr threw a stick into the water. "In March we had nothing less than a national disaster. That police riot in *Bydgoszcz* set off the crisis throughout the country. And with this event as backdrop, what we all had feared most looked bound to happen: Soviet invasion. It was like '68 and the tanks in Prague all over again. So we compromised. Yeah, the crisis was resolved at the last minute, but I wonder, I'm still wondering, at what cost?"

Piotr sighed again, then laughed uncomfortably. "Enough of all this serious stuff. Why don't we go find something to eat? Tomku, you think you're too big to ride on my shoulders?"

"No, sir!" As Jan hoisted Tomek onto Piotr's shoulders, he thought, this was great. Now he was taller than any of the men and could look clear across the lake. He didn't know his uncle was so strong. "I'll be careful to keep my hands out of your eyes," he said.

Piotr laughed. "Much appreciated. You *are* a big boy," he said as the three of them headed back to the others.

But as they came closer to the women, Tomek could hear Halina's shrill tone. "Oh, sure this freedom is such a relief. Now we can breathe. We can talk, we can use the phones, we can make love loudly in our bedrooms." Then she laughed scornfully. "Oh, I'm glad Piotr didn't hear that one."

As she said his name, Piotr hesitated. Tomek could feel his change of pace. He could also tell the women hadn't seen them yet from where they sat under the trees. Then he wondered why his uncle and father stopped walking. Jan looked confused.

"So now I know why he brought me here to propose. It's the *family's* special spot."

Right then Halina looked up and saw them. She turned in the other direction as Amy stepped over to her and put an arm around Halina's shoulders. "Halina, you sound so bitter. It's none of our business, but if you want to talk about anything with Hanna or me, we're both good listeners. You talked about family, but that's what families are for, after all."

Amy and Hanna had their backs to them, but Halina looked over her shoulder, straight at Piotr as she blurted out, "Oh, you're one to talk. *Your name* is the one on Piotr's lips, even when he sleeps. 'Amy this, Amy that. She takes care of my mother, she's so good with her children, she's always supporting my brother.' Well, I'll tell you something. When he woke up calling your name, I made him tell me every single time he's seen you before the wedding. There was your father's funeral, of course, right, Piotr?" Now she nodded at him, and Amy whirled, her face drawn and pale.

Tomek could tell something was desperately wrong. His mother looked awful. Slowly, Piotr's hands came up to help Tomek off his shoulders. He looked at all the adults. They all looked at the ground, except his grandmother. And she didn't look happy, either.

Don't let this be happening, he thought desperately. Did this mean the picnic was ruined? His own Name Day picnic?

But Halina's voice would not stop. "Oh, and let's not forget some mysterious afternoon five years ago when the family was negotiating some sort of deal. Oh, are you surprised that I know these things, too? That's called openness. It's what marriage is about, according to Piotr. Aren't you open with Jan about these things, Amy? Piotr, did I quote you right?"

Piotr reached her in two strides. "That's enough!"

Gonia looked up at him, startled by the sudden movement, and began crying. Żanetka put an arm around her and reached up to touch Hanna's wheelchair.

With Piotr standing between Amy and Jan, Tomek now looked from one to the other. This was worse than what his mother called "tension." The strained looks on his parents' faces as they finally glanced at each other now were caused by more than just the tension Tomek had seen etched there sometimes when he made too much noise in their small apartment.

Tomek sensed something even worse had come to take its place. His worst fears were only confirmed when it seemed that everyone just pretended to be nice for the rest of the picnic, and they went home way too early.

That night, not for the first time, Tomek caught himself wishing his bed wasn't right next to the wall of his parents' bedroom. His grandmother slept on the other side of his room, also the living room and kitchen. In the room next door slept his parents and sisters. At night all the sofas folded out into beds. Now Tomek wished he could fold himself back into the sofa so he didn't have to hear the anguished voices next door. He was glad Babcia was snoring and couldn't hear what was going on.

"Jan, you have to believe me! Oh, are we going to have this torment again? Don't do this to us. Please forgive me. Yes, I saw him that day the government minister came to visit. He slipped in so quickly and took me by surprise, I didn't know what to do. All of you were being so secretive about what we should say in front of that man. And he was offering to help me find my father. I was all confused. . . . No, that's a lie."

"What do you mean 'a lie'?"

"Well, most of it is true, but what I mean is, I *was* confused. And . . . I was afraid of how you'd react."

"Amy . . ."

"I thought you'd react like you are now. By shutting me out the same way you did when you found his letters. If it hadn't been for little Żanetka being born, I don't know if we would have grown close again."

Tomek didn't want to hear any more, but the pain in his father's voice kept him from putting the pillow over his head as he did at other times.

"Amy, *I'm* the one who is confused here. You must learn to believe in us. Otherwise we *are* doomed to repeat these same mistakes. I wonder..."

"What?"

"I wonder why I feel like the one who should be asking forgiveness. Don't you see? There's something wrong with the messages I'm sending you if you didn't feel free to tell me about Piotr's visit. I'm sorry, Amy. All I want is for us to be close again."

Now his mother was crying. And then Tomek heard Żanetka, who must have been pretending to sleep just like Tomek. "Tatuś still loves Mamusia?" *Daddy still loves Mommy?* Tomek thought in English. Yes, that was the question the whole household had been waiting for ever since the disaster of the picnic. Tomek wished they'd never even gone that morning.

From the other bedroom he heard both his parents talking to his sister.

"Oh, sweetie, of course I still love Mamusia."

"Your forgiving heart, Jan, is yet another reason why I love you so much."

"Shh, the children."

His mother laughed softly. "Who knows? Maybe this incident with Halina has brought us even closer. Now we truly have no more secrets from each other."

"Truly?"

"Yes."

"And Piotr?"

Tomek could not hear his mother's answer. Yet he took their assuring words and loving tone and wrapped each one around him like an extra blanket on a winter night.

Even in Jacek's wildest dreams, he had never imagined this. "Absolutely incredible," he mumbled, shaking his head. "Ten million." The latest figures were in, and even the government's propaganda machine wouldn't know how to doctor such extremes. As of September 1981, at the Solidarność First National Congress held that month, the trade union enjoyed overwhelming success nationwide. Over ten million of the Polish population registered as members. It had only been a year and the movement had exploded.

Delegates met in Gdańsk, where Wałęsa had set it all into motion. They pounded out a program and elected a National Commission.

"I'll admit. We entirely underestimated the opposition's organizational skills. But now it's too much, too fast." Roman's words spoken behind Jacek echoed his own fears.

"You think so?"

"I *know* so, Comrade."

"This isn't '68 anymore," Jacek said. "Soviet tanks can't come crashing into Poland now."

"That's what you think. No, this *openness* has served its purpose. But it's gone on long enough."

"The Soviets wouldn't dare crack down now. Not after a year of freedom."

"Drastic support like this calls for drastic measures. Not Soviet tanks. . . ."

Jacek knew it was going to happen before it did. But that didn't help ease the terrible ache of anticipation he had to carry around. Why did it never go right in Poland? Why did history always change the rules, just when it looked as if Poland would finally get a break?

There must be a reason for the line in the national anthem, *"Poland is not yet lost."* Jacek thought of the optimistic verses of the anthem he had had to recite as a boy, almost arrogant in contrast to the desperate entreaty to be left alone that the Poles sang.

On December 13, 1981, the defense minister, General Wojciech Jaruzelski, replaced Kania as head of Poland. As swift as any sword thrust, he imposed martial law on the country, calling it a "State of War." Not Soviet tanks but Polish milicja interned thousands of activists, including Lech Wałęsa and almost all those who had attended the National Commission meeting the day before in Gdańsk, only three months after the commission was elected.

10

Tomek brought the ball right up next to his nose. *Going for two points at the free-throw line to win the game. He aims. He shoots!* The orange basketball arched up and over, then slammed against the backboard and bounced off to the left.

He misses. "The story of my life," Tomek mumbled. He shot as many baskets as fast as he could until he was too tired to think. His breath came out in gusts of steam. He looked like a smoking dragon on the court.

When he finally took a break, Tomek leaned over at his waist as he'd seen the pros do and put his hands on his hips. *Only a serious player would be out on a winter day practicing like this. Temperatures are near zero, and the Baltic Sea wind has brought the chill factor even lower.*

Tomek didn't even remember what the fight had been about. Lately his father had been picking on him more than usual. His grandmother said it was because the apartment was so small, and on the dark, cold days, everyone got on everyone's nerves. It had been her idea that he go outside and shoot a few baskets, even if it was December.

"But he's right. I never do it right. I can't even shoot baskets right." Tomek straightened up and tried spinning the ball on his fingertips. He loved the ball, a present from his uncle. And there was no way either of his sisters was going to get their hands on it.

That was it. Gonia had been rolling it around the room when he took it away from her. And immediately she had started screaming like most three-year-olds do. Then, of course, he had gotten in trouble.

"I wonder why it's so hard for *him* to understand when I say it's not my fault."

But a part of Tomek wondered if maybe it really was his fault. He was seven and should have known better. When he was by himself like this, he sometimes thought maybe there *was* something wrong with him. Something different? He wasn't quiet and good like Żanetka. And he didn't pray nearly as much as everyone else in the family. In fact, he spent most of the prayer time sneaking looks at everyone when their eyes were closed.

It's almost as if I don't belong in this family.

He wished he could be more like his uncle. Piotr always seemed to know what to say and how and when, and he ended up getting everyone to agree with him. *Well, except for his stupid wife, but she doesn't count.* She was weird.

Then a thought occurred to Tomek. Wouldn't it be great if *Piotr* were his father? "Yeah, we'd play basketball. He'd take me to his important meetings, and I'd meet Wałęsa and could help him shape the New Poland."

Piotr burst through the door and stood there panting. Tomek was still making his bed, putting away the linen so he could make it into a sofa. Mamusia was giving his grandmother a bath. Tomek looked up surprised, but he was always glad to see his uncle.

"Where's Jan?"

Tomek didn't like the look on his uncle's face. "He's with one of the old ladies from the church. She fell down some stairs and needed someone to go with her to the hospital. What is it?"

"Where's your mother?"

"In the bathroom with Babcia. Why? What's wrong?"

Piotr came inside and closed the door, then double-bolted it behind him. He sat down. Then he got up and started to make a cup of tea in the kitchen corner. Then he sat down again.

"Tomku!" his mother called. "Tomku, can you get the girls out of here and give them some breakfast? I'll be out in a minute."

Since he wasn't getting any answers from his uncle, Tomek tried his mother. "Mamusiu, Uncle Piotr is here, and I think he has bad news." His message had the right effect. He had his mother's undivided attention and felt very important saying it.

He heard Babcia's voice. "Go, Amy. Find out what's happened."

Amy emerged in the doorway, wiping her hands on a towel. "Piotr? It's not Jan or Halina, is it?"

"What?" He looked dazed.

"There hasn't been an accident, has there?"

Tomek watched his uncle stare at his mother. It was as if he were taking a good long drink before he dared to say his message. "No, no. I . . . they're fine. I don't know how to even say it. It's over, Amy. Everything we worked for. We had one year and now it's over. Oh, God!" He buried his face in his hands, moaning.

Tomek looked at his mother. She seemed uncertain, so he went over to his uncle and put a hand on his shoulder as he'd seen his father do.

"Your marriage with Halina?" Amy asked softly. Tomek wondered why his mother would say such a thing.

Again Piotr looked up, confused. But after a moment, he shook his head slowly and repeated, "No, no. Solidarność. Last night it all came crashing down around us. They must have been planning it for months. It couldn't have been timed better. *Everyone* was in Gdańsk for the National Commission meeting. It ended yesterday. Then in the middle of the night, the SB raided all the leaders' homes and arrested them. We don't even know who's been taken, or where they've gone. Or if they're still alive!"

"Wałęsa?" Tomek asked.

"He was one of the first. I don't have a phone, so I didn't find out until this morning. And the first thing I thought of was you and Jan and the children. I was so afraid . . ."

"Piotr, they wouldn't come here. . . . Oh, I wish Jan were home. We have to get you to safety."

Tomek's eyes grew wide. "Will they take you away, too?" His grip on his uncle's arm tightened.

"No, Tomku, no one's taking me away." Again, his uncle and his mother locked gazes.

———— ∽ ————

His uncle's friend Ewa sat with them around their table, and Tomek heard words he thought meant the end of the world.

"It's war. The Polish government has declared war on its own people," Ewa said.

"It's far worse than we first thought. *Thousands* were arrested last night," Piotr said.

"If only I knew Bogdan was still alive, it would help." Ewa's voice cracked and she turned away.

Jan said, "No one is telling where they've been taken."

"It's all so familiar," his grandmother said, looking out the window. Tomek sat on the couch beside her, a book open on his lap. It was the first time he had ever heard words like "war" and "still alive" about times that were his own and not his parents' or grandmother's.

"I can't believe there was no warning," Jan said.

Piotr shook his head. "Oh, we knew there was tension. The government has been giving us ultimatums all year. And especially during the last months, while the new commission scrambled to get itself organized."

Ewa pitched in, "We couldn't afford to lose the popular support, or the momentum. The threat of *Soviet* invasion still hung over us all. We never dreamed *Polish* forces would be used against their own people. The men in the milicja are traitors. How can they do this?"

"You should have heard some of the speakers two days ago at the National Commission meeting. We thought the sooner Poland could show the world that they had a viable, workable government option to what the communists offered, the more secure its freedom would be," Piotr said.

"Yes, Bogdan told me they were all aware a crisis was brewing. But we managed to stave it off in March, so we thought it wouldn't be so serious. How long can it last? They can't get away with it, can they? I mean, the world won't let them?"

As the adults' voices and their big words washed over Tomek, he watched his grandmother slowly roll her wheelchair into the other room and close the door.

11

Lord, be my wisdom and be my true word

As they entered his uncle's apartment building in Gdańsk, Tomek looked up at his mother and said, "Żanetka said she had a nightmare about Uncle Piotr."

"Did she?" his mother said. "Oh, it's good to get out of the wind. I know it's February, but this time of year we should have snow, not just this incessant freezing wind."

As usual, it didn't sound as if she was listening. Tomek bounded up the stairs two at a time. But he waited for his mother before he rang the buzzer. He liked his aunt and uncle's apartment. It was even smaller than theirs, but nice. Piotr worked as a carpenter, and he had fixed up all sorts of clever things, like bookcases along all the walls.

It took a few minutes before Halina answered the door. She didn't take the chain off until his mother called out who was there.

When she opened the door wide, Tomek couldn't believe his eyes. "What a mess!" he said.

"Tomku," his mother hissed.

"Oh, Amy, I was wondering who they'd send," Halina said.

Tomek was surprised she still wore her bathrobe. It was nearly noon.

"What happened, Halina? What do you mean 'who they'd send'? No one sent us. I brought Tomek over because he and Piotr were going somewhere together. What's wrong? I'm sorry if we woke you up. If you want us to leave . . ."

Halina picked up the couch cushions off the floor. Books were strewn everywhere. The wallpaper had been torn off in slashes. The

109

armchair stuffing lay on the ground. Tomek thought it was a glorious mess.

Then his mother said, "Halina? Halina, did the SB do this? Halina, answer me. What happened?"

"Yeah, the SB did this. They stormed in here in the middle of the night and arrested Piotr. He's gone." Then she sat down on their couch and started to cry.

Tomek couldn't believe his ears. "What? They took Uncle Piotr?" He shook her arm. "What happened?"

She pushed him away, but at least she finally gave them an answer. "I woke up to the sound of men pounding on the door. Then I heard Piotr switching on the light in this room. It was around 3:30. I heard Piotr call out. He was angry about something. So I slowly opened my door just a crack, and I saw three men pushing their way past him as a fourth shoved him up against the wall.

"They said they were going to arrest him. But when he asked the charges, they said for treason against the State. Then they let him get dressed."

"And then what?" Tomek asked. His world was shifting shapes.

"Then he was gone."

Ewa walked arm in arm with Amy along the boardwalk. Żanetka pushed Gonia's stroller, and Tomek walked on the other side. He was under strict orders not to throw snowballs at the girls, but it would be hard to resist the temptation. Maybe at the end of the walk. . . .

"Who else?" his mother asked.

Ewa answered, "The ones who got away? Let's see . . . *Bogdan Lis, Władysław Frasyniuk, Zbigniew Bujak, and Bogdan Borusewicz.* They've put together an underground Temporary Coordinating Commission or *TKK*. It's an emergency group with one goal: to keep the flame of Solidarność burning no matter what."

"What about you, Ewa? I was so afraid when they had Piotr, they'd take you, too."

"I seem to have been left off the lists. I don't know why, but it puts me in a unique position. I don't know what I'd do without your and Jan's support, though. Your family has saved me. I go crazy at home with Bogdan still gone. It's been two months now, and still almost no news. I can't help but wonder what's happening. . . ."

"Yes, but at least you know he's alive. Maybe it's because you're a woman. Perhaps that's why you weren't arrested."

"No. Other women were taken. Some *couples* were arrested and their children put into state orphanages."

This caught Tomek's attention. There was *no way* anyone was going to put him and his sisters into an orphanage. He'd visited one once with his mother to take some clothes. It smelled funny inside the building, and it was even more crowded than their home.

Amy shook her head. "I was *so sure* America and the other countries in the West would respond. I'll start sounding like I'm the reactionary if you don't stop me. Really, everyone gets used to it, but what's going on is such a blatant violation of human rights. I mean, this is *Europe, in 1982.*"

Ewa smiled at Amy. "That's what I love about you, Amy. Your righteous anger. Well, to be fair, in a limited way, the West did respond. Because of martial law, a food embargo was called, and remember? In December trucks loaded with food, winter clothing, and blankets barreled their way over to us from all over Western Europe, through the East German borders and into Poland."

Amy sighed. "But we still don't even know where they're keeping Bogdan and Piotr! Even Jan admits the communists' bluff paid off. It isn't the first time the West has forgotten its promises to Poland."

For Jacek, the order meant the fulfillment of a five-year obsession. He finally had Piotr Piekarz where he wanted him, in prison. He had his own reasons for wanting the outlaw behind bars, but it had worked out beautifully that history played right into his hands. *Maybe the only bloody advantage of martial law,* he thought as he heard the prison doors lock behind him.

Now, finally, Piekarz was out of the way and unable to expose Jacek as a spy for the West. Most important, he could no longer harass Amy.

Jacek had made sure Piotr's name remained high up on the SB list. He'd been there ever since November 1977. And initially, in December 1981, as the net closed in around anyone involved in the Solidarność leadership, Jacek had patiently waited. Just a few more months. Then he stepped up the hunt for Piotr, and now, in February 1982, Jacek had had him arrested like all the rest and thrown into prison.

He could have had Piotr tortured for information and shot, but Jacek left word that this particular prisoner was to be kept locked up for a very long time. There would be no early release, but the man was also not to be physically harmed.

A few days after the arrest, Jacek went to visit Piotr. He entered the prison in Gdańsk and arranged for a private audience with the prisoner. As he stood waiting, Jacek took out his cigarettes. He had waited a long time for this moment. Now he wanted this man to know exactly where he stood, and that he never, ever could threaten Jacek's family again. He looked down at the cigarette in his hand, an old man's hand.

The door swung open and Jacek nodded at the guard. They would not be disturbed. He had seen to that with a generous bribe for the man that now ushered Piotr in through the door.

"You! I should have known," Piotr said.

Jacek was pleased that Piotr remembered him. He hoped he'd given the man some nightmares. *Well, let him have a few more*, he thought now. "Glad to see me?" he asked, thinking, *Finally, confrontation*.

Piotr's eyes narrowed. "Oh, I've seen you. I've seen you more than you know. I saw you at my father's funeral. And I saw you outside the hotel where Carter spoke. One of our men was a waiter there. He claims nothing of what happened there reached the press, and *you* were at the center of it all. So you see, no matter what you might hold against me, I'm not the only one under surveillance."

"Oh, this goes way beyond a grudge," Jacek said. He felt disturbed that Piotr knew these things about him, but it didn't matter. Nothing mattered now that he had him where he wanted, now that Jacek could have this man "accidently" killed during interrogation. *Now I'm in charge*, he told himself.

He stepped toward the outlaw and blew smoke in his face. "Consider it a last warning. I want only one thing from you, Piekarz. Listen closely. *You stay away from your sister-in-law, Amy. You leave her alone*. I've seen what you do to her life, and you bring her nothing but misery. The only reason you're not dead is because of me."

Piotr opened his mouth to speak, but Jacek held up a hand. "You may think you know who I am. Fine. That's our secret and it stays that way. Do you understand? Oh, I haven't forgotten our little encounter on the stairs of your parents' apartment building. I'll keep you in here where you can't harm her for as long as it takes. In fact, I hope you *rot* in this place. You deserve no better."

Shaking from the emotion, Jacek left the cell. His feelings had taken him by surprise. Only when he walked outside and could breathe again did he realize he must have been focusing all his pent-up frustration of being excluded from Amy's life at this man.

Well, let him suffer for a change.

12

April 1982

Dear Amy,

I write this to you now. From me, in this dark place to you. It seems I'm destined always to write you and nothing more. If that is to be our sole means of communicating, then I hold fast to it. For in doing so, in my mind at least, you are close, as close as our embrace today.

They don't let us write much here, which could mean that if we've succeeded in nothing else, we've succeeded in convincing them that words are power. One word, Solidarność. How that word thrills my heart. It is everything I have worked for these eight years since I joined the underground.

Then I think of what has now been lost, and my heart. . . Oh, Amy, how does your heart bear this ripping away? I can't . . . So many, so very many losses, and for what gain?

It began at my father's funeral, the loss, my own loss of love.

Our second clandestine meeting happened over four years ago. Yes, I knew, I knew of his sickness. Knew more than you through my contacts. I had only intended to watch you all at the funeral, then leave, a face in the crowd. I missed him every day of our estrangement. And it ate away at me bitterly that we never had the chance to talk before he died.

I saw you, and I saw the three children you've given Jan. It was confirmation of what the long silence had told me. I knew after three children, I could never stand a chance. Only a fool keeps caring for no reason.

I must learn to focus. This man has haunted me, dogged my steps, been as an infection of the blood, reappearing whenever I was weak or unaware, vulnerable.

But I have learned to see his face in a crowd, too. Only a month before

Tatuś's death, I recognized him as one of the guests entering the hotel where President Carter spoke.

But I'm getting ahead of myself.

Yes, then again, I saw him at the funeral, and I saw you watching him. Ironic how we all keep observing one another. I've discovered that this man has very interesting connections. Did you know he has come back to watch you, and in watching him, I learned a devastating truth about you, something I first guessed, a wild gamble really, two years before that. Now I know it is true. And the truth, unlike my father's God who allowed him to suffer and die, that truth did not set me free. Because of that knowledge, I am imprisoned. Convenient for him, wasn't it, that I also happened to belong to the wrong political movement.

When you told me that day, at my father's graveside, to hope, I did. I accepted it as a gift at the same time that my mind gave you up as lost. You couldn't know it, but that was a very dark time for me. Those three children, I had lost you for good, lost as a lover.

And I was deeply disillusioned with the movement. We couldn't get past the impasse between the intelligentsia and workers. How to get the two together? That was a question which would not be answered until the connection made through the development of KOR that same year could begin to be felt. And the economy was far too strong. Who can enkindle revolution when the shops are full? It didn't matter that it was a false prosperity, based on nothing but government loans. Freedom had lost its attraction in the face of plenty. All of Poland was pointing to the election of our own archbishop of Kraków as pope, back in October, as a sign of improving times. Then, eight months later, when Pope John Paul II made his first pilgrimage to his home country, the people adored him. They were ecstatic. God was with Poland. Who needed the underground anymore?

I couldn't know it when you spoke that word of hope to me, of course. Not until today, really, did I realize you might have meant to encourage me in another way. But now I know better. I was so blind, not for the first time.

Despite everything, after Tatuś's funeral I went back to the movement with renewed hope, your gift to me. And then in August 1980, a year and a half later . . .

Piotr did not think the man looked very impressive. His mus1tache was too long and his legs too short. And he spoke with a strange accent, often mispronouncing the endings of words. But when he spoke—and this was the amazing thing—the entire world listened.

Piotr was seeing Lech Wałęsa for the first time in person. The occupation *strajk* at the Lenin Shipyard was already two weeks old. Labor disturbances throughout Poland had kept Piotr away from Gdańsk. This first summer of a new decade promised to be the start of a new season in Poland's fight for freedom. If the shipyard workers could hold on long enough, if the Soviets didn't invade Poland like they did Czechoslovakia in '68, if the KOR and other underground leadership could forge some sort of agreement with the workers, *if, if, if,* thought Piotr. Still, there was a chance they just might pull it off this time. For the first time in thirty-five years, *if* everything came together in the right way, they just might break the communist curse on Poland.

Like a land waking from a long sleep, Poland was shaking itself and slowly daring to fight back. Piotr had seen it himself this summer. Everywhere, he had witnessed mine workers striking, housewives marching, students protesting. Poland was rising, and much of it was due to this unlikely Prince Charming, the engineer from Gdańsk.

Piotr took a closer look at Wałęsa, fascinated to watch him in action. Here, behind the strajk lines, Wałęsa had climbed on top of the wrought-iron fence surrounding the shipyard, a structure that both protected them from milicja guns and formed a cage around the workers for as long as they insisted on occupying the shipyard. They were prisoners as much as liberators.

Wałęsa hung from the fence with one arm and called out to his fellow workers to endure in their fight, called on the world to witness Poland's courage, called on the communists to surrender a lost battle.

The crowd loved him. They roared each time his voice rose. And the journalists that Piotr could pick out on the other side of the gate were scribbling madly, some leaning toward their interpreters, writing down the translation as fast as they could.

"Solidarność! Solidarność!" the workers chanted in time to Wałęsa's lead, waving their fists back and forth.

"We *are* the first free trade union in Poland *since the war!*" His voice rang out. Piotr looked at the upturned faces of men, their features charged with emotion, men in working clothes with rolled-up sleeves, strong arms bare and upraised, the men of his generation. The power of the moment grabbed hold of Piotr as Wałęsa's words echoed his own thoughts.

"*This* is what we've worked so long and hard for."

"Solidarność! Solidarność!"

"*This* is Poland's moment in history! No one, not even *they* can take it away from us!"

He had guts, they all did. Piotr felt it happening around him, the raw emotion of the moment, the smell of sweating men in the summer heat, most of all, the hope, as tangible as any first day of a new season.

Three days later Wałęsa called an end to the strajk; the government had met his terms. His face emerged on the cover of major newspapers and magazines all over the world as Poland's new national leader. And on August 31, 1980, the signing of the Gdańsk agreements set the stage for the legalization of Solidarność, the Eastern bloc's first independent trade union.

Against all odds, they had won. After nearly ten years, Edward Gierek was no longer the First Secretary of the Polish People's Republic. Stanisław Kania took his place. The people of Poland had let their voice be heard.

Every town and city of Poland celebrated wildly. People poured onto the streets, waving flags. The Polish eagle wore its crown again, often painted on by hand. This crown symbolized self-governance, and the crowned eagle had not been seen since 1939, when Germany invaded Poland at the start of World War II.

Piotr wandered through the streets of Gdańsk in a daze. It was as if someone had remembered to turn on the lights. After so many decades of darkness, they had almost forgotten how bright it could be. This then was the color of freedom.

Young people danced with old people on the cobblestone streets. The King Neptune fountain wore a crown of dandelions. Ships in the harbor blinked Christmas lights from mast to mast, despite it being the middle of summer. Old women leaned out of top-story windows calling to their neighbors.

Piotr found himself standing beside the Crane, a huge wooden structure on the waterfront. He crossed the bridge and stood looking out over the water. Ships behind him, the city in front of him. A group of students danced their way onto his bridge, vodka bottles in hand. He couldn't help but smile at their laughter and think, *This is how it should be.*

"Hey, come join us!"

A pretty blonde grabbed hold of Piotr's elbow and pulled him into the fray. He laughed but felt embarrassed. She was petite and he could see in the eyes of at least two young men standing near her that she was desirable. "Hey, I'm ten years too old for you."

She turned a pert smile his way and giggled. "I'm twenty-two. How old are you?"

"Ages," he answered, realizing with a start that his twenty-seven years didn't sound so ancient after all. "Where are you taking me?" She had hooked her arm through his and, by the feel of it, didn't intend on letting him go.

That was the first time I met Halina. When does love enter a heart? I don't know. I do know she made me laugh. And she made the loneliness I had learned to wear like an old coat of armor seem lighter. I loved many things about Halina, especially her youth. She will still be just as young even when she turns sixty. That's how she is, young at heart, always looking for a good time, so willing to please, laughing.

After we had gone out for a few weeks, and the peace Solidarność had secured seemed firm, I told her about my involvement in the underground. A part of me wanted to scare her off. I think I knew, even then, that she wasn't right for me. What would dark and disappointed me do with such a bundle of light and joy? Looking back, it was probably this dark side of me that attracted her, though. When she heard my news, it backfired, and she only became that much more intrigued with her latest catch.

No, that's not fair. I was much more than that to her. But she didn't love me any more than I loved her. What I mean is, we thought we loved each other. Even worse, we wanted to love each other so much, we talked ourselves into it.

Halina loved to be surrounded by people. It didn't take long before I was accompanying her to plenty of parties, all the birthdays and Name Day celebrations of her many friends. She loved nothing better than dressing up and going out to have fun for a night. And I loved basking in the warmth of her optimism.

In October, when our own poet Czesław Miłosz was awarded the Nobel Prize for Literature, we felt as if the world had crowned all of our efforts with glory. All Poles had won that prize, and this was the rest of the world's way of commending our accomplishments that year. At the same time, the award was also a signal to the Soviet Union that the world was watching.

I took Halina to a party at Bogdan and Ewa's. She was so full of admiration for what she thought I had done for Poland's cause, I thought it was time she met some of the real heroes of the story. . . .

Ewa gave Piotr one of her meaningful looks as he helped her with the dishes. They could hear the party in full swing in the room next door. "Bogdan and I have known you for several years now, Piotr. You know you've always been one of my favorite partisans."

He smiled. It was an old joke between them. *What is Ewa getting at that she's trying to soften me up like this*, Piotr wondered.

She went on, "I'm so happy you've finally found someone. Mind you, I had heard rumors you were going out with some bright, young thing, but, Piotr, I had no idea."

"You don't approve?" He tried to sound abashed, but the truth was, he valued Ewa and Bogdan's opinion. They were two of his closest friends. And he *had* put off introducing them to Halina. Now he wondered why.

"Approve? Of course I approve. Anyone who can make you smile and laugh like she does *has* to be good for you. I'm happy for you, Piotr. You're finally being good to yourself by taking this girl into your heart."

It's what Piotr wanted to do, too. He had, in fact, been thinking about doing it for a long time—taking Halina into his heart. The next day he borrowed Bogdan's car and drove Halina a few hours south to the *Kaszuby* lake district. Halina had balked when he told her they were going hiking for a day. "I still have a hangover from last night. Just the two of us? No one else?"

"It's called being romantic, Halina," he teased her.

"Well, if you put it *that* way," she said and gave him a kiss.

They spent the morning walking hand in hand among tall pines and high grass, row upon row of silver birch and oaks, all changing colors and waving at them in the early-autumn breezes, branches creating golden space. They even passed a stream with a beaver dam. "What a glorious day," Piotr said, squeezing Halina's hand. His words sounded more confident than he felt.

"Yes, but I'm wondering where you're taking me."

"You'll see," Piotr said. "The truth is, we're almost there." He looked down at Halina and thought she had never looked more beautiful. He stopped and picked a tiny pinecone out of her hair.

"You know you could look like this every day and I wouldn't mind," he said.

"What? I don't even have any makeup on today. You picked me up way too early. I overslept anyway, so I didn't have time to get ready at all."

"Still, you look great in those jeans. A workshirt and jeans and an oversized sweater, preferably one of my own, that's what I want to see you in from now on," he teased her. "And you're so beautiful, you don't need any makeup."

"Right. Now come on. Stop trying to make me mad and show me where we're going."

Piotr laughed. They walked a little longer and finally came to a lake, tucked between the gold and red hills around them like a hidden jewel. "Oh, Piotr, it *is* beautiful," Halina said.

He put his arm around her and drew her close. "See, I told you it was worth a little effort. And look, Halina, there are even people."

"Oh, you're mean," she jabbed him in the ribs.

They walked down to the shore and found a small group of families having a picnic. At one end of the lake was a lifeguard, and along the beach were sailboats and rowboats for hire.

"You! We could have driven to this place." Halina's eyes flashed at Piotr.

"Of course, but I thought you wanted to go on a hike and enjoy nature. Besides, I have big plans for today."

"Piotr Piekarz, you will always be a mystery to me. Hey, wait up!"

He was walking fast on purpose, just to make her run along to keep up. They reached the shore, and in no time, he had rented one of the boats and lifted Halina into it so she wouldn't get her feet wet. Then he took off the backpack he had been carrying, threw that into the boat, and climbed in himself.

"I hope you know that even though the sun is shining, the summer's over," she said. "If we fall out of this thing, that water's going to be *very* cold."

"I know." Piotr shut his eyes and rowed, pouring his strength into the motion. Soon they reached the middle of the lake, with no one around them. The breeze died down, and all they could hear were the sounds of the children laughing on the shore and geese flying overhead. He looked up and pointed out the birds to Halina.

"Oh, I thought they were storks," she said.

Piotr took a deep breath. He was a nest of knots inside. "Halina, I've brought you out here for a reason. I wanted to ask you something, and this place is special to me, so I wanted to share it with you."

He stopped. She was staring at Piotr, her eyes wide. "Halina, you have brought something into my life these last months I had almost forgotten to miss. And I love you for that. I love you for so many things. It's like I've been waking up and discovering my senses since I met you. You've helped me see and taste life in a whole new way. I don't ever want to lose that again. Sweet Halina, will you marry me?"

She gasped and looked down as he leaned forward and took her hands in his, thinking how small they seemed. He waited, and with each passing second, it became more difficult to silence the thought, *This can't be happening again. No, it can't. . . .*

"Piotr, you're always so formal. I've been wondering for a while if we were going anywhere, and then out of nowhere, this. I don't know what to say, really. I mean . . . I thought the next step would be for you to move in with me. I have my own apartment, thanks to my grandmother, remember? That is, if you want that. But marriage? It seems so . . . final."

"But you're not saying no?" he whispered, hearing himself and thinking he sounded like a boy all over again.

"No, I'm not saying no. Piotr, what? Why? You're so *deep* sometimes."

"I hadn't even thought of us moving in together," he said, shaking his head, a little baffled.

"You didn't? Well, welcome to the eighties. Do you want to?"

It didn't take long for Piotr to decide. He shook his head. "No, I want to do this right."

"You must come from a very strict background," she said, pushing a wisp of hair impatiently out of her eyes.

He nodded. "Yeah, I must." His heart was sinking. It hadn't worked. When did anything he tried that had to do with women and emotions ever work? He thought about Amy, hoping he really was over her, and then Halina's voice interrupted him.

"Hello? Sorry, you were so far away. Piotr, listen. I *am* honored that you asked me. I guess you took me by surprise. I just needed a few moments to think about it and get my bearings. If you don't want to live together, that's fine. Let's get married. Yes." She smiled like a child who had just found a coin on the street.

He looked up, unable to believe. As the conversation had dragged on, he had slowly let go of hope. And here it was again, right in front of him. He reached out to Halina and drew her to him, kissing her, and wanting with all his heart to love as he had always longed to.

I confess to you, I lied to myself. Yes, I tried to love another woman, I even married her. It was time to move on and get past you. I married Halina, despite what I knew about myself, and, in the end, drove her away as well. What was I to do? That loneliness, all those years of giving up on you, knowing you had given up on me, it was worse than what I now feel in the physical solitude of this prison cell.

I know the silence after today will be the worst. Silence and uncertainty are hard for me to handle.

I'm looking at myself now in a slab of mirror, cracked and crooked on these prison walls. Shall I tell you what I see? A dark, troubled, almost arrogant expression, confident and cocky, shoulders broad and thrown back, black eyes, unshaven chin, black hair tight and curly. This man staring back at me is dressed in blue overalls, workers' clothes, a prisoner's clothes, sleeves rolled up.

Guilt shadows his eyes red.

Thoughts of you have walked beside me. You haunt me still. I am broken by what has happened. These events . . . this horrible year 1982.

The scent of your hair, your touch, the love in your eyes. I couldn't help myself. It was on impulse, an instinctive response to all those years of longing. I didn't mean it!

And now this loss, the price you must pay. Just as truth has not set me free, so love has wrung a terrible sacrifice from you and my brother. Our entire family will suffer and I am to blame. The guilt is worse than anything I've ever known. What is forgiveness in the face of such loss? My anger and bitterness, the armor of yesterday, is but a shifting shadow, nothing in the face of such devastation.

I am empty. I have only been able to love you in words, through letters on paper, and now I've tried a higher love in my mind . . . and failed. God's curse on me: love with words alone. Then I am the cursed one, for they say He is the Word.

PART III

―――――――――― ⨍ ――――――――――

BROKEN BREAD
1 Corinthians 10:16

April 1982 – March 1985

As a Chinese brother once said, "Faith is like a bird, which sings when the night is still dark."

13

I ever with you and you with me, Lord

Żaneta's very first memory was of her sister's death. It was as if Gonia's exit from life marked Żanetka's own entrance into consciousness; she was the first entry into her memory. What did she remember?

Żaneta could remember the entire day. She knew she had turned five a month earlier in March, and Gonia was already four in January. It was as if to compensate for a dark infant past, no longer remembered, Żaneta could remember events of her fifth year with startling clarity.

In the morning she played with clay, blue and yellow clay, and got it under each of her nails. She sat at the table while her grandmother and mother played school. The house smelled like tomato soup.

Her mother said, "I know. I just still can't believe how everything is so different. It's as if someone has turned a page, no, has put away something like a book of freedom and taken out an old volume of injustice, dog-eared and too familiar in the annals of Poland's history. And, and we just don't know how the story will end."

She was quiet, and then she said, "I know it's only been four months, but the state of siege Jaruzelski imposed on his own country has gagged and blindfolded us all. These last months of curfew and sudden arrests have the whole country stirred up."

"You sound like Ewa," Hanna said. But her voice was kind.

"Well, think about it, Mamusiu. The shops are empty. Like a lost dream, the personal freedom we waited so long for is gone. We *had* it, for one precious year, we had it.

125

"It's as if our world has just been turned inside out, purely because of the whims of some men in Warszawa. You know, Mamusiu, I've always believed Poland would free itself. And ever since I moved here, the country's been making slow and steady progress in that direction. Now with a jerk, we're being yanked back into the sixties, or fifties even, with shades of the Stalinist terror coming back to haunt us in the form of night arrests and cloaking censorship."

Hanna looked at her, and Amy had to laugh at herself. "I *do* get carried away, don't I? I probably think about it too much. It's driving me crazy not knowing where Piotr is. I don't know how you stand the uncertainty. Well, I suppose I've lectured enough," Amy sighed as she closed the English grammar book.

Żanetka looked up. Twice a week her mother talked to Babcia in English, teaching her the words. Her grandmother sat in her wheelchair with a pillow on her lap. A board covered her lap, and papers covered the board. She had set herself the goal of learning ten new vocabulary words each day.

Żanetka once asked her mother why she was so good at taking care of Babcia. She said it was because she used to nurse her stepfather. Żanetka thought it was sad that her mother had no real parents.

On that particular morning, the window was open and birdsongs mingled with the sounds of traffic down below. Already the leaves of the chestnuts lining the street below them shone bright green.

Her mother asked, "How many times have you been caught up by events in history, then been forced to experience changes in your own life because of those incidents?"

"You need to ask me this? Oh, Amy, I think it's the fate of Poland and her people to always be victims of history. It's a question of geography. We are trapped between Russia and Germany, always the invaded, rarely free. For one brief period between the two world wars, we were allowed to breathe. Then Germany attacked, then Russia attacked. Six years of war, and afterward all we did was exchange one occupying power for another. The Soviets are far more manipulative and damaging to our spirits and our country than the Germans ever were. Now who has let this latest blow fall? A Pole, one of our own. Jaruzelski. That's the most bitter and ironic part of this new chapter, as you like to call it. After all, there is nothing new under the sun. Nothing at all."

"How long do you think it will last?" Amy asked.

"Child, none of us dared dream the nightmare that the war would last six years. Who can tell? In '68 so many thought they were close to freedom. Last year we were closer than then, but now it seems that we have lost much more than was gained. I remember when they took Tadeusz away in the fifties. I thought I would die. But I didn't, and he came home safe. You know what Tadeusz would say now?"

Amy shook her head.

" 'Things are not as they seem.' "

Amy put away the books and papers. "You're right, I know. Listen, I'm going downstairs to see how the children are. Żanetko, you want to come with me?"

At the bottom of the stairs, the heavy outer door banged shut behind them. Żanetka slipped her hand into her mother's. They were headed for the space of green between their apartment building and the other two. Some of the parents had dug a pit there and filled it with sand. The children of both buildings used it, and the bars of the fence surrounding it, as a playground.

As soon as they rounded the corner, Żanetka noticed a group of children standing in a circle around two boys. They were fighting and rolling on the ground. Amy let go of Żanetka and broke into a run. "Tomku! Tomku, stop that right now." When she reached them, she bent over and pulled him away from the other boy. He didn't look hurt. "What is this all about? Tomku, calm down. Stop that right now!" Amy shook Tomasz hard. Then she hauled him over to a nearby bench and put him on it.

"Tomku, what have you been doing? Say something."

Żanetka's brother pushed his hair out of his eyes and said, "What do you care?"

"What do you mean, 'What do I care?' Where is your sister? I told you to watch her." Amy straightened up, suddenly alarmed. "Goniu!" She saw the boy Tomasz had been fighting now standing on the opposite side of the sandpit. He had a crowd of the rough boys in the neighborhood around him as he pointed in their direction.

Żanetka looked around the playground and saw her little sister, bent over and picking yellow flowers from the grass. She went over and did the same, then, holding on to Gonia's hand, brought her back to their mother. In both their free hands they clutched yellow buttercups. "Mamusiu! Look, for you!" Żanetka called out.

Amy smiled. She stooped down and let little Gonia run into her arms. "Look at the two of you! Where did you come from? Where were you? Mamusia was worried. Such pretty flowers. Thank you, Gonia."

She placed the flowers on the bench, and right away Tomasz grabbed them and started tearing them apart, throwing them onto the ground. "Tomku! Stop that!" Too late, Gonia started crying, and Amy heaved her up onto her hip, trying to quiet her.

Żanetka tugged on her mother's jacket. "Mamusiu, my flowers."

Amy took Żanetka's gift and shoved the yellow flowers into the pudgy hand kneading her arm. Gonia stopped crying immediately. "Oh, poor Goniu, my poor, poor baby," Amy crooned as she used her fingers to comb Goniu's brown curls behind her ears and out of her eyes.

Żanetka knew Tomasz was in trouble again, but she didn't know how to fix it. He still sat sullenly on the bench.

Their mother called, "C'mon, you. We're going back home to get you cleaned up. Let's go!" Amy grabbed his arm and pulled him upright, then shifted Gonia onto the other hip.

Żanetka followed a few steps behind, her head hanging slightly lower than that of Tomasz. "But my flowers were for Mamusia," she mumbled.

Her mother turned, and just then, Żanetka heard Tatuś calling to them. "Amy!" He crossed the street and joined them, smiling at the children. "I'm glad I caught you all. Hey, what happened?"

Amy opened her mouth, but before she could speak, Żanetka said, "Tomasz beat up that boy who is always saying bad things. He was very strong. And I had flowers for Mamusia. But now I don't."

Her father said to Tomasz, "Come here. What have we told you about fighting?" Without waiting for an answer, he continued, "Walk away from it. Just walk away from the fight, do you understand?" He lifted the boy's chin up with his fingers.

"But he was good, Tatusiu," Żanetka piped up. No one answered.

After a moment, Jan sighed. "All right, Tomku, upstairs with you. And get cleaned up!" he called after him.

Amy smiled weakly at Jan. "He's not as difficult as he seems," she said.

Jan shook his head. "I don't know. I never would have dreamed of behaving like he does at his age."

"Times were different then. I suppose we should be glad that he feels free enough to let off steam like this."

"No, Amy, it has nothing to do with freedom. It has to do with self-control. And respect. The boy is almost eight years old. When I was his age . . ." Jan stopped and smiled.

Żanetka smiled back. She was glad he had stopped.

Then he said, "All right, listen, I need to talk to you."

Her mother put Gonia back on the ground. "What is it, Jan?"

"It's Piotr. We've found out where they're keeping him."

Żanetka raced up the seven flights of stairs as fast as she could. *Wait until Tomasz hears. Wait until Babcia hears.* She knew she had important news, and she knew they'd be as excited to hear it as she was to tell it.

"Żanetko, wait!"

She could hear Gonia wailing two flights below her, but Gonia was four now and could climb the stairs herself. Żanetka rang their buzzer twice. It was the signal that someone from the family wanted to come in. When Tomasz finally opened the door, she flew in and announced, "Tatuś says they know where Uncle Piotr is being kept. They've found him! He's all right. He's safe. They found him!"

Żanetka ran to Babcia and gave her a big hug. She knew her grandmother was crying, and it was all right because Żanetka was also crying a little. "Good tears, right, Babciu?"

"Yes, dear. Good tears, not bad tears."

Żanetka especially enjoyed the look on her brother's face. She knew their uncle was a special friend of Tomasz. They needed each other. And this was very good news. The only better news would have been that Piotr was out of prison.

Soon Gonia tumbled into the room all angry and out of breath. "You should have *waited*, Żanetko!"

"Yes, you should have waited for your sister," her father said.

"The news is so good, Jan. Is it true, Amy?" Hanna looked breathless.

Jan smiled and nodded. "Yes. I was contacted by a man, some-one I don't know, who must be in the underground. I was on my way back from the train station, and he walked beside me and said, 'Your brother was arrested in February. He was in an internment camp in the south somewhere. Then a priest who knew Piotr was able to find him. The conditions were bad, but it could have been worse. Overcrowding, sometimes up to twenty people in a cell. But now he's been moved to a prison with criminals. It looks like the government's way of humiliating these men and women, putting them in with murderers and prostitutes.' "

The family was quiet. Żanetka couldn't imagine what it would be like to live in prison.

"Anyway, now he's in a prison near here, in Gdańsk, and they'll allow short visits."

"Oh, Jan. At least we know he's alive," Amy beamed. Then she motioned to the walls and asked more softly, "Should we be talking about this here? Do you think we've been under surveillance again?"

"I don't know." He stroked his chin. "Probably. But we're not talking about anything the SB doesn't already know. *They* arrested him, remember?"

"Mamusiu, Jan and I think I should be the one to visit Piotr. And I want to go right away, in case they move him again."

"Oh, Amy. Do you think that's wise. . . ?"

Żanetka could not believe her ears. The thought of her mother going to a prison, even for a visit, brought the tears dangerously close again.

Jan said, "The man who contacted me suggested it. He said I could become a target if I'm not very careful. Don't forget I'm teach-ing in the university, the so-called center of intellectual Solidarność leadership. Worst of all, thanks to the freedom we thought we were living in last year, the secret police now know Piotr is my brother *and* that Bogdan and I *did* know each other in 1968. And still know each other. Remember the wedding? That makes two connections we have with Solidarność leadership."

"Yes, all the secrets came out in 1981, and now the SB has even more information on everyone. I was talking to Mamusia about that earlier this morning," Amy said.

"More than a few think they let us pretend to be free so they could glean new information. We lowered our guard and played like children with our new toy. Look where it got us."

"Jan, you sound like Piotr."

"I *am* bitter," Jan said. "I'm so upset by these arrests. I was hoping my children would not have to live through a time like I did. I pray my *grandchildren* will live in a free Poland." Then he sighed. "Listen, Mamusiu. I've talked it over with Amy. If I go to the prison to meet Piotr, I may not come home. I can't do that to you or the children."

Żanetka looked up. She had never known her father to be afraid of anything.

He continued, "The underground man said to me that they wouldn't dare restrain Amy, and especially not if she took Gonia with her. Piotr *needs* us now. Do you remember how happy he looked at his wedding? When was it? Not even a year and a half ago. He's had a tremendous year. This whole country has. He was happy with Halina, wasn't he? He looked happy, and then at that picnic. . . ? And now this. It drives me crazy. I pray not to become bitter, but I can't forget all the times Piotr has had something given to him, then taken away."

Żanetka knew the story of Piotr's violin scholarship, withdrawn from Piotr when he was a teenager because his father had been arrested in the fifties. She wondered if now was the same kind of time.

Her mother said, "Please, Mamusiu. I look more innocent with Gonia. And remember, we both have the added protection of being U.S. citizens. They'd never dream of arresting us."

"All right," Babcia said. "Yes. All right. Let him know we're praying for him. I don't want him thinking he's all alone. I *know* that loneliness. And take a Bible with you," Hanna told her.

Żanetka watched as Amy bundled Gonia up to leave amid shouts of protest from Tomasz.

"I want to go to Gdańsk! Please take me instead. I *have* to see him! Gonia's too small. *Please* let me go with you, Mamusiu, and I promise I'll be good."

Amy sent a desperate look to Jan, but he just shook his head and turned away. Instead, Babcia said, "Come here, Tomku, and stop making so much noise. Your mother has an errand to run, and she needs Gonia with her."

"But the girls always . . ." he sputtered.

"No, the girls don't *always*," Hanna said, patting the couch beside her wheelchair. "Now, come here and keep me company. I want to hear how your reading is coming along."

"Mamusiu?" Żanetka had to at least try. She sensed the urgency of this mission. Softly she asked, "Mamusiu, can *I* go with you and Gonia?"

But now her mother looked annoyed. "Jan, can't you ever help with the children? No, Żanetko, you can't. Now, all of you stop hanging on me. I have to go."

Żanetka turned away and walked quietly over to Gonia. "You be good for Mamusia, and give me a good-bye hug." The two girls hugged each other. Then Żanetka added, "And Tatuś, too, and Babcia, and Tomasz." Obediently, Gonia made the rounds, until she kissed Tomasz, who licked her face in response, which set Gonia crying again.

"All right!" Amy said impatiently. "I'm just going away for a few hours. Cześć, everyone!"

Żanetka stood watching her mother and sister leave, followed by her father, carrying the old stroller. Then she dashed over to the window so she could watch her mother pushing Gonia down the street.

She stood on the chair, breathing against the glass, still watching, even long after they were out of sight.

Żanetka could even remember the feel of the sun on her face that late afternoon when Ewa brought her mother home. She had not left the window, except to get her pens and paper so she could draw. And she waited. The longer she waited, the quieter she became inside.

No one else seemed to feel the same way. That afternoon, the apartment was full of noise and movement, her father coming and going. Babcia reading stories and trying to keep Tomasz happy. A few times her grandmother asked, "Żanetko, do you feel well?" Then she had felt her forehead. But she had no fever.

Żanetka felt warm, it was true, but it was warm from inside, a sort of tightness, not like good tears.

And then, just before dark, she saw them.

Her mother was limping toward their building as she leaned on Ewa. Żanetka jumped from her spot by the window and flew to her grandmother's chair. Her hands ran up and down the wheel. She shifted her weight from one foot to the other. "Babciu?"

Her grandmother's eyes fluttered open. "I just had the strangest dream . . . but I don't remember what it was. It's a wonder I could sleep with all the noise around here. What is it, Żanetko?"

"Mamusia is coming home. I saw her." Żanetka wanted to say more, but her throat felt as if it couldn't open right.

"Go knock on your father's door and tell him, would you? I know he's as anxious as the rest of us."

Żanetka knocked on the bedroom door. When Jan opened it, he had his Bible in his hands. "Yes? I've almost got the sermon finished. . . ."

"Mamusia is home. And, Tatusiu, there's something wrong." There, she'd said it.

"All right," Jan said. He put down his Bible and rushed out the door and down the steps, leaving the door open behind him.

When Żanetka moved to close the door, her grandmother said, "It's all right, you can leave it. They'll be up in a moment."

Then they heard it. A wail, a keening sound from the ground floor. And Jan calling, "Amy!" Both Żanetka and Tomasz ran to the top of the stairs and leaned over the railing.

"That sound . . . was Mamusia," Tomasz said.

"I know. It sounded awful," Żanetka said.

"Something terrible has happened. Come on, we better go inside." The two children retreated to their grandmother's side as all three steeled themselves for the parents' arrival.

Amy staggered up the stairs, leaning heavily on both Ewa and Jan. Her father's face looked white. Both Ewa's and Amy's mascara smeared down their cheeks.

Still Żanetka waited. Tomasz was the one to get a glass of water for his mother. He stood there looking at his shoes. Babcia said only two words, "God, no."

When Żanetka could not stand it any longer, she said the word that had been burning on her lips all afternoon. "Gonia? Where is Gonia, Mamusiu?"

Amy looked up at her, and Żanetka thought her heart would break at the strangled look on her mother's face. "She's gone. My baby is gone."

"Amy, tell us what happened." Hanna's words sounded stern.

Amy stared at them all, her eyes wide. "I dashed out the door and went as fast as I could, but I was too late. I heard them beat Piotr when he tried to follow after I left. Other women gathered around me. All I could hear was them gasping over and over, 'Look!' They pointed downward.

"I saw, but didn't want to see. I just couldn't believe it could be true. I went down the stairs myself, thinking with each step, *No! No, please! Not this!*

"And all I could see was the pink mound on the tiles at the bottom of the stairway. A pink bundle topped by brown hair. Our Gonia." Then her eyes focused, and she looked directly at Żanetka and Tomasz, as if she owed them both an apology. "She was dead. She's gone. Your baby sister is gone."

And only then did she start to sob. It was the strangest sort of crying Żanetka had ever witnessed. Silent tears. No more wailing. Just tears, as if her mother were being choked. She leaned on Jan, and he half carried her to the other bedroom and closed the door behind them.

Żanetka felt a hand in hers, and to her surprise, it was her brother's. He looked as shattered as Żanetka felt.

Babcia said, "I cannot bear this life anymore. One son in prison, and a granddaughter dead. Child, can you help me go to bed?" she asked Ewa.

"I'll get your bed ready, Babciu," Tomasz offered.

Żanetka moved nearer to Ewa and said, "You found her."

Ewa looked at her and bent down, taking Żanetka's cold hands into her warm ones. "Yes. I was at the same prison, trying to see Bogdan. I know he's in there, but they won't let him have any visitors yet. As I was coming out, I heard the commotion. Oh, I'm so sorry. I heard several women screaming. And then I found poor Amy bent over little Gonia, rocking her back and forth. And not saying anything. Just like she is now. I . . . the guards came, and somebody official, I don't know who. And they took the body. Only then could I get Amy to get off the floor and come home with me. She didn't say anything until you told her to," she said to Hanna.

Hanna nodded. Żanetka thought her face looked so sad, older and whiter. Everything happening around Żanetka seemed to be happening in slow motion.

"Thank you, Tomku," Babcia said. "You're a good boy. Your parents will need your help in the next weeks. Can you be a big boy?"

"Yes, Babciu."

"And, little Żanetko, you are so still. Come give your grandmother a hug. I need a hug from my granddaughter."

"I'm not Gonia," Żanetka said, and then she started shaking.

"No, you're not. You're my other granddaughter. My first one."

Ewa said, "Is there anything I can do to help you get ready for bed? Or anything else I can do for any of you?"

"Yes, if you'd just help me into the bed over there. Thank you." Hanna reached out and took Ewa's hands. "You've done so much. And you have your own problems. I'm sure you'll get to see Bogdan very soon now. It's a good sign that Piotr is in the same prison. Maybe they will have contact with each other." Babcia's voice was so strange. No feeling.

"Yes. Maybe. All right. All settled? I'll leave you, then. A family should be alone at a time like this." Ewa slipped out the door.

Then their grandmother told her and Tomasz, "Losing little Gonia will be the hardest thing you have ever done in your lives. These next days and the changes you will see in your parents will be difficult to understand. Remember to pray to God about how you feel. He knows. . . . Now I think we should all go to bed early. There's nothing left of this day. A terrible, terrible, dark day."

Żanetka didn't want to go into her parents' bedroom that night, but her grandmother insisted. So she quietly entered and heard nothing, then got ready for bed. Her father had pulled out the bed and made it for her. All she had to do was get undressed and crawl between the sheets.

It was their bed. They shared it. And now she could smell the baby sweat of her little sister. At first she thought, *She's back. She wasn't really dead, just gone for an afternoon. And now she's asleep next to me. I can smell her.* Żanetka turned her pillow over, and rolled over to face the wall.

Then she heard her mother whisper, "Jan, I'm so sorry. I'm so sorry."

"Shh, it's not your fault. It was an accident."

"But, Jan . . ."

"Shh."

But her mother insisted. And in that same strange voice with no emotion, this time so soft Żanetka could hardly hear it, Amy said, "Your brother. Piotr and I . . . that's when Gonia fell down the stairs. And now she's . . . gone." The last word she choked out. Then again, "Jan, I'm so sorry."

Żanetka held her breath, hoping for something she couldn't name. Then she heard her father say, "Come here." And she could tell he was holding her. "It would be too easy to grieve privately, to bleed alone. We won't do that. We will cling to each other as if our lives depended on it. Because they do. It's the only way, Amy."

Żanetka remembered from that day on, there was the crying. Her crying and her mother's, and no one would hold her, so she just kept on crying. And on that night, for the first of many, many times, Żanetka cried herself to sleep.

She cried herself to sleep while listening to the sounds of her mother dreaming restlessly and calling out Gonia's name.

She cried herself to sleep, missing her little sister in their bed next to her, her warmth, her softness, her little kicking feet when she dreamed.

She cried herself to sleep whenever she heard her mother wake up screaming over and over in the dark.

Jacek had left word that he wanted to know who visited the prisoner Piekarz and when. Thanks to martial law, it was easy to arrange such things. And so it was that he received a written report of another woman visitor. Amy Piekarz.

He stared at the name and shook his head. But as he read on, his hands flew to his face. *No! Not this. Not little Gonia.* An accident, a stupid oversight, the fools. Jacek shook his head, his two worlds now jostling each other, overlapping, mutually exclusive, as volatile as the day he first faced Amy and knew her as his daughter.

He rushed to the prison and demanded a second audience. This time, when he saw the criminal, it took all of Jacek's self-control to keep from flying at his throat. "You!" It was his turn to accuse. "I should have had you killed when I had the chance! Did you think the last time I was here I was making idle threats? That I didn't *know* the potential you had for hurting her? Or that you could undo it all this way? *Don't you know there is no greater pain than to lose a child?*" Jacek fairly screamed.

His heart pounded . . . too fast. Through the sound of blood rushing through his ears, he heard the man slouched in the chair on the other side of the room mumble something. "What? What did you say?"

And now Jacek looked at the man. Piotr dragged his hands from his face, and Jacek saw the bruise on his cheek. More serious was the pain etched in dark lines around his eyes and mouth.

"I said, of course I won't tell her you're her father. You're right, you *were* right all along. I . . . can't . . . hurt . . . her any worse than this."

Never before had anyone called Jacek a father. The word startled him. But in the face of this tragedy, no more games could be played. He acknowledged that together with the man sitting across from him. It was the first time he would agree with Piotr Piekarz.

"Do you realize the devastation you've caused by . . . her death?" he whispered. Just saying the name that represented the little bundle of life he had watched grow for a year and a half seemed an act of betrayal in itself. *Gonia.* How often had Jacek recited her name in his little apartment. "Gonia," he said it now, wishing with all his being that the word might summon the child back to life.

Then he said slowly, his voice shaking with emotion, "What happened?"

Piotr spoke in a monotone. "Amy. I saw her waiting for me. The child was asleep in the stroller, parked in the corner. She took my hand and asked how I was, what I needed. I asked for notebooks and pens to write with. I told her the food was killing me, soup and stale bread. I told her . . ." His voice choked.

"I told her about Halina leaving me, wanting to move to Germany. I told her about the humiliation."

"The child," Jacek interrupted. "What happened to the child?"

"We heard a woman scream. Then we both saw the stroller was empty. Gonia had climbed out without us noticing. Then Amy dashed out the door, and I heard Amy's own voice crying out. I tried to follow, but the guard held me back, and finally had to beat me with his club. When I came to, a cellmate told me they had found a small child at the bottom of the stone stairs leading up here. She had slipped and fallen. . . ."

"And died," Jacek finished for him. "What were you doing that neither of you noticed her leave the room?" He paused a moment, then realized what Piotr's dark look meant.

Jacek shook his head in disbelief.

Piotr gasped. "She was so near. Her eyes. You don't understand. I've *always* loved her. I didn't mean . . ." His voice died, and Jacek saw the brokenness in Piotr mirror his own.

Jacek said quietly, his spirit cold like stone, "Gonia is gone, and you're still alive. Amy is broken. You stay here and die," he hissed.

Let the man find a place to suffer worse even than what I now know. As he passed by a dark window, Jacek caught sight of his face, no longer arrogant, but instead aghast and appalled.

Yet again, he had tied his own hands worse than before. Especially in his rediscovered position of power, Jacek presented more of a threat to Amy than ever. And precisely for that reason, Jacek could not do what everything in him screamed to do.

He could never comfort his daughter in her crushing loss.

14

It felt to Żanetka as if a darkness hung over them all. Darkness and tears. Never, ever in all the stories Babcia had told them did a child die. Even Babcia cried as she helped Amy fold up Gonia's little dresses and pack them away in a box. "Do we bury the dresses, too?" Żanetka asked.

"No, they go into the storage cell in the basement," Babcia said.

A month after the funeral, Żanetka still could not shake the dark and heavy feeling. It was one of the reasons she kept crying in her bed. Her father had told them they needed to talk about whatever they felt. So Żanetka finally blurted it out when Tomasz was at school and she was alone with her mother and grandmother.

"I think Gonia died because of me." Just saying the words hurt.

Her mother looked up, startled. Żanetka's hand flew to her mouth as Mamusia dropped the last slab of bacon into the pan and the grease splattered upward, burning her neck and arm. She yelled in surprise and ran to the bathroom, crying, "I have to get cold water on this."

"Oh, Amy!" Hanna cried.

Żanetka never expected her words to have such an effect. When her mother returned to the room, the ointment soaking through her blouse around her neck looked oily. Żanetka hurried to say, "I'm sorry, Mamusiu. I made you do it when I scared you like that."

"You didn't scare me, Żanetko." She sighed. "Here, let me get this cleaned up, then we'll sit down and have some tea."

"I don't want any, thank you," Hanna said.

"Are you sure you're all right?" she asked her mother again. But

Amy wouldn't look her in the eye, and Żanetka knew she wasn't all right. Not at all.

Żanetka knew this even when a few moments later, Amy said, "The burn isn't deep. I'll be fine."

Żanetka already regretted bringing up the subject. Today wasn't a good day for Babcia, either. Her mother had tried to get her medicine at the *apteka*, but it was all gone. So now she tried something different, but it didn't make the pain go away so well.

"What do you mean that Gonia died because of you?" Amy asked.

Żanetka said, "No, it's okay. Really. I think I'll go find my sketchbook." She started to leave, when she felt her mother's hand on her shoulder.

"Not so fast, young lady. Now you didn't say something like that for no reason. Come sit down and tell me why you would say such a thing."

Żanetka felt trapped. She ran into the other room and got her notebook anyway. Then she brought it over to her mother and started turning the pages so she could see the pictures. She looked up at her mother's face, hoping the pictures would explain what she could not.

After a few moments, Amy said, "I see. Have you shown these to anyone else?"

"Just Babcia."

Hanna looked up from where she sat reading in the corner by the window. She shifted uncomfortably but said nothing. Żanetka could tell by her look that she was going to have to do this on her own. Babcia had said she'd have to show her mother the pictures, and now she had.

"Do you want to tell me about what you've drawn, Żanetko?"

"Well, it's why I think Gonia died because of me." She sighed. *Doesn't she see?* "It's my fault that Gonia thought she was safe on the stairs. Don't you remember that day?"

"Yes. I remember."

"No, I mean, don't you remember how you and Tatuś followed me and Gonia up the stairs? How I let her climb them by herself? How I said she was four and old enough to do it alone, without help? *She heard me*. So she must have thought she *could* climb stairs by herself. And that's why she thought she could go down by herself. She probably woke up in the stroller and didn't know where you were and went looking for you."

Amy sighed and rubbed her eyes. "No, baby, it wasn't your fault. It *isn't* your fault. Do you hear me? If it's anyone's fault, it's mine. I should have been paying better attention."

Her mother looked over at Hanna. Żanetka saw them stare at each other for a few minutes. Then suddenly, Amy scraped back the chair and took Żanetka by the hand. "Come on, we're going for a walk. Just you and me. It's long overdue, don't you think?"

"What about our tea?" Żanetka said.

"We'll make a fresh pot when we get back. Mamusiu, will you be all right for a little while?"

She nodded. "Yes. You go on."

The only time Żanetka had left the apartment since the funeral was to go play with a girl downstairs. She had three Barbie dolls. Żanetka felt all excited. *A walk, yes, and alone with Mamusia. That's what we need.*

Once outside, they headed for the waterfront. On the way they passed a small park, and Żanetka stopped to point up at the purple blooms hanging from the bushes along the wall. "What are they called, Mamusiu?"

"Those? Lilacs. They smell sweet. Here, I'll pick you some." Her mother pulled down a branch and broke off one of the fragrant flowers. "We'll put this in a vase at home, and it will make the whole apartment smell good."

"You're feeling better?" Żanetka had to ask it.

"Well, yes and no. Now, where do you want to go?"

"I want to feed the swans." Żanetka knew this right away.

"Aren't you a little old for that? It's what . . ."

"I know. That's *why* I want to feed the swans. It's what Gonia liked to do. I want to do it for her. I think this is better than putting flowers at her grave."

Her mother nodded slowly. "Makes sense." Together they walked down to the pier, where at least fifty of the large birds swam up and down to the rhythm of the waves. Necks arched, they paddled gracefully through the surf.

"Look, there's a young one. You can tell because he's not white yet," Żanetka said.

"I don't have any bread. We didn't bring any with us," her mother said.

"That's all right. It's good just to be here and watch them. It's

141

funny how ugly they are when they waddle on land, and how pretty they become when they're swimming," Żanetka said. She squinted her eyes up at the sunlight. It felt as if she hadn't been outside for years and years. That's what Gonia's death felt like. Like being locked indoors during the summer.

"Żanetko, it's important that you believe what I told you back at home. *You are not to blame for what happened to Gonia.* Do you understand?"

Żanetka shifted her gaze to her mother's face. She moved around two steps so her mother blocked the sun. Now the light shone through her hair. Żanetka smiled and nodded. "I understand." Then she hesitated. "And you?"

"What about me?"

"Tatuś says it was an accident. So then you're not to blame either. 'Understand?' "

She must have said something wrong because her mother knelt down to her level and the sun burst into Żanetka's eyes, blinding her for a few seconds. All she could feel were her mother's arms holding her tight for the very first time since that day none of them would ever, ever forget.

Żanetka sat in the family's little garden. Located on a strip of land along the train tracks, these garden plots were tended by people in apartment buildings who wanted a little piece of land.

She and her father looked out over the broken tulip stems, stripped of color and nodding in the breeze like forgotten flagpoles. "This garden is like the swans," she said.

"Oh, really? In what way?" her father asked.

"The swans are better than going to Gonia's grave. And you come here instead of visiting your father's grave. This was the flower garden you planted for him when he was so sick, isn't it? That's what Babcia told me."

"Yes." Her father was smiling. "And if I were true to his memory, I should have clipped back the stalks and prepared the ground properly and planted some vegetables."

"We can still do that. It's still spring. A little. When it rains," Żanetka said. "If I help you, can I have a corner for my own flowers and plants?"

"I think that's a very good idea. It will get both our minds off all the bad news."

"Do you still miss him, your father?" Żanetka asked.

"Yes, I do. Some times more than others."

"Sometimes it hurts in my tummy when I think of Gonia. Especially at night. Will I always miss her?"

"Yes. Yes, I'm afraid so. You're too young for all of this. It shouldn't have happened. Another *shouldn't have*. But remember one thing, Żanetko. The pain dulls with time. You won't always miss her with that sharp pain you have now. But you will always miss her."

In the days that followed, Żanetka wanted to block out the voices. Ewa asking her mother, "Can you talk about it? Can you remember? Would it help to talk? Do you remember me telling everyone to get back and leave you alone?"

"Yes, I heard a woman's voice from a faraway place, a place void of feeling, a barren place, empty of everything but loss. I could not even say my baby's name anymore. The sound of that word hurt too much. I just held my little girl, my little girl, in my arms, and rocked her back and forth, back and forth, back and forth, mouthing the name only, in a whisper, willing the child back to life."

"Anything else?"

"I saw no one, felt only the loss, like an enemy had finally found me, besieged and surrounded, there was only loss."

15

You my great father and I your true child

Being with Ewa was different than being with her mother. Different and the same. Ewa was happier, and she didn't get tired as fast, especially when they were waiting in line for something. And the same because they both liked to shop for the same things. They were both fun to be with and at times bought Żanetka something special for her hair or from the bakery.

Żanetka was all excited about Christmas. Every night she opened another window in the advent calendar her mother had made for her. Now there were only six more windows, or six more nights, and it would be Christmas Eve. That was the best day of all. That night she could stay up late, and they would have their big family meal and open presents.

The only problem was that this year there would be no Piotr and Halina. And no Gonia.

But Ewa would join them.

She and Ewa were in charge of shopping for the last-minute things. Żanetka didn't know what this meant, but Ewa did. And while Mamusia took her grandmother to the clinic, she and Ewa were going to "spend all day," if they had to, finding her mother's "last-minute" things for the Christmas feast.

Ewa was raised in Gdańsk, but had also lived in Gdynia a long time, so she knew many of the best places to shop. And whenever they needed anything, she always knew who might know somebody who could help them.

Żanetka clapped her mittened hands together to make a muffled, smacking noise.

"What are you so happy about?" Ewa asked her.

"I just like the sound. Uh, and I'm happy about Christmas."

"Yeah, me too." Ewa knelt down and gave her a quick hug, then took her hand. Żanetka smiled. "So you think waiting in line after line is fun, huh?" Ewa asked.

Żanetka nodded. "With you it is. And I like looking at the people."

"Well, you're the only child I know who has the patience for this. Just three years ago we could go into a shop, find what we wanted, buy it, and leave. Now here we are," Ewa started ticking off her fingers, "standing in line for fish, only to hear they don't have what we want, standing in line at the green grocer's, but they don't have the nice vegetables your mother would like, standing in line at the apteka, but they don't have the right medicine, standing in line for pantyhose and shaving cream and . . ."

"Toilet paper!" Żanetka joined in the game. "But they don't have any at all!"

"That's right. You get the idea. By the way, was that on your mother's list?"

"I don't know. I thought *you* had the list," Żanetka said.

"I thought *you* had the list!" They both laughed.

Żanetka skipped along beside Ewa, reciting out loud all the names of the signs they passed. If she said it fast enough, it sounded like another language.

"You know, young lady. There won't be anything left for you to learn when you go to school. You're already reading so well," Ewa said.

"It's all right. Babcia says Tatuś taught himself how to read too, just like me. And *he* says when he finally turned seven and went to school, there were still plenty of things to learn."

Ewa looked down at Żanetka, then squeezed her hand. "Yes, I suppose there are. Oh, look, they have nothing left. The sign says so on the window. And I still had coupons for meat, lard, and flour. It looks like we'll have to try the open market. You don't mind walking some more in this cold, do you?"

Żanetka shook her head. Seeing all these people and the colors and sounds was *much* better than spending the day in the apartment. Christmas was supposed to be fun, but everyone was so gloomy this year. She knew it was because of Gonia, but still, it was Christmas. "What are those people doing?" Żanetka pointed at a group on the corner ahead of them. Cars were honking their horns at men gathered around something in the grass.

Ewa slowed down and said, "Maybe we should go back. We can go this way another time. . . ."

"Look! There, across the street!" Żanetka cried. Two milicja vans were parked on the curb, and out of their doors now sprang eight police with helmets and shields.

"Oh, Żanetko, I need to get you out of here," Ewa said. She pulled the girl close and turned around. But Żanetka could still see the police pulling out their sticks. People in the group shouted at the police. More men ran past her and Ewa toward the group. A woman screamed.

Then the police began beating the men. Now Żanetka screamed, then clapped a mitten over her mouth. The people ahead of them shouted some more. Someone threw something at the police. A rock. It hit him on the helmet. Then Ewa was dragging her down a side street and away from the noise. On the way, they ran into people all running toward the noise, not away. Żanetka wanted to go back and see what happened to the men.

"Are you all right?" Ewa was panting. She looked right and left, as if she were still scared.

"What happened? What were they doing? *Why* were they doing that?"

"Here, come with me. Let's not get upset now. Wait until I find a less crowded place, then we can talk."

Żanetka was shaking. She couldn't stop thinking about the milicja and their glass masks that shielded their faces. *And those poor men! What if they had little girls like me? What would their little girls say when they didn't come home. . . ?*

They climbed a hill that overlooked the waterfront. Under pine trees and in a bitter cold wind, Ewa stooped down to Żanetka's level. "I don't know what you can understand," she began.

"I *want* to know," Żanetka said.

"Those men were trying to put up crosses to mark a place where other men died when they were fighting for Poland to be free."

"Like you and Bogdan and Piotr. Who killed the men who died there?"

"Milicja forces."

"And that's who was hurting *these* men."

"Yes, that's right. They don't want anyone to remember what those brave men died for."

Żanetka was quiet for a moment. Then Ewa said, "I'm going to ask you something, Żanetka. You just said how Bogdan and Piotr and I help fight for Poland. But you must *never* say that to anyone. Not even at home."

"But everyone knows. . . ."

"We think the secret police can hear what we say at home. Now promise me. *No* talking about what I do to anyone, all right?"

Żanetka nodded. "I don't want you to go to prison, too."

"I'm not going to, not if I can help it. For one thing, I don't think I could bear to be away from you for so long."

Żanetka looked at her eyes. "Really?"

"Really. You know that Bogdan and I have no children. Well, your mother and I have grown so close that she lets me borrow you and Tomek. Especially now with Bogdan gone, I *need* your family. Otherwise I'd have no one. So you see how important you are to me, little Żanetko?"

Żanetka threw her arms around Ewa and started crying.

"Hey, what are those tears for?"

"Good tears," Żanetka sniffed. "And scared tears." Her voice muffled in Ewa's collar, Żanetka said, "I want to go home. I'm cold."

"It isn't what I wanted. I wrote down on the list what I wanted, and it isn't what I wrote down!"

Tomasz was spoiling Christmas Eve. He was mad because the race car under the tree was not the kind he had asked for.

"I said I wanted one with remote control. I've been asking for it since before *last* Christmas. You should have known. I don't want *this*."

Żanetka felt as if she was going to throw up. She didn't want more fighting. Not on Christmas. Not when Ewa was with them, and Mamusia and Babcia had worked so hard with the "last-minute things" to make such a special dinner.

"That's enough," her father said.

"Come, Tomku," Babcia said. "Don't get so angry. Everyone is trying to make do with what they can find this year."

"But I . . ."

"I said that's enough." Her father's voice was even softer, stone soft.

Żanetka ran for the bathroom and was sick. From the other room she could hear her parents yelling at Tomasz, and him yelling back. Then she heard the other bedroom door slam. She came back into the room and everyone was quiet. Then she bent under the tree and pulled out a scroll with a ribbon around it. She walked over to Ewa and gave it to her.

"Merry Christmas. It's not for you, it's for Bogdan. I drew it myself. And there's a second one inside. That one is for my uncle."

"You look so pale, Żanetko," Ewa said, running the back of her cool hand along Żanetka's cheek. Then she opened the scroll and said, "Thank you very much. I'll make sure both Bogdan and Piotr get your pretty pictures."

"I tried again earlier this week," Jan said. "He refuses to see any of us. Ever since . . ."

"You have to give him time," Ewa said. "I speak to him whenever I see Bogdan. And at least they have each other. He told me he did not want to see any of you. I try each time to change his mind, but . . . well, you know Piotr."

"But I won't stop trying," Jan said. "I can't imagine how he must have suffered. And it's been ten months since he was arrested. We've had each other to get through the grief, eight months long, but he's alone. What does he think? That it's his fault?"

"I'll go check on Tomasz," Amy said and left the room.

16

Żanetka was writing a book. Her first book, but there would be more. Żanetka had a plan. First she would write about her family, then about ponies, and then about dolphins. These were her favorite subjects.

And flowers. She liked flowers and trees and birds, so she also liked to press petals and bits of bark and feathers into another book, a scrapbook. But this was not a real book like the one she was writing now.

They had walked from the road to the garden plot, Żanetka and her father. This was their special place, their special time alone together. For the last year Żanetka had been coming here sometimes to help him, other times to work in her own corner while he read or wrote his sermons, or when he slept in the sun.

Now it was her turn to write, and he was going to work. First, though, she stood beside him and looked proudly at the block of color produced by five years of multiplying bulbs. Each spring the flowers returned, first hyacinth, then daffodils, and finally the tulips, all a memorial to her grandfather.

And to Gonia. Żanetka hadn't told anyone, but her corner was for Gonia. And now that it had been exactly a year since her four-year-old sister went to heaven, it was a good time to come and look at what she had planted for her sister.

"Your roses are already budding. Look, that one even has a flower opening," her father said.

Żanetka had not wanted to cut back the plants last month. In fact, she had gotten very mad and even yelled at Tatuś when he started pruning, but he had insisted. Since she had chosen to plant rosebushes in that corner, he said she would have to give them the care that roses needed.

"There will be more flowers because you cut them back," he said now.

She smiled up at him to let him know he had read her mind. Then she walked over to the one open bloom and cupped it in the palm of her hand.

Yellow, her favorite color.

The girls were fixing each other's hair. Ewa, Mamusia, Babcia, and Żanetka. Babcia and Żanetka were giggling because Żanetka's red hair stuck straight up in twenty tiny tufts, all tied with ribbons. "I look like that little dog that lives downstairs."

"Oh, not that white one. He always growls at my wheelchair," Babcia said.

"Grrr," Żanetka said.

Ewa and Amy laughed from the other side of the room, where they were painstakingly dyeing each other's hair. "We just look so gray because we have black hair. Blondes don't have this problem."

"Yes, they do, but they can ignore it longer," Ewa said.

"Well, I think the package said that hiding the gray hair on a regular basis would make us younger," Amy said.

"No, you read it wrong. 'Would make us *look* younger.' It won't make us younger, but that's all right. We can pretend," Ewa said.

"Well, I'm older than you, so I need it worse. Just be thankful our hair is the same tone or you'd have to go out and buy your own dye."

"Are you two fighting over there?" Babcia called.

"No. Just Ewa. She's causing trouble."

"Me? Your daughter-in-law thinks she's the only one here with gray hairs. And she can't read."

"Well, then you haven't taken a look at my hair," Babcia said. "I win the prize in that department. Maybe I should transfer over from the dog department side of this beauty parlor to the anti-aging one."

"No, Babciu, stay here. We're not done yet," Żanetka said. "Maybe I should dye *your* hair red."

She had the flu, so she got to stay in bed all day while Mamusia brought her toast and tea. Żanetka fell asleep in the middle of the day, then opened her eyes just as the shadows were filling her parents' room with dancing patterns of light on the other wall.

She stared at the shadowplay and slowly woke up, only half realizing that both her parents were talking in hushed tones in the other room. She was hot and thirsty and felt as if she were still in a dream, waiting for the late-evening sunlight to fade away.

Then she saw the shapes change. The light came from the far window in the other room. Her door was open. In a perfect silhouette, she saw her father kiss her mother. She couldn't tell where one ended and the other began. It was just a figure of a couple holding each other and whispering.

Then her mother's words, "I just feel so empty."

Jacek laughed cynically. "I'm getting too old for this, Roman. Why don't you let me just ride off into the sunset?"

"I don't even know how old you are. Did you know your file doesn't contain that information?" Roman said. Since martial law had been enforced, he had switched from cigarettes to cigars from Havana. He offered one to Jacek now, and Jacek accepted it, cutting off the tip and smelling the length of the cigar.

"Since when have you been looking at my file?"

"Oh, just doing some housecleaning. We don't know how old you were when you first reported for duty back—when was it now? Just before the Soviets liberated Gdańsk. Didn't you just walk into Rokossovski's camp and sort of volunteer your spy services to the Soviets?"

Jacek frowned. *Where on earth is all of this leading?* "Yeah," he answered.

"What do you remember about Gdańsk? I mean, what do you remember most?"

Jacek did not even hesitate. It was a safe answer. And it would show Roman how serious he was in this perpetual cat-and-mouse game he insisted on playing with Jacek during the years. And it was the truth. "A woman."

"Ah, yes. The women during the war were the sweetest and bravest. Sometimes I think all the really good women died in the war. What was yours called?"

"Monika."

"What happened to her?"

Jacek took a deep drag on the cigar, then slowly blew the smoke out through pursed lips. "We didn't even have a chance. Our friends the Soviets took care of her in Gdańsk." Jacek said the words calmly enough, but he had long ago had to reconcile his awful guilt with the woman he had loved and lost. He had left her behind, abandoned and betrayed, when the Soviets poured into Gdańsk. The city's liberators had torched it systematically, street by street. Gang rapes, murder, theft. Jacek had witnessed the terror he had helped usher in. For in those final weeks, Jacek had lived in Gdańsk, obtaining information about the German fortifications, spying for the Russians. And only after he had done his job had he returned to his lover. After what the Soviets had done to her, her eyes—eyes more dead than alive—had been staring at him ever since.

"Ah, Gdańsk. No trace of what really happened there in the history books."

The two men smoked in silence for a few moments. Then Jacek asked, "How old are *you*?"

"Older than your sixty-five and even longer due for that ride into the sunset, that's for sure."

Jacek smiled to himself. He had just turned seventy-four the week before.

17

Once far away, but by love reconciled

April 1983

Dear Amy and Jan,

What does it mean, change of heart? I will entitle this "States of Heart" and hope you understand.

I have read about losing heart, a whole heart, the secrets of the heart, a clean heart. There is the broken and contrite heart, joyful or troubled heart; a heart can be searched by God. Things can be treasured in a woman's heart, one can be slow of heart to believe, pain can pierce to the heart. Search a heart, a heart can be guarded, directed, sincere, or deceived. But there is only One who may dwell in a heart. And today, as a man who once wore my name wrote, the morning star arose in my heart. A lamp is finally shining in this dark place where I have lived for over a year.

See what can happen in a year? Dark and light. Looking back, I know there will never be a year like 1981 again in the history of Poland. We will never trust as children like that, the lessons of the war so long forgotten. This golden year, a golden fifteen months, was Poland's romp in the sunshine. . . .

And then in December, martial law. I couldn't help but remember, hadn't Britain and France both pledged their aid in the summer of 1939 if Hitler ever dared to invade? We've seen it all happen before. It seems some promises of worldwide solidarity were as empty as the very wind now threatening to extinguish Solidarność.

I've heard even here how Poland fought back that first year. The demonstrations scheduled for May 1 and August 31 all occurred. Then, in October 1982, there were more police arrests, among them Frasyniuk of the TKK. Three days later the Sejm, or Polish lower house of parliament, formally "delegalized" Solidarność. Ha! The joke of their language. The TKK called for a four-hour protest strike on November 10, but when that proved to be the fateful date of Leonid Brezhnev's death, the strike fizzled out. The next day, Wałęsa was released from prison. We who remained behind rejoiced, even though we knew full well nothing he says or does goes unnoticed by the secret police.

Just as in 1939 when Poland held out longer than any other Western country against Germany's tanks, so now, there is only so much the country can do.

Even now, four months into 1983, Jaruzelski is still waging a war against his own people.

And so nothing changes. Well, at least we don't believe the words anymore. We have learned the hard way that lies can be told more easily than truth. Never again. If martial law has taught us anything, it is that we will never have another golden year like 1981.

When I was first imprisoned over a year ago, I had two visitors. The one came on the day after my arrest, only confirming what I had suspected . . . and dreaded. And then a month later, Halina came to see me, and because she knew better where to strike, she inflicted the greater wound.

She sat across from me and said she was leaving me, would try leaving Poland. She had sold the apartment and taken my personal things to Ewa. What could I do? I was in prison. My time had run out.

"Where will you go?" I asked.

I could tell she was nervous by all the things she tried to say. "I have cousins in Germany, West Germany. It's easy to get a job there. They'll send me an invitation, and I can try to leave here and make more money than I'd ever see in Poland. There's nothing here. It's a lost country. We can't do anything right."

Here I thought she was talking about the underground's efforts, but then she went on, "You should see it now, Piotr. Everyone has to stand in lines. There's nothing in the shops anymore. The government is choking the country to death. I've got to get out of here before I suffocate.

"I got the idea to leave the night they came to take you away. It was too much. I mean, I had had enough. Enough broken promises, enough waiting." *She was quiet for a moment. I think she wanted to ask for a divorce, but she didn't. Then she didn't say anything. She just stood up and left.*

That's not how I like to remember Halina. I would rather picture in my mind what she looked like on the night they took me away. Just before the police and I reached the staircase, I looked back and saw Halina standing there in the open doorway, wearing her bathrobe and rubbing her eyes. That's the image I prefer to think of when I remember my wife now. So small and con-

fused, surprised at how complicated I turned out to be.

Only after she left me, and I was thinking of her standing like that, clutching her robe around her neck, did I finally realize why the entire scene that night had all seemed so familiar to me. It was your nightmare all over again, Jan. Remember the one you had so often when we were boys, the memory of when they came to take away Tatuś?

Ironic, isn't it, I come from a long line of prisoners. And I tell myself because it's in my blood, I will endure. I may even break all their records. When Tatuś was arrested in the fifties, it wasn't the first time. Remember Mamusia's stories? When the Soviet army took Kraków, they arrested her father, Johann, because he was German, and Tatuś for collaborating, since he would not leave Johann's side. They both ended up inside a Soviet labor camp somewhere on the steppes of Kazakhstan.

I remember those stories now so vividly. I have nothing else to do but remember in this lonely place. I remember hearing how my grandfather died out there, but not until God did miracles through him and touched the hearts of other prisoners in that hellhole.

Hearts were touched.

Last April when you visited, Amy, I wrote you another sort of letter, one you will never see. Now I have been in this place much longer. It has been a long year, all the emptier because I would not let you near. I know Jan has tried to contact me, but I would not see him. I told Ewa to tell you both to stay away.

Now, with this letter, I beg you both to forgive me. Amy and Jan, you have to understand, I never meant for any of this to happen. I beg your forgiveness. If there has been one stumbling block in your love for each other, I'm so ashamed it had to be me. If you can forgive me, there is the chance of a miracle that I can forgive myself. . . .

I can imagine your shock at the sight of my writing these words. I have brought you only misery. Can you forgive me? Can you ever forgive me?

My heart has softened, although there is no one moment I can point to, I was never blinded by light. If my heart changing is conversion, then yes, with each word I read in the Bible you brought me, I have been touched.

Much of that book was still familiar to me from when I memorized verses for Mamusia and Tatuś, trying to please them, or recorded translations of taped sermons for Aad. I thought the least I could do was read what you had left behind. So during the empty months that stretched on either side of me, all I could do was remember and read. I saw my own arrogance, spoiled childishness, the stubbornness of my anger, but most of all, my hardness of heart. My state of heart.

I am that angry young man. I am arrogant Jacob, wrestling more with my own demons, rather demons of my own making, than with the Almighty himself.

You were right, Amy, all along. I was desperate though, desperate with loss. Halina had left me. The movement had been crushed. I had nothing but you. And now I've discovered new life in the darkness of this prison cell.

That's why I'm writing this to you and Jan now. After your great loss, I know nothing can compensate. But if it helps, rest in the knowledge that your loss was not wasted. It has brought me to the very feet of Christ.

18

Today was the day Żanetka had waited seven and a half years for, her first day of school. She walked proudly beside her big brother. Tomasz said, "You'll be all right. I'll come check on you during the break."

She loved her new square case riding on her back, but most of all, she loved the clean notebooks and new pens her parents had given her. Just thinking of all the exciting things she was going to learn and write down in those notebooks made her feel how she did every time she visited the library for new books.

Żanetka sat in a class with many children. She knew two or three of the girls. They lived in the same building, and she had played with them a few times. So she wasn't a stranger.

During the long break she stood watching the other children and wondering what she should do. Then she heard giggling behind her. She turned around and saw the older sister of the girl downstairs who had three Barbie dolls.

"My mother says she's a little strange. She never wants to play. Look at her standing there, doing nothing. And look at her funny hair. It looks like someone put her head into a bucket of carrot juice."

"Hey, Żanetko, is that all you drink, carrot juice?"

She stared at the girls. *Carrot juice?* "No," she said.

"And look at her funny shoes."

Żanetka looked down and saw only her normal shoes, which her mother had polished for her the night before.

"With those shoes and that hair, she could be a clown. A clown in a circus! A gypsy! She's a stinking gypsy who steals and lies. Her father's always tipsy!"

Tipsy? Did they mean drunk? "My father doesn't get drunk." She could feel the color rising in her cheeks. She felt hot. She looked around for the teacher, but she was talking to the other teachers over by the door. All the other children had stopped playing and were staring at her.

"Dirty little gypsy!"

"Or maybe she's a vampire, sucking blood! That's what my Serbian uncle says about people with that funny-colored hair!"

Żanetka started to run toward the teacher but turned and ran smack into her brother instead. "Oh, Tomku, listen to them!" She started to cry.

But then as soon as she said the words, she regretted them. Tomasz flew at the girls, fists flying. He knocked two of them down and fell on top of one, hitting her in the shoulder.

"Get him off! Get him off!" she screamed. They all screamed.

Żanetka ran after Tomasz and pulled on the hood of his jacket. "No, Tomku! Stop! No, don't!" The girl Tomasz sat on top of kicked Żanetka, and she fell against the second girl, knocking her down on the ground.

Then two teachers came running. "That's enough!" They pulled Tomasz off the girl while he was still kicking, his fists flying in the empty air.

The big girl under Żanetka said, "She pushed me. She hit me." The teachers pulled her up off the ground and put her in the corner next to Tomasz.

"It's the Piekarz children," said one teacher.

"It's *her* first day."

"Both of you should be ashamed of yourselves. Tomasz Piekarz, hasn't anyone taught you not to hit girls? And you, young lady, what's your name?"

"Elżbieta." She didn't want the teacher or anyone outside her family calling her by her favorite name.

"Well, Elżbieta, didn't anyone teach you that girls don't fight? Now inside, both of you. And go to your classrooms and sit at your desks and think about what bad children you've been."

They led Tomasz away to the other door. Before he went inside, though, he turned and nodded at Żanetka, like they had done something right, not wrong. She entered the door nearest her own classroom but then wasn't sure which room was hers. It was next to the bathroom, she knew that.

Then she saw the door with the shape of a girl in a dress on it. She went in and sat down on the toilet. Only when it was too late did she remember. She hadn't pulled down her panties.

Her mother's voice didn't sound right. "But dear, sweet Żanetko, you *are* beautiful, both inside and out. Those girls were just being mean. Or maybe they were jealous. Don't you know, your father had reddish hair when he was younger. That's where you get it from. Now go get that little hand mirror and bring it to me."

Żanetka returned with the mirror and held it up for her mother. "Let's both take a good look at you. Hold it up to your face, and I'll tell you what I see. I see an angel-white face framed in red curls and crowned with the darkest green eyes I've ever seen."

"Angel-white?"

"Yes. Do you still remember what I told you Jesus said about the angels of the little ones?"

"That they're the closest to the Father."

Żanetka said, "Tell me the garden story, Babciu. Tell it to me again. And then *I promise* I'll go to sleep."

Babcia smiled. "Well, it happened during an autumn just like this one. We had lovely warm sunshine, and the trees around Gdynia were bright with color, just like now. We were all very excited because your grandfather suddenly seemed much better—that's called remission. And you were such a good baby and—"

"You could still walk," Żanetka blurted out. "And Mamusia had Gonia safe in her tummy."

· Hanna ran her hand through Żanetka's hair. "That's right. Well, anyway, Tadeusz was strong enough to go down the stairs. So one day, we all went to the garden by the train tracks. He sat down in that old chair we keep in the garden shed, and your mother told him, 'You look just like a king surveying your kingdom.' And he laughed and said, 'That's just how I feel!' And then do you know what he said? He said, 'On a day like this, I feel like redigging the garden and filling it with flowers.'

"Well, then your mother winked at me and said, 'Why don't

we?' And your father said, 'Why don't we what?' He hadn't really been paying that much attention because he was playing with Tomek. I remember Tomek was riding on his father's shoulders. We were all laughing because Tomek kept putting his hands over Jan's eyes. Every time he'd do that, Jan would pretend to walk into a tree. And Tomek was laughing so hard he almost fell off. Tadeusz told them they should try out for the circus."

"Where was I?" Żanetka asked.

"Well, *you* were sound asleep in your baby buggy, parked under a tree. Now, what was I telling you? Oh yes. Tadeusz had been talking about getting rid of the vegetables and planting flowers, and your mamusia said, 'Why don't we, Jan? Why don't we plant flowers?' And then she took your tatuś's hand and they walked over in front of Tadeusz and stood there and waited.

"Your grandfather just sat there, looking at them. Then, he said in that soft voice of his—oh, Żanetko, I wish you had known him—anyway, he said, 'Flowers. Yes, I'd like that. We can't use the plot for much during the winter, anyway. Most everything has already been harvested.'

"Then your father said, 'And we have the bulbs Aad sent us in boxes from Holland. We can plant tulips and daffodils.' Do you remember Aad? Anyway, that idea of using Aad's tulips really pleased Tadeusz. I remember that he leaned over and crumbled a clod of dirt between his fingers, and he said again, 'Yes, flowers from our brother in Holland.' "

"And you did plant the tulips!" Żanetka said.

Babcia nodded. "It took part of that day and many more during the rest of the month. We had to dig the beds and plant the bulbs. Whenever he could manage to summon the strength, Tadeusz would go with Amy and Jan and you babies, and it would be a family outing.

"It took us three weeks to get the garden ready. Most of the time we spent laughing at Tomek's antics or Jan's bad jokes or playing with you. Oh, Żanetko, it took some work, but it was so much fun. And the weather didn't turn cold until we had finished emptying the last box of bulbs. But then the wind came whipping across from Siberia, and Gdynia had her first snowfall of the winter. About the same time, Tadeusz's period of remission ended."

Żanetka didn't say it, but she thought, *And then he died.*

Żanetka handed the reused envelope, sealed with a sticker, to her father. "Give this to my uncle. It's very special and comes from my book. Tell him I will write a story about it for his package next week."

"All right, any other messages?" Jan asked.

"I wrote him a letter," Tomasz said.

"Good boy. I know he treasures all your letters." Jan looked at them both.

"Give him our love," Babcia said. "I'm so thankful you and Amy are able to visit him so often. Once a week, and having him in Gdańsk, it almost makes these two and a half years bearable."

"It's been that long," Amy said.

"Incredible. Sometimes I think this madness can't go on any longer. And then it does," Jan said.

"What's in the envelope?" Tomasz asked her as the two of them finished up the dishes. She was drying and he was washing.

"A swan's feather."

19

Lord, be my breastplate, my sword for the fight

Żaneta stopped and stared at the turned-over dirt on the street corner. *Again* they had ripped out the wooden crosses. Ewa would be *livid*.

It was one of her new English words. "Livid," she said it out loud as she looked over her shoulder. No one had seen her stop here. She kicked a dirt clod and continued on to the market.

It wasn't the same at home anymore now that Ewa didn't keep popping in for visits, or to take her shopping, or to show her some new pair of shoes she had found that would be perfect.

Last month, during a secret meeting with Wałęsa, the milicja broke in and arrested Ewa together with some others in the TKK. And now she was in a prison in the south, somewhere in *Śląsk*.

A part of Żaneta knew this, but she didn't want to know it. She took a detour and walked by the flower stand just to say hello to the old woman there. Sometimes at the end of the day, she could get free flowers, the ones that wouldn't still look nice enough to sell tomorrow. At least that was one thing they didn't have to wait in line for. She liked the bright-colored ones best.

"*Livid.*"

The family had different language days. Polish on Mondays, Wednesdays, and Fridays, and German on Tuesdays and Thursdays, then English on the weekends. It started out as a game, but because Tomasz now insisted on speaking only Polish, it wasn't fun anymore.

"Then you'll just have to show me that you've learned ten new

162

words of the language for that day," his father said.

Żaneta hated the dark look on Tomasz's face. It meant more yelling and slamming of doors.

"You need four thousand words for a working vocabulary. Think about it. If you learned ten words a day for a year, you'd have almost four thousand words. And then you could speak a new language," her father said.

"A Russian tourist asked me for directions today, and I pretended I didn't know what she said," Tomasz said. "Even though I have to learn it at school, it's still the language of the oppressor."

Żanetka liked the sound of that.

"No, that's not good. Not at all," Jan sighed, so Żaneta knew he wasn't really mad.

"I'm so tired of this resistance, Tomku. You have to start working more within the family. Taking responsibility and making an effort. Now turn that television off and . . ."

"All right, but name me one good reason *why* I should memorize all these words. I've got my regular school homework too, you know."

"So you can travel someday and know what people are saying to you," Mamusia said.

"So you can understand other cultures," Babcia said.

"So you can ask where the bathroom is," Żaneta said. But no one laughed.

Instead, Tomasz said, "Right. As if any of us will be going anywhere. Our passports have to be turned in each time to the police. Oh, sure it's okay if we go somewhere, as long as someone we love stays behind to make sure we come back. Our money is so worthless. We count it in hundreds and thousands and can't even keep track of all the zeroes. There are no good shoes, no good meat, no good fruit—I haven't eaten a banana in years. You can't even get film anymore. We've been on the waiting list for a phone for seven years, and for a bigger apartment for forty years! How much worse can it get? This is such a *loser* country. . . ."

"That's enough, Tomku. Your uncle is in prison for the sake of this 'loser' country," Jan said.

"If we lived in America, we wouldn't have these problems. Mamusia knows. *I'm* an American. When I grow up, I'm moving to America."

"You're half-American. When you grow up you can do whatever you please. But for now you had better realize that *things* are not what's most important."

"Oh, now you're going to preach to me? I'm not some old congregation."

"I'm not preaching, Tomku. And if you don't change your attitude, you'll be heading for a rough time in this life. Not everything American is good, and not everything Polish is bad."

"Right." Tomasz left the apartment, slamming the door behind him.

Roman squinted at Jacek. "Ever seen him before?"

Roman had asked to see Jacek at the entrance to the forest outside of Warszawa. Jacek didn't mind. He spent most evenings walking these same paths between the silver birch and oaks. Lately it was his only escape from the madness all around him. When had it all gotten so out of hand? He asked himself every day again. And when, when would it ever end? In one sweep of injustice, he and Roman and all the men they worked for had managed to throw the country they supposedly served back into the Stalinist period of fear and suspicion. Martial law.

Roman pointed out the tracks in the dust. They had paused to take a break, and two bikers whizzed past them. Then Roman asked again about the old man in the photo. "Do you know him?"

"He looks like someone I haven't seen since the war," Jacek said. *I'm weary of the game.* Where would it stop? And yet he had to stay on. For Amy's sake. Every day, he said it to himself again.

"We picked him up in February during a meeting where Wałęsa was stirring up trouble again. Letting that man out of prison and putting a tail on him has led us to more jackpots. He's much more useful outside of prison than he ever was inside. Now he's lost his status as a martyr. So who does this fellow remind you of again?"

"Someone I worked with in the Polish underground. It's hard to say, so much time has passed. People's faces change."

"What was his name?"

"What? Then? Everyone used a fake name. You know that."

"Well, what did you call him? In Kraków, wasn't it?"

Jacek nodded, feeling old and tired. Beaten. "His name was Jurek."

PART IV

———————— ✍ ————————

BREAD ALONE
Matthew 4:4

January 1986 – June 1987

Such proof of the Almighty God remembering us
are very, very many in these difficult times.

20

It was easy. Usually Tomasz took the train into Gdańsk. But he wanted to try hitchhiking to see if it really worked. Maybe he could even get into the city faster. He'd seen lots of other kids do it, especially in the countryside.

He walked along the two-lane road and lingered near a spot where a car could easily turn in and stop. He was just outside Gdynia and put his hand out and waved as he'd seen others do. Sure enough, a red *Polski Fiat* slowed down and pulled over. He ran up to it and opened the door. The man inside smiled and said, "Going to Gdańsk? Want a lift?"

"That would be great. Thanks," Tomasz said. *Not bad for a first try.* He leaned back and enjoyed the ride. This was much better than riding the smelly train, anyway. And probably faster, if they didn't hit too much traffic.

Tomasz had the man let him off near the city center. He wondered how he would have reacted if he'd asked him to take him to the prison. Tomasz knew the way. He'd studied it on the map.

The place where Gonia died. The thought slipped into his mind as he reached his destination. He stopped and looked up at the building behind the stone wall.

He even knew what time and what days they allowed visitors because both his parents took turns visiting. And today neither of them would be here. *Okay, go in like you own the place.* Tomasz squared his shoulders and tried to look four years older than eleven.

"I've come to visit my father," he told the first guard who stopped him.

"There has to be an adult with you."

167

"I'm over fifteen."

"Oh. All right. Up those stairs and to the right."

Gonia's stairs. It was Tomasz's first time inside a prison. He had expected it to smell differently, and for men to be moaning and groaning and crying out loud, "Let me out!" He didn't get to see any cells. When he looked down the long corridor, he could hear classical music playing from somewhere, and he saw a man with a book in his hands. But maybe it was a guard.

He told the man at the door, "I've come to visit Piotr Piekarz. He's my father." It had worked the first time.

Ten minutes later, his uncle came walking through the door.

"You?" he said. "Tomku, is that you?"

Tomasz stared. His uncle's dark hair was shaved very short. He had lost a lot of weight, and his cheekbones stuck out. But his eyes were bright, and Tomasz could tell he was pleased to see him.

"Yeah, it's me. Tomasz." He grinned. He had waited a long time for this moment. And if he'd known how easy it was, he would have tried it even sooner.

"You've changed so much, Tomku."

"So have you. But four years is a long time."

When his uncle didn't reply, Tomasz thought he probably shouldn't talk about how long he'd been locked away in this hole. Instead, he said, "Do you get my letters?"

"Yes. Thank you. You've been so faithful. The whole family has. I can't tell you what they've meant. And I hear the news every week from your parents of how you and your sister are. I was . . . sorry to read in your letters that you're having such a hard time with Jan. It will pass, you know. These things always do."

He was quiet, then said, "Tomku. I can't believe I'm looking at you. How did they let you in?"

"I lied." He grinned again.

Slowly, very slowly, a smile crawled across his uncle's gaunt face. "You lied. And I suppose no one knows you're here now."

Tomasz shook his head. "And I hitchhiked here from Gdynia."

"Well, well, it's been quite a day for you then, hasn't it?" Now his uncle was definitely smiling.

"What's it like?" Tomasz asked, then realized it was probably another forbidden subject, like how long he'd been here. But it was too late, and he really wanted to know, so he went ahead and dove in with both feet. "In here, I mean. What's it like?"

Piotr shook his head. "Well, I suppose it's good that you hear these things. It's no secret. In the beginning they hid us all away in buildings that weren't even prisons. No one knew where we were."

"I remember that. It was a long time before Ewa knew that Bogdan was being kept here, too."

"That's right. The priests helped locate us for our families. I don't think people wanted the same kind of disappearances to occur as what happened during the war, when people just vanished. At first we were put into rooms, twenty people in a cell of twenty square meters. Then we were moved into prisons."

"And kept with common criminals."

"That's right. Some were. My cellmate is all right. I had one who died, though. He was a diabetic. And the food is terrible, stale bread, a watered-down milk soup, no fruit or vegetables. When I get visitors, there's always a guard present."

"Don't you ever get to go outside?"

Piotr nodded. "It's the highlight of my day, unless I get visitors. I go out for half an hour a day. Oh yeah, and everything I receive is read first."

"Even my letters?"

"Even your letters."

A hot, beautiful day at the end of April. Tomasz sat on the bench lining the *Sopot* pier, his face turned into the sun. He had come there with a friend from school and his parents. They were off looking at the fishermen at the end of the pier. Tomasz couldn't get enough of the sun. He fantasized that someday he would sail around the world and come home with skin turned brown by the sea and sun, hardened like leather.

Two boys stood next to the girl sitting opposite him. Her skin was the tone of golden honey. A radio blared from the bench beside them. Tomasz was watching the boys flirt with the girl when an official-sounding voice interrupted the music.

Nuclear accident . . . meltdown . . . emergency . . . radiation . . . no danger. . . . Tomasz sat up straighter, then caught one word, *Czernobyl.* He had never heard of the place. He squinted at the people around him. No one seemed to be taking any notice. Then his eyes caught those of the two boys with the radio. They had heard the announcement as well but didn't react. No one did anything. Then the music started again, and it was as if the interruption had never occurred.

At school a few days later, they were all issued iodine drops. The news bulletins insisted that even Poles along the Ukrainian border were not in any danger. The drops were "just in case."

"They say *if* there is any radiation in the food and water, the drops will take it out," Tomasz explained to his grandmother. She held up the small bottles of dark fluid and looked doubtful.

His mother interrupted from the sink, where she was preparing dinner. Her voice shook. " '*They* say.' Oh, it's one of the things that infuriates me so much about this country. *Big Brother* Russia, *they* always know what's best for Poland. Our greatest friend," she laughed sarcastically. "Why, the authorities had no intention of informing us about Czernobyl. If it hadn't been for the Swedes asking questions about the high levels of radiation, we still wouldn't know anything had happened."

"I heard they thought all the radiation was coming from Poland," Tomasz piped up.

"Well, that just tells you how much we've been exposed to."

"What color is radiation?" Żaneta asked.

Tomasz groaned. "You can't *see* it."

"That's what makes it so frightening," his grandmother mumbled.

"Yes," Mamusia said, "that and the way the government has issued no warnings, no instructions. *They* have forbidden any releases about anything. Two days later, *two days*, we find out we've been exposing our children to . . . " Her voice trailed off. Then she added, "And now the only reliable information is from other countries' radio stations. That's how I heard that these iodine drops would only have done some good right away. Not days later. And keeping you children indoors, that's what I should have done last week. The government insists there is no danger, and that just makes me think the danger's all the worse."

Tomasz caught his grandmother's eyes. Mamusia was nervous. And scared. "If it's bad here, just think what it must be like in Belarus and the Ukraine," he said. "Now would be a good time for one of your stories," he whispered to Babcia.

She nodded, then shook her head and said, "I remember a Ukrainian soldier who thought the toilet was a washbasin and put his potatoes into it. When he flushed the toilet and the potatoes disappeared, he thought the man downstairs had stolen his food.

Those poor people in the Ukraine. This man had undoubtedly suffered during *shtuchnyl holod*, that horrible famine between 1932 and 1933. Stalin caused the deaths of between six and eleven million Ukrainians then. Those poor, poor people. What will happen to them now?"

"What happened to the man downstairs?" Tomasz asked.

"The Ukrainian shot him."

"Really?"

"Tomku," Mamusia corrected him as she peeled the apples and gave them slices.

Tomasz wondered if they were going to make an apple pie.

His mother said, "I remember when I was growing up in America everyone was scared the communists would attack. It was a lot of propaganda, of course, but some people built bomb shelters in their backyards. Can you imagine?"

Then her voice dropped as she brushed past Tomasz. "And at school we learned not to eat anything with skin on it if the bomb was dropped."

Well, this was it. Tomasz had officially reached adolescence. He felt as if he'd been ready to stop being called a child for years. On his twelfth birthday, they made him close his eyes. Then the door opened, and he could hear Żaneta going next door to Irena's, then giggling, then coming back in and putting something in front of him.

"I still don't know if this is such a good idea," he heard his grandmother say.

"Can I open my eyes?" he asked.

"I think you'd better," his mother laughed.

Tomasz opened his eyes and looked down. A cardboard box. A cardboard box that shook and made scuffling sounds. He reached down and opened one corner, and a little white head with a black spot covering one eye poked out.

"A puppy?" He had never expected this.

"I thought you could use an extra friend," Jan said.

Tomasz reached in and pulled the little shaking creature out of the box. He had floppy ears and a Pluto-like tail. He was black and white and so excited, he climbed up Tomasz's chest and started licking his ears.

Everyone laughed. Tomasz caught his father's eye. He couldn't believe his father had thought of a gift like this. It was a good idea. He liked the puppy.

Then his mother said, "We have another gift for you, but you'll have to wait about a month until it's finished."

"Finished?" He had the puppy down on his back now and was scratching his tiny tummy.

His father answered. "Yes. I've hired a carpenter to come into the apartment and build a dividing wall halfway down our bedroom, the other room. You'll be needing your own space now that you're twelve," his father said to him.

Tomasz couldn't believe his parents would actually do something like that just for him. "Well, what about Babcia? She should be the first one to have her own room. She's waited the longest."

Tomasz could tell he had said something right. All the adults beamed at him.

"Thank you for offering, Tomku. But I don't want a little room like that. We've discussed this all behind your back and everyone agrees. Żaneta will move in here with me. I like to wake up in a big space and be nearer the bathroom. With your parents' room split in half like that, it will just barely be large enough for their bed. So Żaneta's bed wouldn't fit in there, anyway. Besides, your parents need their privacy."

Tomasz knew what that meant.

"What will you call the puppy?"

"Azor."

"All right," his father said. "Now remember, Azor is your responsibility, and he's counting on you to take care of him. This will be a good way for you to learn to think of someone besides yourself."

Tomasz shook his head cynically. *So much for the truce.*

For five long years Jacek helped oil the machine of martial law that tortured Poland into becoming a country at siege with itself. He grew to hate himself, the men he worked for, the system they represented. No longer did he have the excuse of spying for a so-called better cause, since the CIA had thought him long since dead after the Carter incident. Now he had been successful in fooling their people inside Poland, but in doing so, Jacek had also removed the last vestige of any excuse that might have made his present existence worthwhile.

All this time he had been hoping Poland would throw off the chains Jaruzelski had shackled it with. Yet with each passing year, the irons keeping the country in bondage became that much tighter. And in the process, Jacek finally lost sight of his own cause.

An old man of seventy-seven, Jacek Duch had simply had enough. The taste of retirement he had enjoyed during the season in Gdynia had now soured and spoiled in denial, leaving him ruined. He now knew what he could have, what he could have had. And the realization had left him bitter and empty.

In September 1986, Jacek returned to Piotr for the third time. They met outside, in the prison yard, alone. Jacek had difficulty breathing in confined spaces lately and tried to stay in the fresh air as much as possible. When Piotr came up alongside Jacek, he didn't even look up.

Piotr began, "Amy has visited me often during the years, so I know how Gonia's death has scarred her." Then he paused and added, "I can also guess how the increased surveillance and hardship of your martial law will have only made her life more difficult."

Jacek listened to Piotr, and although he *still* blamed this man for Gonia's death and Amy's unbearable pain, the anger and vindictive hatred had deserted him. Even standing next to him, Jacek no longer felt the old, old rage toward him. Only emptiness reigned.

Instead of looking at the prisoner, Jacek kept his eyes focused on the figures in the dust when he said, "It's gone on long enough. I thought imprisoning you would fulfill my last goal in life. But I've changed during these last years." As Poland had become more bowed and broken, so had he. "And slowly, I've realized there is only one more thing I want."

Here he stopped and looked up. The dark eyes waiting for him could have been his own. Jacek stared. Piotr Piekarz was a different man than the cowed one he had last cursed at four years earlier.

He said it out loud for the first time. "I want Poland to be free." He swallowed. "You think you know everything about me, but you don't. Yes, I am Amy's father. And yes, I was a spy for the West. But now I am nothing but a tool being used to perpetuate the madness overtaking this country. And once ... once I fought for Poland's freedom.

"I've thought long and hard about this. Your people were doing it right. You almost had it! Do you understand how close you were to freedom?" He waved his fist in Piotr's face.

"All the economic prosperity of the seventies was a sham. Everything's collapsed, and now, whether it's because of the sanctions or the crippling debt run up during these years while you've been in prison, the country has been thrown into disaster. I have seen things, I have *done* things . . ." Then Jacek stopped. Why was he confessing to this man?

And then the revelation dawned on him as he stared at Piotr. He *has* changed. Where was the torment Jacek saw in his own eyes each morning? Why didn't the man responsible for Gonia's death suffer as intensely as Jacek did? What had happened? Carefully, he continued, "In light of what I have witnessed these last years, what I've been party to, I've made a decision." He stopped one more time to check himself. But this also was true. The more he had seen, the more appalled he became. What had he been working for all his life but the cause of Poland? And where had it gotten him or the country? They were both bound by tighter chains than ever.

"This is what I want. Everyone is to be released. Do you understand? All of you will be getting out soon. Then, you work with me and vouch for me with your Solidarność friends. I need an inside contact to convince the SB I should stay on. Give me information you can afford for them to know. Give me misinformation, I don't care."

Only then did Piotr speak. "How do I know I can trust you?"

"You know who I am, so you know whose side I was always on. I'm useful. And know one thing. I want the same as you. We're more alike than you think. I love her, too, and the children. And I want Poland free. Work with me. I promise I'll do anything to protect her. I admit I wanted you killed for what you did to her, but we've both changed since then."

And all the while Jacek was thinking, *I was already tired. Now I'm more tired. My old dream to free Poland might still be possible. When I was young and served the Home Army, I wanted that.* He repeated, "We are more alike than you think."

In this way, then, Jacek fought off the legion still haunting him. For years he had felt tormented and betrayed that his life had involved so much sacrifice. For years he had carried the secret of who his daughter and grandchildren were. His only respite in the torment had been his brief time in Gdynia. The years following that period had been hollow of all meaning. And now suddenly he had discovered a new sensation. He was no longer alone.

Piotr returned his steady gaze and nodded. "Yes, I can understand what you mean. I think we should have been working together all along."

Despite his inherent pessimism, Jacek felt a rush of hope. Maybe in these few months or years left to him, he could make something right. All he wanted now was to somehow glean some good out of the dirty work he'd done for the secret police. *Justification.* "I am willing to work together with you to do whatever it takes. Do you understand? Me from within the SB, and you from within Solidarność. Can you trust me?"

Piotr responded, "In some ways you could say I've also switched causes, but not in the way you think. I cannot imagine all your pain and loneliness."

Jacek was powerless to deflect the kind words. They caught him unaware, cutting deep. "Pain" and "loneliness" were the names of his lifelong companions.

And at that moment, Jacek recognized in Piotr the unlikely comrade he had never known. He heard himself speaking again, against his will, confiding his deepest wish to this man, a former enemy, this *altered* former enemy, he corrected himself, even as he blurted out, "I am tormented with the decision of whether or not to tell Amy who I am. I have imagined that moment many times." In the telling, Jacek suddenly released the hold the secret had on him. He felt a physical relief at Piotr's visible surprise.

Piotr said, "Only you can decide that. She is strong. You know that from watching her. But as far as you and I are concerned, I release you from any hold you think I might have had over you. We'll try it. Besides, we're family."

Jacek left with those words ringing in his ears. And he could not help but reflect on this strange love-hate relationship he had stumbled onto in these final years of his life.

21

Be my strong armor, for you are my might

Tomasz was pulling on his socks when the buzzer sounded twice. All of them were home. It was still early on a Saturday morning, and he had gotten up to do his "chore," as his father called it, walking to the bakery with Azor for fresh bread and rolls for breakfast.

He slipped into the living room and saw his grandmother awake, her eyes blinking blindly as she reached for her glasses. Żaneta's bed showed only a mound topped by red curls.

"Tomku, who could that be?"

"I don't know, Babciu." And in that moment, he *did* know. There was only one person who wasn't inside the apartment who would buzz twice like that.

His heart began to race, and he wished with all his heart as he slipped the deadbolts back. Then he opened the door and gasped, crying out, "Piotr!"

His uncle buried Tomasz in his burly hug, and Tomasz held him just as tightly, only dimly aware that he had one sock on. The dog kept jumping up and down, dancing all around them, and his grandmother was calling out behind him.

"Tomku? Tomku? Piotr! Amy, Jan, it's Piotr! Oh, my heart, it's our Piotr!"

Tomasz turned to the others, his arm still around his uncle. The door to the other room flew open, and his parents cried out loud. But Piotr went straight to his own mother. He engulfed her in a hug, kneeling down beside her bed, rocking her back and forth.

"Oh, Mamusiu. I was so afraid I wouldn't get to see you again. Seeing your face was the one thing I prayed for."

Tomasz was still holding on to his arm. His parents came and hugged them both. Then Żaneta crawled onto their grandmother's bed and hugged Piotr as well. Amy and Żaneta were crying. Tomasz was surprised to see tears on his father's face, but then he thought maybe they had come from his mother.

"So that's why I'm still not with your father," Hanna said. "It's all your fault. I should have known."

"Four and a half years is a long time," Jan said.

"It is indeed," Hanna sighed. "Oh, look at me. I can't stop crying."

"Me neither," piped Żaneta.

And then as if they had rehearsed it, they all said together, "Good tears." The laughter washed over the entire family like a cool sea breeze.

Later that morning, as they sat around eating the rolls Tomasz had brought them for breakfast, Piotr said, "Many, many times I dreamed of how this morning would be. I knew I'd surprise you all this way. No phone calls to the neighbor. Jan, I've never forgotten the stories you told me when we were little of what it was like when you came home from school and found Mamusia crying at the sink. Then you went into that other room and saw our father playing with me as a baby. He was back home, as if he'd never been gone. That's how I wanted it to be today."

In the basement, beside their family's storage cell, Tomasz could work on his bike in peace. It was second-hand, but he had stripped the paint off and was putting the last coat on.

"Can I help?"

Tomasz looked up. *Tatuś?* "No, it's okay," Tomasz said. "I may take this over to show Piotr. He said he's got the right-sized wrench for tightening the bolts."

"I think I probably do, too."

Tomasz sighed and said again, "No, it's okay."

"Tomku, lately I get the feeling that quite a wall has grown up between us."

Tomasz looked up, then quickly down. He couldn't afford eye contact when his father spoke like this.

"I feel like no matter what I do, it's not good enough," Jan said.

"Funny, that's the message I get from *you*." Tomasz couldn't let that one slip by.

"Why are you so critical of me, Tomku? I know you think your uncle is a hero, and he is. But we can't all be heroes. I have something to offer you, as well."

Tomasz faced his father. "Why? I'm not the one who is critical. *You* are. I can do *nothing* right. Nothing!"

"Well, maybe you get that impression because I expect so much more from you. You're the eldest, and I have to admit, I don't know where you get this dark side. I'm not asking much. You don't rely on the Lord like you should. Lean on Him more. Pray more. You must tell the truth and not always be making up excuses."

"Then stop practicing your sermons on me." Tomasz shoved past his father and ran up the stairs.

"Where are you going?"

"To basketball practice." Maybe there he could get away from him.

Piotr, Bogdan, and Ewa squeezed themselves around the Christmas Eve table. *"Wesołych Świąt!* Merry Christmas," they toasted, clinking glasses. Carp and herring. Somewhere, someone had found fresh fish. It was Amy's secret, and she said, "I'm not telling you which fisherman sold it to me while the microphones are on."

They all laughed. "No one can touch us now," Ewa said, squeezing Bogdan's arm.

When Tomasz looked at them, he swelled with pride that such brave people were all in his home. Ewa had been separated from her husband for five years. That's how long Bogdan had been in prison. Piotr for almost as long. And Ewa herself for the last year and a half. The way everyone just kept smiling, it was as if they were all living in a dream-come-true.

Bogdan said, "I cannot tell you how often I described to myself and my cellmates my fantasies of food."

"Yes," Piotr said. "It was sort of a self-imposed torture. We all did it—the ideal meal."

"Bogdan, tell us what you imagined," Jan said.

He rubbed his hands together. "Well, you may not believe it, but almost exactly what I see on the table now. Slices of carp fried in butter, a delicious *barszcz*, or beetroot soup, the herring marinated in a dill pickle sauce, a little olive oil, grated apples, dumplings, onions, and this cabbage! Sweet and sour, cooked with dried mushrooms. Let me guess? A pinch of sugar and marjoram to taste?"

Amy laughed. "Bogdan, you amaze me. You should be a chef."

"Now tell me you're serving poppyseed cake and honey cakes covered in chocolate and I'll know I've died and gone to heaven."

"He peeked in the kitchen," Żaneta said.

"What about you, Ewa?" Jan asked.

"The worst part was the boredom," she said. "How to fill the long, empty days. We lived for meals, as awful as they were. And worried about loved ones," she added. "Every day I thought of my 'family' here—the children, Jan, and you, dear Amy. I was so afraid they would arrest you, as well, and so relieved when I got out and found you all here safe and sound. Amy, I can just imagine the trouble you went to for all this food. The lines you waited in. How did you find it all?"

"I had my helpers." She winked at Żaneta and Tomasz. "And a certain friend whose cousin has a fishing boat." She laughed.

The meal stood steaming on the table, waiting for them to dish it up. But first, as on every Christmas Eve, they waited for the Christmas story. Babcia always asked one of the grandchildren to read it, and this year it would be Tomasz's turn. Everyone turned to her, and Tomasz thought he had never seen his grandmother look so radiant.

"I'm just soaking it all in," she said. "There are so many answers to prayer sitting around this table, it's literally pressed-down and overflowing."

"We've never had a Christmas like this one," Żaneta said.

Now Babcia looked at Tomasz, and he thought it was his cue to start reading. He opened the Bible, but Babcia said, "Just a moment, Tomku. You know, I've been thinking. Mostly about past Christmases. And Żaneta is right. We've never had one like this. Most of you know I have a hard time with Christmas because it's the time of year when my Tadeusz was so sick. That particular December, we didn't even celebrate. Now it occurs to me that Piotr has never heard the story of how his father died."

"Mamusiu, it's all right, you don't have to . . ." Piotr interrupted. "I was the one who—"

"No, no, I want to. I tell these stories to keep your grandfather alive in our hearts. Just like we remember little Gonia and all the sweet things she said and did. This story needs to be told. And it needs to be told now, for more reasons than you know, Piotr."

She looked at Jan, then she looked at Tomasz. And as her words began to spin a spell around them, Tomasz had the feeling that though she addressed his uncle, the story was really meant for him.

"You see, Piotr, I had only one regret as the time for your father to leave this world grew closer. It was too soon. We were still praying for *you*. Tadeusz so wanted his youngest son to discover the same Way of bearing his bitterness as he once did."

"He was bitter?" Tomasz asked.

"A bitter young man like no other. Even Piotr's stubbornness didn't match that of his father when he was younger. When I first met him, Tadeusz was filled with hate. It's true," she said in answer to their protests. "He hated my father because we were German, he hated the war, he hated himself for being a prisoner during the war, he even hated Poland for being so helpless at the hands of the Nazis. And when he received word that the Germans had killed his parents, I thought I'd lost him forever."

Babcia's description didn't sound at all like the man Tomasz had been taught to know as his grandfather. "What happened?" he asked.

" 'What happened?' Love happened. I was so young, and Tadeusz's raw anger touched me very deeply. He was so lost, and I was too young to know better. My heart chose to love a difficult man, a complicated, hurting, bitter young man. Not that I ever regretted it, mind you. But you mustn't think we've always had the kind of joy and peace we shared when your mother married Jan and joined us. That was God's gift to us in later years. In the beginning of our relationship, Tadeusz and I had to learn many hard lessons about trusting the Lord, and forgiving our enemies, and hope." She paused.

"Amy, do you remember when he was dying, you asked me if I had given up?"

"Oh yes," Amy said.

Babcia's eyes took on a dreamy look, as if she were seeing it all over again. "I took Tadeusz's hand and held it against my cheek. And I said that I hadn't given up, but that I knew that where he was going would be an infinitely better place than here. Because, you see, he was hurting so.

"And then that night, while you little ones slept, we all gathered around Tadeusz's bed—Amy, Jan, and I. We were praying quietly, one at a time, and whispering words of comfort to one another. Because we knew what we were waiting for. Oh, it was so hard. Every breath was a struggle, a battle, and the doctor had told us he could not live through the night—the cancer was in his blood, in his bones."

Tomasz could hardly bear to hear Babcia talk this way. He looked around the table and caught Piotr's eyes as Hanna continued. "We listened to him breathe, and we held one another's hands, and we were touching him and stroking him. Amy, you were crying without making a sound—just the tears rolling down your face."

"I remember." Tomasz's mother reached for his father's hand. The room was so still, Tomasz could hear all of them breathing.

"And then Tadeusz drew one more breath and stopped. We were waiting for him to exhale. I reached a hand across and laid two fingers against his neck—just to see. But then there was a groan. It was his lungs emptying themselves. That's when I knew he was gone. My mother breathed like that when she died at the end of the war. In my arms."

Now Tomasz's father spoke up, nodding. "I remember that you told us that. And I was thinking about her, and I spoke her name: 'Helena.'"

"Yes, I remember," Amy said. "Then I said it, too. I said the names of my parents who adopted me—John and Ruth. And Ron."

"And Johann." Jan said his grandfather's name, the man whose name he carried in Polish. It was almost as if they were reliving the scene, reciting again the litany of saints.

"That's right," Hanna said. "We were thinking about all those who had gone before us, and that my Tadeusz had joined them all with our Savior. And I *knew* the angels were taking better care of him than I ever could. He was finally gone from this place of . . ." Hanna's voice cracked.

Piotr got up and came around behind her wheelchair. He held her close until she could look up and speak again. She never finished the sentence, but left the unspoken word *pain* hanging in the air. She simply stated, "Then I reached out one more time and held my Tadeusz in my arms. And it was over."

When his grandmother finished talking, they all sat there, silent for a few moments. Tomasz didn't know if he should read the Christmas story or not. "Babciu?" he asked tentatively.

She looked up and smiled, her gaze a blessing, staring into each of their faces, one at a time. "We don't know what awaits us here on earth or in heaven. But I *know* that the joy and happiness and love and caring and relief and love around this table is only a fraction of what we will have in heaven. And so now, as our Tomek reads the story of our Lord's birth to us, I think we should consider all that we share tonight, on this most special of Christmas Eves, as *'but a mere shadow of what is to come.'* "

22

Tomasz looked in the mirror and knew he was still one of those boys who could say he was five years older than his actual age, and no one would suspect differently. He nodded as he stroked the stubble on his chin. He could pass for eighteen. The hair helped. His father would have a fit when he saw the new cut. He smiled.

"Hey, Tomasz! Think it's long enough to shave? Ha!" Stefan shoved him away from the sink and rubbed his own chin with his hand, imitating Tomasz. "Hmm, should I shave once a day or twice? You better hurry. The others are almost ready, and that includes your lovely *Zosia*."

"She's not *my lovely Zosia*. I don't know where you get this idea, Stefan." But Tomasz smiled nonetheless. He and Stefan were close. More than once Stefan had gotten into fights right beside Tomasz and been pretty beat up for it, too. In fact, Stefan was one of the few guys Tomasz could count on as a real friend.

He pushed Stefan aside, picked up the shaving foam, and squirted it onto his hand. Only a little came out when he pushed the button.

"Guess you've been shaving too often, huh, Tomasz?" Stefan grinned at him in the mirror.

Tomasz ignored him. "Think they sell shaving foam in Kraków?"

"Sure, it's the 'city of kings,' according to Mrs. Mustache. And even kings have to shave. Sure wish she would. No, I wish we could stay here another two nights, don't you? I'm just starting to figure out where the right places are. You know, the action."

Tomasz nodded. As far as he was concerned, the longer he

stayed away from home, the better. This week was the highlight of their school year, a four-day trip to Kraków, sleeping in a youth hostel. They'd already spent one day in the bus, and two days here. Today was their last morning, then it was back to Gdynia.

"The 'action.' What do you know about action? I'm the one who just turned thirteen. And I'm at least twenty centimeters taller than you."

"Ohhh! He's annoyed!" Stefan punched Tomasz, and as Tomasz reached over to grab him, they knocked over his shaving kit.

"Hey, what's this?" Stefan picked up a round, green-colored piece of cardboard.

"You mean for someone who knows where the *action* is, you don't recognize a beer pad? I picked it up in Holland over Easter break when I went there with my family."

"What was it like there?"

"Flat. Oh, and they were making this real big deal about how the spinach couldn't be sold in the shops because it still had radiation from Czernobyl. When I asked my parents' friend about it, he said it still wasn't safe to eat mushrooms. The French aren't eating theirs, and they're farther west. He said mushrooms absorb radiation and retain it longer than other plants. Even a year afterward."

"Cool." Stefan turned the beer pad over. "Maybe it glows in the dark. No, I mean, what was it *really* like? Come on, let me help you pick this stuff up. Listen, we've got to get out of here, or our favorite teacher will be here calling us all our favorite names again. Bet they didn't have anyone as ugly as old Mrs. Mustache in Holland. I hear the girls are gorgeous there," Stefan said.

Tomasz laughed as together they cleaned up his things and returned to the dorm bedroom. "Yeah, they're okay," Tomasz said. "Mostly blondes. I guess the trip was okay."

"Why'd you go there? Do you have family or something?"

"No, just a good friend of my parents . . . well, and of my grandparents. My parents were busy with their usual stuff, though. I wanted to go to this huge computer shop, but all my father could talk about with our friends there was some deal about Bibles."

"Bibles?" Stefan looked at him funny. "Oh yeah, I forgot. He's a pastor, right?"

"Well, more than that. My father's been taking Bibles and medicine and other stuff into Albania and Russia for years. Smuggling." Tomasz thought he might as well make it sound good. Stefan would believe anything, and it never hurt to make the most of a bad situation, in this case, his father's occupation.

"Cool. So what was this all about, these Bibles?"

"Some deal with the International Bible Society, where you could always buy Bibles in Warszawa, but not more than fifteen at a time. So now my father has figured out that Bibles can also be sold on the street. He's tried it, too. The police don't know what to do about it as long as my father's church can prove that it isn't making a profit. And since that meant no taxes, bingo. My parents were in Bible heaven."

"Hey, I wonder if that would work with comic strips. Or *other* magazines," Stefan said with a lecherous grin on his face.

"You have only one thing on your mind," Tomasz said.

"Yeah, the same thing you do. Well, did you see any movies there?"

"One with Meryl Streep, called *Sophie's Choice*. It was about the war, but her Polish accent was really fake. Oh, and this friend we stayed with, Aad, he had a video machine. I saw this really long movie that was a TV series in English called *Winds of War*. You're not going to believe this, but the Polish uniforms were really Yugoslavian!"

"You always were a history freak. I swear, you're the only one who would notice those sorts of things," Stefan said. "Hey, look, there are the girls."

Stefan batted his eyelashes at Tomasz. "Hi, Tomasz. My name is Zosia."

Tomasz heard the bus honking its horn outside and broke into a run. "C'mon, they're leaving!"

Stefan took off down the hall and passed him by in a few strides, calling back, "You might be bigger, but I'm faster!"

That morning their class was visiting what Tomasz considered the best part of the trip: Wawel Castle. Once they arrived, he let the others rush through the castle entrance ahead of him and walked slowly through the courtyard by himself. He squinted his eyes into the warm sun and tried to picture what it used to be like when knights and horses filled this place with the clatter of hooves and shouts of men. There, along the balconies, would have been servants walking, or ladies-in-waiting promenading. The yellow stone seemed to reflect the sunlight right back at him. Within these walls had reigned Polish kings for hundreds and hundreds of years.

A door slammed somewhere on the upper balcony behind him. Tomasz whirled around but saw no one. "Where's my group gone?" he mumbled and jogged in the direction of the main entrance.

When he found them, his class was milling around a room where a receded safe showed a jeweled sword behind glass. The guide explained, ". . . but unfortunately, when Frank—the Nazi head of Poland during the war, remember—left his residence here because the Soviet Army had surprised the Germans and was due to liberate Kraków at any time, he ordered his men to take most of our Polish national treasures with him back to Germany. Unfortunately, we have only very few such jeweled swords. Many other national art treasures are still missing."

Sword fights! That's what the courtyard was missing when he walked through it, thought Tomasz.

The tour continued outside and into the Royal Chapel, lined in marble and smelling very old. He and Stefan found a slate staircase going underground and followed it. "Look," Stefan whispered. "The royal dead."

They wandered from one catacomb to another, until they heard their class coming down a set of stairs in front of them.

"We must have crossed all the way under the chapel," Tomasz whispered. "C'mon, let's hide."

They stooped down behind a statue of an angel and waited until the same guide entered, followed by their classmates. Then, while the guide and Mrs. Mustache stood with their backs to them, facing the rest, Tomasz and Stefan played out an imaginary sword fight and death scene. Just as Tomasz had thrust his own sword into his stomach and was doubled over with pain, a few of the other students couldn't control their laughter anymore and giggled. Especially the girls. Mrs. Mustache turned around and grabbed Stefan by the ear.

"There you two are. I should have known you'd be down here, up to no good." She pushed him toward the group, and Tomasz joined him, amidst general clapping and cheers from his friends. Tomasz gave their teacher one of his best scowls and noticed that in this dim light, she already looked dead.

Once outside, they walked down the hill to the bus that was waiting for the rest. He loved this city, the gold-colored stone, the hundreds of churches, the student cafés, the cobblestone streets and square, the color, the sunshine, the *history*.

Some of the others wanted to buy postcards at the gift shop. Tomasz looked up and down the wall running around the bottom of the hill and noticed a recession in the stone, probably a hole for a statue. "Hey, Stefan, look at this," he called. When his friend didn't hear him, Tomasz checked it out himself. It looked really old and would make a great hiding place, since two grown men could easily have fit inside.

Just then, he heard Stefan calling him. He was across the street talking to what looked like a couple of tourists. *German or American?* Tomasz always played that game. In Gdańsk there was a better chance that they were Germans, but here, he wasn't so sure. Well, they had on the white sport shoes, and they were an expensive brand. He took in the woman's sweatshirt knotted around her neck and the man's black hip bag and thought, *Americans. What's Stefan up to?*

He crossed over to where they were standing and heard Stefan say, "Moment, please. My friend *po angielsku.*" Then to Tomasz, he said in Polish, "They're looking for Wawel Castle and don't know it's right in front of them. Come on, let's have some fun. See if you can sell them a leather jacket like yours. Why not? Your English is good enough. Then tell them some political jokes or something and scare them, like the last time we tried it." His eyes twinkled dangerously.

Why not? Tomasz thought. It was good for a laugh. When he tried it once in Gdańsk, the people had walked away without a word, scared he was going to rob them or something. Now he had his hair . . .

"Hi," he said, using his mother's accent. "My friend here said you wanted to change money. I can give you a really good rate for dollars. Better than what you get anywhere else. And then, if you want, I can show you where you can buy a leather jacket, even nicer than mine, and cheap."

"Come on, George. Don't listen to him," the woman said.

"Hold on, honey. Maybe the kid knows something we don't. A nice leather jacket is bound to be cheaper here than back home. Go ahead, boy, show us what you've got."

Tomasz looked at Stefan, dumbfounded. He hadn't expected this. Suddenly embarrassed, Tomasz said to the couple, "No, it's okay. Really. Sorry. If you're looking for Wawel Castle, it's right here, up this little hill. I'm sorry. This was just a joke." He grabbed

Stefan and walked as fast as he could in the other direction.

As they turned away, Tomasz heard the woman say, "See, I *told* you not to ask. We were right here all along."

Stefan said, "Man, why'd you say that? We could have led those two all over Kraków, then asked them for twenty dollars or something and left them lost. They never would have known the difference."

"Twenty dollars? That's more money than your father makes in a month. No, it's not right."

Stefan snorted, "Since when do you care what's right?"

"Hey, now who's bothered?"

"It's okay. It's just that I thought we had some easy money."

"Right. You're just still sore because The Mustache yanked on your ear."

"Sorry, I'm deaf. What did you say?" Stefan asked, and they raced each other back to the bus.

During the long trip back home, Tomasz stared out the window at the little villages and towns they passed through. Poland all looked so shabby, so run-down.

"What are you thinking?" Stefan asked from the seat beside him.

"About Holland. It's so different there. Everything is new. You don't see horse-drawn carts or ploughs there. It's modern."

"Yeah, what about that computer shop you mentioned. Did you buy anything?"

"No. It was all too expensive. I did see a Game Boy I wanted, though. But there was no way my father would get it for me. He doesn't even hear me these days. That trip was okay, but I'll tell you one thing. These few days in Kraków were a lot better."

"Even with all the museums and art lectures and other dumb stuff we've had to do?"

"Yeah. Here at least we had a little freedom. You know, lately, my father has been all over me about everything. He doesn't even *try* to listen to me. I don't get it."

"I know what you mean. My parents are the same. Yeah, but you know what we say at moments like this?"

It was the cue for their life's motto. In unison, they recited, "Life is brutal and full of *zasadskas*." The last word meant ambush, trap, or betrayal, a dark place you don't expect. Tomasz wasn't too sure how he would translate that one into English.

He stared out the window again, thinking about what he'd just been saying. In another few weeks, school would be out for the summer. He wasn't looking forward to vacation at all. And now, with this punk haircut, he was bound to have his parents whining at him every day. He'd have to find a reason to get out of the house. Hey, maybe his uncle could help him get a job. It was an idea, and Tomasz fell asleep with the sun on his face as he thought about it.

That evening, when the bus pulled into their school's street in Gdynia, Tomasz saw his parents waiting. "Brace yourself for World War Three," he said to Stefan. His friend nodded sympathetically.

As Tomasz climbed down the steps, he took a deep breath. Then he walked up to his parents and said, "Hey, thanks for coming to meet me."

Jan's eyes grew huge and he turned to Amy. "I can't handle this. You bring him home."

Tomasz made a point of putting his hand out at his father's receding back and shouting after him, "Yeah, we had a great trip. And I'm *so* glad to be back. Thanks for asking."

"Tomku," his mother said. "Don't embarrass him like that. Come on. You must have known you'd get a reaction like this. When did you have it done?" She reached up and stroked the scalp around his ears, shaved bald. The only hair left was a dark strip running from his forehead over his head to his neck.

"My first day in Kraków. It was cheap."

"I'll bet," she said.

Tomasz felt grateful that she didn't yell at him. But he knew once they were back in the privacy of their apartment, his father would start in on him. *What would people think?*

"How was Kraków?" Amy asked.

Tomasz looked at his mother to see if she meant it. He had wanted to tell her about the castle and the crypts and his and Stefan's joke, and even how they'd all gone to a student disco the first night, but he didn't. It would be letting her in too much. *Have to play it safe. She always sides with him.* "Fine," he answered.

"Just fine?" She gave him one of her looks.

Tomasz noticed she needed to dye her hair again. The gray was showing through. Well, that's what they say happens when you've got black hair. He'd probably go gray early, too. How old was his mother now, forty-eight? Well, not so young then. "Yeah, just fine."

Once home, Tomasz went straight to his grandmother's wheelchair and kissed her. "What's this?" she asked, shaking her head as her hand ran over what was left of his hair. "Oh, Tomku, always the rebel." But she was smiling a little.

"You know me better than anyone, Babciu. Hey, where's little sister? And where's my dog?"

"Guess," Hanna said. "That girl has been taking poor Azor for so many walks, he's nothing but skin and bones. I think they both missed you," she said softly.

"Good," Tomasz said, then went into his room and closed the door.

He took his jacket off and looked around his room, feeling proud that he had made it so much his own. The walls were plastered with posters of American NBA basketball stars, and he had even mounted a hoop on the wall over his closet so he could practice with wadded-up paper weighted down with tape. A sponge ball would have been better, but Azor had eaten that.

"Where is he?"

Enter my loving father, he thought, knowing before it happened that Jan wouldn't knock.

Sure enough, the door to Tomasz's room swung open, then shut, and Tomasz stood face-to-face with his father. *Same height*, he noticed with pride.

"What were you thinking, Tomasz? A haircut like this! Just another way of getting attention? Don't you know how foolish this makes me and your mother look? We head a *church*, and I teach at the *university*."

Always so concerned with what others think. "Well, if you looked around that *university* of yours, you might see that this is the fashion right now," Tomasz said.

"You just don't understand."

YOU just don't understand. "Try me," Tomasz said.

Jan took a deep breath and began, "When I was away at school..."

Here we go again.

"... all I could think of was trying to take care of the family. I attended my lectures, worked the night shift in a restaurant, scraping off other people's leftovers..."

And worked in the church.

"... and I worked in the church. I thought about how Mamusia used to stay up late every night, crocheting at one in the morning so I could study."

Crocheting?

"Why do you always have to be so difficult? When I was your age . . ."

And here we go one more time.

". . . I wouldn't have dreamed of . . . of *mutilating* myself like what you've done. It's such a sign of disrespect. If you were trying to embarrass us, then you did a good job of it."

Catch your breath for the next round. "You're not listening to me," Tomasz said. "This haircut's the *fashion.*"

"No, you're not listening to me, young man. This time you've gone too far, and there *will* be consequences." His father turned and left Tomasz's room, slamming the door behind him.

Consequences. Right, what can you do? Take away all the things I don't have? Not let me play on the nonexistent computer? Not give me that tremendous amount of pocket money I don't earn by doing the dishes every night for five people? It's not like we have so many great things that could be used against me as consequences.

Tomasz took two steps over to the window, opened it wide, and then threw himself onto his bed. He reached into his pocket and pulled out a pack of Caro cigarettes. He lit one, breathing in deeply, and tried to blow the perfect ring every time he exhaled. He heard the front door slam open again and thought, *Oh no! That's all I need.* He quickly put out the cigarette, hid the pack under his mattress, and popped a peppermint into his mouth. Then he started waving the air, trying to push the smoke out the window. But there was no breeze.

A soft knock sounded on his door, then came his little sister's voice. "Can I come in, Tomasz? There's a little dog here who wants to see . . ."

The door slammed open, and his father stood in the doorway again, this time with Żaneta behind him. Azor leaped past them both and hurled his little black-and-white body straight at Tomasz's middle. He had to laugh, despite the ominous accusation of his father.

"You've been smoking!"

Yeah, I've been smoking.

"You know that's not allowed. You know I've strictly forbidden you to *ever* smoke. We have rules in this family, Tomasz, and they're the only way we can all live together with respect for one another. You've broken so many rules, I can't remember how many."

One.

"You've shown no respect for the rules I've set down. And I warned you. Since you've chosen to disobey, you'll have to pay the price for your actions. Your uncle had asked if you could stay with him during the summer vacation and help out, maybe do some typing for him. But after this, I'd be ashamed to have anyone see what kind of no-good boy you've become. You don't listen and you refuse to carry any responsibility around here. No, you're staying home this summer, where I can keep an eye on you. And all twelve weeks you'll spend cleaning up apartments for some of the elderly in our church who can't do it themselves."

His father was gone as suddenly as he appeared. Tomasz watched him go, his head spinning. Piotr had asked for *him*? His uncle had only been released from prison last October. Since then, Tomasz had seen Piotr at least once a week.

There was no one on earth as brave as his uncle. Tomasz couldn't even imagine spending a week in prison. *Four and a half years*. Piotr was amazing. He had vision, too.

And he always understood, even when Tomasz talked to him about how difficult it was getting along with his father. He wasn't really allowed to go outside the family with their problems. That's what his mother said. But Piotr was family, so Tomasz had figured it was all right. He just wished they could spend more time together. This summer would have been a perfect chance ... living with him!

"Tomasz?" Żaneta had pushed open the door his father must not have closed again. She stood there, probably waiting to see if he was going to blow up. But his father's punishment had taken the wind right out of Tomasz.

And deep down he did feel mad, really mad. He was so disappointed at not being able to spend the summer with Piotr that he vowed to himself to think of the perfect way to hurt his father back. "Yeah?"

"Hi. Welcome home." His ten-year-old sister had this way of talking and looking up at him from under her eyelashes that always made him smile. And she knew it. That was the worst part.

"Yeah. Come on in. And close the door behind you!" he said extra loud so his father might get the hint.

"Were you really smoking?"

"It's nice that someone asks. Yeah, I was." He shrugged his shoulders.

"Can I see?"

"No. And if I *ever* catch you smoking, Żanetko . . ."

She laughed at him. "Now *you* sound just like Tatuś. Tell me about the trip."

What's the use? She's trying to pretend that nothing's happened, but this time he's really gone too far. "Uh, Żanetko, I really don't feel like it now. I'm kind of tired. Go on. Isn't it past your bedtime or something?" He didn't even feel guilty when he saw her disappointment. Instead he just thought, *Yeah, little sister, life is brutal and full of zasadskas.*

A few days later, his uncle joined them for the main meal. Piotr wouldn't say anything about the secret meeting with the apartment bugged. The SB knew they were his family and were probably hoping to find out what the Solidarność leadership were up to by following the men and women they had released. Piotr didn't need to say he had a secret meeting. Tomasz knew it when Piotr excused himself earlier than normal, and his parents nodded at him when he left.

Tomasz told his parents, "I'm going over to Stefan's," then waited until the main door downstairs slammed shut and flew after his uncle. He was surprised when Piotr didn't head for the train station. *So the meeting's not in Gdańsk.* Tomasz hoped he wouldn't have to take a taxi. He didn't have enough money for that.

Piotr walked down one street, turned up an alley, crossed the square, turned left, and ducked into an old hotel. "They've probably rented a room in there," Tomasz mumbled to himself.

He entered the lobby and headed for the elevator, when he felt a hand on his shoulder. He nearly screamed, but with the hand came a voice, his uncle's.

"What do you think you're doing?"

The hand whirled Tomasz around, and the face he saw did not look happy. "Hi," Tomasz said.

"No, not 'hi.' What do you think you're doing, Tomku, following me?"

Tomasz nodded.

"Why on earth. . . ?"

Tomasz stepped backward, bringing them both into a corner with a palm plant so they wouldn't be so obvious. "I wanted to see where your secret meeting was. And I thought . . ."

"What did you think? That you could join us? Just pull up a chair and be one of the boys? No, Tomku, you weren't *thinking*. That's just it."

He had never seen his uncle so angry. "But I—"

Piotr cut him off. "Come on, we're attracting too much attention here. I have to find a post office."

Tomasz walked a little behind his uncle until they reached the main post office. Inside, Piotr stood in line at the window for *telefon i telegraf*. When it was his turn and a booth became vacant, the lady behind the window nodded at him, and he disappeared inside. All along the wall people were phoning and talking loudly, motioning with their hands. On the bench beside Tomasz sat an old lady waiting for someone.

Piotr had to redial several times, but after five minutes he was finished. Then Tomasz stood up and they went back outside. As they walked, Piotr said, "I get a worse line calling locally than when I call outside the country. Yes, Tomku, I *did* have a meeting, but I won't be going now. I can't be sure who followed you when you were following me. See how it works?"

Tomasz felt miserable. "I really didn't mean to make a mess of it like this. I'm sorry."

They had reached the hill near Tomasz's school. Piotr stopped and turned to him. "Listen, it's not at all as adventurous as you think. These meetings are boring, about policy and economic strategy. But it doesn't matter. You've gone too far this time. I kept your hitching a ride to the prison a secret because you asked me to. But this endangers more than just yourself. You know, you really need to think more of others and not be so selfish like your father says."

23

You are my shelter and you my high tower

I am that angry young man. I am arrogant Jacob, wrestling more with my own demons, rather, demons of my own making, than with the Almighty himself.

You were right, Amy, all along. I was desperate though, desperate with loss. Halina had left me. The movement was crushed. I had nothing but you. And now I've discovered new life in the darkness of this prison cell.

That's why I'm writing this to you and Jan now. After your great loss, I know nothing can compensate. But if it helps, rest in the knowledge that your loss was not wasted. It has brought me to the very feet of Christ.

Tomasz sat on the floor of his uncle's apartment, surrounded by sheaves of paper. The letter he held in his hand was obviously some sort of rough draft, sentences crossed out, notes in the margin. Tomasz tried to picture his uncle painstakingly copying it over, and his parents' reactions to such words.

The words. That was it. Now he mumbled out loud, "Oh, so that's why. He's become one of *them*. That's why he sided with Tatuś. He's just like him. They're both the same."

Still, the words on these papers had moved Tomasz. He didn't know how to handle Piotr's admission of love for his mother, but its connection with Gonia's accident and the description of a change of heart had touched Tomasz deeply.

He looked around guiltily. He hadn't meant to get into Piotr's private papers. Piotr had invited him over for the weekend, probably to make up for their argument yesterday when Tomasz had followed him. Then he went out to get them some dinner. All

Tomasz had meant to do was look for his own letters he had sent to Piotr when he was in prison. He saw this drawer full of papers and had assumed his letters were in there somewhere. Tomasz didn't want Piotr showing his father what he had written. After that comment yesterday that maybe his father was right, Tomasz wasn't sure if he could trust Piotr anymore.

So Tomasz had started searching through the drawer. He could see Piotr was putting together notes for a book. And then he'd found these two letters, dated April 1982 and April 1983. He hadn't meant to pry, but the words had tumbled one over the other, and before he knew it, Tomasz was caught up in the fall.

Just as he thought these things, the buzzer sounded. Tomasz nearly jumped out of his skin. He grabbed a handful of papers and shoved them back in the drawer. Then keys turned in the locks and the door flew open. Tomasz saw he had missed some pages and said, "Hi, sorry about the mess. I was just looking for those letters I sent you. . . ."

"Tomasz?"

Tomasz whirled and stared straight into the eyes of his father. "Tomasz Piekarz, what have you been doing? Going through your uncle's personal papers?"

"No, really. I . . . well, what are *you* doing here?"

"Don't try to change the subject. I came looking for Piotr, obviously. And he's given me a key, just as he has one for our home. But I don't have to justify myself to you. I can't believe . . ."

And then, to Tomasz's mortification, he heard Piotr's voice. "Jan? Is there a problem?" His uncle came running up behind Jan and stood there taking in the scene. Tomasz with pages in his hands, the open drawer, and a few papers still on the floor. "When I saw the open door, I was afraid I'd had another unwanted visit from the SB."

"No, nothing so drastic, I'm afraid. But you have had an unwanted visitor. I'm sorry, Piotr, but I caught my son going through your private papers."

"I wasn't," Tomasz protested. "And he invited me here! I'm not unwanted, except by *you*. What am I saying, you're both in this together!" Then Tomasz blew past both men and hurled himself down the stairs.

He ran and ran. He ran until he could hardly breathe. He ran outside the city limits, all the way to the forest. Then he kept on running.

He had never felt so naked and ashamed. The longer he ran, the more he realized there was no place he could go and hide from that shame. It kept hounding him. The shame he felt wasn't his alone. It was also shame for his mother, and his uncle, and his father for being so weak. Shame and confusion were the names of what hunted him now.

Finally Tomasz stumbled to a stop. He stared straight into the setting sun and watched a stork feeding in a field. Then he looked around him and knew he'd have a long walk back home. He shook his head. He had no desire to go home. If only there was somewhere else he could go.

He had passed a sign at the last crossroads. He headed back there and saw it pointed toward a campground in the woods. As he approached the place, he heard music. It was already dark, and he told himself he could probably hitch a ride from there. But when he entered the campground, it was obvious a disco had just gotten started, complete with lamps hanging in the trees.

In five minutes flat Tomasz was helping himself to a beer and talking to one of the girls playing the music. The kids were his age, and it felt good to be with strangers.

Long after the moon had risen, Tomasz tried to hitchhike back home. It was way after midnight. In fact, he had no idea what time it was, and he didn't care. He kept following the road, his head turned upward to watch the moon and stars duck in and out from between the trees.

He heard a pounding noise ahead of him. A rhythm in the dark. He stood still, not sure if he should be afraid. Hadn't he heard there were tanks parked somewhere in these woods? A deer ran across the road. She stopped in the full stream of moonlight and stared right at him. Then she was gone.

Tomasz yelled at Żaneta, "I said give it to me!"

"There's nothing on, I told you," she said.

"I don't care. Give the remote control to me. It's my turn to decide what we watch." He snatched the thin, dark box from his sister's hand and started pushing buttons, jumping back and forth between the channels. There weren't many to choose from, but it was the feeling of having the thing in his hands that he liked.

It was no secret. Despite the persecution, despite the secret police, despite the informers in their midst, Hanna and Tadeusz Piekarz had never failed to hold the Tuesday night prayer meetings. Their home had been open to friend and stranger alike. They lived what Tadeusz preached, a Gospel straight out of the Bible, based on God's own forgiveness.

Tomasz knew the score. He had the myth memorized.

His father's voice droned on. "And you have always attended these prayer meetings, and you will continue to do so."

That Tuesday night Piotr came and sat beside Babcia. Tomasz avoided any eye contact with his uncle. No one was even talking about his disappearing act four nights earlier. Although he tried to tune out his father's sermon, when Jan mentioned Gonia's name, Tomasz grew interested.

". . . It is healing, never whole. I felt like I had nothing when Amy and I lost our youngest daughter, Gonia. You see, the loss was simply too great to combat. But I did recognize my own brokenness in my wife, and how I ached to love her back into life. She knows I was planning to say these things tonight. We thought it was time, especially since so many of you let us lean on you these past five years.

"Amy and I clung to each other like two children alone, and slowly, one by one, God gave us the words and the ways to reach out to each other. Together we have healed, in different ways, while the loss has still remained.

"You see, I was so completely incapable of being strong on my own. I could do nothing but lie at Christ's feet, broken, and right there, God gave to me the very strength I lacked. I knew Amy loved me. I know this, just like I know the sun will come up every morning. I trust in her love, and that trust, too, God has given me. Maybe my previous trials in doubt were somehow a preparation. But today I give thanks not only for these things, but for my brother's freedom, and that often it is in the darkest places that our hearts may perceive the truth."

Tomasz was confused. As the meeting dragged on, he couldn't stop thinking about the implications of the words he had read in his uncle's letters. How were those words related to what he was hearing now? Was his father's sermon his parents' way of telling Piotr off, or not? Were they being honest, or making fun of Piotr? Was his father just playing the hypocrite again? What kind of twisted game was being played here? Was he messing with their minds? Did they *know* about the letters? They had never been sent. . . .

"Let us pray for our enemies."

When Tomasz heard the last prayer of the meeting, he thought, *Then I pray for you, Tatusiu. Then I pray for you.*

24

On the first morning after school was out, Tomasz woke up to his father's hand shaking him roughly. "Time to get up. I need you to help out at old Mrs. Stok's apartment. Come on, Tomku, let's go."

"But it's vacation," he moaned. And then with a shock he woke up enough to remember his father's threat. So he *had* been serious. Tomasz had hoped since no one had mentioned it again, maybe his father had forgotten the punishment. No such luck.

Tomasz spent the entire day sweeping and scrubbing and feeling thoroughly humiliated, like some servant. You could tell old Mrs. Stok hadn't had anyone in to help her with the apartment for a long time. And the bathroom was awful. At the end of the afternoon, with her thanks ringing after him in the stairwell, Tomasz took the long way back home.

On the way, he passed a place where they were piercing ears for a reduced price. All you had to do was pay for the gold earrings. *Or earring,* Tomasz thought. He saw some other boys from his class hanging around outside the window. He had money. Mrs. Stok had insisted on paying him, even though his father had strictly forbidden him to accept anything from her. *Why not? It's a good way of getting back at him.* Tomasz entered the shop, making sure the other boys saw him.

Fifteen minutes later he emerged with a small gold-colored ring hanging out of his right ear. That, plus his leather jacket and the haircut, it all fit nicely together, he told himself.

When he got home, his father was waiting for him outside their building. Tomasz saw him pacing back and forth like a dumb bull. *How can he be angry already?* he thought. For a split second he considered sneaking around the other way before his father saw him. But he was hungry and knew his grandmother and mother would have cooked something he liked to try to make up for his having to work all day.

"Where were you? I stopped by Mrs. Stok's and she said you'd already left. She also admitted that you'd taken money from her."

"I didn't *take money from her*. She gave it to me. Practically shoved it into my hands. And I did a good job, so I thought, yeah, I'd earned it." *Not that you noticed how clean everything was.*

"All right, give me the money, then." He stuck out his hand.

"I can't. I spent it already." Tomasz enjoyed the sight of his father turning a slight shade of purple as he caught sight of the earring.

"You spent it on *that*? After I told you how I feel about mutilating your body? You did *that* with Mrs. Stok's money?"

Meltdown time. But to Tomasz's surprise, his father just turned around and headed up the stairs. Stone silent. All evening long, no one said anything about the money or the earring. When Tomasz went to bed, he thought, *Maybe I should have tried something like this sooner.*

The next morning, Tomasz got up early to leave the house before his father could get to him. As he tiptoed through the living room where his grandmother still slept, Żaneta whispered, "Where are you going?"

"To the bakery. Can't sleep anymore. You owe me one."

"Thanks." They had switched jobs, and now it was Żaneta's job to wait in line at the bakery. Every day, without complaining, she got up before everyone else and made sure they had fresh bread for breakfast. Tomasz didn't know how she did it. Sleeping in was one of his favorite things to do, which was why he'd switched with her, but now that his father had started this latest vendetta against him, he couldn't wait to get out of the house.

Tomasz went down to the cellar, where they shared locked storage space with the rest of the building's occupants. He had taken the key to the storage cell off the wall by the stove on his way out of the apartment. Now he unlocked the little room and opened the door. He wanted to get his bike out and combine the trip to the bakery with a little time alone, maybe along the waterfront, looking at the ships.

Tomasz flipped on the light switch and looked around. *It's been stolen*, was his first thought. Then he realized, *But the lock wasn't broken*. A terrible premonition crept over Tomasz as he methodically looked around the cell one more time, turned out the light, and locked the door behind him. He headed back upstairs.

A cold rage had taken hold of Tomasz. But *he* would ask first before deciding who was guilty. He stood outside his parents' bedroom and knocked. *Control. Now you need control*, he told himself.

A small voice said, "Tomku, think again before you say these things."

He whirled, expecting his angelic sister to be the one interfering again, but her eyes were closed. The eyes staring back at him from bed, clear gray as the dawn, were his grandmother's.

He shook his head. "No," he hissed.

At the sound of his father's voice saying, "Come in," Tomasz pushed the door open.

He stood there panting, angry, struggling even to find his voice. Then he asked, "Did you sell my bike?"

His father sat up in bed. "Did you have to wake us up at this hour for that? Yes, I sold your bike. I sold your bike to earn back the money you took from Mrs. Stok so we could pay her back. She has next to nothing, do you understand? And since you're the one she has to thank for having even less now, I thought it only right that your bike should be the means of repaying her."

"You . . . had . . . no . . . right."

"I had every right. Every right, do you hear me, Tomasz? You have been walking around here blatantly disobeying me, disregarding our rules, making a fool of yourself by looking the way you do, and showing no sign of respect for anyone but yourself for long enough. It's time you grew up and learned there is a price to pay for the choices you make."

Amy said, "Tomasz, I wish you'd listen to your father."

" 'Father?' You call him a father? Why are you always siding with him? I'll tell you what I wish. Speaking of fathers . . ." Here Tomasz took a very deep breath because something inside told him that his next words would cut deep, would hurt back in exactly the way he had been hurt.

He said slowly, "I wish *Piotr* were my father. I wish I had someone brave who stood for something and was willing to suffer like he has, and does. I look like him, don't I? You know what I've often wondered? I mean, I don't belong in this family, do I? Everyone agrees on that. *I* think that Piotr maybe really *is* my father."

Amy covered her mouth with a trembling hand.

"Don't you dare talk that way to your mother. What's wrong with you?"

Tomasz barely understood the words through his blind rage. "I'll tell you what's wrong with me. I . . . don't . . . belong . . . here." And now the anger, white-hot as the words, hurled furiously out of his mouth. "What about it?" He glared at his mother. "What did you have with him anyway? And what was going on at the prayer meeting?"

"What do you mean?" Amy asked. "Piotr knew your father was going to say those things. He didn't mind. Your father was just referring to Piotr accepting the Lord into his heart." Then she took a deep breath and said slowly, "As far as any . . . other types of feelings he had for me . . ."

"Amy, don't," Jan warned.

Tomasz looked at her, begging for the truth, but at the same time not wanting to hear it, even as he added, "Don't deny it. I read Piotr's letters he wrote in prison. And I *know* the sick thing you two share is what killed my baby sister."

There. The words were out. Poison hung in the air between Tomasz and his parents. He saw the devastation on his father's face. What he hadn't counted on was his mother's voice, continuing word by word, a soft monotone.

"I admit, after Gonia's death, all three of us could see clearly what was truly important. It was . . . a wake-up call. And since then, we've talked it out and forgiven each other." She sighed and tears coursed down her cheeks. "You move on, Tomku."

"What about Halina and all her claims?"

"Halina was a mistake, but she had nothing to do with me."

"That's not what Halina said. You don't think I remember that disaster of a picnic when I was seven? I heard my aunt yelling that Piotr kept waking her up calling out *your* name? I didn't know what it meant at the time, but I have an idea now."

"No, you *don't understand*. Halina was superficial, always interrupting and complaining. She tried to cause trouble."

"I don't believe you."

"But, Tomasz—"

"No! You know what? I don't even want to know all your stinking secrets. I just want to be somewhere I belong!"

Hot tears burned behind his eyes. He whirled blindly and stumbled away from the door, hardly even seeing the wrinkled hand silently reaching out to him as he stormed into his own bedroom.

He had never dreamed she'd actually *admit* to what he had discovered in Piotr's letters. All day he thought about it, and for once, no one bothered him. He played his *Lady Punk* record over and over, and no one told him to turn it down. Even when it came time for the afternoon meal, he didn't come out, although he could hear every word that was spoken and smell his mother's cooking.

Instead, Tomasz paced the small confines of his room back and forth. Over and over the words *she admits it's true* dogged his steps. He managed to twist the story slightly so Piotr emerged the injured third party. After all, he'd been punished, had spent over four years in prison. Piotr couldn't help it if his mother had led him on.

Tomasz finally realized his parents' guilty secret provided him with fuel for a fire he had been trying to inflame for some time. Add this terrible knowledge to the malicious act of his father selling his bike behind Tomasz's back, and a blaze had kindled.

It's all right, he told himself. He knew what he had to do. That knowledge contained the fire raging within Tomasz. After the meal, he heard them all leave to go for a walk. Then he waited ten minutes, just to be sure. As he sat on the edge of his bed, Tomasz could picture his father and grandmother waiting for the elevator.

Tomasz slowly pushed his door open, half hoping that Azor would still be there to greet him. But Żaneta must have taken him along. He moved quickly to the opposite corner and, one by one, opened the drawers of the storage cupboard against the wall. *It's got to be in here somewhere.*

Tomasz went through every drawer and then crossed to his parents' room. On a whim, he searched under their mattress. *Bingo.* He checked each of the three blue passports. His was the last one he opened. It was valid for another two years. Tomasz thought of how his mother had always insisted on keeping their U.S. passports valid, "just in case," she said. He slipped Żaneta's and his mother's back in the manila envelope and replaced it under the mattress. Then he carefully placed his own U.S. passport in his hip pocket with the button.

Tomasz looked at his watch. He had already wasted an hour searching the apartment. He had run out of time. Returning to his room, he grabbed his jacket and the duffel bag he used for basketball practice, then crossed to the main door and slowly pulled back the latches of the door. When he closed it behind him, he purposely did not look back.

Tomasz had to dash for it, but he caught the express to Gdańsk. Once there, he went straight to his uncle's little apartment in the city center. When he knocked on the door, he heard voices inside and felt excited. What if he got to be part of some secret meeting?

Piotr's voice called out, "Just a moment," as Tomasz heard all the locks being undone. The door swung open and Tomasz was surprised at how relieved he felt to see his uncle. *He really is more like a father to me*, he thought.

As he walked inside, he looked past Piotr and, to his dismay, saw his parents sitting around the table. "No!" he yelled, backing away, but Piotr stood behind him and closed the door.

"Tomku, look. Listen, your parents have told me everything. They're as upset as you are. Why don't you sit down with them, and we can talk this out."

"What are you doing here?" his father asked.

Tomasz looked at him, the hate burning a hole in his heart. "What are *you* doing here? I've come somewhere I belong." He looked at Piotr. "I've come here to stay with you. They don't want me, and I thought you might." He laughed to cover his embarrassment.

"No, Tomku," Piotr said. "You can't do that. You can't come here. You belong at home. I know it's been hard, but you really need to go back with your parents to Gdynia. I can't let you stay here, not under these circumstances."

"What lies have they told you about me? I was sure you'd take me in. I spent the weekend here. You wanted me for the summer, didn't you?"

"Yes, but that's different."

"Come on, Tomasz. It's time to go home," his father said

A slow clamminess crept over Tomasz. *So this is what it feels like.* "Did he tell you how he wants me to work like a slave, cleaning old people's apartments? How I don't deserve anything better? And that he can't stand to look at me? How I'm a constant disappointment? How I can't do anything right? How I'm a failure? How I don't belong in this twisted, messed-up family?"

"Tomku, your father is right." Piotr raised a hand.

"Do you really think so? You're not even listening to me!"

Tomasz yelled in exasperation. He felt his throat choke. At that moment his father scraped his chair back, and Piotr reached out toward him. " 'My father is right'? How can you say that? You traitor. You're worse than they are!" he screamed at Piotr.

And in one movement, Tomasz ducked under his uncle's arm, swung the door open, and flew down the staircase, his mother's voice still ringing in his ears, still calling his name.

PART V

———————— ✧ ————————

LIVING BREAD
John 6:51

June 1987 – August 1988

Tell me what you believe. Why did Jesus, who was
perfect, have to suffer on the cross?

25

Raise me to heaven, O Power of my power

Żaneta didn't even want to think about those horrible words Tomasz had spoken early that morning. Now she had other things to concentrate on. She held on to her grandmother's hand. Żaneta could tell Babcia was in great pain by the tight look in her eyes. "Babciu, they'll be back soon." She hoped she was right. She kept watching for the little white Polski Fiat her father had bought six years earlier. Żaneta could remember because he bought it the same month and year she had turned four. He had given it to Mamusia on her birthday, which was also in March.

But none of this is important now, Żaneta told herself. Babcia had to get home, and fast. The whole family, everyone but Tomasz, had left the apartment to go shopping at the street market. They had heard someone was selling oranges. Then Żaneta had volunteered to stay with her grandmother near the market while her parents drove to Gdańsk.

It had been Hanna's idea that they go to Piotr about Tomasz. She had said, "Invite him for dinner. Maybe he can talk to Tomasz and reach him. This tension in the home has to stop. I know you're doing your best, Jan, but we have to find another way to reach the boy."

The words Tomasz and their mother had spoken that morning still rang in all their ears like a death knell. Żaneta knew Babcia was troubled. They all were. And she was right. Things *were* very tense at home because of all the fighting.

Żaneta had steered Hanna to a cool place by the fountain in front of Gdynia's main hotel. Now Hanna sat in the shade, but the warm temperature was still proving too much for her. "They said they would just go over to Uncle Piotr's, then be right back."

"I know, I know," Hanna sighed. "Talk to me, Żanetko. What are you thinking about with that frown on your pretty lips?"

"Oh, just Tomasz." She reached down absentmindedly and pet Azor, who lay panting at her feet. His look told her he also felt glad for a bit of cool shade.

Her grandmother sighed and said again, "I know. It can't be easy for you, either. You may wonder sometimes, but I see all the little things you do at home to try to smooth things between your parents and Tomasz. You try to play the peacemaker, and it's an honorable role, but be careful that you don't become a victim yourself."

Żaneta looked at her grandmother, wanting to understand. She knew one thing. Whenever she felt like crying when everyone was yelling, she would do almost anything to get them to stop. The worst part was not knowing *how*.

Hanna continued. "Tomasz is always trying to fight back. He's a rebel, and that's all right if his rebellion is directed in a healthy direction. I know some of this is too hard for you to understand, but in a few years, you'll be hitting that difficult age and wanting to rebel as well. So maybe if a little of what I say now sticks in that lovely head of yours, it will make that time easier for you."

"But you'll be around then, too."

Hanna blinked at her. "Yes, of course. I'll always be in your heart, and you'll always be in mine." She coughed, then said, "All I want to say to you about your brother is that some of his rebellion is very normal. So when you get around to rebelling, you'll know that's normal too. Much of Tomasz is honestly searching, and he's a smart and clever boy."

"And funny sometimes," Żaneta offered.

Hanna smiled. "Yes, and funny. But your father is right. Tomasz should show more respect. And the things he was saying this morning, well, he had no right to interfere in something that doesn't concern him and that has been resolved. It's a pity he doesn't listen better."

"Did Tatuś not listen to *Dziadek*?"

"Jan and your grandfather? Yes, your father always listened and obeyed. A little too well. But Piotr was another matter. It's all right now, though. Dear Piotr may be the only one who can reach our Tomek now."

"And you, Babciu. He listens to you." Żaneta squeezed Hanna's hand, then looked up and saw her parents' car pulling up beside them. "Mamusiu, oh, I'm so glad to see you. We were waiting *so* long, and . . ." Żaneta stopped when her mother got out of the car and rushed right past her to Hanna. Azor barked and leaped on them both, so Żaneta had to pull him away from the wheelchair.

Her mother cried, "He's gone. Hanna, he's gone. He's run away. That's why it took so long. We went home first to see if he'd come back, but he wasn't there."

"Amy, calm down. It will be all right." Hanna turned to Jan. "What's this all about? Can someone tell me that?"

Żaneta was relieved when Jan finally bent over her grandmother to lift her out of the chair. But as he made the effort, Hanna went rigid with pain. He said, "Amy, come help me. Mamusia needs to get home."

"Yes, that's what I was trying to tell you. . . ." Żaneta said, her voice trailing off again as she suddenly understood what her mother's words might mean. "Tomasz has run away from home?"

"Well, we don't know that for sure," Jan said. He spoke as Amy helped him get Hanna settled in the car. Żaneta folded up the chair and brought it over to them as her father continued. She wished Azor would stop pulling on his leash. "We were at Piotr's, when Tomasz showed up, just like that. He had a small bag with him, and he exploded when he saw Amy and me. Evidently, he had left home this afternoon and was planning on moving in with Piotr."

"What happened, then? He's not there now, is he?" Hanna asked.

"No, he must have thought it was a trap. I don't know. He took off like a scared animal. The three of us searched the nearby streets, but we didn't find him. Piotr is still combing Gdańsk. We thought maybe he might have come home."

Żaneta looked at her mother, waiting for her to say something. But her mouth remained tightly fixed in a pained and rigid line. "Mamusiu, are you all right?" Żaneta asked, reaching out a hand for her mother's arm.

"No, I'm . . . not."

Żaneta saw the tears in her mother's eyes. She looked back and forth between both parents.

"Come on, Amy. You climb in here through my side. This isn't a good place—"

But Amy cut him off. "There is no good place, Jan. I know, I *know* in my heart that we've lost him." Żaneta heard the panic rising in her voice. "I've already lost one child. I can't lose another!" Jan engulfed Amy in his arms and let her sob.

As he stood there holding her, Żaneta could tell he didn't care anymore about the people walking by, staring at them strangely. And it must have looked odd, her mother standing there crying in her father's arms, her grandmother in the car, so pale, the wheelchair against the car, and a funny red-haired girl, watching it all, not knowing what to say or do.

Żaneta broke the spell of stillness on herself and stepped forward, touching both her parents. She said nothing, but tears ran down her face, too. And she wasn't even sure why. She just hurt that her mother hurt so much.

A few moments later, Jan said, "Amy, come home with me now. You haven't lost Tomasz. *We* haven't lost him. We can't give up like that. Don't worry, we'll find him. Żanetko, you want to help me put the chair in the back?"

"You okay, Mamusiu?" She asked it again, and this time her mother gave her hand a squeeze and nodded. Then she climbed into the backseat through the driver's side as Żaneta helped her father.

When they had finished, Jan said quietly, "Your mother's so upset. I know the two of you were going to walk home together, but I should get her home right away. And since there's no room for you with the wheelchair in the car, do you mind walking the little ways home alone? We'll meet you there. There's a good girl. Azor, you take good care of her."

Żaneta gave Tatuś a smile and said, "Sure, no problem. We'll see you at home." She waited until the car had pulled away and she had waved before she started walking up the hill. She was a little bit glad she had a few moments alone. It didn't happen often in their crowded apartment. That's why she liked to take Tomasz's dog out so much. It gave her time to think. And it made her feel closer to her brother. Now Żaneta had a lot to think about.

Would Tomasz really run away from home? *Yes.* She had never heard so much anger in him as she had that morning when he woke them all up. That had been terrible.

But what about Mamusia? She hardly ever cried. What was it she had said? *"I've already lost one child. I can't lose another!"* Such words. Żaneta knew exactly what she was talking about. *Gonia*.

Gonia's death had left its mark on their family. In some ways, the scars were even deeper than those left by the war. Żaneta had heard her grandmother's stories and noticed how she marked time with "before the war" and "after the war." In the same way, they often referred to things in the past by saying, "When Gonia was alive, we . . ." Żaneta thought it was right to do that because since the death of Gonia, their family had never been the same.

Żaneta had hated hearing the pain in her mother's voice when she cried out like that. *It means she still blames herself for the accident.*

Żaneta was only five when Gonia died. But she still remembered. Oh, she remembered so well. She remembered where she was sitting when her mother came into the apartment with the empty stroller, hanging limply in her hands. She remembered that her face was white, her eyes empty.

Yet Żaneta still had the feeling that Gonia was with her somehow. She'd always had that feeling. Once when she told her grandmother about it, Babcia had said the two of them had been like twins. And they say twins know things about each other and are very close. Żaneta had wondered if she really was that much like Gonia. She didn't know for sure.

Babcia had also told her that she always took good care of Gonia. That Żaneta could also remember. She knew that Gonia's bib had had a teddy bear on it, and they both had pajamas with little red bows as the print. She could remember waking up beside Gonia in the mornings and watching her suck her thumb. And Żaneta could remember the smell of the sea whenever the three of them used to go and feed the swans with Mamusia.

Deep inside Żaneta's heart, in that hidden part of her, she still felt her little sister's presence. Not like a ghost, but just in a way that meant Żaneta never felt alone. When she'd been younger, she had even talked out loud to Gonia, believing she could hear her from where she sat playing with the angels in heaven.

When Żaneta reached their apartment building, she looked up all the way to the seventh floor. *That window* belonged to the kitchen side of the room she shared with Babcia.

Żaneta trudged up the stairs flight by flight, since now there was a sign saying the elevator was broken again. This meant her poor father had to carry Babcia the whole way up. On the fourth floor landing, she heard the main door slam shut. She stopped and leaned over the bannister, looking down all the way to the ground floor. The man's head she saw looked familiar. When Azor began to bark, Żaneta knew it must be someone their family knew. "Who's there?" she called down the stairwell, peering over all the floors where the stairs turned a corner.

"It's me." Her uncle Piotr's face peered up at her. "Cześć, Żanetko!"

She waited for him to catch up with her and gave him a big hug. She didn't remember anything about her uncle before he went into prison. So even though she knew him from everyone's stories, she didn't really *know* him, hadn't really met him until a little over a half year ago, when he finally got out of prison. She liked him, though. He was very different from her father most of the time. He also never talked down to her but treated her like an adult.

Now he said, "Please tell me your brother's upstairs."

She shook her head. "I don't think so. I'm just getting home myself. But everyone else is up there. And Mamusia is very upset." He nodded, but said nothing more until they reached their door and Żaneta buzzed twice.

Jan swung it open right away, then looked at both their faces and frowned. Żaneta thought now he did look like his brother, after all. They both had the same sad expression on their faces.

The family spent the rest of the evening sitting around the table, talking about what could be done. Piotr had contacted several friends who promised to continue searching for Tomasz. He said in the morning he would walk through Gdańsk again and show Tomasz's photo to anyone who would look. Unless someone recognized him and told them about it, all they could do was wait. Many times that night, Żaneta heard the words, "He'll come home. He won't stay away."

Żaneta had the idea of checking with Stefan's family downstairs to see if Stefan knew anything. Her father went with her. But Stefan looked as surprised as his parents. He said he'd be glad to contact their other friends, though. Maybe someone else had heard something.

Żaneta was also worried about her grandmother. Babcia took some of her new pills and was able to fall asleep on her parents' bed. They told Żaneta to go to bed in Tomasz's room, and that was something she'd been afraid of. "No, I can't do that," she said.

"But it's just for tonight," her father said. "You'll see. We'll find him tomorrow, and then you'll have to fall asleep with all of us talking here until late at night and bothering you like we always do."

"You don't bother me. And neither does the noise."

"Come on, Żanetko, it's late." She knew what that tone meant. She kissed everyone good-night and took her pajamas into the little room.

Through the thin wall, she could hear her uncle say to her parents, "I feel so responsible. I never should have encouraged him. I've been everywhere. I even went over to Ewa and Bogdan's, thinking he's so obsessed with Solidarność he might turn to them."

The adults' voices droned on, and Żaneta looked around the room, Tomasz's room. She didn't like being here without him. It didn't feel right, her being glad for some privacy, almost as if there might be a reason why she would be pleased that her brother was gone. It wasn't that way, she told herself, and sighed.

Azor lay in a little ball at the foot of Tomasz's bed. "You know you're not supposed to be there," she scolded him. He looked at her with sorrowful eyes and wagged his tail slowly up and down. "I know, I miss him, too." Żaneta knew she should kick him off the bed, but instead she curled herself around the dog. One arm over his chest, she fell sound asleep beneath the gaze of basketball stars from another land.

26

Tomasz ran. His heart beating wildly, he felt everything and everyone closing in on him. He ran and ran and ran. With each pounding step the fury in his soul grew more focused. What did they think they were trying to do? They had lied to Piotr, the only adult who'd ever really cared. And now he didn't care anymore, because of their lies. *I was a fool to go to him in the first place.*

The realization dawned on Tomasz just as he began to notice his surroundings had changed drastically. He was out of the city and on a main road running through the countryside. Tall chestnuts lined the lane, and a flock of geese crossed the road ahead. He slowed to a jog, not really surprised. Stefan might be faster, but he had better stamina.

Stefan. He stopped to pick up a few stones, then threw them at the geese as he walked by them. Tomasz wondered if maybe he should go back and tell his friend what he'd done. He didn't feel quite so explosively angry anymore. It had become more of a simmering rage. *Stefan. What for?* He had the clothes he needed, and money, although not much, but enough to buy a few meals until he found a job somewhere. And he had something else. Tomasz tapped the U.S. passport in his hip pocket. *Like gold.* It gave him a comforting feeling.

He'd miss his friend, but Stefan wouldn't understand. He liked to talk big, but that's where it stopped. Tomasz looked up at the canopy of leaves above him, intertwined together in branches crossing over the road. He squinted his eyes, then let out a whoop. A flock of crows rose out of the trees, cawing in protest.

Tomasz looked around, a little self-consciously, but no one had heard him. The pastures on both sides of the road were deserted. The sun was setting behind a distant stand of trees in red and pink swirls. That meant tomorrow would be warm as well.

Tomasz checked his watch, almost ten. Way too early to go to bed if he'd been home, but he felt as if he'd just played four rounds of basketball. *You wish*, he thought. The more he thought about it, the more tired Tomasz felt. And then he realized he hadn't had anything to eat all day. He'd packed bread and sausage, so now he looked around and saw the next field over was dotted with newly harvested hay, all stacked neatly in regular rows. *A perfect place to spend the night.*

Tomasz settled down behind one haystack so that no one could see him from the road. He ate his meal and gazed up at the sky, wondering if it was Venus or Mars he saw in the corner farthest from where the sun had set. His mother would have known. She had learned it from her stepfather, who, she said, had served in the U.S. Navy. Tomasz was right in the middle of trying to remember the names of the other stars when he fell sound asleep, his mind full of the broad night sky.

The next time Tomasz opened his eyes, the sun was already up. His muscles were stiff. He had to think a moment to remember the events of the previous day, then he told himself it was all right. His watch read 7 A.M., yet the air already felt warm. He ate the rest of his food and wandered back to the road.

He had wondered if his resolve would lessen any after a night's sleep in the open, away from home. He thought of his family now, as sort of a test. Although the rage that had caused him to jog quite a few kilometers the day before had died down, he did not doubt his decision. It had been a long time coming. Tomasz thought of how often this last year he'd been fighting with his parents and told himself it was better for everyone this way. It was time.

And, he had to admit, he had never felt so good. He said it out loud, "I've never felt so good." It was true. He heard a truck coming up behind him and turned to wave it down. The truck roared by, not even slowing.

It's okay, Tomasz told himself. *I'm not in a hurry*. The truth was, he had a plan. It wasn't according to any timetable, but he certainly had a destination. When he'd gone with his parents to Holland, they'd driven on this same road. It ended at the border in *Szczecin*. And that's where the road to Berlin began.

Berlin. They had only spent one night there in an apartment on the West side of the city with friends of his parents, but what Tomasz had seen that one day and night was enough to lure him back. The city was so alive, so colorful and moving. No, it was more than that. He'd sneaked off that night under the guise of getting something out of the car and discovered a rock concert only three blocks away. The bands were playing on raised podiums so students on the Eastern side of the Wall could hear the music as well. He spent all that night soaking up the wild side of Berlin and loving it. When he got back to the apartment, his father had been furious and embarrassed for their friends, of course, but what else was new?

Berlin had gotten into Tomasz's blood and he wanted more. It was the only place that had ever dazzled him like that. He'd felt so *free*. And the shops were bursting with things you couldn't get in Poland. With the discos, it had all been one big party-city. That night in Berlin Tomasz had made up his mind. No matter what, someday, somehow, he would get back to West Berlin.

He just hadn't thought it would be so soon. Tomasz shrugged his shoulders. *Who cares?* He could take care of himself.

Then, as proof that he was right, another truck came rumbling up behind him. Tomasz stuck out his hand and listened with satisfaction as the brakes screeched. He ran up to the cab and threw the right-hand door open.

"Thanks. Can you give me a lift maybe?"

A middle-aged man with a gigantic mustache grunted at him. "Sure. Get in. Where are you going?"

"Where are you heading?"

"Szczecin."

"That's perfect. Thanks again," Tomasz said. He climbed up into the cab and tucked his bag between his legs. Tomasz glanced over at the driver. He didn't look very interested in conversation. *It's just as well*, Tomasz thought. He pulled out his pack of cigarettes and offered the driver one, then lit up as he stretched in the sun and put his head back against the big seat. The huge motor lulled on and on. They headed west, the sun at the truck's back, casting a long shadow along the road before them. Tomasz tried not to watch the crucifixes hanging from the mirror, bouncing around like little dolls.

By the end of the morning, they had reached the border. Tomasz showed the driver his U.S. passport and asked if he could stay in the cab.

"Sure. If that doesn't get you across, nothing will. You'll have to buy an East German transit visa, though."

Tomasz nodded. There went some of his cash. Well, it hardly mattered. The driver had proven something to Tomasz. He really *could* go where he wanted and do what he pleased.

It was important to remind himself of this, now that he would have to be extra careful at the border. The uniformed guards, the guns, seeing the cars being pulled over to the side and searched by East German guards just beyond the Polish post, it all made him nervous. His family had a bad history at border crossings.

Tomasz told himself he had nothing to hide. He took a deep breath and handed the passport to the guard. He looked at him, showed the passport to his colleague, and said, "Look at this one. He doesn't look anything like the photo."

The colleague looked up at Tomasz, then laughed, "You're right." The first guard reached for the red ink pad, then stamped the date and location of *Kołbaskowo* on the page and handed the passport back at Tomasz. Only after he'd accepted it back and was heading toward the East German post did it dawn on Tomasz that the guards might have thought he couldn't understand them, since he had an American passport. He had been a little kid when the photo was taken.

This next part should go all right, he reminded himself. *Just look normal. You have nothing to feel guilty about.* Still, anything East German scared him. He'd grown up on stories that always ended with, "At least we're better off than the East Germans. We can travel, and we're not all spying on each other like they do."

When it was his turn, the guard asked him, *"Wo sind deinen Eltern? Du bist doch dreizehn?"*

He nodded. He'd been ready for this. *"Das stimmt.* My aunt is meeting me. She lives in a village near here."

"Which village?"

Tomasz broke into a sweat. He hadn't anticipated that question. Just then the phone rang in the booth, and the guard had to turn away from him. Tomasz waited, and whispered desperately, "What should I answer?"

The driver shrugged his shoulders. "Leave me out of this."

Then another guard appeared and took over. He looked at Tomasz's passport, had him fill out a visa form, took his money, looked at him, and stamped it without another word.

Right, Tomasz thought. *I'm in. Now all I have to do is get out.* That had been too risky. He decided he needed some extra insurance. Tomasz thanked the driver, got out of the cab, and wandered around the parking lot until he saw what he needed. At the *wechsel* stand, an American man was arguing in loud English with the woman behind the little window.

Tomasz remembered the trick he and Stefan had played in Kraków and thought how childish that seemed, compared with what he needed to pull off now. He took one more drag on his cigarette, then flicked it downward and ground it out with his heel.

Then he took out his earring, slipped it into his pocket, and walked up to the man. "Excuse me, can I help maybe?" he asked in English.

The man didn't look very friendly, but Tomasz told himself that was because of his hair. He put his hands up and backed away a few steps. "Sorry, I just heard you were having some problems. I thought maybe I could translate or something. I don't want anything in return. My dad's based in Germany, and I know how hard it is sometimes getting people here to understand what you want."

That did the trick. The man's eyes opened a little wider and he nodded. "I want to exchange all these *złotys* into deutschmarks, but they won't take them."

"No, I'm sorry, they won't. And there's nothing you can do about it. I'm afraid Polish money can't be exchanged outside of Poland. If you need *Deutschmarks*—I mean West German marks—you could give her dollars. I'll bet she'll take those."

"You mean I'm stuck with all this?" The man held up a fistful of faded bills. "If I'd known that, I wouldn't have exchanged so much. Okay, guess I can't do anything about it now. Right." The man turned back to the woman in the window and said, "Well, then give me twenty dollars' worth. That will pay for gas until I get to Berlin."

That's what I was hoping, Tomasz thought. He stepped away politely until the man had finished his transaction. Then the man walked toward him, stuffing the new bills into his wallet. He fell into stride beside Tomasz. "Hey, thanks. I can't speak any German. And this place gives me the creeps."

"Me, too," Tomasz said honestly.

"Did you say your father was stationed in Germany?" The man's eyes narrowed again.

"Yeah. I don't understand it. We have family in Poland. My mom's Polish, and they brought me to the border. My dad was supposed to pick me up, but I bet he got delayed, or maybe didn't even get the message. I'm coming home earlier than we'd expected. He's based in Berlin. I don't know what to do, if I should wait here or . . ."

"Yeah, okay, listen." The man looked at him closely. "You say you're a military brat?"

Tomasz didn't know the term, but he nodded. It sounded right.

"Show me your U.S. passport, then."

He started to feel the panic rising up his back again. "No, it's okay, really," he said to the man and started walking away.

"No, wait. I'm just trying to help. I wouldn't want my son waiting around a border post. I just want to see if you really are a U.S. citizen."

And if he looks inside and sees I actually live in Poland and am thirteen, I've had it. Then he had an idea. Tomasz slowly took out the passport, turning the gold-colored eagle emblem upward. Then he said, "I don't know . . . my dad told me not to let anyone get their hands on this. These things go for a fortune on the black market over here."

The man nodded. "You're right. I can see you are who you say you are. Listen, I'm going to Berlin. If you want, you can hitch a ride. But once we're in the city, you're on your own."

"I don't want to impose. Are you sure? Thanks, that would be great," Tomasz said.

"It's okay. I used to be in the marines myself. Maybe when I stop for gas, you can give your father a call and tell him where you are."

"What?"

"That you'll be in Berlin by nightfall. So he doesn't go looking for you, or worse, drive all the way out here and pass us going the other way."

"Oh, right. Yeah, good idea. That way he won't worry." *Tell him anything, just so he takes you along.* Tomasz couldn't believe his good luck.

This meant the next time he had to cross a border was four hours later, in Berlin itself, at Checkpoint Charlie. As they crossed *Unter den Linden*, Tomasz looked right and saw the *Brandenburger Tor*, or Brandenburg Gate. Behind it loomed the Wall. They slowly drove up the *Friedrichstrasse* and got in line to cross the *Kontrollpunkt*. He tried not to stare, but the watchtower and guard dogs and grim-faced East German guards frightened him anyway.

"I guess you're used to this," the man said.

Tomasz had since found out his name was Bob and he had been in Poland on business for some farming company. He had told the man he was seventeen and would be finishing high school at the base next year.

"Not really," Tomasz said. "I mean, I don't think anyone *could* get used to all this."

Bob nodded. The part of East Berlin they had just driven through was drab and colorless. Tomasz thought the gray high-rises here looked even less habitable than what they had in Poland. It was all just as he'd remembered. As they slowly drove through the narrow gap in the Wall, Tomasz held his breath. *How many people have they shot here as they hid in cars or made a run for it?* he asked himself. *That's all I'm doing. Running away.* The thought came out of nowhere, and Tomasz shoved it aside as they started making their way through West Berlin. He had to stay focused.

He couldn't help feeling more than a little satisfied with himself, though. Only yesterday he'd left Gdańsk, and now here he was driving down the neon-lit street of the *Kurfürstendamm*. He'd made good time. And Berlin was everything he remembered and better.

"Where do you want me to let you off?" Bob asked.

"Anywhere's okay. I can take public transport, I mean, a bus or something."

"Well, now that we're here, I might as well go the whole nine yards. Wouldn't mind being on a base again. Although I don't know how you ever got a military father to go along with that haircut."

Tomasz looked at him, appalled. *He wants to go to the base? This has gone on long enough.* At the next stoplight, he said, "There's the bus I need to take. I'll get out here. Hey, thanks, really. You saved me. Bye."

"Yeah, sure. Bye, have a nice life," Bob called after him. He sounded a little baffled, but Tomasz thought he'd handled it well.

Berlin. I'm back.

27

I need no riches, nor earth's empty praise

The morning after Tomasz ran away, Amy's best friend Ewa came to visit them. Żaneta woke up to the sound of the women's voices. For a few moments longer she lay in bed, eavesdropping on her mother and Ewa. She didn't want to get up yet. She had a feeling it wasn't going to be a very good day. Ewa was telling Amy that she had been helping Piotr and Bogdan and the others look for Tomasz.

"I don't think he wants to be found," she said now.

"I don't want to admit that," Amy said. "But this morning I discovered he's taken his U.S. passport with him. Oh, Ewa, he could be anywhere!"

That's what Żaneta had been thinking ever since she had heard the news at the fountain yesterday. She knew Tomasz, and he was really mad, had been for a long time. *Yes, he wanted to run away, probably far away, and now he has.*

Żaneta waited until Ewa had left and she heard her mother getting Hanna up and into her chair before she left Tomasz's room. A little later, her father showed up. Everyone turned to look at him expectantly when he walked through the door, but he just shook his head. Żaneta thought, *They're not going to find Tomasz. Not today.* She didn't know how she knew, but she did.

At their afternoon meal, her father kept rubbing his head. "We've been searching for him everywhere. I'm desperate. All I wanted to do was reason with him at Piotr's apartment. I was even ready to apologize. I never dreamed he'd run away from home," he said weakly.

They were all quiet for a few moments until Babcia said softly,

"I hardly dare to say it again. But I think we can battle this in the same way we've taken on every fight, with prayer and with hope, and by being smart."

Jan took his cue from his mother. "You're right. It's going to be very hard, but we will keep faith that God has our Tomasz in His hands. Let's pray for his safety now." And to Żaneta's surprise, he began the prayer by saying, "Lord, forgive me for my hardness of heart. My son . . ."

And then his voice cracked, and Żaneta opened her eyes just a little bit to peek. She saw Amy reach over and take his hand, then they both opened their eyes and looked at each other, so Żaneta closed hers quickly.

Her grandmother continued praying. "Our Tomasz is lost to us, Lord, but You see him even now. Thank You for sending angels to his side. . . ."

Listening to her, Żaneta felt as if her grandmother could see things they could not.

The day passed, and then a week went by, and they still had no word from Tomasz. Żaneta didn't want to stay in Tomasz's room, but her parents insisted she sleep there for the little while her brother would be gone. Since Tomasz's room was too small for Hanna, they traded with Hanna and moved into the living room, which she didn't like, even though the arrangement did give her more privacy. "I want to be where I can see what's going on in this family. My room has always been the hub of activity."

Jan said, "It's all right, Mamusiu. You're just going to sleep in our old room. Every morning we'll bring you back out here to your usual spot between the window above the trees and the couch." It was easier for everyone this way, but no one said so.

The summer dragged on. Her uncle was very busy, and always dropping in at the strangest times. The same rule of not talking about certain things applied to his visits as to Ewa's. Even though Żaneta knew her parents didn't want her knowing anything about the underground, she couldn't help but know. She was often around when they went for walks and talked about what Uncle Piotr and Ewa and Bogdan were trying to do. Besides, she thought, it was part of her history, too.

For instance, Żaneta knew her uncle was involved in many activities, still trying to wake up the old feeling of Solidarność and get the country out from under martial law. Żaneta tried to understand, but whenever they talked about things like a Poland with a worsening economy riddled with shortages, she thought about it in terms of standing in line for everything. This Poland was the only one Żaneta had ever known. Martial law, the arrests, and the shortages had lasted five long years. The first time Żaneta had ever eaten a banana was when her parents took her to The Netherlands last Easter.

That was when she learned just how different her country really was. It wasn't only that they had more things in the West, but they had more *freedom*. The concept took on real meaning when Żaneta realized what it was to be rid of the constant worry of who was listening or watching. In The Netherlands, you could do what you wanted. People were paid better and could buy much more with what they earned.

One day during their Easter trip, they had met another Pole, a man they had heard speaking Polish in one of the shops in Rotterdam. When they all started talking together, this man told them how he was a surgeon from Łódź. He came to The Netherlands each year to pick cucumbers in the greenhouses for three months. In that time he made more than he did all year round following his medical calling back home. "I have to feed my family somehow," he had said.

And they had met Polish sailors who gladly fished on boats all over the world, sometimes not seeing their families for years at a time. With the Western currency they earned, they could afford to buy an apartment in a high-rise somewhere in Poland. That was the only way married children could get a place of their own, unless they inherited an apartment. Otherwise, everyone lived together, three generations under one roof, like Żaneta's family.

When Żaneta saw how much *room* people in other countries had, that was when she realized what a housing shortage really meant. In Poland, people had been on waiting lists for decades!

Żaneta heard all the talk about worsening conditions whenever the adults sat around. Yet whenever someone complained that Poland had to rise up and *do* something, Piotr was always there to point out that things were being *done*.

During each of the long years of martial law, there had been more protests, more demonstrations. Those who longed for Poland's freedom weren't giving up. Of course, it hadn't helped when most of the leadership was in jail. But even then, they had managed to keep the fire burning. That's how Piotr put it.

When she was alone with him, they often went over the dates together. He said it was part of her education, one she wouldn't be learning at school or out of a book. But he was wrong.

She could learn these things from *his* book. Żaneta had never known anyone who had written a book before. But her uncle Piotr had. That summer the book was published in Paris and by the underground press in Poland.

Piotr showed her a copy one day when he took her to a circus that was in Gdynia for the week. And there, while the ringmaster from Romania yelled at the bears to waltz around the center ring, Żaneta saw those same dates he'd been teaching her in print for the first time.

Żaneta turned to the pages preceding Chapter 1. There was a timeline showing the first date as *December 13, 1981—declaration of martial law*. Then she read what followed, a long litany of arrests and demonstrations, year after year after year, all stretched across the next several pages, with every year outlined in its own little box.

1983
April 9–11—Wałęsa holds secret meetings with the TKK
May 1 and 3—major demonstrations
June—Pope John Paul II's second visit to Poland
July—"Termination" of State of War; partial amnesty, though show trial
    of major figures is still pending
October 5—Lech Wałęsa awarded Nobel Peace Prize

Piotr was reading over her shoulder and pointed now at the last entry. "We thought certainly that 1983 would be a turning point. When Wałęsa won the Nobel Prize, it was as if the world was standing there cheering us on. But in the end, that's all they did, was stand there. Look, in 1984, there were even more arrests in June. . . ."

Żaneta read on,

July—limited amnesty includes several key figures in Solidarność lead-
    ership, but not all. Some still facing charges of high treason and
    possible death penalty
August 31—more demonstrations
October—kidnapping and murder of Father Jerzy Popiełuszko

"This . . . this was another moment when we could not comprehend how the government could continue. It was incredible. The pope had visited his homeland twice. And they *dared* to kidnap and beat up a Roman Catholic priest. I think your grandmother would say that's when you learn to know the face of evil. You won't understand that now, and I hope you never do."

Żaneta looked at her uncle.

"I'm sorry," he said. "Your mother wouldn't be happy if she thought I was scaring you."

"You're not scaring me," she said simply. And he wasn't. The next pages listed more arrests, more demonstrations, each year piling up more and more, looking as if it would never end.

1985
February—rearrested while meeting with Wałęsa, face serious new
 charges

"That's when they arrested Ewa, isn't it?" Piotr nodded.

1985
March—Mikhail Gorbachev becomes new Soviet First Secretary
May 1 and 3—demonstrations
May-June—arrests, trials, and new convictions. . . .

1986
—additional arrests. . . .
May 1—demonstrations
May 31—arrested. . . .
July 17—new so-called "amnesty" for political prisoners announced

September 1986—virtually all prisoners released; Wałęsa establishes a
 Temporary Solidarity Council, including . . . Borusewicz, Bujak,
 Frasyniuk, Jedynak, Lis. . . .

And there was almost the same list of names as those who had been arrested, released, and rearrested during the previous years.

"This was when you got out, too," Żaneta said, pointing at *September 1986*. "Almost a year ago now, you know."

As she thumbed through the rest of the book, Piotr said, "That's all commentary and interviews with some of the people mentioned in the timeline. Probably too serious for your little head."

She turned to him and asked, "Who did you write this for?"

Piotr looked at Żaneta oddly, then smiled. "My little niece, this is for you and all the children of your generation. And it's for the future generations, for your grandchildren. Because, you see, my prayer is that when *your* children are free and you are the parents teaching the true history of our country, you will know these dates in your hearts."

He stopped and chuckled to himself. "That sounds lofty, but what I was really thinking when I wrote it was that it's for all those stubborn Poles who say no one is fighting back, so why should they?"

"Aren't you afraid they'll arrest you again, especially when they find this?"

"I'd like to see them try," Piotr said. "No, I don't think we need to worry. It can't last much longer."

Żaneta didn't want to be the one to say that's what they'd all been saying for over five years now. Instead, she sat up straighter to watch the ponies prance around the center ring.

Despite the book, and the solemn masses held in all the cities in Poland way back during the first week of May, it still seemed to Żaneta that the world had forgotten them. Now that she'd been outside of Poland, she knew a little better what was at stake. In June, the pope had visited Poland a third time. Now, at the end of August, there were more demonstrations.

"It's another chapter in Uncle Piotr's book," Żaneta said that night. The heat had sent her grandmother to bed early, and she was alone with her parents. They were all nervous that Piotr or one of their other friends might be rearrested because of the demonstrations going on in Gdańsk.

Żaneta asked, "Weren't you afraid the police would come and search the apartment?" She pointed at the ceiling. "Aren't you still?" she whispered.

Her mother answered, "When he was writing it, we never hid any of the chapters here. If they come and find his book now, they get a free copy and a chance to read what's been really happening in this country. The men who serve in the milicja and the army are all Poles. I wonder how many have chosen not to know the very things Piotr has written about. It would do them good if they found Piotr's book. On the other hand, maybe it would be no surprise to them, after all."

Then Żaneta asked her mother a question she had been thinking about since their trip at Easter. "Isn't it hard being here, I mean staying in Poland when it's so different and so hard to get things. I don't know. You're not *from* here, Mamusiu. Why do you stay?"

"What kind of a question is that?" Amy looked at her alarmed. "It's funny. Your father asked me the same thing after his trip to America. Remember, Jan? I think sometimes this Piekarz family thinks too much. Żanetko, it might be hard to explain to a stranger why I stay. But don't *you* know? Materialism doesn't matter to me. I'm here because it's where God gave me Jan and my childre . . ." Her voice broke and she swallowed, then smiled bravely for Żaneta and said, ". . . my precious children."

What she didn't need to say was that none of them had forgotten Tomasz. It wasn't that they didn't talk about him very much anymore. They had just stopped telling one another that it would be all right, that he would come home soon, that they would hear some news.

She got up from the table and turned on the television. One channel had a movie, a love story. But just like all the foreign films on television, there was no sound of voices or dialogue. Instead, a man's voice started speaking as the pictures were shown. Żaneta could barely hear a little of the original soundtrack in the background, and sometimes even a little music. But the different character voices were hard to understand because throughout the film, a male voice kept translating both the men's and women's parts.

Żaneta had a vague familiar feeling about what her mother had said. She'd been thinking it for the last months. It was almost as if Tomasz's running away had hung a cloud over them in the same way Gonia's death did so many years earlier. *Can you mourn someone who's still alive?* she wondered as the monotone voice on the television droned on and on and on.

28

As Tomasz walked up and down West Berlin's shopping district of *Wilmersdorf*, he felt this was the place he had always wanted to be. Stronger, as though this was where he was *meant* to be. Televisions filled an entire shop window, all of them tuned to different channels. Tomasz stopped and counted them. Sixteen. That must be what they called cable.

The broad sidewalk was packed with people, many coming home from work, well dressed and carrying briefcases. There were a lot of tourists, and Tomasz had trained himself to pick them out. Most of the people looked as though they belonged here and were taking an evening stroll, looking in through all the windows, just like Tomasz. *I belong here, too.*

The flashing lights fascinated him. Everything sparkled. He was glad he'd arrived just as it was getting dark. When a whole street full of lamps lit up right before him, Tomasz took it as a sign of the city coming alive just for him.

Thanks to his grandmother, he had thought that the language would be no problem. But now as the crowd all around passed him by, their German sounded different, another dialect, he realized. That was no problem. He'd pick that up, too.

Tomasz had thought to take the mini-tourist guidebook he'd found when looking through his parents' papers. He'd also taken the envelope of leftover deutschmarks he'd found in the same folder. *Payment for my bike,* he'd thought at the time. It was more than 100 deutschmarks, which would get him by for a while, as long as he was careful.

He took out the guidebook and looked up the location of the

nearest youth hostel. He knew this was the cheapest way. He had given himself the mental deadline of two weeks to find a job. That's how long he figured his money would pay for food and his nights at a youth hostel. If he hadn't proven to himself by then that he could make it, he'd go back. No, he wouldn't go back, he told himself. *I'll make it work, no matter what.*

The youth hostel was located on the other side of the *Tiergarten*, or zoo. Actually, it was a huge park with a zoo somewhere inside it, as Tomasz soon found out. He kept walking and walking. He didn't like that it was so empty in the park, and when he found himself in a corner with hardly any lamps, he began to feel nervous. *Isn't the Wall near here? I've got to get out of here.* The trick was being careful. It was the rule for everything, for how he handled his money, and for how he took care of himself. If he was careful, he'd be all right.

"Hey! You!" a police agent shouted.

Tomasz stopped and turned and reminded himself, *At least it's West German this time.*

"What are you doing here?"

"I'm lost."

"What do you mean 'lost'? Don't give me that. I've been chasing your gang of friends out of these woods ever since the weather turned warm. I warned you all the last time that if I saw you here again, you'd have to spend a night in jail."

Tomasz couldn't believe what he was hearing. He tried to come up with the right German words, stammering, "No, really, please. I *am* lost. I'm looking for the youth hostel, and I got all turned around. Look...." He started to pull out the guidebook to offer some sort of proof that he was unfamiliar with the city. The next moment, he found his face flat down in the gravel. The agent had his arm twisted so tightly against his back that Tomasz could hardly breathe.

"The last time one of you punks tried that trick, my partner was stabbed. Now he's got a scar to prove it."

Tomasz shook with fear. He didn't know what to say. The agent kept him pinned down with one hand, while the other undid the zipper of his bag and dumped the contents on the ground. The guidebook fell out last. "See?" Tomasz mumbled, his mouth full of dust.

Then the man ran a hand down both his legs, feeling around the ankles. Tomasz lifted his head slightly and said, "I *don't* have a knife."

"No, you don't."

"And I'm not one of your gang of punks. I'm not even German. I'm Polish."

"Well, that's worse then, isn't it? Because so are they. But all right, I don't see anything here you shouldn't have. The youth hostel?"

"Yeah, that's what I was looking for."

"Right, well, just walk in that direction until you come out of the park, then turn right. It's on the left. Hey, how old are you anyway?"

"Eighteen."

The agent raised an eyebrow but said nothing more. Tomasz didn't stay around to see if he had any other questions. He scooped up his things and stuffed them back into his bag as fast as could, then took off at a jog in the direction the man had pointed out.

Tomasz spent the next few days visiting every restaurant and office building he could find, asking for work. Every night he returned to the youth hostel, and although he tried not to eat very much, the 100 deutschmarks quickly dwindled. Everywhere he went, it was the same story. If they asked for identification, and he showed them the passport, he was too young. If they didn't ask for ID, then they didn't want "his sort" around, which either meant they didn't like his haircut and leather jacket, or they didn't like his being Polish.

And then on his tenth day in Berlin, his luck changed. The owner of a Greek restaurant said he needed a dishwasher. Tomasz was overjoyed. The man didn't ask any uncomfortable questions. But he did say, "You know what I'm looking for. I need someone working *schwartz*, you understand?"

Tomasz understood. No taxes, no questions asked, but also no insurance coverage of any kind, no protection. And he would be paid in cash every other Sunday night. When Tomasz asked how long the job was for, the man shrugged and answered as long as the tourist season lasted. Tomasz figured that should be at least a few months. And he didn't care about working illegally. This was the break he'd been waiting for, and it had come just in time. Now all he had to do was hold on a little longer than he'd budgeted for, until his first payday.

That turned out to be harder than he had planned. After his fifth night of work, Tomasz waited for a good moment, then asked his new boss, "Do you think it might be possible to get 50 DM as an advance?"

The man just laughed. "You think you got problems? You should hear mine someday. Don't make jokes like that. And get back to work."

The work was more than just washing dishes. Tomasz also had to sweep and clean the restaurant after closing time, and scrub the bathrooms. He kept telling himself he didn't mind.

In order to make it until payday, Tomasz was forced to take his watch to a pawn shop. He'd been around the city enough during his job search to know that whatever he did, he should make sure he slept in a safe place. Well, safe was relative. He found that out the second day he'd left his things at the youth hostel. While he was out, someone stole most of his clothes and his towel, leaving him only the underwear. Luckily, he'd had his money and passport on him. But it had served to warn Tomasz that he couldn't be too careful. He'd heard that although the few shelters around the city were cheaper, they were much less safe. Romanian refugees, gypsies, and countless others from any country in Eastern Europe that allowed travel had all come to Berlin as the gateway into the West, a place shining with its promise of prosperity. Tomasz quickly found out during his rounds of the city that he wasn't the only one who'd come here to run away.

The few deutschmarks he managed to get for his watch meant Tomasz had barely enough to pay for the hostel during his second week of work. But that was all. So he made a deal with himself and ate the food off the plates he cleaned. He told himself that was all right, too, since it was temporary. Come Sunday, he'd have enough marks to buy his own meals. And come two Sundays after that, he might even be able to rent a room somewhere.

Tomasz made it through to Sunday. That night he had to work especially late because of a large party. The patrons threw plates and sang songs and danced on the tables until two A.M. By the time Tomasz had cleaned everything up, it was an hour later. The owner gave him an envelope of cash when he was finished and told him he'd done a good job.

Tomasz was too tired to care about the man's praise. He just wanted that money. It was all he'd been focusing on for fourteen days straight. He checked the amount and said good-night, relieved to finally put the smell of roast lamb behind him. There were no more buses, so he'd have to walk back to the hostel. But he'd done that the past few nights as well, since he didn't have money for the bus fare. He wouldn't have to wake up the concierge again, since after the first late night, when he'd explained that he was working, the man had shown him where a spare key was hidden. So now he was set.

Tomasz had waited so long for the money, and felt such relief at finally having it in his pocket, he toyed with the idea of spending part of it on a cab only for a split second. No, he'd walk, and in a half hour's time, he'd be in bed. That thought kept him going, dragging his feet, fighting the exhaustion.

Tomasz was only a few streets from the hostel when he noticed the sound of footsteps behind him. He turned around and saw a group of boys around his own age. They kept walking straight toward him. Not one of them said a word, but they stared straight at him, wearing the eeriest grins on their faces.

A more brightly lit street lay up ahead to the left, and an all-night petrol station was just around the corner. If he could reach that, he'd have a better chance of asking for help, or even better, waving down a passing patrol car. This was his thought as he forced himself to start running. The adrenalin took over and he turned this way and that, all the time trying to gauge if he was gaining or losing in the race toward safer ground.

He risked a quick glance behind him and saw two boys had broken ahead of the pack. Their chase was silent. He panted into a sprint. Tomasz poured all his energy into his legs, pumping as hard as he could. *Not tonight, not now*, he thought desperately. He had just one street to go, and then, right before he reached the corner, Tomasz heard a grunt and felt hands grabbing at his ankles. The two boys tackled Tomasz, and he went down with a huge, desperate thud. In the next second, he felt cold metal pressing against his neck.

"*Nein, nein!*" he begged them. He'd been afraid for his money, but now he realized much, much more was at stake. To die like this, here? *No, please!* A tiny part of him that did not give into the panic kept him paralyzed on the ground, at the mercy of the knife blade. As he lay there, he noticed now that the other boys who were jogging up to join their friends were talking Polish.

He switched languages, begging them to tell him what they wanted. The boy who had run the fastest had a scar running across his left cheek. He laughed scornfully and kicked Tomasz square in the stomach. "Ha! He wants to know what we want. Well, for starters, we'll take your jacket. How are his shoes, boys? No good? Try his pockets."

Tomasz curled up in pain, tears springing from his eyes. A sinking feeling of dread overwhelmed him. With one hand he instinctively tried to push the rough hands away. He opened his eyes for a split second, saw the toe of a cowboy boot aimed straight at his forehead, cried out, and then felt one searing shot of pain in his skull before everything went black.

As it turned out, there was precious little Jacek could do to reverse the prisoner-of-war trend he had helped inflict on Poland through the secret police. Even after Piotr's release, and that of so many of his comrades, Jacek tried a few times to warn Piotr and his colleagues of upcoming rearrest campaigns, but the information he passed along to the underground was always something they already knew.

The important thing was that Piotr held true to his promise. He did not betray Jacek.

And then that June, during the pope's third visit to Poland, Piotr sought Jacek out. They agreed to meet in the middle of the square packed with people who had turned out to see the pope. Jacek was curious, since he hadn't seen Piotr for several months. And he still had nothing to offer, nothing to bargain for, nothing with which to pay back his debt to Poland.

When Jacek caught sight of Piotr working his way through the unbelievable mass of people to their meeting place, Jacek's first reaction was that Piotr looked like the defeated man he had visited shortly after Gonia's accident. And then Jacek had a premonition, and his gut wrenched so hard, he nearly doubled over with the pain. When Piotr was finally beside him, Jacek could barely get the words out. "Not one of the children. Not again."

At the same time, he wondered yet again who this man was with whom he shared such a strange pact? Only Piotr knew Jacek was Amy's father. Only Piotr knew Jacek's true political allegiance. Only Piotr knew Jacek would do anything for Amy and her children.

And very, very strangely, Jacek trusted Piotr, as unlikely an ally as he had turned out to be.

So there, amidst tremendous crowds, Piotr began to speak. "I have a favor to ask."

"You're ignoring my question," Jacek said.

Piotr sighed. "Yes," he said.

And in saying it, he slew Jacek's hopes of somehow averting any further disaster from striking those he loved. He wondered desperately if he had brought this curse on his family by ignoring the laws of life and betraying and lying his entire life? It was a random thought, but Jacek could not silence its accusation as Piotr's words tumbled one over the other.

"I know who you are. You told me in that cell. It's your choice whether or not you tell Amy, but I'm begging you to help us find the boy. We don't know where he is, but he has his American passport with him. His parents say he was obsessed with Berlin. We've contacted the police . . . so many young people on the streets now . . . the authorities know. We've done all we could, but we've heard nothing for weeks."

When he finally stopped talking, Jacek shook his head, still refusing to accept what Piotr had said. "Tomek. Our Tomasz. You're telling me he ran away?" Jacek hadn't seen the boy for years. He had thought of him often though, every day loving his dark looks and ways as his own. "He can't be old enough to run away."

"Thirteen."

Jacek recalled his own childhood drifting in and out of foster homes and realized with a jolt that he had been even younger the first time he ran away. "Of course. Yes, I'll do whatever I have to. But on one condition."

Piotr squinted at him in the sunlight. The people around them began to pray out loud. The wind picked up, and Jacek had to lean forward to say the last words to Piotr. "You must never tell anyone that I helped look for the boy. Even if I'm successful. Agreed?" Piotr nodded. "Then we'll contact each other again as soon as one of us hears something."

Piotr reached out a hand and squeezed Jacek's shoulder. Then he shoved a photo into Jacek's hand and melted away into the crowd.

Jacek looked down and uncurled his fist. The face of his only grandson stared up at him.

29

You my inheritance through all my days

From very, very far away, Tomasz heard someone yelling. And then he felt himself being rolled over, and a hand touching his forehead, but then he lost consciousness again. The sun shone bright, everything throbbed, and he felt as though he was going to throw up.

"I know him."

No one knows me here, the thought penetrated his pain and made him curious enough to challenge the sun again. He saw the face of the police agent who had frisked him his first night in Berlin.

"Didn't make it to the hostel this time, huh? Come on, I'll give you a hand up."

The thought of standing proved too much for Tomasz. He groaned and twisted over, retching until he had nothing left. Then he wiped his mouth with the back of his hand and heaved himself onto his knees.

"That's it, come on, let me help you. They really gave it to you, didn't they?"

Only at that moment did Tomasz remember what had happened. He dragged his head up to look at the ground around him. Dried blood marked his spot on the pavement. In panic, he patted his hip pocket, then his other pockets. He looked desperately around, breathing hard, trying to concentrate through the pain. He stood barefoot. His fingers flew to his ear and felt a bloody mass. Even the gold earring was gone. They had ripped it right out of the bottom of his ear.

"What did they take?"

"Everything. My money, my passport . . . it was American."

The police agent whistled softly. "Come on, on your feet. You okay? You can walk?"

"Yeah, thanks." Tomasz felt far from okay. He ran his hand over his forehead and winced from the pain.

"Yeah, you've got quite a lump. You need a ride anywhere? Listen . . . I could call your parents."

"No, it's okay. Thanks." Tomasz stumbled down the street, discovering to his dismay as he felt his ribs that nothing was broken. When he arrived at the hostel, the concierge met him at the door.

"Oh no, you don't. You didn't show up, and you haven't paid. This is my busiest season, so I gave your place away. I couldn't find anything in your locker. *Auf Wiedersehen*. And don't get any ideas about the spare key, because I've moved it!" he called after him.

Dismayed, Tomasz turned away from the hostel and stumbled back down the street.

Tomasz didn't know how long he wandered around before it occurred to him that he should get himself cleaned up. He ducked into a public bathroom, stinking of urine, and leaned against the sink. The cool water hurt at first as he splashed it onto his face, but when he had done it a few times, it began to soothe his raw nerves. When Tomasz looked in the cracked mirror in front of him, he almost laughed.

One eye had already turned purple. His left side showed a black bruise where they'd kicked him, his ear lobe was swollen and covered in a bloody crust, and his forehead looked awful. He told himself that none of his injuries were serious. Now that he felt a little better, Tomasz started thinking about his situation. He only had the one set of clothing, torn and soaked in his own blood. He rinsed everything out as best he could and put it on wet, hoping it would dry in a few hours. He was exhausted and had to find somewhere to sleep before he went back to the restaurant that afternoon.

He remembered seeing a little park back one street and returned there. Tomasz stretched out on the bench in the shade and fell asleep with the summer breeze cooling his sore body. A few hours later Tomasz woke up to the sound of a dog barking somewhere. He had no idea what time it was, but a gut feeling told him he was late for work.

Tomasz started walking in the direction of the restaurant, trying to keep to the shade so the pavement wouldn't burn his bare feet. He told himself, at least at the restaurant, he could get something to eat. Then he caught sight of a church clock. Five o'clock! Two hours late. Tomasz started running, now ignoring the sun and the people who turned to stare as he passed them by.

When he reached the restaurant, he went in through the back door, only to see someone else standing in his place at the sink. Tomasz entered the dining room, where he found the owner. "I'm so sorry I'm late. Please, I got beat up last night, and they stole my money. I'm really sorry. It won't happen again."

His boss shook his head but looked sympathetic. "Sorry. When you didn't show up, I gave it to that guy who's been coming around here every day now. What was I going to do? I didn't know if you were coming back. When you didn't show up today, and you had your money, I thought maybe you had had enough. Sorry." He stood with both hands turned upward and shrugged his shoulders.

Tomasz looked at him, incredulous. *How can all this be happening? I don't believe it.*

He stumbled his way up one street and down another. Before long his feet were bleeding, cut open by broken glass. Everywhere he went, Tomasz asked if they needed help. "I can wash or clean. I'm a hard worker." He said it so often, he didn't even sound convincing to himself anymore.

Finally, he ducked down a stairway and found an empty bench in the corner of an *S-bahn* metro station. He curled up on a bench and fell asleep, trying not to notice the gnawing hunger he felt.

When Tomasz woke up, it was to the hammering sound of a dog barking in his face. He sat up with a start, not knowing where he was at first. His head throbbed. A police agent pulled the dog back and yelled over the barking, "Get out of here. You're not allowed to sleep in public places. Go on!"

Tomasz caught sight of a clock as he left the metro, 11 P.M. He still had the entire night to go. He resumed his march around the city, stumbling from one alley into the next. Now there were two sensations foremost on his mind. His hunger and his anger. He foraged through the garbage he found outside restaurants and ate whatever he could find. He hadn't eaten in almost twenty-four hours, and his gut felt turned inside-out. He was hoping that once he had filled it, the pain in his side and his head might lessen.

And Tomasz was angry. He had never let on then that he could speak German, or that his grandmother was German. But now, surrounded by the language, in this strange place, he needed someone to blame for his predicament. Why did the police have to be so strict and kick him out of the one place he'd found where he could get some rest? Typically German.

His grandmother. Tomasz didn't really want to think of her at that moment, but she would not leave his thoughts. He missed her. Hanna was always the only one who would listen to him. They'd had some good laughs together, and also some good talks. At that moment, for the very first time since leaving home, Tomasz's tough resolve faltered, and he felt a twinge of homesickness.

But then his anger rose up again. He remembered his anger at his grandmother's sickness and his anger at his parents. And if he thought the Germans were bad, the Poles were even worse, nothing but losers. Look at them, letting themselves be held captive during martial law for almost five years. There was a time when Tomasz had dreamed of nothing else but joining forces with his uncle in the ranks of Solidarność. But who was fighting back now? He felt the shame of coming from a country where its own soldiers had been at war with its people for five years now. Who could be proud of a place like that? Tomasz asked himself. Losers, they were all losers.

At that moment Tomasz caught sight of a sportswear shop. He crossed the street and stared at the posters of American basketball players, recognizing his own personal heroes. These were the winners, the Americans. They knew how to get things done. Tomasz felt proud. *I'm half-American, better than all these losers put together.*

Then he curled up at the corner of an alley where he'd found some uneaten pizzas and fell asleep again.

Tomasz's days and nights became a long series of searches for food and places to rest. All he did was wander from one quiet, stinking corner of the city to the next. He lost track of how many days had gone by since his mugging. He was sick to his stomach most of the time. Once or twice it occurred to him that he should try asking for help, maybe try to contact home, but each time, the anger and pride in him proved too strong. Besides, now he had no way of getting across the border. He had no papers, no passport, no identification. No money. When the panic rose in his throat at the thought of being just one more nameless, homeless street kid, he swallowed it back down. Tomasz just kept telling himself that his luck would change the next day, and he'd find a job and be all right.

One rainy night, he stumbled into an empty, abandoned building, relieved to find somewhere dry. Inside he found at least fifty kids like himself, their faces thin and pale, dark circles around their eyes. Like him, they were just looking for a place to spend the night. Despite the coughing all around him, Tomasz slept well that night, feeling safe for the first time in weeks.

In the next days, he got to know a few of the kids, and one girl in particular, named Heike.

Heike wanted to sleep with him, and at first he said no, but after a few weeks of being around her and her friends, he saw that many of them had sex together. The kids laughed at him and said he was lucky she wanted him, so Tomasz thought, *Why not?* He felt proud she had chosen to pursue him like that.

Heike became the focal point of Tomasz's days and nights. He loved her long blond hair, and how she tossed it over her left shoulder. When she smiled, it seemed meant just for him.

He liked some of her friends less, but they all operated together. Most of the kids spent the days and nights working the streets as pickpockets, while others searched through piles of garbage around the city. Some begged at the tourist spots, and more than a few stood at street corners, washing the windshields of cars that were stopped. At the end of each day, they pooled their resources. Their combined efforts meant that everyone at least had something to eat every day.

At first, Tomasz opted for the salvaging work, but the others made fun of him and said that was kids' stuff. Heike showed him how they could work as a team, one asking directions or accidentally bumping into and distracting the target, while the other took the bag or wallet.

Once, he caught sight of a busload of Polish tourists. He wandered over to them and overheard how East Germans had thrown stones and rotten eggs at the bus as it passed through on its way to Berlin. *Typical*, he thought.

The weeks went by, and it rained more and more. It didn't matter too much to Tomasz, since he had his shelter. Even when the temperature dove down to near zero, he told himself he didn't mind because it was the holiday season. Christmastime brought the group their biggest takes yet. During the last weeks of 1987, they could even afford some extra food for the pack of dogs that had adopted them, and for cigarettes.

Their temporary added wealth meant the group fought more

about who got what. A few left. Then between Christmas and New Year's Day when the winter really set in with snowfalls almost every day, the city government finally got around to destroying their building. The group split up, and each of them became desperate to find anywhere to stay out of the cold.

Jacek used his various ranks and identification passes to make full use of the secret police's searching machine. He checked with local police throughout Poland and with the hospitals. He had to be careful, but thorough. He crisscrossed the country under the auspices of an SB assignment. Everywhere he went, Jacek showed the photo to young people and old, anyone hanging around a street corner. Thankful for his new autonomy, a privilege of his latest high rank, Jacek exhausted every means he could think of looking for the boy.

He spent six months searching for Tomasz. And the more he searched, the more desperate Jacek grew. He listened as literally thousands of people told him they had never seen this boy. He visited nightclubs and dark alleys. He saw corners of Poland he had never visited before. He became appalled at the number of street children, their apathy, their disuse. And with each question, each passing month, each potential exposure of mixing professional means for private ends, his position at the SB became increasingly vulnerable.

By the end of 1987, even the government had to admit that Solidarność was slowly making a comeback. Jaruzelski did not want a replay of 1981, and Jacek did not think he could stomach another round of military measures pitting Polish milicja against the people. He hadn't really expected to find Tomasz in Poland, but he had to be sure before he took the following step and risked everything. When all his inquiries turned up nothing, he knew what he had to do. There would be no turning back once he began searching abroad. It was time to follow the lead Piotr had given him concerning Berlin.

Jacek feared that if the boy had ended up in East Germany, there would be no finding him there. Jacek's credentials would not get him far within the Stasi. No, he had decided to gamble it all and go directly to West Berlin. He berated himself for wasting half a year in the search already. Jacek had not seen Amy or any other members of her family, except for Piotr, in years. He could not afford to jeopardize their safety. But he could only imagine what the loss of a second child would mean to his daughter.

When he finally left the country in February 1988, Jacek knew full well what his actions would condemn him to, the unanswerable questions. It was the reason he had waited so long. For in making this trip, he risked it all.

30

As the winter weeks of the new year of 1988 went by, Tomasz and Heike continued to work the streets together. Tomasz used the trick of speaking English as often as he could, offering to give directions or asking about something, while Heike bumped into the person he was talking to. But as the weather grew more grim, the streets became emptier, and everything grew more difficult.

Then one morning Heike came back to the bridge under which they'd been spending the last few nights, and she had money. A whole fistful of coins, at least 10 deutschmarks.

"Where did you find it?" Tomasz asked as he kissed her.

"A man gave it to me."

Tomasz looked at her, but she would not meet his gaze. He knew several girls in their old group had worked as prostitutes during the summer. He'd never asked Heike if she'd done that, but now it hurt to know the truth for certain.

"Ah, Heike, we would have found a way."

"Oh yeah? You say that all the time, but it's not true. And look. He gave me these, too, and said I could come back for more, free." She opened her fist and showed him multicolored capsules. "He said they'd drive out the cold, make me feel good. I thought, they're free, so why not? And you know what, Tomasz? They work."

Tomasz looked down at the pills, then swallowed three of them, one at a time. Heike's stranger was right. After a few minutes, for the first time in months, he didn't feel the ball knotting up his stomach, and he felt warm.

When Heike said she wanted to go back for more, though, Tomasz insisted on going with her. The place was in a run-down neighborhood. Tomasz had never been able to find food in any of the bins along that particular street. She led him to a door behind a shop and knocked.

The man who opened it looked them over and said, "So, you were a good girl and brought your boyfriend. We can have a party. He'll be worth more each time than you, anyway. Now get in here before anyone sees you."

Tomasz saw yellow eyes and a smile with no warmth.

That night, Tomasz felt the small hand of Gonia in his own. She came to him, still a little girl of four, even though he was his real age. She said nothing but just took him by the hand and wanted him to follow. He couldn't, though, and he cried out, over and over again, "I'm sorry. I'm sorry, I didn't mean it. No, not there, I'm sorry. . . ."

He woke up to the sound of cruel laughter. How much time had passed? Days? Weeks? There had been pills. And then something else. He had learned fast.

The man who had taught Tomasz how to burn the powder and then inject the rest—that man had Heike in his arms. How long ago had that been? Tomasz tried to get himself standing, but his legs didn't work. He stumbled around the room like a drunk, and all the while the cruel laughter grew louder and louder. It followed him down into his dreams.

Jacek flew to *Tempelhof* airport, West Berlin, then went straight to the U.S. embassy. "I'm from the State Department." *The magic words.* Using his old CIA credentials, which the security man duly noted, he was able to get inside.

"I'm sorry, sir, the consul is out this afternoon. And his assistant is sick. But if, as you say, all you want is access to passport and missing-persons records, I can get someone else to help you with the computer."

"Yes, please," he nodded, determined to act as if he knew what he was doing. A secretary showed up and showed him into an empty office. Jacek looked around at the uncluttered bookshelves, the diplomas on the wall, and the man's coat on the coatrack while she turned on the computer. "Whose office is this?" he asked.

"Mr. Brown, the military attaché," she said, standing up. "If you'll come around here, sir, I'll show you how to scroll for the information you're looking for."

Jacek sat down in the leather chair and listened carefully as she showed him which files to call up on the computer. Then she left him alone and closed the door behind her.

It all went so smoothly. It was better than anything Jacek had hoped for. Here he could read the names of passports confiscated from people using them illegally, people who had been arrested at borders throughout Europe, not just in Berlin. And he could see who had reported a stolen passport within the same area. He scanned and searched but turned up nothing.

At the same time, he was thinking that the standard procedure would be to check his identification papers as he worked. He was thankful that the pass he had kept was still valid, even a decade after his so-called death, and still carried such a high security clearance. With everything becoming computerized, he had been afraid they wouldn't even let him in the door.

After an hour, Jacek heard a knock on the door. The same woman entered with a tray of coffee, creamer, and sugar. "I thought you might like something to drink," she said.

Jacek leaned back in the chair and took off his reading glasses to rub his eyes. "Thank you, yes." The woman spoke German, and so did he. He noticed she wore a well-tailored gray suit and polished pumps. She did not look him in the eyes but placed the tray on the desk and then left again.

Well-trained, Jacek thought. As he reached for the coffee, his eyes caught on something behind the tray. A framed photo. He paused, then picked up the picture to look at it more closely.

The woman smiling in the photo had blond hair, a nondescript face, brown eyes, a sad sort of smile. *Mrs. Brown?* Jacek wondered.

Something registered in the recesses of his memory. He *had* seen her before. Take away the blond hair, add a few years—no, subtract a few, it was hard to say. Jacek felt confused. The eyes staring back at him from the photo looked so familiar. And then it hit him.

Gabi. Oh no, it couldn't be. He looked closer. No, it wasn't. Surely not. A strange, tingling feeling crept up Jacek's spine. He put the photo in front of the tray and stood to stretch. Then he looked up. Sure enough, a video camera in the far corner of the room blinked its green light at him as he stared in its direction.

Don't panic. Just think for a moment. He wasn't sure it was Gabi.

Under the scrutiny of the camera, he didn't want to pick up the picture a second time. Instead, he walked around the office under the pretense of stretching his legs. Now Jacek was alert for anything in the room that might give away the identity of this Mr. Brown. Jacek knew an embassy's military attaché could easily be just a cover title for the local intelligence officer. Every embassy had one. Jacek's own bosses had operated out of Berlin. There was a better-than-average chance that Mr. Brown was one of these bosses.

Former bosses, he reminded himself. And then he realized: *the computer.* That was his key. He sat back down at the desk and tried to remember what the secretary had shown him. It was all very simple and logical. He exited the file he had been working in and entered the personnel files. But there was no entry under *Brown.*

On a whim, Jacek looked up the name *Jurek.* He remembered Roman telling him about Jurek's arrest back in February of 1985. *Surely he should have been released by now,* Jacek thought. It had been during a meeting with Wałęsa. So maybe, then, Jurek was acting as advisor for the State Department. But he had no last name, and Jurek's name alone was not listed, either.

Then something occurred to Jacek as he thought of a phrase Jurek had let drop during their encounter in the park, back in 1976. He typed in *Guardian Angel* and pressed *search.* This time the computer asked for a password.

So Guardian Angel exists, Jacek thought. He had no way of knowing the password, so he returned to the missing-persons files and continued his search for Tomasz's name. At the same time, he could not let go of the uneasiness the photo had conjured up. And what was *Guardian Angel*? When he thought about it, it didn't even make sense that the title of an intelligence mission should be in the computer. Or did it?

As he perused the list of stolen passports, then confiscated when the wrong bearers had tried to cross a border illegally, Jacek knew full well that each minute tightened the noose around his neck, a rope he had put there himself. *But it is a risk worth taking,* he told himself.

He tried to concentrate on scrutinizing the lists of names, but even while part of him searched for *Piekarz,* another part insisted on struggling with something he could not quite put his finger on. He was missing something. What was it?

The door opened and the secretary approached him with a marine guard behind her. She held his intelligence identification in her right hand. Watching her approach, Jacek suddenly realized the question that had been trying to surface from his subconscious.

Is Jurek Mr. Brown?

His next thought, while watching the guard take position by the door, was, *Well, I knew I'd be discovered eventually.* He had been aware of it going into Berlin and become certain of it when the guard at the entrance wrote down the details of his card. He just hadn't figured it would happen this soon.

"Here you are, sir," the secretary said as she put the papers on his desk. Jacek looked expectantly at the young marine.

"I'm sorry to disturb you, sir, but we'll be closing the embassy shortly. The computers shut down five minutes beforehand. Would you like me to take measures to make sure this terminal remains open?"

Jacek smiled at how his own suspicions had almost given him away. "No. No, thank you. I'm finished here. Would you like to turn this thing off for me?" he asked the secretary. "I'm not very good with computers, I'm afraid."

As she smiled and took his place, Jacek replaced his coffee cup on the tray. His hand tripped over the photo and knocked it off the desk. "Oh, how clumsy of me. Here, let me get that," he said. He stooped over and picked up the picture frame. On the back he saw the letters scrawled, *To Du.* A German-English pun—though not a grammatical one.

"I'm sure Mr. Brown would not want anything to happen to his wife's photo." *If it is his wife.*

The secretary smiled at him but would not volunteer any information. *Too well-trained,* he corrected himself. Then he gathered his coat and turned to the guard and secretary. "Thank you again for all your help." A sense of urgency settled over Jacek as the same professional instinct that had associated Jurek's identity with Mr. Brown's took over.

He had already spent too much time in a room where a security camera recorded his every movement. Now they even had him on video. He had told himself the gamble would pay off. Yet here he was, still with nothing. Not one sign of Tomasz Piekarz, no trace of his name anywhere, not in West Berlin or any other western European country.

So Jacek left the embassy dispirited and discouraged. And bemused. Back and forth went his thoughts, from Tomasz to the photo. *To Du.* "To you." He recollected the handwriting. He had only had time to glance at the letters. He retraced the second capital. *To Du.* It could have been a "Y." *To Yu.* Another play on words. Or a capital "J." *To Ju.*

Jurek.

"Ah," Jacek sighed out loud. *Gabi and Jurek?* He shook his head. "What am I thinking? Only I could put those two together. I *must* be paranoid." Jacek shook his head. *Focus.* That's what he had to do now. He made a conscious effort to set aside his questions about the mysterious Mr. Brown. He had left that world behind. Tomasz was all that counted now.

Eight full months the boy had been gone from home. In eight months he could have been murdered and left in some ditch . . . or worse. Jacek knew too well from his search so far just how terrible life on the streets could become for a young person these days. He had been appalled to find so many teenage girls and boys throughout Poland doing nothing, believing in nothing. Now, here in Berlin, he could already see the problem multiplied exponentially. Here they were, so young, so indifferent, sitting on church steps, hanging around on street corners, and waiting for what?

Could Tomasz be in East Germany? *No, not that. Not yet. One step at a time.*

Jacek told himself he had no choice. He got out the dog-eared photo and started showing it to a group of kids around the corner from the embassy.

"Hey, look at the old man!"

He looked up at them, thinking, *Yes, I am old.* Maybe it was the lack of fear they saw in his face, but two of the boys sauntered over to where Jacek was showing the photo to a girl and shoved her away. "Hey, you don't know who he is. Listen to his accent. He's not from here."

"Well, neither are you," Jacek said, sizing up the teenager. He had purple hair and a nose ring. The photo he carried of Tomasz showed him with neatly combed hair. Somehow Jacek doubted that's how he still looked. "But that's all right. Just tell me if you've seen someone who looks like this boy anywhere around the city."

"What's in it for me?"

"Your heart's desire." Jacek said the first thing he could think of. There was no way he was going to offer this group money. If they ever found out how much he had on him, they'd be all over him in a second. And he really *was* an old man now, though still relatively vigorous for his age. He didn't think he'd be equal to a physical fight with a group of street kids. Besides, he chose to fight his battles in other ways these days.

The teenagers didn't recognize the photo, and Jacek resumed his search. He tuned all his years of training into picking up the feel and messages of the street.

Where would I go if I were Tomasz? Who would I ask for help?

The answers were simple. *Food and shelter.* The basics.

At some point, the boy's money must have run out. If Berlin was where he really wanted to go, then his passport would have gotten him into the Western half. But what then? A job? A place to stay? Jacek decided those should be his own first steps as well.

So he found a private boardinghouse with a *Zimmer frei* sign in the window and moved into the spare room the family was renting. He had nowhere else to look, and Berlin had always been their best bet. He should have come much sooner. The more he thought about it, the more convinced Jacek became that this was where Tomasz should be. He had nothing else to go on besides Piotr's word that this was where the boy had wanted to go in the first place. *Now we've both gone underground*, he thought, realizing this city had now become Jacek's own hiding place from both the SB and CIA.

Jacek spent every night after that roaming West Berlin. He learned to recognize the places where young people hung out. Most of them surprised him with their willingness to talk with him and look at the photo. They seemed so bored—almost thankful for some sort of attention. One young girl put it best when he asked her why she was willing to help. "I wish someone was looking for me," she said.

Jacek also checked with the police officers who had street beats. And in this way he found a man who *thought* he recognized the picture. "It could have been a boy I found beat up last summer. But I have no idea where he is now."

It was all Jacek had to go on. Last summer would have been about right. He kept searching, and the weeks became two months. He learned to gravitate toward the streets that ended abruptly at the Wall. Young people hung out beside the stone separator, their graffiti a colorful backdrop, as if the proximity of others in a darker prison than their own could somehow console them.

He slept in the mornings, and every afternoon he woke up aching, all his muscles sore from walking so much. Yet he could not face the thought that here, too, he might fail. Already, Tomasz had been missing for almost a year.

Sometimes Jacek wondered how his life had taken such an unexpected turn. The thought dogged him as he checked the back alleys and under bridges, all the hiding places smelling of urine. He roamed the red-light district and lurked in dark corners around the *Hauptbahnhof*, the main train station. And all the while he promised himself, *I only want to tell my daughter who I am. I only want to right all the wrongs. If I can find the boy, if I can do that one thing right, it would help pay the debt.*

And part of paying off a private debt was the requirement that no one know. Somewhere in all his reading during his sojourn in Gdynia, he had understood that giving should be done in private. *Let me do this one thing, to make it all right.*

It was more of a cry from the heart than a prayer. And he uttered it again as he stumbled through the snow on a particularly cold night at the end of the April, during yet another winter storm. A bitter wind whipped through the streets of Berlin, sent straight from Siberia, cutting even through the Wall that carved the city in half. Jacek walked with his head bent down, his cheeks cracked from the cold. On that particular night, all he could think about was how Tomasz could be anywhere, literally anywhere. Why, the boy might have even completed the circle and returned to America, finishing what Jacek himself had started two generations earlier.

Jacek heard the wind. It moaned in and out of the small streets, catching him by surprise as he turned one corner, leaving him in peace when he passed another. It would be light soon. He could already see some older women, heads bent into the wind, heading for their cleaning jobs. He walked on, unwilling for the hundredth time to give up and turn back.

Bitte.

Had Jacek thought the word or heard it? The plea for help might have come from behind a heap of rubbish, piled against a deserted building. Jacek turned so the wind would not hit him head on, so he could hear better.

"Please."

There it was again. He sighed. How many times had he given a hand up to a drunk or an addict, only to have them sneer in his face when he could give them only a few deutschmarks. He rummaged around the garbage bags and saw a foot. He felt up the leg, throwing aside the oil-soaked rags he found. He was near some sort of car garage. Then he caught sight of black hair. Hands came up as he removed the last cover from the face. Jacek was unsure. He hadn't seen Tomasz in so many years. This was a teenager with dark features, but it couldn't be the same boy whose photo he had carried for so many months.

Or could it?

He reached down and found two hands, nails bitten to the nub. His hands fastened on the arms, bare in this weather, and noticed track marks up and down the underside. *Just another addict*, he thought.

As he pushed the arms aside, a voice cried out in German, "No! Please no! Don't hurt me. Not again, please." And then the boy began to sob.

Jacek felt his heart open up to the anguish curled up in the trash before him. He hardly dared to speak. "Are you Tomasz Piekarz?"

The boy squinted up, shading his eyes despite the early dawn shadows. "What did you say?" he asked, his hands shaking. "Do you . . . do you have some money? Just some spare change maybe? I need . . ." He didn't get any further but started throwing up. He was too weak to even turn aside as he spread filth all over himself.

Jacek bent down and put a few coins in the boy's hand. "Here. It's not enough for what you really want, but it will buy you a meal." Then he turned away. He was looking for a Polish boy, not a German one. And this boy's German had been flawless, showing no trace of a foreign accent. He had even spoken in the Berlin dialect.

He started to walk away, but he could not get the boy's eyes out of his mind. He had seen them for only an instant, but there had been something there, something he recognized. . . .

What if . . . Dangerous words in Jacek's life. He turned slowly around and watched the boy retching again, this time all over one of his hands. Then Jacek called out one word, *"Tomasz!"*

The boy looked up, but not at Jacek. He looked away from Jacek, as if he were trying to remember something, like someone listening to the distant call of horns. Then he collapsed.

It was enough for Jacek. He found a taxi at the next street and returned to the spot, afraid at first that the boy had disappeared.

But he and the driver found him reburied under the plastic bags. When the driver agreed to lift the unconscious boy into the car, he came to again, moaning, *"No! No! Don't take me back! No, don't touch me!"*

But this time he cried out in Polish.

31

All of your treasure to me you impart

Tomasz felt the down crashing around him. He couldn't be sure what Helmut had shot him up with, or how much, but it had been some awful stuff. He knew by the churned-up state of his stomach. Before he'd even opened his eyes, he could smell his own vomit. And only then did he become aware of the motion. Was that why he'd been sick?

He *was* moving. In a car. He heard the motor. And changing directions. Winding roads. The back streets of Berlin. He smelled cigarettes. He *needed* a cigarette. *What I need is a needle and a high.*

Tomasz opened his eyes. He was lying down in the back of a car. City apartments, small windows, white curtains, rising around him. He swallowed, then heaved. Nothing came up. He groaned, cradling his gut.

"You all right back there?"

The voice slam-dunked him into fear. *One of Helmut's men?* Not for the best stuff on the streets would he go back to that maniac. "Hey, who are you?" he answered in German. "What am I doing in this car? Where are you taking me?"

"Let me ask the questions here. How old are you?"

Tomasz coughed, trying to make his voice deeper. "Eighteen."

"Right. And so am I. Let's see . . . I'd put you at thirteen. Am I right?"

Tomasz swallowed more brine. He sat up and the world swiveled right. He squinted at the eyes on the passenger side in the rearview mirror. *Who is he? And how did he know my right age?* Old eyes, but the back of his neck folded over into thick muscles. Tomasz swore. "You can believe me or not. Now answer *my* questions, or

254

I'll jump out of here. I feel sick anyway."

"Let's just say I'm a friend. I put you in the car. And we're going to a nice hotel I know."

Tomasz's gut reaction told him everything he needed to know. Without hesitation, he lunged for the door. Anything would be better than what Helmut and his friends had been doing to him. This was his chance to escape, maybe for good. In a dizzy daze, he threw himself out of the car, tumbled, more pain, rolled, dirt in his mouth. Then he blacked out.

Tomasz came to, feeling cotton sheets all around him. For a devastating moment, he thought he might be back home in his own bed. He waited, wondering if the dream would fade as he woke up more.

"Tomasz?"

An old man's voice. His eyes flew open. Tomasz recognized the voice, the eyes of the man sitting beside his bed, remembered the passenger in the car.

"Let's just say I played a hunch." The man had an evil smile. Tomasz studied his face, strange, no laugh wrinkles, but plenty of the other kind.

"I don't know *who* you are," Tomasz said. "And I don't want you knowing who I am. Look, I don't know why you got me all cleaned up and brought me here, and I don't know what Helmut told you, but I'm not what you think. There's *no way* I'm going to repay you in any way. Got it?"

The old man's smile melted, and he looked down at the floor. Tomasz thought, *Struck a nerve, did I?*

"You're a fighter. That's good," the man mumbled, so Tomasz had to lean forward on one elbow to hear the words. "You'll need that in the weeks to come."

"What 'weeks to come'? You're not hearing me. I didn't ask to be found. You should have just let me go when I rolled out of the car. I won't be anything but trouble. I don't even know who you are, man. And as soon as I'm dressed, I'll be gone again." Tomasz sat up all the way and swung his feet onto the floor. He started to stand, then felt himself fading fast and decided to sit for a few moments longer.

"See," the man said. "You can't go anywhere. Listen, I'm not going to hurt you. I won't even touch you. . . ."

"You undressed me."

The old man blinked. "Let's just say a mutual friend wanted me to get you a little cleaned up."

Tomasz peered at the face. No evil in the eyes, but the rest was just a mask. There was no way to read what he might really be thinking.

"And give you some food."

The moment Tomasz heard the word, he knew he was hungry. Deep-down starving. Like the cool sheets, he hadn't felt a good, warm meal in ages. He hesitated.

The man turned and left the room, then came back pushing a cart with toast and fruit and a hard-boiled egg and bacon. The scent of bacon wafted through the room, instantly clearing Tomasz's lightheadedness. "I'll leave you alone while you think about it," the man said. Before he had even closed the door behind him, Tomasz was pulling the cart up closer to the bed.

Jacek knew he would have to act fast. He had to get the boy out of Berlin, to a safe house, and confirm what his outcry in Polish had indicated. *This is my Tomasz.* He thought the forbidden words as he looked down on the sleeping man-boy in his own bedroom at the boardinghouse. Then he noticed Tomasz had finished every last crumb of his breakfast.

A good sign, but Jacek knew the worst was still to come. Soon they would have to endure the nightmare of withdrawal . . . together. The marks inside the boy's arms and behind his knees told Jacek more than he wanted to know.

One step at a time. Jacek had spent his nearly three months in Berlin figuring out where he could get what he needed now that the time had come to leave. He waited until Tomasz slept soundly, then made quick work of the list he had put together long ago.

He bought a second-hand car from a market just outside the city center where he could pay in cash and get all the papers in order. A three-year-old Opel. Not too noticeable in Berlin, although it might stand out where he was going. No matter.

Then he met with a man whose highest recommendation was that both sides bought passports from him. East and West. It didn't matter to Jacek. The important thing was, for a price, this man could sell him two Swedish passports. Jacek gave him photos of Tomasz taken just after he had brought him his breakfast, during one of the few moments Tomasz had been coherent, when he returned suddenly with his camera. Tomasz hadn't been happy then, and the photo showed it.

Jacek smiled at the picture, slapped the passports against his palm, then slipped them into his inside coat pocket. The likeness was good enough, and certainly better than the photo Piotr had given him. As far as Jacek was concerned, the Polish and American passports he still carried could too easily target him for the two antagonists he was still running from. The Polish SB and the American CIA.

As he drove back to the boardinghouse, Jacek thought how lucky he had been while in Berlin not to be discovered by the U.S. intelligence network. It was the reason why he'd waited so long to buy a car. The less of a paper trail he left behind, the better. When he logged on to that computer in the embassy on his first day in the city, it should have sounded all sorts of alarms. He had been a hunted man ever since, even as he hunted for Tomasz those last months. With the video film and maybe even fingerprints, they should have found him and locked him away forever. *Maybe they have more important things to do,* he thought. All the same, he'd be glad to finally escape Berlin. Spending these past months in a rented private room, instead of staying in a hotel, had probably been what saved him.

"You! I need you to help me get my car loaded! Watch my car, then come up in ten minutes." Jacek threw his keys at the boardinghouse owner's son, a young man around twenty. Then Jacek turned to the owner.

"I'll be checking out today. I'd like to settle the account . . . er . . . plus some extra in case anyone asks any questions after I'm gone. Understand?"

"Yes, sir." The man's eye's lit up when he saw the 100 DM note.

"Let me just get upstairs and packed. I need to get my young friend to a hospital, so you'll have to carry him down for me, all right?"

"My son will do it, no problem," said the owner.

As Jacek started up the familiar stairs, he felt a premonition creep up his spine. He knew enough about his own instincts to trust them. Despite his fatigue, Jacek charged up the stairs two at a time, crushing his packages under his arm as he ran.

He fumbled with the key. When Jacek entered his room, his heart flew into his mouth. *No Tomasz.* The bed was empty, sheets lay askew, and the cart was knocked over. Jacek swallowed hard as he closed the door behind him and went down a mental checklist. The door had been locked. The window was too high. He stood in the room, turning in a circle, his heart beating hard. He checked the closet, then thought of the bathroom. A tiny corner of the room, it was barely large enough to house a toilet and shower behind one door. As he pushed the door open, it jammed.

Relief flooded over Jacek as he stooped down to feel with one hand around the door and felt Tomasz's head leaning up against the wall. He maneuvered the boy around the toilet and out of the little cubicle. He'd been sick again. Jacek quickly cleaned him up, an act already reassuring in its familiarity. When Tomasz remained unconscious, Jacek put the new clothes on Tomasz he had just bought. Then he threw the rest of the packages he'd acquired at the department store that morning into his suitcase. He was packed in five minutes.

It was hard to believe he had only found Tomasz late last night. *Early this morning*, he corrected himself as he let the owner's son into the room and followed him as he carried Tomasz to the car. After the man carefully lay Tomasz across the backseat, Jacek covered him with a blanket, tipped the man, locked the doors, and slid in behind the steering wheel.

"Here we go, Tomasz. We're both going back home."

Less than an hour later, while waiting in line at the border, Jacek felt nervous. How often in his long and tortuous life had he done something like this, something illegal, something clandestine, something wrong for a greater good? He'd managed it then, he told himself. Now, with everything riding on his getting through the border crossings, he'd manage again.

The car crawled forward. He slipped the two passports out of the window and nodded at the green-uniformed West German guard. *Stamp, stamp. Stamp, stamp.*

Then across no-man's-land. High watchtowers. Barbed wire, guards, and dogs. He thought of a story in the newspaper he had bought that morning of an East German student who had tunneled to the river *Spree*, tried swimming across, but was shot down like a dog and left to drown by an East German boat patrol. Jacek shook his head. *Think like a Swedish businessman bringing a sick cousin back with him to Poland.*

Guards peering into his car. Into everyone's car. More lines, more dogs, guns, surrounded by guns. Jacek had gone to Berlin unarmed for a reason. *East Germans*, he thought bitterly. *Their propaganda blames the West Germans for the war.*

When it was finally the turn of the car in front of him, Jacek heard a groan from the backseat. *Oh no, not now.* He pulled up into the next slot and rolled his window down. In his rearview mirror he could see the blanketed bundle stirring on the backseat.

He told himself to be calm. They wouldn't be strict about going *into* East Germany from the West. He gave the guard his story and explained that the boy in the back was sick. The guard grunted and stamped both their passports. Then he was through.

Jacek passed by a line of trucks on the opposite side of the road, waiting to get out of East Germany. One of the drivers disappeared into the woods. A helicopter patrolled the periphery. Jacek sailed by them all and tuned the radio to a classical station. He heard no more sounds coming from the backseat.

As Jacek drove the hobbled cement slabs laid by Hitler and not improved since, he smiled. *I'm like the East German roads*, he thought. *Old and obsolete, too much trouble to replace, but I get the job done.*

He had to admit to himself he had been shocked at the drastic difference between East and West. His visit to West Berlin had been Jacek's first time out from behind the Iron Curtain in . . . he thought back. Since before the war? The trip to Berlin in August 1939, when he had tried to show them a way of ending the pending war swiftly.

"So much for following my advice," he said out loud.

"What's that?"

"Ah, you're awake."

"Yeah, I'm awake. Where am I? And what are these clothes I'm wearing? Where are you taking me?"

Jacek had checked the child-lock function inside the back doors before he bought the car that morning. There would be no repeat of the taxi escape fiasco earlier that day. If need be, Jacek had tranquilizers with him. He hated to use them with all the other stuff in Tomasz's system, but he would if it meant keeping the boy safe. Tomasz wouldn't be jumping out of this car. He saw Tomasz sit up and rub his head.

"Man, I feel awful."

"I can imagine. Are you hungry?"

"No."

"Good, because I don't feel like cleaning you up again."

No reaction. Jacek held his foot down and pulled out to pass a string of trucks, diesel spewing out of their exhausts. When he looked in the mirror again, he was surprised to see Tomasz staring at him in a mixture of admiration and fear. "Never gone that fast before?" Jacek asked. But his hope of finding some common ground failed as Tomasz turned to stare out the window.

They drove on in silence for the rest of the afternoon. He'd spent the morning getting ready. They left Berlin at eleven and pulled into a hotel just north of *Cottbus*, west of *Olszyna*, the southern border crossing with Poland, just as it was getting dark.

Tomasz had said nothing more the rest of the trip. Now he meekly followed Jacek into the huge lobby, then the elevator, and then the simple room with two narrow, hard beds. A shower was at one end of the hall and a toilet at the other. Their room shared closet space with two other rooms in a sort-of entryway. Jacek was careful to park the car under the window of the room so he could keep an eye on it.

It was a huge beast of a hotel, and it looked as though they had it all to themselves. *Probably something used for Party congresses,* Jacek thought. The towel in the bathroom was dirty. No hot water in the shower. The sink in their room was cracked. The faucet contained only rust-colored water.

Tomasz had refused to eat anything since breakfast. When he dozed off again, Jacek sneaked downstairs to the lobby. He saw a huge dining room with all the tables set and thought, *It's as if they expect half the Politburo.* One waitress, sitting on a wooden chair in the corner, smoking, looked up as Jacek entered.

"I'd like to buy some food."

"Don't have any. Kitchen's closed."

"What about some bottled water, then," Jacek said.

She grunted and shuffled across the room to a small refrigerator. Jacek shook his head at her apron and slippers. She returned with a small glass bottle. "Do you have a bigger size?"

"No, this is all we have."

"All right. And some soda. Put it on my tab."

"You have to pay here for the drinks."

Jacek sighed. He didn't like leaving Tomasz alone for so long.

While he waited, he checked the parking lot one more time. It was still vacant around Jacek's car.

As Jacek returned to his room, he reflected on how Tomasz had spent most of the day sleeping off whatever it was he had done, *or had done to him*, Jacek thought. He knew he couldn't count on much more than a day or two before . . . *one step at a time*, he reminded himself.

He was beat. Jacek hadn't felt a pillow under his head for more than twenty-four hours. The elevator halted at Jacek's floor, and he pushed the outer door open. When he looked up, he saw Tomasz's bare back disappearing around the corner of the hall.

Jacek did not run after him. After all, there was nowhere Tomasz could go. He picked up his pace, noticing the bright red carpet with *fleur-de-lis* patterns in gold, and mildew along the edges in brown. As he caught up with Tomasz, Jacek thought it was such a strange sight, this half-dressed, lost teenager wandering down the empty hall of a hotel like this, no one inside, with all those doors to empty rooms.

"Tomasz?" He matched Tomasz's stride, then reached out a hand to touch his elbow.

The boy didn't stop, didn't even turn to acknowledge Jacek's face. "Hey," Jacek said louder. "Where are you going? Stop. Look, you're not dressed. You're shaking from the cold."

Tomasz slowed and stood still, then looked down at his body. He was dressed only in his underwear and socks. "Who are you? Where am I?" he asked.

"I'm a . . . doctor. A special doctor. I've been sent to take care of you."

Tomasz shook his head slowly back and forth. But he allowed Jacek now to lead him back to their room as Jacek continued. "Don't you remember? I found you early this morning, and you've been in the car all day. Tomasz, don't you remember this morning? Do you remember what we did today?"

The boy looked blankly at Jacek. He was glad when they reached the room and he could lock the door behind them. "Here, why don't you just go to bed? I'll get ready too." Jacek didn't quite know what to do with the comatose gaze staring at him. He sat Tomasz on his bed and turned around to get undressed, when he heard the voice.

"Why do you call me Tomasz?"

"I thought that was your name." Jacek was pulling off his pants when he turned around to look at Tomasz. The boy looked him up and down as a slow terror crept into his stare.

"Unless, is this like when Gonia came? *Who are you?*" Tomasz started to back away from Jacek, then stopped when his back hit the wall. He crouched on the bed and looked at himself, registering that he was undressed, then he looked at Jacek and realized the same of him.

Jacek could see the panic pounding against him. Tomasz looked desperately to the side, eyed the window, then started sliding in that direction. Jacek hated to do it, but he was afraid of what Tomasz might try. He knew he was not stronger than the boy. Not anymore. He quickly reached into his bag and pulled out the hypodermic needle and one of the tranquilizer vials he had bought that morning.

"No! Please, no! Not again. I promise I'll be good!" His screaming echoed through the empty stone building.

"It's all right, Tomasz. This is just to help you sleep. Please trust me." Jacek was desperate. He filled the needle to the right amount, then squirted a few drops out. As he approached Tomasz, the boy held up his hands to push Jacek away. Then Tomasz tripped on the pillow and tumbled onto the bed. Jacek moved fast. He aimed at the boy's shoulder and pushed the needle in, moved the fluid forward with his thumb, then removed the needle.

"No! No more, I said! No!" Tomasz crept away into a corner and sobbed.

Jacek was panting. He waited. The doctor who sold him the medicine had said it would take twenty seconds. He waited and counted, not saying anything, shaking from the effort, the room charged with emotion.

When Tomasz's head started to bob, Jacek slid over beside him. Old man's body against young man's, his sagging muscles and gray chest hairs pressed up against Tomasz's back. His gnarled arms around the smooth arms of Tomasz. He wrapped his own old body around him and held the boy beside his heart, willing him to make it through a worse torture than any enemy ever wreaked on Jacek. Jacek smelled his adolescent sweat and felt the tremors run up and down the boy's spine as the muscle relaxant took effect.

Let us shiver in the shadows together, Jacek thought suddenly. The boy's acknowledgment of Gonia had been Jacek's first definite confirmation of who Tomasz really was.

Worse still was who Tomasz thought Jacek embodied. For Jacek, it was the ultimate irony. In Jacek's twisted world of playing all the sides and none, he had become his grandson's worst enemy.

Tomasz woke up from a dream about Heike. *Or was it a dream?* He saw her long, blond hair, could almost feel it. And she was speaking to him in Polish, instead of German. He didn't want to wake up, to face what his body was asking of him.

Now Tomasz blinked, wide awake, and said out loud to himself, "I have to find Heike." Tomasz knew why he had been dreaming of her. He needed Heike. She always knew how and where to score. His right hand stroked the inside of his left elbow, tracing the track marks up and down. How long had it been since he'd last shot up? He couldn't be sure. His hands shook uncontrollably. *Bad sign*, he thought.

Tomasz scratched his head, then cried out in surprise. "What the. . . ?" His hair was all gone, shaven to a short stubble. He ran his hand over the butch cut and felt only the even length. "Hey!" he called out. No sound. He slowly got himself out of bed and walked over to the door, but when he pulled the handle down, nothing gave. "You mean I'm locked in here?" he shouted again. Still no answer.

The effort had brought back the thudding sensation in his head. He'd have to move slower. Tomasz turned and faced the room. Wasn't this place different from the last place he'd been put in? He shook his head. He couldn't be sure. Across the room, a curtain darkened the window. He didn't hear any traffic.

He thought of how real the dream seemed. He missed Heike. Her softness. It was almost as if she'd been in that bed with him. That's how close she still felt after the dream.

He staggered over to the sink and smiled at the reflection in the mirror. *Now you even look like a smack-head.* It was worse than he'd imagined. His hand rose again to the top of his head, unbelieving. His punk cut, with a strip of black hair running down the middle of his head, had been one of the few things Tomasz was proud of about himself. The dark eyes, ringed with shadows, what else was different with his face? A little bit of stubble.

Then Tomasz knew. *Hey, I'm not dirty*, he realized suddenly, followed by, *So he washed me, as well as undressed me.*

Tomasz's knees gave out and he sagged, holding on to the wash-basin to keep from falling. *I have to get out of here. I've gone without way too long.* Against his will, Tomasz felt his body folding onto the floor. He knew what was ahead. Helmut had played this game with him before. The shakes, the hallucinations, wanting it more than wanting to breathe, until he *would* do anything for that needle blessedly back in his arm.

"*No!*" Tomasz yelled, despite the pounding in his head. Never again would he let himself be used like that again. The door opened slowly, and he saw a man's legs and feet walk in. Walk toward him. "No! No, go away!" he screamed.

How much time has passed? Tomasz can still feel he is on the floor. He feels his cheeks, wet with tears. He hears a little girl's voice, again speaking Polish. Everyone here does. He just knows that. She comes skipping around the end of the bed. Brown curls hang in her eyes. He hears her voice, calling out his name as a little boy, "Tomku, Tomku, I found where you are hiding!"

She looks so happy. Doesn't she know? Tomasz wonders. Doesn't she know what? He tries to remember, tries hard to re-member what it is she doesn't know. He watches the little hands clapping back and forth, back and forth. He reaches toward her, and then remembers. "Gonia?" The girl looks up and smiles at Tomasz. "Gonia, how old are you now?"

"I'm four." One of the pudgy hands goes up while the other holds the thumb down.

"Gonia!" This time he shouts at her, and she backs away a few steps. "Gonia!" What didn't she know? "Gonia! Gonia!"

Tomasz finds himself in a bed. Not cold. Hands on his forehead.

He opens his eyes and tries to focus on his mother as she says, "It's all right. Hush now. It's hard, I know. But you can do this, Tomku. You're strong. It's not the first time you've been through withdrawal, is it?"

How does she know? he wonders. Where is he? Another voice, his father's. "You're a good boy, Tomku. A little wild, but a good boy." No, he thinks, that can't be his father. He blinks, more tears.

He groaned and looked up again. A stranger. An old man. That old man from the car . . .

Tomasz tried to talk, tried to say he wanted to go. He needed something more than bed. "More smack," he heard his voice croak. He motioned with his forefinger and thumb as if he were shooting a needle into his shoulder.

He wants to say something more, but when he opens his mouth, the man puts a spider on his tongue. Tomasz is sure of it. He struggles to get away. He spits the spider out. He feels it crawling up his arm. He hits at it. Over and over.

Then he looks across the room and sees Gonia and Żaneta and both his parents just standing there, watching him, spiders on their faces. Crawling everywhere. He looks up at the ceiling and sees more spiders. *Everywhere. Everywhere!* He starts to brush them off his own face, his arms, even in the bed with him. He screams and screams and screams, "Make them go away! Please, make them go away!"

Then, in a lucid flash, he grabs at the hand on his face again and feels the wrist in his grasp. *Who is this man?* "You have to help me," he hisses.

The man is gone. Tomasz throws himself out of bed and runs for the door. The handle goes down and he can pull the door open.

He sees nothing but darkness. He is afraid to take another step. He leans forward. *What is out there?* Then he is falling, madly reaching out for anything to hold on to, anything at all.

And now he sees himself from very far away, crying in a corner, back beneath the sink.

The strange old man sat beside him. His arm was around Tomasz's shoulders. "You're okay. For now. A rough ride. It's all right. Look at me now."

Tomasz felt the warm hands on his cheeks. Neck turning, facing such dark, empty eyes. Eyes he knew somehow, the same eyes he had seen staring back at him somewhere else.

Old man's voice again. "Tomasz. It *is* all right. Do you hear me? I won't harm you. It's my job to get you through this so you can kick this habit. You want that, don't you?"

"No, I . . . can't." Tomasz panted. He ran his hand over his head and looked at his palm, covered with sweat. His own.

"You can. Come here. I've got you. I'm *here* to help you through this. You're safe here. No one can get you." The old man folded Tomasz into his arms and held him with an iron grip. He smelled of cool cotton and cigarette smoke. He pulled Tomasz's head down against his shoulder, muffling his ears, but Tomasz could have sworn the last words he heard before the shakes started again were, "I won't let you go, son."

Tomasz looks down at himself and sees that his clothes are on. Not his clothes, someone else's, but he is dressed. This is a good thing because he has to leave, has to get out of this hospital or clinic, or whatever sort of place it is.

The doctor isn't anywhere around. When he tries the handle, the door opens. No black void waiting. The smell of food hangs in the air. He is ravenous, but he has to leave. He's waited for the perfect moment. Now is the time to go. He dashes across the floor and heads for a larger door. Wood looms all around him, the floor, the walls, a low, dark roof. Not tiled like a hospital, Tomasz thinks.

He stands, quietly panting, listening. No one around. Where are the nurses in this place? He wonders where the doctor could be. His plan is simple. Get out, get away. Then steal something and score some smack. He knows the streets of Berlin well enough by now to know just the right places where he can jimmy open a car door and steal a stereo. He can almost feel the high already coursing through his veins.

He breathes deep. He knows he doesn't have long before the shakes catch up with him again. Slowly Tomasz jerks open the door, then without looking, he takes off. He runs right, then left, down a hill.

He thinks, *The cars, where are the cars?* Tomasz feels desperate. Soon someone will be after him. That old man. Or maybe Helmut. *No*, he reminds himself. Helmut isn't in this place.

Where am I? He can't get his bearings. *Focus*, Tomasz tells himself. He is having problems seeing the images he passes. He settles into a quiet jog, proud that he's outrun everyone so far. He feels the pounding rhythm of his feet. He is getting tired. He looks down. No shoes. *Just like when that gang beat me up.* He looks behind and sees no one. There are tall, narrow buildings all around him.

He veers left. The cobblestones hurt his feet here. Tomasz is now quite sure he has lost them all. *Who was following me?* He looks right and sees a steeple. Finds a church.

Mamusia had a trick with her hands and fingers. Used to play it with me when I was little and we sang in English.

The church is at the top of a hill. When he finally reaches it, the church looks strange. It is made of wood, colored dark brown and black. The door is locked. The walls are covered in shingles and the domed tower is shaped like an onion. *Like the buildings in Red Square in Moscow.* He always liked the swirling patterns on those towers when he saw the pictures.

What am I thinking? This isn't Moscow. Tomasz stops running and doubles over, panting. *Where are the cars?* When he straightens up, his body begins to tremble.

"Where are the cars?" he says out loud. No one answers. There is no sound of cars. No honking. No sirens. No fumes. He needs a car so he can take something and score. He has to steal something. Maybe back at the clinic, from that doctor. Maybe he has a watch. . . .

Tomasz already knows he can never find his way back there. It is too far away. He staggers around the church and sees an iron gate to the left. He enters through it, shaking even more, and wonders why there are so many weeds. Gravestones rear up to meet him. Stone slabs of death.

Tomasz stumbles on a tree root, then trips. Sobbing, he looks up and sees a name on the granite rising before him. *"Tomasz."* My name? "What's my name doing here?" he calls out. He hears nothing but wind rushing around him.

Tomasz cries out one more time, a sound like a lost animal, before he collapses, sobbing, in the graveyard.

32

He heard the voice calling, "Tomasz! Tomasz, you've got to help me here. I can't carry you by myself."

Tomasz wondered how his life had become such a series of awakenings. His grandmother would have liked that one. It sounded poetic. It seemed all he did lately was wake up from another dark nightmare . . . and every time again, this old doctor was there, nagging him about something.

"That's it. Now open your eyes. Look around, boy. I had quite a time finding you."

Tomasz tried to remember where it was he had gone so he wouldn't be found. Berlin, streets, no cars . . . it came back in chunks. Now, as Tomasz leaned on the strength of the doctor, he struggled to his feet.

"Shall we try again? You okay now?"

Tomasz nodded and looked around. Trees, tall pines and cedars. Oaks, silver birches. His feet were cold, despite the sun. Weeds and wild bluebells with yellow dandelions surrounded him. He turned slowly and saw blackberry bushes, thorns, wild roses, grass, more weeds, moss-covered stones, marble gravestones, names in a script he'd learned at school. *Russian.*

Then he remembered something else. "You didn't take me to Russia, did you?"

The doctor chuckled softly. "That would have been a good one. No, but we're close by. Another twenty kilometers east, and we'd be in the Soviet Union, all right. That's the Ukrainian border." He pointed.

Tomasz blinked. *What happened to Berlin?* He stepped away from

268

the doctor to lean up against a tree.

"You're still weak," the doctor said, "and it's bit of a walk back to the cabin. We'll take it slow. Tomasz," he said more softly. "I'm glad you're back with us. You were somewhere else for so long, I was beginning to wonder if you'd ever come back."

Tomasz looked up, surprised. "Yeah," he answered. "I still can't figure it out. I mean . . ." Then slowly a lovely truth dawned on Tomasz, and he smiled. "I'm back home, aren't I? I'm in Poland?"

The doctor nodded, looking pleased. "Yes, we're both back home." He paused. "You don't mind that I kidnapped you?"

Tomasz shook his head slowly. *Back in Poland?* It took some getting used to. The thought alone was reassuring, almost enough so to erase those nagging little traces of fear at the back of his mind. *What will I have to do to pay him back?*

He was thinking clearly now. If the doctor hadn't tried anything when Tomasz was so sick, there was a good chance he really was safe. *For now.* "I'm back in Poland," he said one more time, just to check out the words. Then in Polish, *"Polska."*

And as if the old German doctor did nothing else every day, he, too, suddenly switched from speaking German to Polish. "Come on. I'm not strong enough to carry you, and your newfound strength could give way anytime."

Tomasz put his arm around the doctor's shoulders, surprised again at how lean and muscled he felt. Then together they negotiated the narrow path between hedges of nettles and wild berries. "Where is this place? What was that building?" Tomasz asked. The path didn't look anything like the route he could remember taking after he fled the hospital.

"Don't you know? I thought maybe you went there because you recognized it. That was a church. A Russian Orthodox church. And this area where we are now was a place where people were tortured during the war."

"Great," Tomasz said unenthusiastically. He saved his breath. It looked as though it would be a while before they reached the main road. *Was* there even a main road? Then he remembered something else. "Hey, how come I don't see any cars?"

The doctor shot a rare smile at Tomasz, then stopped and nodded over his shoulder. Tomasz looked in that direction and didn't see anything at first. Then far, far off, on the third or fourth hillside, he saw a horse-drawn plough to his left. A farmer with a horse?

Tomasz said slowly, "There *are* no cars here."

"Good guess. Now come on, Tomasz. It's a long way back, and I've got to get you back inside."

Tomasz knew why. He was already starting to feel clammy again. He stumbled his way beside the doctor for what seemed an eternity of stones and dirt, only rarely looking up to take in the summer countryside. They were somewhere up high. Mountain-tops to the left with snow still on them. Hills rolling on and on. *There's no one here. No one.* Even though it scared him a little to be so cut off from the rest of the world, Tomasz also felt deeply grateful to be out of Germany and back in Poland.

Then he remembered something else. The *big* disadvantage, of course, would be there was no way he could score out here. The doctor had chosen this place well. Tomasz would have to go cold turkey or die, whichever came first.

"One more hill. Look, there it is," he said.

Tomasz stopped. The thudding in his head pumped in time with his heart. "High altitude, right?" he asked, but the doctor didn't seem to hear him. He was looking down the hill. Tomasz followed his gaze but saw only a small building that looked like a glorified cowshed, with a chimney poking out of one end. Again, a small truth slowly dawned on him. *"That's* where I've been staying?"

"You didn't know, did you?" the doctor asked. "I mean, you thought you knew, wherever it was, Tomasz, you were hallucinating. It's been almost four weeks since you've been this lucid for this long. I think you may have put the worst of withdrawal behind you. Tomasz, look at me. You believe me? Look at you, you're in shock again. Why didn't you tell me you felt so cold?"

Tomasz looked down and saw his entire body tremble uncontrollably. All those things, the people who had come to see him, the sounds, *the smells*, none of it had been real?

Suddenly he knew something else, too. An awful realization dawned on him. If this doctor was any good, he would realize it as well and not try to lie to Tomasz.

The worst *wasn't* over. There would be more visits to his place of torture. For a long time to come, the hallucinations would still be there, lurking in the shadows.

———— ✑ ————

Tomasz had never owned his own pair of hiking boots. And

these were the best brand, authentic *Dachstein*. Tomasz stretched the sock so it lay smoothly in the shoe, then laced up his boot. He enjoyed the new laces, the smell of the leather. The night before, he and the doctor had smeared paraffin on the boots and put them near the fire to bake in the wax layer as waterproofing.

Tomasz took a few steps and enjoyed the heavy clomping noise he now made.

"Ready?" The doctor stood before him, a gnarled walking stick in his right hand.

Tomasz nodded at the piece of wood. "Looks like that's been around a while."

"It has. Just like me. Come on. These walks will be good for you, get you out into the fresh air, let your body concentrate on something besides controlled substances, get you to sweat for a different reason than the shakes."

"You say that a lot to me," Tomasz said quietly.

"What do I say a lot?"

" 'Come on.' It's like you're always trying to get me to go somewhere."

"Maybe I am, maybe I am. Humor an old man, all right? Now . . . *shall we?*"

Tomasz smiled at the last two words spoken in a posh British accent. The doctor wouldn't know Tomasz had an American mother and could speak fluent English. In fact, all the doctor had seemed to know was what he asked in the car that first day, Tomasz's name and age. After that, there had been no more questions at all. *Fine with me*, Tomasz thought.

The two struck out in the opposite direction of the old church. Tomasz was still amazed to walk around in the middle of nowhere like this. The sun shone, birds sang, and there was *no one* in sight. "How'd you find this place?" Tomasz asked as they walked along a small river, following the treeline.

"How are the boots?" the doctor asked.

I guess not asking questions works both ways. "Great," Tomasz answered. He concentrated on keeping up with the doctor. "You move pretty good for an old man. How old are you, anyway?"

The two picked their way across the river, jumping from stone to stone, then set off through the trees, the scent of pines all around them.

"See, I told you it would feel good to be outside," the doctor said.

"Yeah, well, you still haven't answered my question."

The doctor was quiet for so long, Tomasz thought he was ignoring the question as he had so many others. But then, after a few minutes, Tomasz heard one word, "Seventy-nine."

"What?" Tomasz stared at the broad-backed man walking in front of him. There was no way. He wasn't even slightly bent. Why, *Babcia*, his own grandmother, was only sixty-eight, and she was in awful shape. Well, she was sick, too. Still. On the other hand, his hair *was* snow-white. "You're almost eighty?" He ran up and took the doctor by the arm, forcing him to stop.

The doctor turned, and Tomasz was surprised by a look of such longing, it almost hurt to watch. Then it was gone and Tomasz wondered if he'd seen right.

The doctor said, "Yeah, hard to believe, isn't it?"

Tomasz didn't want to give away what he thought he'd caught a glimpse of. He said quickly, "Well, this clinic. I mean, this isn't a clinic at all, not a hospital. It's just you and me here in the middle of nowhere."

"Your point being. . . ?"

"Who are you, and what are we doing here? Admit it. You're not really a doctor, are you?" The old man walked away from Tomasz without a word. Tomasz had trouble keeping up. *He's in great shape for almost eighty.* When no answer came, he tried another tack. "And is that really true? Are you really seventy-nine?"

"Yes, I am. You know what? Now *I* just thought of something. I think you're the only person in the world who knows my real age. And that's the truth as well. As far as who I am and what we're doing here, I've told you already." As Tomasz came alongside, he added, "Look, Tomasz, what better place to quit a habit? Here, no one heard your screaming. I'm the only one you have to worry about. Most important, there's no one to smuggle smack in when I'm not looking, and there's absolutely no place you can find it around here. Just what *any* doctor would order, wouldn't you say?"

"I guess we're even now," Tomasz said. "That's only fair. You know my real age, too."

"Yeah, thirteen, right?"

Tomasz looked up. They had just reached a level point, and through the trees, Tomasz could see an alpine meadow, grass moving gently in waves of wind. He stopped to catch his breath, but also because a thought had just dawned on him.

"What is it?" the doctor asked.

"I was just thinking. You said I've been here awhile. What month is it now?"

"June."

Tomasz looked across the meadow blanketed in wildflowers. The colors and smells washed over him in a sea of sunshine. White, yellow, purple, he could hardly count all the different shades and colors. "Then I've had another birthday. I'm *fourteen*." Tomasz grinned as if he'd just discovered something remarkable.

The doctor reached out and shook his hand, laughing. "Well, well, congratulations to you then, Tomasz. And may your fourteenth year be a better one than your thirteenth."

Tomasz glanced at the doctor. How could he know what kind of year Tomasz had had? Well, he could probably guess, given the circumstances. He returned the smile. "Thanks." He stroked his chin, wondering if now he'd be growing more of a beard, although he'd never want one as big and bushy as the doctor's. "Fourteen. Not bad, huh?"

"Not bad, Tomasz, not bad."

Tomasz lay down in the tall grass. Somewhere to the right lay the good doctor. It was like being in a fort. They couldn't see each other, despite only being a meter apart. Gold and green grass swayed above his head, while he chewed on one strand, trying to feel like Huckleberry Finn in one of his mother's books. Beyond the grass, he could see a hawk circling. *Hunting field mice, probably.*

"Doc?"

"What did you call me?" the voice in the grass to his right said.

"Doc? I've done this before. And, well, there's more. I'm not better yet."

"I know."

"What I mean is, I'm going to be getting these crazy attacks, you know, when I trip out and don't know where I am, and, well, you know. I'm going to be getting them for a while, aren't I? That's how it was the last time, until I finally scored. And then that felt *so* rich." Tomasz hadn't meant to give away so much. But he could almost taste that first high when Helmut finally had given him the stuff. It had been sweet.

"I know. One day at a time."

Tomasz thought about this while watching a ladybug crawl across his stomach. It sounded good, but he just didn't think he could make it work. Here, Tomasz was more afraid of himself and what he might do than anyone else, least of all a seventy-nine-year-old man.

33

High King of heaven, the first in my heart

An odyssey, my last one. Jacek stood in the doorway and gazed on the cloud of July wildflowers engulfing them, surrounding them, spread right and left. Then he turned around to check the inside of what had been their home for nearly three months.

The little low, sprawling cabin Jacek had rented for them contained one main room with a wood-burning stove, candlelight, mattresses of straw, and clear running water pumped in from the spring at the back of the house. His pack leaned against the fireplace wall. The single bedroom contained a sink. The outhouse was near the woodpile out back.

Jacek leaned over to poke the fireplace and make sure no embers lingered. As he straightened up, a wave of nostalgia washed over him. Here, in this place, he had tried to make up for all the years of no contact. He had condensed a lifetime of longing into a few months of nursing Tomasz as tenderly as he knew how.

Gabi. Why think of her—why now? Yes, she had been the one to care for Jacek, as he had cared for Tomasz. In fact, the only time Jacek ever had someone take care of him was when Gabi nursed him after both his legs had been broken by Roman's men. And this season with Tomasz had been Jacek's only time in his life when he, in turn, had cared for another.

Jacek had to admit that he had subconsciously imitated Gabi's skills when learning how to make Tomasz comfortable. Strange how the inconsequential acts of cleaning and taking care of the physical needs of someone weaker could bring about healing. Jacek thought of all the little things Gabi had done for him and realized she had been a good teacher. The proof stood outside now, waiting for him. And Gabi? Where was she?

It doesn't matter, he thought. *Nothing matters. After where I'm going now and what I will do afterward, I don't care where Jurek and Gabi and Roman and all the rest of them might be. I just don't care anymore.*

It was time to go. He heaved his pack over one shoulder, took up his walking stick, and closed the door behind him. Tomasz stood beside the gate. As he headed in that direction, Jacek knew an overwhelming sense of anticipation. Tomasz's grin welcomed him as they both shared the excitement of a journey just beginning.

Later that afternoon, Jacek paused to watch the boy forge on ahead of him. The river they crossed raced beneath the wood-and-rope bridge, its rushing current visible from between the slats. He stopped and looked left at the trees and hills, and then to the higher range on the right. Beyond the timberline, snow was still melting, swelling rivers like the one beneath him now.

"If you're scared of heights, we won't get far," Tomasz yelled back at him from the other side.

Jacek waved back at his young companion. The trip had been his idea, a way out of the dark confines of the cabin, a means of pushing onward. *For us both*, he thought.

For although Tomasz had experienced fewer spells of hallucination during the last weeks, his days and nights had been marked by fear. There had even been periods of several days when Tomasz did not dare to venture from the cabin. This trip was his last step in confronting that dread.

In a strange sort of way, Jacek was grateful for the nature of this fear. For somewhere during their time in the cabin, Tomasz had decided to trust him, unwillingly maybe, begrudgingly, but at least Tomasz's fear had not been aimed at Jacek. They had shared a major breakthrough when he had coaxed the boy out for his first hike in the high grass, his first walk to see where he actually was.

Jacek lifted his gaze to above the trees on the other side of the river, to where he heard an eagle call. *And now it's time to venture forth one last time.* Away from darkness, into the light. So if there were any more flashbacks, any more gaps in the boy's conscious perception, any more blackouts, now Tomasz could face them outside, no shadows in sight.

Tomasz started jumping on the other side of the bridge, causing it to sway back and forth. "Now try! Come on, Doc," he shouted at Jacek, laughing.

Jacek couldn't help but smile back. When had he *ever* felt as young as Tomasz now looked? He finished crossing the bridge, then said, "I *knew* there was a reason I gave you the big pack with all the gear. Mine's nice and light."

As they headed up the trail, Tomasz said, "All right. So where are we going?"

"See that ridge to the right? And the one behind it? Well, the one *behind* that is the first summit. There will be three."

"You know where we're going?"

Jacek nodded, then added under his breath, "And by the time we're finished, so will you."

Żaneta and her uncle Piotr crossed the main road on the other side of the parking lot behind the church. The sound of screeching brakes came up right behind them as three milicja vans bounced onto the same curb where they waited for the light to change. Men in masks and bulletproof vests poured out of the van.

Piotr said gently, "Just stand. And when the light changes, we walk on. Just keep going as if nothing is happening."

Żaneta knew full well it was a forbidden place to go. But her parents had told her, "Stay close to Piotr and you'll be fine."

When they finally reached the church and pushed open the doors that morning, Żaneta noticed the building was almost empty. St. Brygida's was more than just another church in Gdańsk. It was the patron church of the illegal Solidarność movement.

"Will we see Wałęsa?" Żaneta whispered, careful to close the doors quietly behind her.

"No," Piotr answered. "I doubt it, although this is Wałęsa's home church. Look, that man praying in the far pew is Tadeusz Mazowiecki."

Żaneta stared at the tall, stooped man with his face cradled in his hands. Piotr led her to the back of the church and whispered, "In some ways, he is even more important than Wałęsa."

"Tatuś says he is a good man."

"He is a good leader, a true statesman. The power of his words stand on their own strength."

"Why is he so important?"

"Because he stands for unity. He has helped the workers of Solidarność join forces with the intelligentsia in the movement. Mark my words. He and Wałęsa are an unbeatable team."

Żaneta watched the man cross himself and stand, then walk slowly out the doors she had just entered through. His face looked drawn and haggard. Her uncle's words sounded strange in this place. She looked up at the ceiling and the banners hanging down all around them. Red-and-white Solidarność flags and posters, all illegal, still hung there for all the world to see. In this church the milicja did not dare to take them down.

"Here," Piotr said. "I'll show you around."

Żaneta walked around the pews. She paused at the shrine to Father Jerzy Popiełuszko, covered with fresh bouquets of flowers. "I can remember when everyone was so upset about his kidnapping," she said.

Then they walked toward the front of the church. On the right-hand side hung a small plaque, commemorating the victims of *Katyń*. She whispered the word softly.

"Yes, another so-called 'illegal' acclaim. A mass grave of Polish officers. The Soviets murdered them during the war but tried to pin it on the Germans. Even today it's forbidden to talk about, but that doesn't make it go away, does it? The loss of an entire generation's captains and leaders. . . ."

Żaneta nodded, but she was thinking of something else as Piotr continued. "This madness of lies and denials and deception has to end. Martial law has gone on long enough. You can't even remember any differently. How old are you? Ten?"

"Eleven," she corrected him. "Babcia says, about the war, God seems to test us in six-year gaps. If that's true, then martial law might end soon."

He raised his eyebrows. "She said that, did she?"

Żaneta looked at her uncle. He was rubbing his forehead. "Go on," she said.

"It's just . . . I once tried to go to Katyń. And I knew a man once . . . I haven't heard from him in a long time. He was probably the only man to escape Katyń alive." He paused. "I think of him every day. Strange, huh?"

"Not so strange, really. I do that, too," she said.

"What?" Piotr asked as they crossed the church, back toward the entrance.

Żaneta could hear their own footsteps and no one else's. With one hand on the heavy door, Piotr turned back to look in the direction of the altar. Żaneta followed his gaze and repeated, "I think of someone every day, too."

He looked down at her, and Żaneta could tell he knew what she meant. Then his eyes lifted, moved, and came to rest on the crucifix. Żaneta watched as Piotr closed them and mouthed the word she thought at that moment, the name she remembered every day, the brother she had lost more than a year earlier.

Tomasz.

A blanket of stars. Now Tomasz knew what the term meant as he stretched out in his sleeping bag and looked up, wiggling his toes. Tonight he would lie here and this would be his blanket. The old man was in the tent. He would lie awake all night, he promised himself, and the stars would keep him company as they rotated from one side of the sky to the other.

"Feel good?" the doctor asked.

Tomasz rolled over onto his elbow. "I thought you'd gone to bed."

"Well, I was just coming back from those bushes over there, and I saw you by the fire. It seemed inviting. Mind if I sit with you a little longer? Will you be all right alone out here like this?"

"You asked me that already."

They were both quiet for a moment. Then the doctor said, "Not bad for a first day, huh? You'll be sore tomorrow."

"No, Doc, *you'll* be sore tomorrow." They both chuckled. Tomasz wouldn't admit it, but he was *way* out of shape. And a part of him looked forward to hardening all the soft muscles he could feel tightening in his legs and back as they tried to relax now.

"Your pack is the heaviest," the doctor said.

"Yeah, well, you're old. And crazy. Who goes backpacking at your age?"

Jacek raised an eyebrow at him. When he didn't answer, Tomasz continued. "But you've done this before, I can tell," Tomasz said.

"No, not really. Not trekking like this."

"Great. But you've *been* here before, you said."

"That's right. I've been here before."

Tomasz waited, but the old man said nothing more. Typical. He'd say something, and then because nothing came after it, he made it sound as if it had a double meaning. Right then, Tomasz didn't mind. He was busy trying to recognize a figure other than Orion. The stars looked close enough to reach down and brush against his cheeks. There were so many of them, he couldn't even figure out the major constellations.

And then a star did fall. And another and another. He caught his breath and heard the doctor do the same, so he knew he had seen it, too. Pinpoints of light showered down from all sides of the sky. Tomasz lost track of the trails. He held his breath, wishing and willing it never to stop.

He wanted it to mean that his one wish would now come true. As Tomasz visualized it, his heart ached in the same way the sky above him seemed to, bleeding drops of light. His one big wish consumed Tomasz, became everything to the boy for those few moments, as big as the meteor shower filling the space above him.

And then, as suddenly as it started, the lights raining down ceased. The stars stayed put, where they belonged, and Tomasz let out a long breath, as filled by the sight as the sky above him. He heard a movement beside him and turned back onto his side just in time to catch the back of the doctor as he stooped and disappeared into the tent.

Tomasz lay in the dark, still from the sight he had just witnessed. Tomasz worked on his plan. He had a wish and he had a plan.

He *had* had a plan. He had thought he'd run away tonight on their first night out. Especially when the doctor said he would sleep in the tent, Tomasz knew he could slip away now. But they had come so far today, Tomasz was afraid he couldn't find his way back, not in the dark anyway.

He had been working on his plan to run away for two weeks. He thought he was ready. Now it occurred to him that maybe the doctor had taken him up into the mountains, only a short while after he had felt confident enough to leave their cabin, as a way of preventing him from running away. The old man was no dummy, that was for sure. But did he really think that leading Tomasz into the mountains would keep him from finding a way home? Yet, now that Tomasz really thought about it, he had to admit, there must be other reasons. Maybe even a trip like this would be good for him. *Good for both of them*, that's what the old man had said. That *he* needed it as much as Tomasz.

Tomasz closed his eyes and still saw the silhouette of pines. He made his decision to stay. *How often will I have the chance to trek through mountains like this? I know where I am. I can head back anytime I choose. Hitch up north.*

But there *was* another reason. Tomasz was afraid. And this he could admit in the dark. Afraid of being alone, afraid of what might happen if he headed off on his own. The doctor had said he would be going home as soon as he was well enough. Maybe it was strange, but Tomasz trusted the old man. And this was his last thought as the moon chased all his other thoughts out from between the shadows of sleep. *There is no need to run away.*

In the days to come, Tomasz did not regret his decision. His plan may have changed, but his wish would remain the same, as swollen as the studded sky that waited for him faithfully every night again.

The wish grew as the days slipped by in an easy rhythm. Sun, wide vistas, new summits, variations of snowscapes, grass blowing in the summer breeze, swollen brooks, trees bowing down to welcome them. Tomasz's body hardened. He slept soundly every night and began to believe there was a life after death, the death of a dying drugs dependence within his own body.

One day, just after they had negotiated a particularly difficult slope, Tomasz stood waiting for the doctor to catch up. He looked out over the panorama and tried to count the different shades of color spread out before him. He was remembering many things hiking in these mountains—his time in Berlin . . . his time home.

When the doctor finally reached him, the old man panted, "Boy, I could really use a cigarette."

Tomasz glanced at him and said, "Me too. When did you give them up?"

"The same time you did. It was the least I could do. Your body was giving up so many things at the time. Solidarność, right?"

"What do you mean?"

"Well, maybe I wanted a way to struggle just a little in the same way you were struggling with your body and kicking your habit."

Tomasz didn't know what he should say. He rubbed his scalp. The hair was growing back in, even if it was all one length. "So you gave up smoking and shaved my head. Bet *that* was difficult."

"You had lice," the doctor said. Then he stood and smiled down at Tomasz. "Rested? Let's go."

As the days slipped away in summer easiness, they sometimes entered tiny villages for supplies. In these places Tomasz noticed only certain things. An old woman crossing the trail, leading a string of cows by chains. Small front gardens overflowing with phlox, white, pink, purple, giant marigolds, dahlias, and zinnias. Outside the villages fields dotted with horses pulling the harvesting machinery. Next to that, an old woman with a scarf and scythe. A whole family busy stacking hay. Houses of brick, tendrils of mist floating between the hills, cedars mixed with oaks.

Other times, whole days would pass when they saw no other hikers on the trail. Only fog-cloaked lakes and startled deer. Trees and light marked their path. He and the doctor played naming games with the different wildflowers they found, new ones each day, purple, yellow, and blue. Meadowed hills and, suddenly, another Russian orthodox chapel, no bigger than a few square meters, tucked on the side of the path, left like an afterthought along the way.

One village was named *Cicha Woda*, Quiet Waters. The mountain names haunted them like a litany, *Berdo, Hyrlata, Rosocha*, and then across the *Puszcza Bukowa* up into the high summits of the *Połonina Bukowska*, calling them by name, reciting them like the beads of a rosary, *Szeroki Wierch, Kopa Bukowska*, and *Wołowe*. Once in the southeasternmost corner, they doubled back, heading north, still stopping at the occasional village for supplies, *Muczne* and tiny *Smolnik*, only a few kilometers from the Ukrainian border.

Whenever they reached another summit, Tomasz got high on the breathless view. Before and behind him was endless gold above the treeline, and above that, snow. Then they'd drop back down again and be surrounded by beech, silver birch, oak, pines, and spruce.

Tomasz noticed on their map that they steered clear of the more crowded areas in the middle of the Bieszczady, where the town of *Solina* split the lake district. The map also showed a string of villages, marked as sites of torture during the war. One was called *Stefkowa*, or *Stefko's Wife's Village*, Tomasz translated to himself.

Day after day, blue sky mixed with a thousand shades of green, all the brighter because of the clear mountain air. And each morning Tomasz felt as though a headache had just lifted again.

As they crisscrossed the range, sometimes they stopped at travel inns and ate *pierogi ruskie*, boiled dumplings with mashed potatoes and cottage cheese. Storks rested on haystacks. Eagles circled above Tomasz. Other times they went church hunting, looking for the wooden steeples hidden in trees, domed crosses peeking out from their hiding places.

In one of the remoter corners of the mountains, away from any villages, the doctor took him on a detour and showed him a large stone lodge on the other side of a valley. "Look at that place."

"Why?"

"I used to live there."

Tomasz looked at him strangely.

"Odd," the doctor said.

"What?" Tomasz asked.

"I just realized. We've seen no wolves on this trip."

That same day they had left the trail and were heading cross-country when Tomasz caught sight of bear tracks. They followed them and only realized they were pursuing two bears when the paths split. The doctor went right and Tomasz went left. Tomasz soon lost the trail and turned back around. Just as he reached the original fork in the trail though, he heard the doctor cry out.

Tomasz didn't even pause. The adrenalin took over as he broke into a sprint despite the heavy pack. When he reached the other side of a copse of trees, he called out, "Doc? Where are you?"

"Down here," came the answer. "Watch your step."

Tomasz looked down, and sure enough, a pit opened up on the other side of the clearing, a few hundred meters ahead of him. He made his way over and looked down. It was a crude animal trap and had been covered in branches until the doctor fell into it.

"Stupid of me. I should have known better."

"What is it?" Tomasz asked.

"Some farmer probably dug it to catch one of the bears we were tracking. The hide would bring a lot of money," the doctor said.

Tomasz started laughing. "You look real official down there. Are you all right? When I heard you yell, I thought you'd broken a hip or something."

The doctor shook his head. "No, I didn't break anything. But I won't be able to get out of here until you throw the rope down and haul me up. Can you do that?"

Tomasz stared down at the doctor and had the strangest sensation, as if he were waking from a long dream. He remembered his plan. And his wish. He hesitated.

"Tomasz? What is it?"

"Zasadska."

"What did you say?"

"That's a zasadska you're in. A real one. A trap, hidden and unsuspected. You fell into one."

"Fine. Now, will you please get me out of here?"

"I did have a plan. There was a time when I would have left you there."

The doctor took off his pack and sat on it. He looked up at Tomasz as if he were resigning himself to something. He sighed, then said, "I never forced you to stay. Once you were no longer a hazard to yourself, I never locked you in any room or building. You always had a choice."

"Right. You just brought me to a godforsaken corner of Poland where there was no possible way for me to go anywhere else. *Then* you let me loose."

"I got you away from the drugs. You were always free to leave whenever you wanted. Especially during these last weeks, I was under the impression that you had *chosen* to stay. This has been a special time for me."

They were both quiet, then the doctor continued. "I thought you stayed because you didn't have anywhere better to go. If you'll get me out of here, I still have one more thing I want to show you."

Tomasz did not answer. But he did take off his pack and unwind the rope hanging from its side. As he lowered it down, he said as firmly as he could manage, "On one condition. I want you to tell me who you are."

Jacek heard the words again. "Who are you?" Tomasz grunted as he slipped in the dirt. And as his face disappeared from Jacek's view, he heard Tomasz say, "It's only what I've been asking ever since I let you get me out of Berlin."

" 'Let you get me out of Berlin?' No, Tomasz. You were in no shape to *let me* do anything. And you stopped asking me who I was." Jacek rubbed his eyes. Without looking up he said, "I am who you want me to be."

"Stop. Just stop, all right? Here, send your pack up. Then hold on to this. But I'm warning you! I'll get you out, but then I need to know *who you are.*"

Jacek threw his strength into climbing up the side of the pit while Tomasz strained to keep the rope from slipping back around the tree. Once on top, he approached Tomasz and laid a hand on his shoulder. Tomasz turned around and smiled at how well he had managed. Then his face clouded over as he said, almost in a whisper, "I know you're not a doctor. I . . . we have seen and shared so much. I wanted to run away but didn't. Because of you. I have one wish, but before I make that wish come true, I really need to know, *Who are you?"*

Jacek thought, *It is time.* He sighed and repeated, "Who do you want me to be?"

Tomasz said. "You're a friend of my family. You said that. Tell me where my mother was born."

Jacek almost choked. *My daughter's birth?* He eased himself down onto a tree stump, mentally refusing to give in to the raw emotions surging through him at that moment. As he rubbed his forehead with one hand, Jacek's face remained a mask. "She's American."

"Are you one of my uncle's friends?"

"Yes."

"From the underground?"

Jacek did not answer.

"I know what those silences mean. *Yes.* So you say you know my uncle Piotr. When did he get out of prison, then?"

And I put him there. I should know, since I signed the release form. "September, almost two years ago now."

"What is your name?

"Jacek Duch."

"Are you really a doctor?"

"No."

"What are you then?"

Jacek paused only long enough to close his eyes, then said, "A spy."

Tomasz spat out the water he was drinking. "What? Oh, man, you must think I'm really dumb."

Then Jacek opened his eyes and met the boy's. *Let him learn. Let the boy learn all he can from the past.*

"No, seriously, not that you have anything to prove after a claim like that, but why don't you try to convince me that you're telling me the truth? Umm, tell me about the war. I assume you were one of the good guys?"

Jacek smiled. "I should begin by telling you I'm more of a friend of your grandfather than of your uncle. Well, I didn't realize I was a friend actually until after he had died. I was more of a . . . guardian, shall we say? You see, a long, long time ago, I saw your grandparents saying good-bye to each other in a train station."

"What city?" Tomasz asked him, interested now and leaning forward.

"Kraków. The Germans had ordered all Poles to stay in the city and help them defend it against the Soviets, so your grandmother escaped, but your grandfather had to remain behind. If he was caught leaving . . ."

"He would have been shot," Tomasz finished for him. "My grandmother told me this. So what you're telling really *is* true."

"It was February 1945. I remember because I believe they were heading for Dresden that night. . . ."

The stories, each one a jewel, ultimately were the only gifts Jacek allowed himself to give his grandson. That day they made camp near the bear pit. And as evening fell, Jacek sat by the fire and told stories of courage and endurance. He brought long-dead heroes back to life. Stories of dark times and Party intrigue, of Poland's undeniable spirit, in spite of its long history of oppression and occupation. Jacek told stories of other spies. Of the Russians and the Germans he had made deals with. He even described the death march he was forced to endure like a driven animal across the frozen steppes before the Soviets let him return to fight the Germans.

As the firelight danced in Tomasz's dark eyes, mirroring his own, so much like his own, Jacek's love for Tomasz grew deeper as he learned to love the boy for who he really was.

All night, the stories knit them together. Jacek told himself he had the relationship of a grandfather with a grandson. It had to be enough. He had told Tomasz everything, everything and nothing. Nothing that could harm him. Nothing that told Tomasz Jacek was his grandfather.

Even as he spoke, Jacek knew that night would be his last with the boy. After tomorrow, he would never see Tomasz again. He could not escape the thought of how all his life had been nothing but mere mime, compared with the stark reality of this moment. Jacek drank in the sight of the boy's face, smelled the fire, heard the night animals around them, and knew this was what he had waited for, what he had waited a lifetime for.

In the morning, Jacek led Tomasz into a small town, saying he wanted to buy supplies. "Come here," Jacek said. "There's something in this place I want to show you."

At the bottom of a hill stood an iron fence with a Star of David on the gate. Jacek pushed open the gate and took off his pack, directing Tomasz to do the same. They left their things behind a tree, then started climbing up a steep hill, surrounded on both sides by trees. As they climbed, they passed clusters of gravestones, growing out of the ground like early-spring crocus.

The stones were covered in moss and twisted every which way, most facing east, some lying facedown, a few broken. The higher they climbed, the more stones surrounded them. To the right, beyond those trees, to the left, a path wound around and between hundreds more.

Tomasz was quiet until they neared the top and he could read the inscription on one of the slabs. He ran his hand over the figures. "It's Hebrew, isn't it?" he asked.

"Yes," Jacek said. "The Jewish community here in *Lesko* is centuries old. 'Was.' Now there is no one left. Last night we talked of history, but this, too, is part of your history, part of Poland's history. I wonder if someday Jews from Israel and America and Canada and all the other places they escaped to will return to spots like this and leave something to remember their former communities by. If they don't, the Poles may. Never forget the tragic history of our country, Tomasz."

"How many families. . . ?"

Jacek turned in a full circle. He couldn't begin to count them. "The synagogue is up that hill over there. I think the oldest graves here date back to the fifteenth century. We are surrounded in this place by families of families, generations of generations, hundreds and hundreds of years."

Tomasz said, "I wish . . ."

"What do you wish?"

"I wish *I* could go home."

"Then go. You're ready." Jacek squinted into the sun.

"You mean it? What if I black out again, like a week ago? What if I can't remember stuff?"

"What is it you told me your father sometimes says? 'It's healing, never whole.' You'll be fine. I knew you'd eventually want to do this. You're ready. Go." Jacek took a deep breath and reached into his pocket. "Here's some money. Catch the train in *Jankowce*. It's not far. You can even take a bus. Go there. Get on that train and go home, Tomasz."

"I don't have a passport. How *did* you get me out of West Berlin?"

"I arranged a false passport, which I've since destroyed, so you can't get into any trouble. By the way, what happened to yours?"

"Stolen." Then he looked up and extended his hand. "I'll tell my uncle his friend took good care of me. You . . . have healed me."

Jacek ignored the outstretched hand and pulled Tomasz to him instead. He hugged the boy, wishing him strength. "Go," he whispered.

Tomasz did not look at him as he descended the hill again, legacies to families long dead and lost rising up on both sides. Jacek watched him come and go from between the shadows. At the gate, Tomasz turned once and waved, then he was gone.

We have healed each other.

PART VI

BREAD OF ANGELS
Psalm 78:2

August 1988

*I would like to finish by expressing great
thankfulness to the Lord for what there was, for
what there is, and for what there is going to be.*

34

Żaneta sat beside her mother and tried counting the number of swans.

"What do you think? A hundred? Two hundred?" Amy asked.

She held up a hand and kept counting. Then she laughed. "It's more than two hundred, that's for sure. Look at them all."

"They come here every year in the summer."

"Where do the swans go in the winter, then?" Żaneta asked.

"I think to Africa. That could be the storks, though. I'm not sure. Anyway, have you finished that ice cream? Do you want to keep on walking or try some more shops?"

"Oh, let's keep walking," Żaneta said. She loved the beach. They had driven to Sopot, the seaside resort between Gdynia and Gdańsk. On a day like this everything sparkled, the water, the waves slapping the pier, the countless swans bobbing in the surf, even the sky.

Żaneta and her mother had gone looking for school supplies. She wanted matching things this year, and a friend of hers had said there was a shop in Sopot with binders and pencil boxes and even day-planners that all matched, with pictures of puppies on the front. Well, they hadn't been able to find them, but they had found a shop with some good bread pans, and even a place with sunscreen in stock. They had spent all their coupons for sugar and candy, as well as fruit and household appliances. And they had to wait in different lines for a good two hours, but it had been worth it. And now they could enjoy the beach and be together.

Żaneta looked over and up at her mother. Their doctor said she probably would be as tall as her mother someday. She opened the tube of sunscreen and smeared it onto her face. "I wish I had skin like yours," she said as they started to walk together.

Amy smiled. "I *do* get dark, but your freckles are so cute."

Żaneta frowned. That was a sore point with her. But red hair and fair skin had doomed her to a lifetime of sunscreen and freckles. "Let's change the subject. I wish I could take my shoes off."

Now it was Amy's turn to frown. "I know. I love to walk in the sand with bare feet, too. But the water is so polluted now. They say there's this bacteria in the sand, and if it gets on your skin, you get a rash that itches. . . ."

". . . And is hard to get rid of, I know," Żaneta said. "But it doesn't seem right, walking on the beach with socks and shoes on in the summer."

"Tell that to the factories that have dumped so many chemicals into the sea."

"It's like no one cares."

"Oh, I think people care, but the government doesn't," Amy said. "I think pollution is a problem everywhere. It's even worse in Russia."

"At school they make jokes about Czernobyl and glow-in-the-dark Russians," Żaneta said.

"Oh, look, there's the restaurant Ewa said we'd meet her at. I'm thirsty. How about you?"

"Sure." Żaneta loved it when they went to a restaurant. They sat down at a table and picked up the menu.

When the waitress came over, she greeted them, then began pointing at item after item on the menu. "We don't have this. We're out of that. We have omelettes and pizzas. You want a pizza?"

"No, we'll just have two sodas then," Amy said.

After the waitress left, Żaneta mimicked her, saying, *"Nie ma*. All gone. Everything is nie ma. I think the *PEWEX* stores are the only places where you don't hear that anymore."

Their drinks arrived in glass bottles. Żaneta put hers against her forehead and continued her train of thought. "But if we want to buy Western clothes, canned food, cosmetics, or wallpaper at the PEWEX stores, we have to pay with Western currency. Well, there's always the black market. Remember in Holland? Everything was so easy, and the shops were full of *everything*."

She looked over at her mother, but she was staring out at the water. *Not listening*, Żaneta thought. It would have been all right except that her mother had one of her frowns on her face. "Mamusiu, are you all right?"

"I'm fine. It's just that Ewa says this is a way of wearing us down day in, day out, with all the standing in lines and other humiliating things we have to put up with. Why, we don't even have a phone."

"Irena does."

"But our other neighbor across the street is always watching us. And I can't get the right medicine for Mamusia. We never are able to buy any nice things from the West, or get fresh good-quality fruit or meat. We're like a country held hostage. That's what Ewa says."

"I think she's right," Żaneta said.

"So do I," Amy said softly. "But I probably shouldn't be talking this way to you."

"Hey," Żaneta said. "It's just us girls, remember? Oh look, there she is."

Żaneta watched her mother's face light up as she rose to greet her friend. "You're early."

Ewa kissed them both on the cheeks and sat down. "I couldn't stay inside any longer on a day like this. So, tell me. How are you?"

Żaneta settled back as the two women started chatting. She was thinking of other things, about her grandmother, her upcoming school year, new shoes. Her mind wandered until a name her mother mentioned caught her attention.

"And no one has heard from Aad since."

"But you just saw him last Easter," Ewa said.

Żaneta leaned forward. "What? What happened?"

"I was telling Ewa something Jan told me yesterday. It's Aad. No one has heard from him for quite some time, and we're afraid he's either in prison or lost at sea."

"What do you mean?" Żaneta asked anxiously.

"He disappeared at sea during a sailing trip taking Bibles into Morocco. The people who told us said there have been more arrests in that country lately. If they have Aad, they might make an example of him. But since the Dutch embassy in Morocco hasn't been able to locate him anywhere, no one knows what to do next."

"Lost at sea," Żaneta mumbled as the conversation moved on to other topics. She squinted into the sun, trying to imagine their friend surrounded by waves and dolphins, sailing into the sunset and never, ever returning again.

"How is Hanna?" Ewa asked.

"Not good. She was so uncomfortable this morning, I could hardly turn her over. She weighs next to nothing these days, poor thing. Jan is with her now."

"You know, someone was asking me how you and I became friends, and I realized it was when I first saw you at Piotr and Halina's wedding. Even then I had a feeling we'd become close."

Amy shook her head and laughed. "Do you realize that was almost eight years ago? I wonder where Halina is now? You know Jan and I had one of our worst fights because of something she said at Tomek's picnic that year."

"I'm not surprised," Ewa said. "She was trouble, Amy. When she left Piotr, she brought his things to me and hardly said two words. Piotr would never say so, but Halina cared too much about Halina and pretty things. She was materialistic and very selfish—"

Amy interrupted Ewa. "Well, she was confused, poor Halina."

"What 'poor Halina'? She was selfish and childish. I'll never forget, she had the most irritating habit of speaking of the weather, as if she wanted the men around her to know how helpless they were. She was always wanting more, and claiming Piotr. But I can tell you don't like me talking this way, Amy. I'm sorry. Not everyone is like you two ladies. Maybe if I lived with a saint like your grandmother, Żanetko, I'd be as forgiving as you and Amy."

Żaneta smiled. "It's okay. I think the things you just said about some of the girls in my class."

Everyone laughed. Then Ewa said, "You know, Amy, your daughter's red hair and green eyes, that sweet face . . . She's going to break a few hearts soon."

Amy looked up surprised. "She's only eleven."

"That's what I mean. Don't worry, though. Żaneta's not dumb. She'll know how to handle herself. Right, Żanetko?"

She nodded. It was definitely time to change the subject. "I heard that the hotel around the corner from here has the *best* pastries."

Amy laughed. "Did you now?"

Żaneta said, "Yes. I know these things."

"All right, then let's go check out this great piece of information your daughter has given us," Ewa said.

As they walked away from the beach, Żaneta lingered a few steps behind. She thought about her mother's best friend and how she never, ever talked about her time in prison, or Bogdan's. She covered it up well. But Żaneta knew from eavesdropping too much that Ewa and Bogdan had paid a high price for their long separation. They both had desperately wanted children but were now too old.

It was almost as if Ewa's loneliness and Amy's grief for Gonia had enabled the two women to open up to each other at an unusually deep level, and that's how they became lifelines for each other.

Her grandmother sighed and turned to Żaneta. "If your mother can bear with me, I think we should be able to finish this today. Why is it that some days are so much harder than others?"

Żaneta gave her a glass with a straw to drink from. Hanna was sitting in what the family liked to call her "throne," the wheelchair with a wooden plank stretched between the arms of the chair and resting on her lap. Spread across the board were the typed sheets of paper Amy had already finished. Despite the summer heat, Babcia's feet were nestled in warm boots. It had been years since she was able to exercise her muscles. Now when Żaneta looked down at the wasted and shriveled legs, it seemed to her like another lifetime when her grandmother had been able to use them to ski and swim countless laps beside Mamusia. It was certainly a lifetime before her own, for she had only heard the stories.

Before Amy had left for the apteka, she and Hanna had been working on a project. Jan had insisted they write down Hanna's life story. Żaneta could tell Hanna felt extremely self-conscious about the whole thing. "Whoever would be interested in *my* life?" That's what she asked every time they worked on the story. But Amy and Jan had convinced her that the stories she told could bring people closer to God. That was a good enough reason to do just about anything, she had told Żaneta.

So when Hanna had a good day, which meant the pain up and down her spine could be numbed somewhat, then she and Amy sat down together, and Amy typed the words as Hanna spoke them.

Hanna said now, "I'm pleased with our progress. When your mother comes back, we're going to do a little more."

"How far are you now?" Żaneta asked.

"We've gotten through my childhood, the war years, and my time as a young wife and mother. This morning we've been finishing the part about Tadeusz's death, and it's been especially hard . . ." Her voice trailed off.

Żaneta took the water from her and placed a cool, damp cloth against her grandmother's cheek. "Your story is so good, though. Tatuś says if even one person's heart is touched by what you're writing now, then this effort would be worth it."

"Yes," Hanna sighed again. Then a flash of pain streaked across her face.

"You don't feel well, Babciu," Żaneta said. "Tell me."

"I don't want to complain. This heat . . . Even my throat is now affected by the paralysis, and all my inner organs. I cannot see and hear well, and yet the Lord has given me clarity of mind."

Żaneta knew the multiple sclerosis had crippled all her grandmother's muscles. She could hardly turn her head now. She helped her mother daily to clean Babcia and change her as if she were a child. Together they also fed and carried Hanna from bed to chair, then back again.

"Talking so much about Tadeusz this morning has made me want to be with him. *Oh, and how I do want to leave*," she sighed. "Well, at least there is one thing we will not be required to do in heaven: praising the Lord in spite of difficulties, because they won't exist."

So the pain is only part of the reason, Żaneta thought. Now beads of sweat dotted her forehead, and Żaneta laid her hand against her grandmother's face.

"Your fever's up, Babciu. Are you sure you don't want to continue tomorrow?"

"No, dear. I just want your mother to write this last bit. But first . . . could you hand me the photos on the wall there?"

Żaneta took down the black-and-whites from where they left dark squares on the wallpaper. One was of her grandfather laughing, while he sat beside Babcia, together on a bench. She smiled into his eyes. So happy, so content to live and love. He was her everything. Here was the one of Tadeusz laughing as he stood behind Hanna, holding her around the waist. It was taken in the days before she became sick. *Oh, they were so young then, younger even than my parents now*, Żaneta realized.

Hanna said, "I think those were precious memories." She fingered the shot of her as a skier, radiant with health. "And it has been good to be able to watch my grandchildren, to watch you. Oh, how I pray for our family. I can only hope now that things will be better for my grandchildren than they were for my children."

"Here, let me move your chair. I should keep your head in the shade." Żaneta saw the tears rising in Babcia's eyes. "Are you sure you're all right?" she asked.

"I miss him, child. Oh, how I miss him. I've spent more than ten years alone now." Her whispered voice choked on the tears. "I've wanted to follow him for every day of those ten years." She reached up to take off her glasses and her hands shook. "You know, some-times, although I cannot sing anymore, I remember many of the wonderful songs that we used to sing as a family, and I sing them in my heart." She paused, then sighed. "Your grandfather and I used to pray daily for revival in Poland. Now I still do, but also that Poles will stop leaving for the West. Why, even the Baptists are mov-ing to West Berlin for a better life!"

Żaneta came up behind her, reached down, and began to softly massage her bare white back, willing her hands to feel cool and strong. She wondered at her grandmother's disjointed conversa-tion, knowing what neither of them said, that Tomasz was most probably among those who had fled to the West. Maybe that thought was the reason Babcia's mind seemed to be going in so many different directions that day. Hanna picked up the little mir-ror beside her chair as if she meant to comb her hair. Instead, she stopped and stared up at Żaneta's reflection, then down at what Żaneta saw, gray eyes, a not-yet smiling face, still knowing, seeing through any pride or pretense.

"Do you remember what I said about how long martial law might last?" Hanna asked.

"Why do you bring that up now?"

"Because I'm not very good at knowing how long something will last. Have you noticed? I never dreamed I would have to sur-vive ten years without my Tadeusz." She swallowed, then added, "You want to hear something funny? I've caught the daughter of the same neighbor watching us, just like her mother did twenty years ago. I would never have guessed that our family could be spied on like that for two generations. I sense that tremendous changes are taking place in our country. Only one thing remains, and it is also our home verse, the rock of our hope: "Jesus Christ, yesterday, today and forever the same." Her voice had risen in strength, but now crackled weakly, "Just don't ask me anymore how long something will last."

"Shh," Żaneta said, her hands softly running up and down Hanna's tortured spine.

35

High King of heaven, when battle is done

Tomasz caught sight of his own reflection in the train window. With his hair cut short, he could have been any teenage boy riding the train straight up the middle of his country from south to north. His eyes stared back at him, and when he squinted, everything both inside and outside the train blurred, all moving, moving, back in time, moving to the sound of the tracks, speeding by beneath him, tempting him back to the past, the memories still jagged and incomplete.

He broke the locked gaze and traced the inside of his arm with the fingers of his other hand. The scarring would go away in time, the doctor—*No*, he corrected himself, *Jacek, Jacek Duch had said this.* It didn't matter. What Tomasz wondered now was whether the same held true for the nightmares. All during the last four months, he had been fighting to hold on to what was real and what was not. But the concrete certainty he sought still eluded him, running past him in a blur, like the objects he watched now.

Tomasz did know that during the last weeks in the mountains, he had found out what he had been running away from, and how to finally stand and make it count. He had learned that much from the man named Jacek.

As the train began to slow down, Tomasz looked out the window, mesmerized again by the clacking rhythm of the tracks.

And this time, instead of his own face, he sees the bent figure of his father. He sits on a bench in the wasted garden his grandfather has planted so long ago.

Tomasz feels his stomach turn over. He cannot leave this place. As he imagines walking the path, Tomasz remembers being there as a boy, riding on his father's shoulders. Tomasz trembles inside. The closer he comes, the more frightened he feels. He tries to call out but can make no sound.

His father's hand is over his face. He can see his Bible held loosely in his other hand, the fingers marking certain spots. When he is within a few paces, Tomasz stands still. He opens his mouth, but the fear has deadened his words. His mind a torment of emotions, Tomasz waits. He has resolved to do this thing. He tells himself this, even as his father raises his head, sighs, and opens his eyes.

When he sees Tomasz, his father turns away.

Tomasz's heart lurched in fear. Suddenly, the train whistle blew. His vision cleared, and his world came back into focus as the conductor came through, announcing the next station.

Jacek glanced nervously in his rearview mirror. The blue Audi was still behind him, three cars back. It had been a long two-day drive, but he was almost in Gdynia. He wasn't sure when he first noticed the Audi, sometime early this morning when he left Warszawa. *I'll lose him when I get off the highway,* Jacek thought. He saw the worry in his eyes, his own reflection surprising him again, a clean-shaven face for the first time in a decade.

He could feel his pulse quickening. He'd have to calm down. The high blood pressure had nothing to do with being followed. Jacek knew the direction he had chosen was suicidal. This was one mission he would not survive.

Like finding the Audi on his tail, he wasn't quite sure when he realized this was where he had to go. It had always been with him, in him, a decision made, a secret unshared. Somewhere in those mountains, together with Tomasz, Jacek had said to himself, *It's not enough. It was never enough. I must tell Amy, because of Tomasz.* And now that day was finally upon him.

Jacek had never, in all his seventy-nine years, been in such deep trouble. It was his old nightmare, fighting the two-front war. He knew full well that during his absence, Roman had missed him.

Even as he completed the thought, he watched the Audi swerve onto the offramp just as Jacek took it. He increased his speed and passed three trucks in a row, then he careened to the right and flew over country roads between farms and forest.

Jacek thought it was a fifty-fifty bet that one of Roman's men sat in that car. He had to shake his pursuer. He had to do one more thing. *Just one more time, let me escape,* he thought.

Left, down a dirt road, bouncing on the potholes, left, then left again. He waited, then saw the dark shape approaching the other way through the trees. With a screech of brakes, then screaming gears, Jacek reversed and took off again.

Every moment of the high-speed chase brought Jacek closer to a full realization that he *must* survive. Only he knew what was at stake, and he could not afford to take this particular secret to his grave. By the same token, he realized he couldn't have chosen a worse time to return.

Even in the mountain villages Jacek had heard enough to know these last six months had been crucial in the war the communist-led government had declared on Solidarność. He had missed the demonstrations in March, and the protests in May. Jacek knew that if Roman still had the manpower at his disposal, if the secret police found him, he would be shot on sight as a Western spy. It was what Roman had always suspected of Jacek. Ironic that just when both men had reached old age, had reached an armistice in their own relationship, they should have to oppose each other one final, fatal time.

If Roman had made the inquiries, a simple security check would have revealed that Jacek had spent the time in West Berlin, not exactly a safe haven for a high-ranking member of the Polish secret police. No, Roman would figure there was only one explanation for such a trip, espionage. Now the SB would know for certain that Jacek was really CIA. And although Roman would be right to charge Jacek with treason against the communist state, he would be wrong about the reason. This time it had nothing to do with his status as a former Western spy.

And this was the second enemy who might be occupying the car stubbornly sticking to Jacek's tail. Not only would the KGB and SB want to kill him because of his counterespionage activities through the years, now the CIA would also be hunting him down. Ever since he had accessed the missing-persons file in the computer at the U.S. embassy in Berlin, he had been a walking target. From his identification card, they now knew he was not dead and would be searching either for Jacek or the imposter who had his ID. His long absences, first in 1977 and now this, and for nearly a decade, all pointed toward one thing. And that was the same crime Roman would suspect him of—he was a double agent.

Once the security in Berlin recorded Jacek's use of his identification, he became a hunted man on both sides of the Iron Curtain. Both sides would think he had been playing the enemy because of his suspicious behavior. Both sides would have reason to eliminate him as soon as possible.

Jacek could almost picture his Company file, closed when they thought he had been killed by the SB after the Carter incident, then reopened. They were probably even now classifying him as a mole who went underground during the eighties, then resurfaced in Berlin briefly, looking for someone for some reason, a lost contact maybe. And where would he place himself? Almost certainly back to Gdańsk.

Yes, Jacek thought as he doubled back and pulled into a wood shed just off the road. *They would have been waiting for me.* How they caught sight of him on the highway, how he had blown his cover so early upon returning to civilization, he would never know. But someone had been waiting for him. Now the only question was, *Who?*

As the Audi flew by him, Jacek caught sight of its driver from his hiding place . . . and gasped. He must have been mistaken. A woman? An elderly woman?

He counted to ten, then slowly pulled out and drove in the opposite direction.

Now he had no choice. Under no circumstances could he afford to lead his enemies to Amy. He must continue to protect her. That remained the prime directive.

He had to go back one final time. Knowing that he would not be allowed to live much longer, Jacek had to go and tell Amy who he was. He did not have much time. And he had something crucial to tell Piotr.

He smiled wryly. If the weight of all his secrets did not break his brittle bones first, and if he could keep outrunning his enemies, today . . . he would tell the truth.

36

Jacek told himself he *had* been in this place during a previous life. It wasn't just that it felt that way. Another man in another time and dimension had walked this street, looked up at the seventh-floor window, followed the woman who lived there to the park around the corner and watched her children play.

Another man, a decade ago. Jacek had purposely chosen the route that passed the playground as he walked to Amy's home. He looked up at the familiar chestnut trees, a little older, a little broader around the trunk. That patch of green up ahead, the empty swing sets, embodied the only place of peace he had ever known, the only season in his life when he could rest and discover what he loved above all, his family.

As Jacek turned the last corner before the park, he stopped short. There, sitting on *his* bench, staring at the sky as he used to, was Amy.

He paused and watched her. Was she waiting for someone? No, she was just sitting. *Thinking of Tomasz and Gonia, no doubt*, he realized. Yes, that's what he would do in this place, the children's former playground. He stood there, acutely aware of the blackbirds singing from the treetops, the seagulls calling to one another from the direction of the waterfront.

He stepped forward, willing himself to do the very thing that had become the most difficult act in his long, long life. He hesitated when he reached the bench. How often had he envisioned this moment, in this very spot? How often had he ached, ached in mental anguish to do what he was now about to do? How often had he awakened at night, thinking this moment that was about to happen already had, a prayer for a dream to come true?

"May I sit down?" he asked.

If only had become a forbidden phrase. Now he pushed it aside impatiently.

"Of course, I was just leaving." She started to reach for the shopping bag under the bench.

"No, please. I don't mind if you stay," he said, seating himself beside her.

She looked at him oddly. *She probably just sees a lonely old man wanting conversation,* he thought. He looked at her more closely now. She'd cut her hair short, and it was gray. Lines framed her eyes and mouth, *not laugh-lines.* Jacek had to think for a moment. Yes, she would be almost fifty now. Age plus the loss of two children had not been kind to her face. Her eyes held no warmth that he could see, only suspicion.

"You don't know me," he began. "And I don't quite know how to say this."

"Wait." Her eyes narrowed. "Yes, I *do* know you."

Without his beard and glasses, Jacek told himself she could not possibly recognize him as the old man who used to sit here.

Still, she gasped and pulled away. "You're the man I met, the man Jan's father introduced me to so many years ago. The government minister." She stared at him, then looked around the playground fearfully. "You're with the government." Her voice changed pitch, and Jacek heard the panic rising in its tone. "Jan thought from the secret police maybe . . ."

"No wait," he held up a hand. "Please . . ."

"What is this?" she cried. "You're not going to have me kidnapped, are you? Arrested? Who are you?" She almost screamed the question, standing up and backing away from him.

Jacek hadn't expected this. He shook his head and said as reassuringly as he could, "Look around you. There's no one else here. We're not being listened to. I'm just an old man . . . just an old man. All right? All I want to do is answer that question you just asked. Please sit down." He closed his eyes for a moment and took a deep breath. Then he said again softly, "Amy, please?"

She turned her head slightly at the sound of her name. Amy returned to the bench but sat straight up, ready to flee at any second. "Why do you know my name? Who *are* you?"

What should he say? What *could* he say? "Amy, I'm your father. I am Jacek Skrzypek."

She leaned backward as if thunderstruck. Her hands flew to her face, shaking, trembling, and tears sprang to her eyes. "Oh, this is some kind of sick joke!" she cried. She stood up and towered over him. "You government people will stop at nothing to keep manipulating people's lives. You think I'm stupid enough to go for this? What is the game here? Tell me that. Just tell me what you're doing. What do you want? *Who* do you want? Is it Piotr?" This last question she asked in a sobbing voice. "Oh, when will you people ever leave us alone?"

Jacek forged on, afraid of what he would find, more afraid of her standing up again and running away, but determined to reveal all. "Piotr knew. I put him in prison and kept him there because he knew . . . I was a spy."

Amy shook her head in disbelief. "No! This can't be true. Go away. Just leave me alone!"

But he would not stop talking. "That's why I'm back. I'm going to find Piotr, no matter what it takes, and finish what I've started. No one must know this. I can't imagine what you're feeling now. But I don't want to . . . to pain you anymore. I will leave right away. . . ." He froze, meeting her eyes for the first time.

Slowly, as a hopeful recognition started dawning on her face, she reached forward with her hand, almost touching him. Her hand hovered by his cheek, and Jacek could see the glint of her wedding ring out of the corner of his eye.

"No! You can't be him!" She whispered. Tears coursed their way down her cheeks. Her hands kept fluttering up to her eyes to wipe them away. Finally, he took her hands in his and steadied them, even as she said again, "No, no, it can't be true."

"Amy, it is true. I *am* your father. You were closer than you thought in those first years of your search. Piotr came dangerously close to exposing my true identity as a U.S. spy. That's why I had to have him hunted down like that. You see, I was told during the war that you had been killed in the same accident that killed Barbara."

She jerked her hands out of his. He could tell by her reaction he had hit a familiar chord. Not for the first time, he wondered just how much Amy did know about her mother.

Now she volunteered, speaking as if in a trance, "Yes, there was an envelope . . . among my mother's things, in a box my stepparents gave me. . . . Did you write my mother during the war? From which country did you write her?"

He tried to speak slowly and carefully, searching for the magic combination of words that might unlock her door of distrust. "From here, from Poland. But I don't think many of my letters reached her. Military intelligence disapproved and intercepted most of our post."

"And where were you born?" she asked.

"Here, in Gdańsk."

It was no use. Amy's face clouded over in doubt. He couldn't prove himself to her, not now. It was too late. Then he added, "The letter you're talking about was probably one of the last ones I wrote during the war." He paused, then said, "Before she asked for a divorce."

She glanced at him sharply. *She is still listening.* Jacek forged on, "After the war, my cover here in Poland was with the Polish secret police. It was all far too dangerous, and I couldn't afford anyone linking you and the children with me."

"The children? You know about the children?" Her eyes grew even wider.

He nodded. "It's all right. Please. All this time, for twelve years now, ever since I first found out *from you* that I was the one you were looking for, I've tried in every way I could to watch out for you. Yes, I know about the children."

"About Gonia?" she asked as more tears came.

The torment etched across her face shocked Jacek. *Isn't it supposed to lessen with time?* He would not have thought it possible, but these jagged edges of grief mirrored the same pain he carried within himself.

Amy must have sensed some of his emotional turmoil. She hesitated. He realized that this, more than his words and knowledge of secret events, this empathy of pain and fear, this could be what would convince Amy that he cared. Her hands steadied and now she did touch him. He wondered what she must think, tracing his bizarre face, with the wrinkles all going in the wrong directions.

He drew back instinctively, then smiled ironically and said, "Please believe me. I have suffered with you, Amy." And then to Jacek's utter astonishment, he heard his voice crack on the last word.

"I don't know what to say," Amy said. "Why now? Why do you come to me now and say these things?"

"Because now, I've run out of time. I've made some terrible mistakes, and I will no doubt soon pay for those mistakes. I am being hunted down for another reason, though. I had to tell you these things before something happened. And now I've spent too much time here as it is." He stood and turned, as if to leave.

"No! You can't do that. I've had too many people come into my life and leave me." Amy sounded desperate. She reached toward him. "Please, I've just . . . found you. Give me time to believe you. Don't leave . . . not again."

Her touch burned through his sleeve. He firmly removed her hand from his arm. "If I brought you into danger after all this time, I would suffer in a hell of my own making. No, let me do this my way. Piotr and I made peace several years ago, but there is something he still must know."

Quickly, he stooped and brushed his lips against her cheeks. "Take this," he said, pushing a small booklet into her hands. "It's money in a dollar account, in your name. I opened the account this morning at a new bank, after closing out my own in Warszawa. Use the money for my grandchildren." Then Jacek turned and walked across the playground, feeling the warmth of her gaze on his back every step of the way.

Tomasz rummaged through his backpack. Somewhere he knew he had some phone tokens. The train was only an hour out of Gdańsk, agonizingly close, but it hadn't moved even slightly for twenty minutes, the latest in two days' worth of delays.

He looked out the window. It was a small station, with a phone booth standing just across the tracks at that platform. A conductor walked down the aisle.

"Excuse me," Tomasz called out. "Do you think I have enough time to go make a phone call? How long will it be until we start moving again?"

The conductor shook his head. "I don't know. At least another half hour. Sure, go make your phone call."

Tomasz relaxed and started groping blindly through his things in a more systematic fashion. The tokens would be on the bottom of his bag. He turned the whole thing upside down and out came everything he owned, most of it dirty laundry.

He smelled campfire smoke and thought of where he had been just a few days earlier. *Another world.* The small brown coins tumbled out, and Tomasz snatched them up, then ran out of the car. He leaped across the tracks, waved at a little girl who smiled at him from farther down the train, and entered the phone booth.

Tomasz swallowed. *This is it.* He didn't know what he would do if he got his father on the line. The closer Tomasz came to home, the more weighed down he felt. And his mother, why was he so afraid of talking to his mother? She had always listened to him.

But Tomasz knew. He had already thought about this. He was afraid of the damage he had inflicted on his mother when he said the terrible words about Piotr being his father. That, and his running away, coupled with the pain she still carried around inside because of Gonia's death, would have proven too much and somehow injured her even worse.

Ever since Tomasz had resolved to go home, he had been afraid to see the damage he had wrought, the pain he had inflicted on those he loved. He could not face how he might have changed his mother.

And what if Babcia. . . ? No, he would not think that. *It's my fault.* Somewhere in these mountains, he had come to see his own guilt in all of this, but it didn't lessen his dread. Tomasz took a deep breath. *Help me do this.*

He dropped the tokens in the slot and waited. Static, then a double ring. *"Proszę?"*

"Irena? It's Tomasz."

He heard screaming on the other end as Irena said his name over and over. He laughed, waiting for her to calm down, then said, "Yes, yes, I know. But listen. I don't have much time. Please, can you get someone from my family?"

The receiver banged as it was dropped and then came the sound of Irena's voice calling his mother. She always could be heard through the walls, he thought.

A few moments later, he heard the soft voice of his sister. "Tomasz, is it really you?"

"Yes."

"Where are you?"

"That's why I'm calling. I'm coming home, Żanetko."

"Oh!"

"It's all right. I'm *almost* home. On the train. But the train has stopped and now it's just sitting here. We're only an hour from Gdańsk. . . . Where's Mamusia?"

"Oh, Tomasz! She's out, and so is Tatuś. . . ."

"Babcia?"

"She's very sick, but I know as soon as I tell her you're all right, she'll feel better. Oh, I can't wait until . . ."

"No, Żanetko, please . . . " Tomasz hated to silence her like this, but he had to do this *his* way. "I'll be home this afternoon. *Please* don't tell anyone. Can you keep it a secret? I want to surprise them."

"Are you sure? Are you all right?"

"Yes, but I . . . I have to do it this way. Please, Żanetko?"

"You *are* coming home?"

"Yes, I am coming home."

"All right. But *hurry*. And, Tomasz, listen . . ."

The tokens ran out and Tomasz heard only a dead hush on the other end. He sighed and walked slowly back to his car, kicking at stones along the way.

When he saw the upturned backpack, at first he thought someone had tried to steal his things. Then he remembered, he had done it. Hearing Żaneta's voice had disoriented him. Tomasz shook his head, thankful that he had the car all to himself.

As he absentmindedly jammed his things back into the pack, Tomasz thought of his sister. He loved her voice. He wondered if his parents would respond so warmly, though. His sister was only a few years younger, but she had understood. When had Żaneta never understood?

His hand fell on a small package, wrapped in brown paper. Where had this come from? Tomasz turned it over. He couldn't remember seeing it before. *But then, when do I remember anything well lately?* It must have fallen out of his pack. That was the only explanation.

He slowly unfolded the paper, unwrapping the parcel, and onto his palm rolled a red fire truck.

37

Grant heaven's joy to me, bright heaven's sun

Jacek had done it. He had realized the goal of a lifetime. His daughter now knew who he was! He felt like shouting it out loud.

He had purposely not said anything about Tomasz's safety. He did not want anyone to know what he had done. It would be yet another secret between him and Piotr. *Besides*, he thought, *let her joy be complete later today when Tomasz arrives.* It was obvious by the sadness still shadowing her eyes that Jacek had made it back to Gdynia before Tomasz.

He had deliberately chosen not to tell Amy several things: About how he had spied on her during the years, about finding Tomasz in an alley in West Berlin. About his relationship with Tomasz during the last four months.

Now it was imperative that Jacek reach Gdańsk before Roman discovered his return to Poland. *I have both the SB and CIA breathing down my neck. Both sides want me dead for being a double agent. And I have one more thing that must be done.*

Piotr still needed to know the circumstances of Tomasz's recovery in case the boy needed more help.

Jacek could not shake the sense of impending doom dogging him even now as he drove down the Gdańsk street leading to Piotr's apartment building.

A young woman emerged from the downstairs door, and Jacek caught it just before it closed. Then he slowly went up the stairs. He knew Piotr's apartment. He knew the address well. He pushed the buzzer. No answer. Then he knocked, still nothing. *Oh, I must find you.*

Defeated and feeling empty and tired, Jacek descended the stairs and returned to his car. He felt suddenly exhausted, his eyes heavy. The confrontation with Amy had taken so much out of him. *But I can't stop now*, he told himself.

He did not relish searching the city for Piotr. He could just wait here for him to come home, and maybe sleep in the meantime. . . .

A sixth sense brought Jacek up with a start. *What am I thinking?* He could feel the danger around him. The worst kind, unseen, but very much present. He glanced in all directions and saw an empty street. *No one.* And yet, his instincts told him he *was* being followed.

He started up his car and left the street slowly. He could not shake the feeling of time running out. Jacek had learned to trust these gut reactions. Something was wrong. He wondered, in his wandering, who would he further endanger? Amy, Piotr, the boy? *No, he is safe. Not even due home yet.*

The city streets were uncannily empty. On impulse, Jacek pulled into a guarded parking lot. He nodded at the attendant, who wrote the time on a slip of paper and put it under his windshield wiper. Jacek scanned the lot but saw no dark-colored Audi.

He walked two streets toward a hotel taxi stand and stepped into the front seat of the first car.

"Just drive around a bit," he told the driver.

The man did not even look at Jacek as he snatched up the 10 DM note he slipped him and pulled out of the lineup. As they criss-crossed the city center, Jacek managed to quell the panic that had threatened him earlier in his own car. He took a deep breath. How to find Piotr? Where would he be? Not back in Gdynia? A meeting somewhere. *Don't let him be in Warszawa.*

"What's going on today?" he asked the driver.

The man's face remained a mask as he answered in a monotone, "There's a Solidarność rally. Rumor has it the milicja will be crashing the party."

"So everyone is steering clear of St. Brygida's?"

"That's right."

"You want to take me there?"

"Not particularly." The man fingered the bill Jacek had given him.

Jacek pulled out another just like it and said, "Why don't you try to find a way?"

"Sure."

Jacek knew he would find Piotr there. And for Tomasz's sake, so the boy might not grow up twisted and scarred from his addiction and abuse, Jacek had to reach Piotr. He was the only one now who could help the boy. He had to tell him that he had found Tomasz, to expect him to arrive in Gdynia today or tomorrow. And he had to tell him that Amy now knew who he was.

In other words, *No more debts owed. A clean slate.*

Tomasz clung anxiously to the window as the train pulled out of *Gdańsk Głowny*, the central station. It was as if he were returning from another planet. Which was worse, the transition from Berlin, or that of the mountains to home? He had been gone for more than a year.

Out of the corner of his eye, he saw two milicja agents yelling at a tourist that it was forbidden to take photos at train stations.

Tomasz wanted only one thing now. *Please, Lord, don't let me be too late.* The prayer came unbidden to Tomasz's thoughts. Funny, a presence as familiar as his own parents' seemed to steady his nerves as he watched at least fifty soldiers pass through his car. Tomasz didn't even look up as the soldiers stamped down the middle aisle.

The Gdańsk-Gdynia line usually only took forty minutes, but on this day there seemed an unusual number of delays. Tomasz stared out the window to the left. A large man had gotten on at the previous stop. He now sat beside him, but Tomasz did not give him much thought until the man started swearing under his breath.

Tomasz looked up at his face and saw the man was watching out the opposite window to the right. The train slowed down in front of the Lenin shipyard entrance, an area strictly forbidden and cordoned off from any public access along the streets. Ironically, though, anyone riding this train could see clearly into the fenced-off shipyard. During Poland's state of war since martial law had been declared, this place had been the battleground. Red-and-white flags fluttered in the wind. The bright, illegal banner of Solidarność stretched across the roof, a salute to the civilian train passengers who secretly supported the movement, and a slap in the face to the milicja soldiers tramping up and down the aisles. Tomasz wondered if the conductor had slowed down on purpose along this particular stretch.

"You there, close that window!" One of the soldiers threatened to ram a teenager around Tomasz's age in the back with the butt of his rifle. The boy was hanging out the window, calling to the men in the shipyard, who were pacing behind the fence, carrying placards with the word "STRAJK" painted across them. The boy's action had caught the attention of the strikers on the roof. They stood and waved at the train, chanting the song that had brought all of Poland together, crying out the words proudly. As the boy whirled, the man sitting beside Tomasz stood. Tomasz could see him tense and realized he might find himself caught in a crossfire.

At that moment two other guards came running into the car, brandishing their rifles. "What's the problem here? Get that window closed, you!"

As the boy lowered his fists, the man sat back down, but Tomasz could still hear him breathing heavily. The boy closed the window without another word. Now Tomasz wondered again about the heavy police presence on this particular day.

"You can bet there's something happening at St Brygida's," the man now said softly, his words addressed to Tomasz.

"Then my uncle will be there," Tomasz said. And immediately, he could have bit his tongue. How did he know this man was safe? Maybe the show of bravado just then had been nothing more than that, a show.

The man looked at him more closely. Tomasz returned the gaze and saw a big face, many chins, black chest hair peeking out of the workshirt, perspiration stains under the man's arms.

"Then you shouldn't be telling me such things," the man said.

Tomasz looked up in surprise, then smiled as he saw the twinkle in the man's eyes. "You're right," Tomasz said. "I forgot myself."

"Rule number one during wartime: Don't forget yourself. When will you youngsters learn that we can never be too careful?" The man looked to the right, then gasped.

Tomasz followed his gaze. As the train picked up speed, they passed a line of tanks, the smaller, artillery version used on city streets during riots.

"I heard the Soviets had parked a few in the woods outside of Gdańsk, courtesy of our own Polish Army," the man said. "But I never dreamed they'd . . ." He stopped as a soldier brushed past them.

"They're headed for the city center," Tomasz said. He glanced at the man, who nodded slowly. "I have to go warn him."

Together, they both stood and made their way to the train door, waiting anxiously for the next stop. The man asked Tomasz softly, "Now the question is whether I'm going to walk with you or not. What do you think?"

"No?" Tomasz asked.

"No. Don't trust me. Don't trust anyone except the Almighty Himself, understood?" And with that the stranger stepped toward the open door and jumped nimbly down from the train.

Tomasz wondered how such a large man could disappear so swiftly. He looked out over the upturned faces watching the windows of the train and saw no one he recognized. How could he? No one expected him here. Then Tomasz remembered again the urgency of his mission, and he sprang out of the car and started pushing his way through the men and women lined up to get on the train. He had to run and warn Piotr.

Żaneta paced up and down the apartment. Ever since the phone call, she had been waiting impatiently for her mother to come home. Her grandmother still slept, but Żaneta didn't like the *way* she slept. So restlessly, and calling out suddenly, then growing very still.

What if Babcia is dying? The thought would not let Żaneta go. Żaneta refused to leave her side. Only for the phone call had she been gone. Her mother had left to get some more painkillers, but she had been gone a long time now, too long.

Azor got up from his corner and went to the door, sniffing and wagging his tail. Then the locks turned in the door, and Żaneta looked up expectantly. Her mother appeared, but her worried expression told her enough. Something had happened.

"Mamusiu?" Her mother jumped at Żaneta's voice. She looked white, as if she'd just seen a ghost.

Then her mother turned and smiled slightly at her. "Żanetko, you startled me."

"Mama." She switched to English, something she did whenever she needed her mother's full attention. "Shall I make us some tea?"

"Ah, sweetie. No, I'm sorry for leaving you here so long alone. But . . . I met someone. Come sit next to me and we'll watch over Babcia together." Żaneta joined her mother beside Babcia's bed.

"At least you will never run away." The words were a whisper, and Żaneta barely heard them. She rested her head on her mother's shoulder and could sense the tiredness there.

"Just us girls," Żaneta said.

Amy nodded.

But Żaneta could not sit still. It had been hours since Tomasz's phone call. He should have been home by now. She stood up and started pacing the room.

"What's wrong? Why are you so restless, Żanetko? Is it because. . . ?" Amy nodded back at Hanna, lying so still in bed. Żaneta thought it was as if she could not say the words, describe an act they, in fact, had all been praying for, for months now.

"Mamusiu," Żaneta's voice shook.

"What, darling, what is it?"

She swallowed. She had to do this. Never mind her promise. He might be in trouble again, and this time it would be her fault. "It's Tomasz."

She could see her mother stop breathing and have to blink back the tears that sprang into her eyes. "Our Tomasz?" she whispered, as if to herself. Żaneta nodded. "Where?" Amy asked. She stood, her hands reaching out, the fingers moving as if the boy stood in the room with them and was within her grasp.

"Home. Here, I mean, he *should* be home. He phoned Irena and I spoke to him. It was early this morning. He should have been home by now."

"*Where?*"

"He said he was an hour from Gdańsk." Żaneta kept pulling at the red lock of hair by her cheek. And she would not look at Amy straight on. "But I don't know where he is now, Mamusiu."

She fought the panic as her mother mumbled, "Not gone. Not again. No, Lord." Amy's hands rolled over limply, palms down, and moved up and down, motioning for Żaneta to stop and wait. "Start from the beginning. Tell me *everything*. Tell me why you are saying this only now. *Please.*"

"I'm sorry, Mamusiu. But Tomasz made me promise not to tell you. He wanted to surprise us all. I thought . . . I thought he would come back by now. He said he would be here, and that was hours ago. . . . I didn't know where you were. You were gone so long. . . ."

Again her mother's face clouded over strangely. Then in that peculiar voice, a monotone that scared Żaneta, her mother said absently, "He can't be gone again?"

"He said he was coming straight home. I don't understand," Żaneta repeated feebly.

Amy burst into tears, then impatiently wiped them away. Anger rose up in her as she said, "How . . . how could you keep this from me? This is the most important news I've waited for, and my daughter doesn't even tell me. Tomasz is finally coming—" She stopped, frustration etched on her face.

Żaneta backed into the corner, her arms crossed, her face averted. How she hated this. Her mother did not lash out often, but when she did, it was almost always in Żaneta's direction. She tried to make her face a mask. It was easier that way. Her mother always apologized afterward, but it didn't take away the hurt whenever Żaneta feared her mother didn't trust her.

Moments passed, and then Amy said softly, "I couldn't find your grandmother's medicine anywhere. Look at her. She has a fever again. Her condition has worsened. The . . . the doctor says she's finally leaving us." Then she started sobbing.

Żaneta gasped at her mother's words. She slowly turned back to the bed and heard the shallow breathing of her grandmother. Babcia lay there so still. Chronic pain crippled her muscles and joints.

Amy continued. "He said her heart muscles can't take the strain much longer. They aren't strong enough. She'll go anytime now. And her family should be here. Piotr should be here. Tomasz should be here." Her voice cracked.

Żaneta's mind was reeling. She had never seen her mother so bad. In the last year since Tomasz had run away, Mamusia had sometimes been reduced to a state, but now she was saying things she shouldn't. *Saying things I don't want to hear.* Her grandmother's breathing changed rhythm, becoming more erratic.

If Tatuś were to walk in now, what would he think? Żaneta thought suddenly. *The three women in his life, his dying mother, his sobbing wife, his silent and shaking daughter.*

Żaneta shook herself. She had to be strong and not hide like this. She stepped forward and looked straight at her mother, a little scared of finding the confusion still in her eyes. She curled her hand into her mother's palm and waited, holding her breath, praying. "*Mamusiu?*"

"I need to find your father. He should be here. Can you stay a little longer alone with Babcia?"

Żaneta nodded. "Mamusiu?" she asked again. Her mother's only answer was to squeeze her hand and leave the room.

Żaneta felt the fear descend on her like a well-worn cloak. An old fear, dredged out of the mud. Fear for Tomasz. Fear of being alone here when Babcia died. Fear for her mother that she would not find her father in time. Fear of all the hurt and uncertainty threatening to drown her as she took the pain of others onto herself.

38

Jacek entered the St. Brygida courtyard and was surprised at the quiet calm that greeted him. Where was the rally? He walked up to a man and two women who were talking in English in hushed tones.

"I heard there was going to be a political rally? What's happening?" he asked.

"There's a press conference inside. The demonstration will be afterward, probably in an hour or so," the man said. He introduced himself. "I'm with the Swedish Press Agency." Surprised at his openness, Jacek shook his hand, then kissed the hands of the two women. The black-haired one looked as though she could have been fifteen.

"We're from the Dutch Press Agency."

He said, "I'm supposed to be at that press conference. Do you think they'll let me in? My press pass was stolen."

The tall redhead laughed. "Well, if you're with the secret police, you've got some nerve. Here, this is all they're using for clearance." She gave him a small rectangle with a black-and-white stamp of the Polish eagle on it and a number. "You can keep it. I have an extra."

Armed with his pass, Jacek entered the building on the other side of the courtyard as if he did so every day. When he reached the meeting room, he was amazed at the number of foreign journalists present. A reporter from an American TV station stood in the corner while two people put makeup on him. Jacek could hear their voices from where he stood. A man posted at the door asked for the pass given to legitimate journalists who had Solidarność clearance. Jacek showed him the slip of cardboard, disconcerted by the lax security, especially when he saw who was speaking at the front of the room.

Tadeusz Mazowiecki stood at the side of Lech Wałęsa, speaking softly as everyone but the Americans listened. He could hear the whispered translations of Polish interpreters for the foreign press all around him, like soft echoes in the wind.

Jacek scanned the room for Piotr, knowing he must be near. He would find him when the press conference broke up. It would attract too much attention to slip out just after arriving. Then, as Jacek listened, he had no doubt whatsoever that he was witnessing a historical moment. He felt a deep pride in his country, in his people, in the unselfishness of these two men, and the many others who had suffered and been imprisoned, and died . . . for Poland.

With pleasure, he leaned up against a wall and listened as Mazowiecki gave a rundown of events leading up to that afternoon's demonstration.

". . . this latest wave of strikes started in Śląsk and has spread to Gdańsk. General Kiszczak, Jaruzelski's top aide, met with Wałęsa earlier and agreed to a series of negotiations on a wide range of issues, including the status of the labor union. Now it is up to the Solidarność leadership to convince the young workers to suspend their strike. We are hoping that during this afternoon's rally, if Wałęsa himself speaks to them, we can avoid taking the fight into the streets and prevent any ensuing chaos or bloodshed.

"In October last year we formed the Solidarność National Executive Committee, comprising, among others, Wałęsa, Bujak, Lis, and Frasyniuk.

"Then, in March, there were the student demonstrations commemorating the twentieth anniversary of the 1968 protests, a turning point when the police attacked students in Kraków, Warszawa, and Lublin. Many of us believed the violence was a good sign. The government was becoming desperate.

"Four months ago, another new wave of strikes began, this time in Bydgoszcz, though it quickly spread to *Nowa Huta* and the Lenin shipyards here in Gdańsk. These latest strikes feature the new generation of very young workers. These teenagers have made the relegalization of Solidarność their principal demand.

"On the first of May, in answer to the traditional communist workers' marches, major demonstrations flared up again throughout the country. The government cracked down on the strikes one by one, their intention clearly one of leaving Gdańsk isolated.

"Today it is the task of the Solidarność leaders to convince these younger shipworkers to agree to suspend the strike without having reached an agreement. We have seen the fire burning in their eyes. The spark has leaped from one generation to the next now. *If they decide to end the strike and the government doesn't comply, the workers will return again. Again, and again, as long as it takes.*

"In the less than two years since many of us were released from prison, we have already learned that a short period of freedom is worth any amount of imprisonment. Despite the thrill that *finally* the country is rousing itself, we cannot afford to ignore the fact that history has rarely allowed Poland to be free for long periods of time. *Then let it be a short period again, but let us be free.*"

Jacek caught himself nodding. A few reporters raised their hands, and as questions were asked and answered, Jacek took a good look around to make sure Piotr wasn't in the room. Then he slipped out to explore the building.

As Jacek walked down the hall, he ducked his head into an office and saw two men asleep on the tables, one on the floor. Then he headed for the stairs, and a voice called out.

"You're not allowed up there." A young man, probably not much older than Tomasz, stood smiling at Jacek.

"Oh, sorry, I must be lost. I was looking for the . . ."

"The toilet is that way," the boy pointed to a door down the hall.

"Right, thank you." Jacek was heading in that direction when a thought occurred to him. "Wait," he called after the boy. "I'm actually looking for someone. Maybe you can help me. Is there anyone upstairs?"

"No, that's just storage area. Why? Who do you want to find?" The boy's smile had melted away and he now looked suspicious.

Jacek had nothing to lose and said, "Piotr Piekarz. Do you know where I can find him?"

The smile returned as the boy said, "Sorry, I can't help you. But if you come back when the rally starts, I know he'll be around then."

"Thank you," Jacek said, then ducked into the tiny room with a toilet and sink. Strips of the communist newspaper hung from the toilet-paper dispenser. This was Solidarność headquarters, after all, he thought almost smiling.

The churchyard Jacek returned to was filling up fast. He noticed the three reporters he had met on his way in were nowhere in sight.

He left by the main entrance and walked around the church. A knot of people stood out in front of the *Orbis* hotel across the street. He thought he saw someone who looked like Piotr and headed in that direction. Then something else caught his eye. A dark car parked to the right. He turned, heading toward it, quickening his pace. Just before he reached the vehicle, it pulled away. He broke into a run, trying to see if it really was a woman sitting behind the wheel.

Out of breath, his hands on his knees, he stopped, telling himself he couldn't give in to paranoia, not now.

I must find Piotr.

Żaneta doubted she had done the right thing. *When do I ever?* she asked herself. She sighed and hung her head. At least now she could be alone with her thoughts.

A dry, brittle hand touched her own. Żaneta gasped. Her grandmother's smile was waiting for her. The tears that had been welling up all afternoon spilled spontaneously down her cheeks. "Oh, Babciu!"

"Żanetko, I saw such light . . . I thought I was finally going to see Him, our Lord. And my Tadeusz." Her voice held the sound of falling frozen leaves. Although Żaneta could barely make out what her grandmother had said, there was no mistaking the brittle disappointment in her voice.

"Mamusia came back and just left again. If I run after her, I might still catch her." Żaneta stood up to leave, but the vicelike grip of the old woman would not release her.

"Don't leave me."

Żaneta could feel the intensity of Hanna's gaze. Her grandmother had always known how to read her thoughts. Żaneta looked deep into the crystalline eyes, ringed with folds of skin, each one a story in itself. *I have nothing to hide,* a voice deep inside the girl assured her.

"Ah. Something has happened. Tell me. Tell me the truth, Żanetko. Amy will be back soon enough."

There was a silence. Then Hanna asked, "Did Amy tell you what the doctor said about me?"

Żaneta nodded, but the words would not come out.

"Ah, praise God, it's finally time," Hanna said. "Yes, I thought as much. I have a terrible pressure on my heart, and now I know why. Oh, I only wish I could have seen Tomek one more time . . . and my own boys."

Żaneta leaned forward and whispered into the old woman's ear, "Mamusia has gone to fetch Tatuś. Tomasz will be here today, Babciu. Really. He's coming home to see you, I'm sure."

"Who brought the lovely flowers?" Hanna nodded at the bouquet of dahlias on the table. Then, as if the questions were related, she asked, "Do you think so, child?"

Żaneta had never seen her grandmother's eyes burn so brightly. Even though Żaneta knew full well the circumstances were much more complicated, that Tomasz might not come home at all now, her words had spilled forth unbidden. It was just she wanted it so badly. Żaneta thought if she said it, it might actually happen. More than anything, Żaneta wanted Babcia now to hang on a little longer, until the whole family could be there.

"I spoke to him on the phone earlier, while you slept." Her words gave them both a reason to hope. She reached out and stroked her grandmother's ivory skin. Not one broken artery marred the cheeks, a clear forehead, dotted with beads of sweat. Her tears threatened to resurface.

"Yes," Hanna sighed. "Our Tomek is safe. Żanetko, look at me. You know where I'm going soon, don't you?"

Żaneta nodded, the tears unheeded. *I should get Mamusia. She should be here*, she thought desperately.

"There will be time enough for me to talk to your mother. This time is yours, dear Żanetko. Listen to me closely now. When I'm in heaven, I'll still be with you. In your heart for the rest of your life. Can you understand? You have been gifted with a sensitivity few adults can claim. But it means you will suffer in the years to come. You will experience deep pain, the pain of others coupled with the inability to do anything but pray. And that is what will make or break you in this life, Żanetko. Prayer. Send the pain to our Savior, and He will spare you. You have an intercessory heart. For together with the pain of others, you are also called to carry their joy. Remember, only through suffering and pain can a person grow close to the Father. Can you understand these things?"

Żaneta sat in wonder of her grandmother's words. Something like this had already been whispered to her at night when she cried herself to sleep, feeling the weight of secrets untold, pasts unforgiven, that stalked their home in dark times. Now she nodded, despite her confusion. A part of her leaped at the words of her grandmother and knew them as truth. "Yes," she gasped.

"Then take these things into your heart and believe them, knowing I will always be there with you. I'm not leaving you, dear girl. I'm just finally joining my Tadeusz. Oh, how I've longed for this day! And soon, so soon now, I will be in the arms of my Lord. No pain, Żanetko. Can you imagine? No more pain. . . ."

As suddenly as it had appeared, the energy seeped away from Hanna. Żaneta watched her close her eyes, that face, glowing with fever as she sighed, *"Come, Lord Jesus, come."*

She felt no panic. Her grandmother had very simply fallen asleep.

When Jacek returned to the churchyard again, it was packed to capacity. Young people even sat on the surrounding walls. A few had shinnied up a lamppost. He surveyed the crowd, mostly young workers, but he sensed no hostility.

And yet . . . He had spent the last hour pacing the streets around the church, crisscrossing his path, checking and double-checking that no one was following him.

And feeling as though he had missed a crucial clue.

Now that he had returned to St. Brygida's, his gaze went to the front, where the podium stood. The speeches had already started. Jacek couldn't pick Piotr out from the row of seated men up front. If he could work his way in that direction, he'd probably find Piotr backstage somewhere. He kept looking back and forth, searching for the tall man with black curls. The crowd was huge and many were chanting with upraised fists.

And then Jacek froze. The passage of time became slow and sluggish. Somewhere in the last seconds, his eyes had caught sight of a pistol barrel pointed straight at him. Jacek tried to retrace his gaze. He looked back toward the podium again. *There. No, not a gun, but was that Tomasz?*

Jacek's heart stopped. He clutched it as he stumbled against a car. He stared down at his hands in disbelief. No, his heart had not stopped. The blood dripping off his hands attested to that. He tried to focus on where the gun must be, tried to find the face in the crowd responsible for shooting him.

And then, in all clarity, he saw her. *Gabi.* Older now, with bitter lines etched around her eyes and mouth. But he could not help but recognize her. The woman who had entered his home for years and cleaned it for him, who had cooked for him, who had even nursed him after Roman and his men had tortured Jacek for the very information they now would soon try to kill him for. There was no mistaking her. But had she been sent here by Roman or by the Company? He had always held her accountable for Izzy's death and assumed she had worked both sides back in the days when Jacek was living in Warszawa. *Who sent her?*

The question danced at the edge of Jacek's fading consciousness. He saw Gabi aiming at him again. Desperately, Jacek lurched so that the car stood between him and her, looking right and left. He heaved his eyes forward and saw Tomasz standing beside Piotr, found them both on the stage, above the mass of people. *No! Tomasz should be in Gdynia.*

And who stood on the other side of Tomasz? His heart stopped then, because Monika stood beside them both, like some guardian angel.

Then the boy pointed right at him.

How is it possible? First Gabi, now Monika. The ghosts have all come back.

Jacek forced his eyes open despite the pain.

The boy, at all costs, I must save the boy.

The age in his body, the ache of his joints, the knifelike pain of the bullet wound—it all hammered home to him a message of loss and death. More than anything now, he wanted to let go. In another place, though, searing through his thoughts, countered the need, the drive to reach Tomasz.

He opened his eyes to a maze of oil-covered metal. He was lying under a car. Had he jumped under it when the shooting started? Jacek could no longer remember. How long had he been out? Not long, evidently, for panic still poisoned the hot, heavy air in the courtyard. He saw feet running—jackboots, cheap heels, sports shoes—heard screaming, shouting, more shots, water cannons outside the walls.

No time . . .

Summoning all his strength, Jacek crawled out from under the car and lifted himself out of the dust. Warm blood shot out from between his fingers, which squeezed the wound in his side. He tripped and staggered as his legs gave way. With his good arm he reached out to grab the car door handle for support. He could feel the darkness rising again.

Jacek shook his head and closed his eyes, refusing to give in. When he opened them again, he saw Gabi taking aim at him once more. Or was it at someone in front of him?

Jacek tried to focus. *Tomasz!* The boy was walking toward him, reaching a hand out and calling something out loud.

Tomasz stands between me and my assassin.

The thought cut through Jacek's fading consciousness, the pain in his side, but not his panic. He must choose, and he must choose soon. Jacek knew with searing certainty that if Gabi saw him show any sign of recognizing Tomasz, he would betray himself, betray the one rule he had held himself true to, that of protecting his family. Any acknowledgment by Jacek would be the boy's death warrant. He must choose to save his grandson, or betray himself.

In icy certainty, Jacek knew by the look in Gabi's eyes that she would not hesitate to murder more than once. If she thought the boy knew him, knew who he really was, she would not hesitate to kill Tomasz.

Amy! I can't do that to Amy! The thought steadied him.

Over all the yelling, Jacek heard Tomasz's voice, the voice of his dreams, the voice he had often woken up to, calling out in the dark.

Calling out afraid.

39

Christ of my own heart, whatever befall

Tomasz ran as fast as he could. He zigzagged through the streets, following the train tracks back toward the city center. He veered down one street and came face-to-face with milicja vans parked with trailers carrying water cannons. As he neared St. Brygida's, he could hear the rally already well underway. Loudspeakers broadcast the speeches across the parking lot.

The tanks and milicja vans were not moving. That was good. The fact that they stayed parked meant they were waiting for the order to move in. That much Tomasz had figured out. If he could reach his uncle and warn him of the pending disaster, he might save some lives. He *had* to reach the rally in time. Was he the only one who knew about the tanks, ominously parked nearby?

He careened around the corner behind St. Brygida's church and saw the courtyard full to overflowing. Then he went around the other way and entered through a side door that led to a building at the back of the churchyard. He approached the crowd from behind the stage.

As Tomasz neared the back of the podium, the noise rolled over him in waves of cheers. He peered around the corner at the vast crowd. Fists raised high framed upturned faces, men and women's voices chanting in time, "Solidarność! Solidarność!" He leaned back and almost closed his eyes. He could *feel* the power rolling over him with the sound.

Then he heard his uncle's voice to the left. He looked up and saw Piotr talking with Ewa. "We have them!"

Tomasz waved and called out, "Piotr!" but his uncle didn't hear him. As he started climbing up the scaffolding, Tomasz couldn't help but feel awed by the people he saw sitting on the stage. All the gifted leaders of the movement. Without them, Solidarność would still be just a whispered word in prison cells.

"What did you say?" Ewa cupped her hands around her mouth.

Piotr shouted again, "We have them! Look at this crowd. Jaruzelski wouldn't dare touch us now."

At that moment Wałęsa walked through the door in the brick building beside them and took his place behind the microphone. The crowd erupted in cheers, then changed its chant to the name of the man, now flanked by the movement's leaders on one side, Catholic priests and a bishop on the other. "Wałęsa! Wałęsa!"

Tomasz wondered at the change in mood. It was almost as if the flame had finally been rekindled, a revelation mirrored on the faces of everyone on the podium. This was the August demonstration to top them all. Even as he thought this, Tomasz felt the goose bumps rise on his arm. From where he stood, he could look out over the crowd, beyond the young people sitting on the churchyard wall, into the streets surrounding St. Brygida's church. The flags on the poles by the parking lot hardly fluttered in the still, summer air.

Then Tomasz saw them. The tanks, *moving* in a gray line, crawling two streets to the left. Since everyone was looking in the opposite direction, toward Wałęsa, no one saw the approaching danger. "Piotr!" he screamed again over the din.

His uncle turned his back to the crowd, looking confused. Then his eyes fell on Tomasz, and Tomasz wondered for the first time if this might not have been such a good idea.

In two bounds his uncle was at his side, pulling him off the scaffolding and behind the podium, back down onto the ground. With the speeches continuing behind them, Tomasz felt only his uncle's iron grip on his arm as Piotr demanded an explanation.

"You're here? What are you doing? Do you have any idea what you've done to this family?"

Tomasz stuttered in fear, "Yes, I know. I mean, I think I do. I . . . I had to come straight here because . . ."

"What? You haven't even been home yet? What are you thinking? Are you still so selfish?"

Even though Tomasz could see Piotr regretted the words, he knew every accusation hurled at him that day would be justified. He had never fought with his uncle before. "You're right," he sniffed. "I'm sorry. I meant to go to Gdynia first, but you've got to listen to me."

Piotr pulled him over to the side and took a deep breath. "Listen, I have to get up on that podium in a few minutes. But I want you to stay put. Do you hear that crowd? Stay put! *Do you understand?* Then I'll take you home myself."

Tomasz understood. A part of him, the old part, whined that his uncle didn't have time for him. "No, please. You're right. But you *have* to listen. Piotr, before you send me away, hear me out. A lot has happened, and I promise I'll make it up to everybody." The roar of the crowd rose as Tomasz tried to yell over it. "But there are tanks!" Tomasz had to scream above the chanting of the crowd just behind them.

Piotr shook his head that he hadn't understood. "I have to go. *You stay here,*" he said to Tomasz. Piotr shot him the strangest look, then turned and climbed the stairs again.

Tomasz was left standing at the bottom of the stage, just out of sight of the crowd. He couldn't believe it! His words of warning to Piotr had been swept away. *He didn't even hear me!*

And he doesn't trust me. Tomasz had seen that much in how Piotr treated him. He tried to remember when he started losing the trust of the adults in his life. There was no one moment when the madness began. Thinking about the young man he used to be, Tomasz felt as if he had been cast under a spell, a power of anger and rebellion. How could he have been so blind?

Tomasz moved forward to get a good look at the crowd. He stood at the left base of the podium. If only he could get a little higher. But when he looked upward, he saw Ewa and Bogdan, and there was Piotr, looking at him oddly. No, he didn't dare try anything with his uncle staring at him like that. Tomasz turned his attention outward.

Then he hesitated, feeling a tremor through his feet. He could see Piotr block out the cheering for a moment, unsure. Had he felt it, too? Then Piotr looked at him, and Tomasz scrambled back onto the stage anyway. He cupped his hands around his mouth and screamed as loud as he could, *"Tanks!"*

Piotr was the only one who had been watching him, the only one who heard him. But now he nodded and echoed the word to Ewa. Tomasz sagged against the side wall, weak with relief. He was so close, he could hear and see all the events he set into motion with his one word.

"What?" Ewa shouted back.

"Tanks! I can feel them. Warn the others!" Piotr broke the formation on view before the crowd and ran to the bodyguard behind Wałęsa. "Do you feel it? Tanks. We've got to get him out of here! And the others, too! Go, go, man!"

The bodyguard sprang into action, and the word of warning passed down the line. Wałęsa and the other leaders of the movement were backed into the building behind them. In a matter of seconds, the cheers died down as a murmur rose from the crowd, first questioning, then calling out fearfully.

"What? What's going on?"

"We want Wałęsa! Where is he?"

Piotr took over the microphone and caught the eye of Ewa, who came to his side. He covered the mike with one hand and said, "We have to avert panic."

"You can't," she said. "Tell them the truth and get them out of here before the milicja slaughters them like sheep."

"May I have your attention, please. Please, everyone, remain calm, but I'm afraid we've had a change . . ." Piotr could not even finish the sentence before the people in front of him knew.

Almost seven years of martial law had taught them to know. Like the first warm wind of a hurricane, the word was whispered among them, then grew to a roar of fury, "Milicja! Milicja!"

As if on cue, a shot rang out. A man cried in pain. And then the panic began. The students on the wall leapt onto the tops of cars and back onto the ground. People cried out in the pandemonium, trampling each other to reach the one entrance to the courtyard.

Tomasz *had* heard a shot. Ewa moved to one side of Piotr, and Tomasz stood at the other. Together they looked over the crowd. He tried to find the direction of the gunfire and saw an old woman taking aim again. "Look!" he shouted at Piotr and pointed.

She held the weapon cupped in one hand while the forefinger of the other hand pulled the trigger. He looked in the direction she was aiming at and then sprang off the podium and began moving against the crowd.

Shots rang out on both sides of Tomasz. Volleys of shots, and sirens, and shouting. Screaming. People pushing and running, trapped by the stone church walls.

Tomasz pushed his way past all the people, straining to see the man standing by the car who looked as though he was searching for someone. And at that moment, the man clutched at his chest, then drew his hand away. Tomasz could see him staring at the blood-stained fingers. But with the crowd, Tomasz could not see his face clearly. The waves of people moving past him pulled Tomasz closer, and just then, the old man doubled over and fell facedown beside the parked car.

Tomasz called out, afraid, yet drawn forward, sucked by the flow of the crowd. Driven, Tomasz had to get nearer. Finally, he almost tripped over the body, half under a car. All thoughts of the snipers, the crowd, their pending danger and the tanks, fled his mind.

He looked down. He knew he had to reach out. He bent down and heaved the man over. When he saw his face, clean-shaven now, Tomasz cried out.

In the same breath, the man opened his eyes, fixed them on Tomasz and gasped one word.

And only then did Tomasz know whose voice it was.

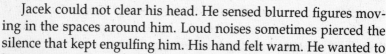

Jacek could not clear his head. He sensed blurred figures moving in the spaces around him. Loud noises sometimes pierced the silence that kept engulfing him. His hand felt warm. He wanted to look down but couldn't move his face. Then he felt a human hand, rolling him over. He looked down and saw blood dripping from between his fingers. Then he looked up.

The young face looking back at him reminded Jacek of his wedding photo with Barbara, torn, hidden, burned, forgotten decades ago. Jacek could not remember. Who was this boy again? Someone important. He had to save him, *had to save him*, that was the thought to hang on to. Then he watched the boy's face, as if in slow motion. The mouth opened, but Jacek could not hear him cry out above the waves of darkness threatening to drown him. He focused on the boy's face and gasped, "Grandson."

Tomasz heard Piotr yell his name and looked up just as his uncle grabbed him.

"No!" Tomasz broke free of Piotr's grip, pulling him away from the car and the fallen man. "No! He's why I'm here. You don't understand!"

Piotr heaved him into the mayhem and started pushing him forward. Tomasz looked up and saw the woman with the gun. She'd moved. He cast a frantic glance at Piotr, pointing. "There! *She* shot him!"

The woman stood on the other side of the courtyard, aiming straight at them. Caught in the crossfire, Tomasz stopped moving and planted his feet squarely in front of Piotr.

"No!" Piotr roared. Now he saw her as well. The old woman's focus shifted slightly as she stared first at Piotr, then Tomasz. Her gun lowered its tip, and then she fired.

Is she trying to kill us, or him? Tomasz wondered wildly.

"Get down!" Piotr tried to push him downward, but the crush of the crowd kept them standing a split second too long.

The shot rang out, then another. Tomasz felt nothing but the dead weight of his uncle as Piotr fell on him, slamming him onto the gravel.

"You're hit!" Tomasz could hardly breathe with his uncle's body on top of him.

"I'm all right. It just grazed my leg," his voice trembled in Tomasz's ear. "Come on, we have to get you out of here." He rolled off of Tomasz, and they crawled back toward the car. For the second time, Tomasz looked at the downed man. He reached out to touch his face.

"You know him?" Piotr asked.

Tomasz nodded and wondered why Piotr said nothing more for a few moments. Instead, he leaned heavily on Tomasz's shoulder, heaved himself to a standing position, then gingerly bent over and picked up the unconscious man. "Help me here, and this time you stick close to me. You understand?"

Tomasz did not even try to answer. The chaos all around him had reached panicked proportions. A surge of people were trying to force through the one gate out of the courtyard. Piotr led him back to the stage, limping under his burden. Water crashed down onto Tomasz just as he ducked under the podium and came out the other side. He could not believe his uncle's strength as they reached the building.

At the same time, his mind reeled around one word. *Grandson.*

Once inside the meeting room, Piotr grunted as he laid the old man on the conference table. "I heard the tanks."

"I tried to warn you," Tomasz said.

"I know. I'm sorry, Tomasz. We knew there was a police presence. But this," he nodded at the table, "this is something different."

With the sounds of water cannons blasting and men and women crying out loud in pain, Tomasz touched his uncle's elbow and repeated Piotr's own question, "You know him?"

"Yes, his name is Jacek Duch."

Tomasz hesitated, then whispered, "He called me grandson. Am I? His, I mean? Is he my mother's father?"

Piotr nodded, the emotions on his face a puzzle to Tomasz. "It's true. But tell no one."

Tomasz let out an involuntary cry, and Piotr looked at him sharply. "Tomasz, listen. I knew, it's all right. He is a good man." He took Tomasz's face in his hands. "Remember when I wrote you from prison that there are moments that make or break us? This is one of them. I need you to be strong now, Tomasz. I'm sorry for accusing you like I did earlier. I should have known you had your reasons. Now the important thing is we have to get help for him and for the others who may be wounded out there. You do know you have nothing to fear from him? Tomasz, he was trying to protect *you.*"

"He did more than that," Tomasz mumbled to himself, unconsciously stroking the wrinkled and spotted hand that lay limp on the table. It suddenly made sense, like figuring out which stars to focus on and seeing the constellations.

"Go out that way." Piotr pointed to another exit. "It will take you to the street. Get help. I'll stay here in case the milicja breaks through."

Tomasz ran out of the room. *Please, God, please, God*, was all he could pray. Only once before in his life had Tomasz felt so afraid, so lost . . . so found. *My grandfather! What should I do?* He stood on the street, hearing sirens blaring from all sides as people ran in panic around him. As he looked left and right, wondering desperately in which direction he should seek help, the death and sudden knowledge of his grandfather hung over Tomasz like a blanket of clouds in a night sky.

At that moment, Tomasz suddenly sensed the presence of his babcia, Hanna. *You've always been closest to me.* No distance could separate them any longer. The nearness came and was gone.

A few moments later, he heard Piotr's voice behind him, "Tomasz! I'm here! Come back. It's too dangerous for you out here." Piotr caught hold of Tomasz and must have seen something that startled him, because his next words were, "Tomasz, I know this is all a shock for you. But you must hold firm."

The words touched Tomasz in a place he had rarely known. Then he looked up and heard the sirens. "Look, ambulances!" At that moment, Tomasz heard a voice to his left. He turned and, as if in one of his deathless dreams, saw his father.

40

Still be my vision, O Ruler of all

"Grandson." Jacek was back in their quiet cabin in the mountains. He bent over to smell the boy as he slept, to kiss him on his forehead. As he said the one word, he fingered the fire truck, placing it on the pillow.

Then there was pain burning up his chest. Someone carried him through a dark place where many people were screaming.

When he opened his eyes, Jacek found himself deposited on a large table like a slab of meat. He looked up into the face of the one man who knew him and who, ironically, had become his protector. His throat croaked open. "Hear me."

"There's help on the way," Piotr said. "You need to rest."

"No. The boy." It was not a question.

"He's all right. And he knows. . . ." Piotr looked away from Jacek, and this was his clue to how much Tomasz knew.

"But *you* don't. I found him—no one must know. I looked everywhere for you." *Finally, I can deliver the message.* "There's something else. He was an addict. He may need professional help later. The mental scarring he experienced . . ." Jacek coughed as what felt like a knife turned in his gut and warm, bitter blood filled his mouth. He spat.

"It's all right," Piotr said quietly. "I saw his arms. We'll be in contact with a clinic."

"No, you don't understand. He has nightmares. He was . . . abused. Repeatedly. The trauma . . . Don't leave him alone!" Jacek fastened Piotr with his eyes, willing him to go after Tomasz. He had seen the boy panic more than once during the past four months. Put him in a stressful situation like this one, and there was no telling where the flashbacks might take him.

Jacek closed his eyes and heard, as if from far away, Piotr open the door and call out, "I'll go after Tomasz and get you an ambulance." He heard the door open and close, open and close. The pain numbed him, lulled him into comfortable waiting.

Open and close.

Jacek smelled familiar perfume. He lifted heavy lids and saw an old woman—not as old as he, but with eyes as tortured or more. "Gabi?" So it wasn't just his aged paranoia. And there was her gun again, pointed straight at his forehead.

He heard her heels clicking on the tile floor, coming closer. *She never wore heels before.* "I'm dying. No more, please," he pleaded.

At the same time he was trying desperately to think. A KGB Gabi would want to kill him because he had secretly left the country against direct orders, defecting to the West, as it were, and confirming all Roman's suspicions over the years that he was indeed a double agent within the SB.

A CIA Gabi would want him dead because the security in Berlin had recorded the use of his identification. Because he was supposed to be dead, they would assume he had been a mole in the Company for all or part of these fifty years, turned somehow, then disappeared for ten years, his very need to hide in such a way an admission of guilt.

Ever since Izzy's murder, he had assumed that Gabi had been working both sides, but defected from where to where?

Her voice was low, murderous. "Well, here we are, together again after so many years. And I'm going to take you out."

He stared at her, uncomprehending.

"You killed him, you know."

"Who?"

"My husband. Jurek. You killed Jurek."

Thunderstruck, Jacek could not tear his eyes from her crazed face.

"You didn't know, did you?" she hissed. "But no matter. You're still to blame. Just couldn't follow the rules, could you?"

All he could do was shake his head weakly. He had no idea what she was trying to tell him. And she seemed torn between an itching desire to pull the trigger again and an equal compulsion to explain herself.

"Oh, there's so much you'd like to know, isn't there? Yes, I killed your Izzy, and do you know why? For the same reason I'm here to eliminate you, Duch. She was a double agent. And here's the funny thing: *she used you*. Your emotional state and drinking problem at the time were the perfect means for her to manipulate herself into your life.

"Operation Guardian Angel was our assignment to protect you. Don't you understand? Jurek and me. We were to stay close to you. *Jacek Duch, the most valuable agent ever to operate behind the Iron Curtain*." She laughed, a dry, bitter snort.

Somewhere behind the haze of his pain, Jacek had the vague sense that he should say something. Do something. But he couldn't move. And she was still talking, still explaining.

"We were your protectors," she was saying. "And we did it faithfully all those years. And then, because of you, we couldn't leave, couldn't go home. When we finally thought you were dead after Carter's visit in 1977, we still had to continue in the field, because a few years later martial law was declared. Then, six months before they were going to pull us out, before we could leave, your people at the SB arrested Jurek."

She had been speaking in a monotone, but now her voice dropped an octave.

She added, "He was too old. They tortured him. He was never the same. And then, after we were posted back to Berlin, the Stasi got him." Her voice faltered, and for the first time the nose of the gun. "If it hadn't been for you, we would have finally been together, finally away from here. . . ."

She caught herself and leveled the gun back at his head. "You do realize your precious Roman was the one lying all along. All those years when I was in your home, I wasn't on the SB's payroll, but the Company's. But Jurek—he was the one who was really devoted to you. He's been a fan since the war."

This last sentence she uttered sarcastically. "Oh yes, you've been used in more ways than you know. You never did discover who fired on Carter, did you? Or how Roman knew you would be acting as assassin? Don't you see? We were there to back you up! That's why we got the ticket to you. It's obvious to me now that you must have lied to us because there *really was* an SB assassin present.

"And yet all the time, Jurek kept saying we could trust you—and look what it brought him. Well, I know better. I knew better after you logged in on Jurek's computer in Berlin. We thought you were trying to make contact—but nothing. That's when we knew you'd crossed over. Then Jurek was murdered. Your fault. I just waited. When you came back yesterday, I had you." She whispered the last word and took a step closer.

"I'm doing both sides a favor, just as I did when I eliminated Izzy. I've seen how you worked both sides, just like she did. You're a double agent. Otherwise, why would you behave this way, working only for the SB and not contacting us?"

As the truth slowly dawned on Jacek that she was actually waiting for an answer, he knew above all else that he could never hint at his family ties. To do so would betray everything he had come to hold important in his life. *Let her think I'm a traitor.* For a moment he could think clearly. *If she doesn't kill me, Roman will.*

She cried, "The bitter truth is, you played both sides for how long? There can be no truer traitor!"

Jacek pleaded, "Let me explain." But a fit of coughing choked the rest of his words.

"It's not true. He was only trying to help," came Piotr's voice. "I went to him and asked his help."

Gabi hissed, "Don't move, any of you."

From far away Jacek heard the exchange. *Any of you.* Tomasz in the room! With a supreme effort, he opened his eyes. He heaved himself onto his side and finally saw the scene. Gabi was wildly waving the gun at him and the entire family. *Żaneta and Amy, too! Not now!* He moved his hand toward his chest, the pain pulling him in.

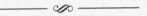

Tomasz watched as if in a trance as his father stumbled toward him, arms outstretched. When Jan staggered forward, Tomasz could finally move. He took a step, but his father was there before him. He cried out like an animal and swept Tomasz into his arms, holding him, holding him tight, holding him in a way that told them both he would never, ever let go.

Tomasz felt his tears, had known they would be in this place in time, waiting for him when he found his family. Then his mother was there, and Żaneta, not little anymore, the four of them together.

Four of us, not five.

"Tomku! Oh, Tomku, my son! My son!"

Tomasz heard his father crying, and through his own tears he said, "Tatusiu, forgive me, please. I'll do anything. Forgive me, please."

In answer, Tomasz heard only the grateful sobbing of both his parents. Still they would not let him go. "You, you are really here?" his mother asked.

Tomasz smiled to himself. How often had he imagined this moment, dreaded it, feared the first question they might ask? But this question he could answer. "Yes, I'm really here." They pulled back from each other, and Tomasz saw with shocked eyes the aging man before him, the lines engraved in his face, the tragic shadows haunting his cheekbones. His mother had gone completely gray, her eyes etched in dark lines. He opened his mouth, but Jan shook his head.

"How I have prayed for this moment, Tomku. And I'm the one who must ask *your* forgiveness. I was stubborn and blind. I was proud. I lost you. Worse, I drove you away. . . ." Jan started to turn away, but Tomasz reached out and pulled him back by one shoulder.

"No," Tomasz said. "It was my choice. I realize that now. They were all my choices. But I . . ." His voice cracked as the shame rose and threatened to drown him again. "I paid a price for those choices."

"Oh, Tomku, none of that matters now," Amy said. "You're home. And you're safe."

Żaneta pulled him down to her level and wrapped her arms around his neck. "We love you," she breathed into his ear. When she refused to let him go, he looked into her face and just grinned.

"You're sopping wet," Jan said. "And you're shaking. Here, take my pullover." His mother's hands helped him out of the wet shirt. As he pulled the cool, dry cotton over his face, the fabric smelling of his father, the good scent reassured Tomasz.

"Tell me," Jan said as he took Tomasz's hand. The same height now, Jan looked Tomasz in the eyes, and Tomasz felt his father lending him strength, the strength coursing through his veins—enough strength, even, to tell his story.

"I was so sorry. I *am* so sorry. That's why I've come back. Besides these," he rolled up the sleeves and held out the underside of both arms like a sacrifice, "I have nothing else to offer." His parents exchanged glances.

Piotr laughed uncomfortably. "Hurry, we have to get inside. There's still sniper fire out here. It's not safe." Shots rang out from the roof of the building opposite them. Together they dashed back into the safety of the building.

Tomasz entered first, then stopped short. Before him he saw the same crazed woman he had glimpsed in the courtyard. Now she shifted her aim and pointed a pistol at all of them. Tomasz put out his hands to stop his family, tried to turn and warn them, but it was too late. Out of the corner of his eye, he saw his father's arm go around his mother. Piotr stepped in front of Żaneta and spoke to the woman. They all stood in the room, waiting. Tomasz held his breath.

The woman held them at gunpoint and cried, "Don't move, any of you!"

Behind her, Jacek rolled over and leaned onto one elbow. The woman swirled and yelled, "I said, 'Don't move!' " But he ignored her and reached into his coat pocket.

Then Tomasz saw his chance. While she was distracted, Tomasz moved. He flew over the table, looked up, and saw a gun pointed right at his head. In the split second that he jumped in the way to save his grandfather, Tomasz remembered it all, everything from Berlin to Lesko, of how he himself had been saved from so much by this man he now so desperately wanted to protect.

Jan lunged after Tomasz, grabbing him by the leg to drag him off the table. Amy screamed, "No!" Tomasz fell onto the ground with a thud.

A shot shattered the room. Tomasz opened his eyes from where he lay on the cool floor beside the table and saw the woman's feet running, running out the door, her voice filling the space, "You're like an old shell of a man that should have died long ago and forgot to."

Tomasz scrambled to his feet and found his father draped across the table. One look at his father's face, and Tomasz could see he was hit.

"Tatusiu!" Żaneta and his mother ran to Jan's side as Piotr dashed for the door. Jan motioned to them all with his hand. "I'm all right. It's just my shoulder."

"Oh, Jan." Amy was crying again, leaning on Tomasz.

Ewa and Bogdan burst into the room. "We heard shots!" They looked wildly from one body to the other.

Piotr called out to them, "Did they. . . ?"

"Yes, it's all right. Everyone is safe and unharmed . . . except

Jan." Bogdan sounded as puzzled as he looked. "And him."

Tomasz looked up and saw that his mother had moved in the direction Bogdan now pointed. She stared down and a strangled cry escaped her throat, like an animal long forgotten and left alone.

Jacek saw the people gathered around him. His grandson—dear, strong Tomasz. Piotr, his outlaw. Amy and her husband. One stranger, a man. Żaneta. And someone else. A woman.

"His eyes are open," he heard Tomasz say.

He rolled his head and could no longer see as clearly. A woman was standing beside him. "Monika?" he groaned.

"What did you say? What did he say?"

He struggled to focus. What was Monika doing here after so many years? After . . .

"Monika is my mother's name."

The woman's words brought him back to himself. He stared at her. The same shy dark beauty, like a deer in the woods—that's how he had thought of Monika during those days of misted fear and waiting.

"My mother . . . you knew my mother?"

Now Jacek's pain blocked him from breathing. He would have to speak slowly. "Gdańsk?"

She leaned over him, the eyes dark pools of light like Amy's. *Where is my Amy?* "Yes, she was from Gdańsk. My grandfather was a tailor, but he died during the war."

The shop with the windows, where sunlight caught dust in its rays when he first saw her. "I was born during the last year of the war."

A clarity woke him out of his stupor. He made the mental effort to push it aside, hold it at bay, and ask once, "Born in '45? Not '46?"

"No, I'm not a child of the liberation."

"Your father?" It was taking all his strength to focus on the pattern emerging from her words.

"My mother said he died when the Soviets took Gdańsk. I was born six months later."

"Your mother, did she look like you?" He did not wait for an answer. He had heard enough.

Now Amy appeared before him. He saw her take Monika's hand.

"This man is my father."

He had waited a lifetime for the sound of those words. He listened to them ring through his soul, attuning to the sound of his own heart beating loudly, the steady rhythm of old women pounding carpets in a Gdańsk courtyard.

"Yes."

Each breath threatened to be his last. "I loved her." He must say it. "Please." He turned away, seeing them no more and whispered one more word, "... Forgive ..."

Forgive ...

The door slammed open as medics pulled a trolley over to Jan's side. In the summer wind that washed over them all, Tomasz heard his grandmother's promise tell his heart, "*... things are but a mere shadow of what is to come.*"

And he knew they would move on, out from under pain and fear, even beyond the shadow cast on them by all history.

They would move on.

Historical Note

On the fourth of June 1989, following re-legalization of the Solidarność labor union two months earlier, semi-democratic elections were held in Poland. Against tremendous odds, Solidarność virtually swept the election, winning almost all the parliamentary seats for which it was eligible.

On the same day in Beijing, Chinese authorities attacked and killed student protesters in Tiananmen Square.

Between July and August of that year, the fall of communism in Poland continued as the communist parliamentary coalition slowly came undone. Although Jaruzelski narrowly won the presidency, Wałęsa's candidate, Tadeusz Mazowiecki, became prime minister of the first non-communist government in Eastern and Central Europe.

As I was writing this series, Wałęsa came and went as president of Poland, and the communists were voted back in power, albeit different communists and a different power. But since the elections of 1997, a coalition has been shaping the new nation, getting it ready for entry to the European Union.

In the new Berlin, government authorities now estimate between three and seven thousand children live on the streets.

Bibliography

The verses in italics following certain chapter-number headings are taken from the hymn sung to an Irish traditional melody, from the Irish (c. eighth century), by Mary E. Byrne (1880–1931) and Eleanor H. Hull (1860–1935), copyright in this version Jubilate Hymns Limited, *Hymns for Today's Church*, first published 1982, Hodder and Stoughton, London.